HELL IN HER WAKE

AND OTHER TWISTED VISIONS

GREG CHAPMAN

HELL IN HER WAKE

AND OTHER TWISTED VISIONS

WEIRD
HOUSE

ISBN: 978-1-937128-47-0

"Hell in Her Wake", "Happiness on Cemetery Street", "Chiaroscuro",
and "Schism" are original to this collection
© 2025 by Greg Chapman.
All other stories previously published as detailed on page 303.

Cover Artwork © 2025 by Greg Chapman
Foreword © by James Chambers

Interior and cover design by César Puch
Editor, James Chambers
Editor and Publisher, Joe Morey

Weird House Press
Central Point, OR 97502
www.weirdhousepress.com

List of Illustrations

Table of Contents

Foreword
Painting Nightmares in Ink

So much of the horror genre is visual.

Ghosts are seen (or unseen). Humans transform their appearance into monsters. Shadows and tricks of light make us doubt what our eyes tell us. Behemoths breach the surface of reality like whales cresting ocean waves. Houses and cenotaphs loom out of the fog. Inhuman eyes watch us from the dark, which hides or reveals terrible things.

What we don't see is often as important as what we do.

In horror movies, jump scares create expectations of shock then deliver something immediately familiar to our eyes—a cat, a windblown branch, a reflection in a mirror. Genre fans and creators debate "how much of the monster" should we see for the most effective scares. Makeup and special effects artists labor to convince viewers that a man might truly transform into a wolf, or an alien being with superior biology might hunt us, or an inhuman entity the size of a small city might rise from the sea or hover in the sky.

What we see or don't see on the screen matters.

In horror literature, vivid and evocative descriptions paint nightmares in readers' imaginations. Writers linger over the right word choices to conjure terrifying, unsettling, and monstrous images. Write just enough to tease the readers' imaginations, to let them fill in the blanks with the worst conceptions of their subconscious. The best augment their descriptions with elements beyond the visual—the sounds, scents, and, shudder, the tastes of a monster or other terror. They appeal to all the senses in ways movies cannot to fashion fully-formed horrors that take root in readers' minds.

Who can forget Edgar Allan Poe's vivid imagery in "The Fall of the House of Usher," "The Masque of the Red Death," and so many other tales?

Who can forget Bram Stoker's description of Jonathan Harker's arrival at Castle Dracula?

Or Shirley Jackson's description of Hill House?

Or Stephen King's depiction of Pennywise, tempting Georgie from the storm drain?

What you hold in your hands is a book of stories by a writer who just happens to be a master of horror in both literary and visual form. As an illustrator, Greg Chapman understands what makes an image that worms under the viewers' skin to intrigue, discomfit, or shock them. As a writer, he knows there is so much more to the story. He comes from a rare breed of storyteller, one capable of fully visualizing, in pen and ink, water colors, pixels, and other media, the frightening vignettes that live inside his mind while also possessing the power to breathe them fully into life with his words.

And bring them to life he does.

In this collection of fourteen of Greg's darkest and most horrifying stories, combined with a selection of his macabre illustrations, readers will encounter many shades of darkness from the monstrous to the tragic to the playful. Greg's knack for quickly sketching in words his characters' lives and conflicts creates, in only a few paragraphs, suspense and anxiety about their fates. From the secrets of an otherworldly notebook discovered by a prison guard to the dark temptations of a mysterious train that offers salvation in a hopeless situation to trick-or-treating in hell with devils both infernal and human, he explores a variety of monsters and nightmares, with poignant, tragic, and shocking outcomes.

Published here for the first time is his novella, "Hell in Her Wake," a witchy work that digs deep into the darkest ideas of family, greed, love, power, and sacrifice, all unfolding with the pace and gory glee of a Sam Raimi horror movie. It tells a tale of escape from and return to dark territories both of the soul and the world.

Together these stories explore the nature of madness grown from seeds of cosmic horror, the betrayals of love and selfishness, the desperation of the artist struggling in a dark, apathetic world, the capacity for horror born of self-deception, and much more. In a Greg Chapman horror story, whether the monsters are real or only perceived, the darkest truths often emerge from within the human heart. Greg's precise, economical style delivers intense bursts of horrifying imagery and emotion that add up to much more than the sum of the words on the page. They will linger in the reader's mind long after the book is closed. Glance at his illustrations and feel a shiver of dread or terror ripple through you. Read his stories, dare the terrifying tableaus and nightmare visions they conjure, and let his words tattoo their darkness on your soul.

James Chambers,
Northport, NY

The Bedlam Stones

Bethlem Royal Hospital, London, 1887.
   To Doctor Edgar Harding, the cries were a symphony, a howling song that struck the soul with the certainty of a tuning fork. Every night he sat in his study and listened to the weeping and gnashing, and every night he recorded the notes in search of its story. The nurses and orderlies despised the din, but to Harding, it was beauty painted upon the air. It was akin to the Gloria sung by angels at the birth of Christ.

Harding returned his quill to its resting place and closed his notebook. The song was calling to him; his patients were calling to him. He left his rooms, stepped into the hall and descended two flights of stairs to the wards. Two orderlies, their heads in cages for protection, wrestled Michael Demmick to the stone floor, while another hosed him with icy water. Demmick shrieked for mercy, for the voices to answer his call, to murder the orderlies where they stood. Harding stooped beside Demmick to help him to his feet, inadvertently receiving a slight spray from the hose.

"Oh, forgive me, Dr. Harding," one of the orderlies said.

Harding ignored the man and concentrated on Demmick's stricken gaze. "Do you forgive them, Michael?" Harding asked his patient.

Demmick glared at the orderlies in their cages as if they were ravenous dogs. "We ... we don't!"

Harding wrapped an arm around Michael and ushered him dripping wet toward his room. The orderlies served as their entourage. Trembling with cold, Demmick kept his eyes locked on Harding as the orderlies stripped him of his wet clothes and dressed him in blue-striped pyjamas. A rat, disturbed by the newcomers, ran out from under Demmick's bed and vanished through a crack in the filthy wall.

"They know not what they do," Harding said. "They're little more than slaves."

Demmick nodded as they ushered him into bed. "We shall kill them!"

"Of course, you will," Harding said, smiling. He stopped one of the orderlies as they left the cell. "Some laudanum for Michael and his friends please, to help them sleep."

The orderly returned with a vial of laudanum, the liquid inside not much different in appearance and fragrance to piss. Demmick took it down like it was a glass of the finest ale in all of England and licked his lips after. Harding nodded for the caged men to wait outside.

"Feeling better now?" Harding said, to which Demmick shook his head in the negative. "How about a story, then? There once was a man named Michael Anthony Demmick, from Birmingham. He grew up in a family of eight children, and he and his brothers and sisters were all flogged by their father—every single day. Sometimes Michael talked to himself to escape the pain. He was always disappointed when no other voice than his father's ever spoke back. One day when Michael's father came home from *The Old Red Lion*, the children were given such a beating that Michael's sister Kate fell down and never got up again. At that moment, something was released from Michael—a scream, so long and loud it took control of his body. It made him so strong he was able to smash a glass bottle over his father's head; even strong enough to stab the man with the shattered end until he, too, was dead. Ever since that day, Michael's head has been filled with the voices of his brothers and sisters, begging him to kill their father, even though they're all long dead."

Harding stroked Demmick's sweat-soaked face. "I'll help you find your true voice again, won't I, Michael?"

Demmick shook his head. Harding chuckled and produced a small stone, about the size of a glass marble.

"All you need to do is keep taking this medicine, and you'll have your voice again."

Demmick shook his head, over and over, but the laudanum was taking hold. His face slackened, his lips parted. The stone went in.

Harding left Demmick to his cell and stepped back into the hall, the song of insanity in his ears.

Dr. Henry Morganstern exited the carriage and beheld the facade of Bethlem Hospital. Blackened with years of London rain, the building resembled a gargantuan tombstone, casting a shadow of decay into the centre of England's capital. He could hear the cries of the patients coming from inside, each one piercing his heart. Yet he had to put such thoughts to one side; he was visiting Bethlem on business, for he had a very special request of one Dr. Edgar Harding.

A nurse escorted Morganstern to Dr. Harding's office on the upper floors. The first thing Morganstern noticed was that the walls failed to muffle the moaning of the patients. In fact, the high ceilings seemed to act as a conductor. Morganstern flinched with each ear-piercing cry and felt tense with so many orderlies running through the corridors in fits of panic.

Regardless, Dr. Harding was smiling when he eventually arrived to greet him. Harding was a tall, wiry, well-dressed man, and Morganstern surmised, judging by his balding pate, he was in his mid-to-late fifties. There was a sharpness in the psychiatrist's eyes that seemed … off-putting. Morganstern accepted the doctor's bony handshake cautiously.

"I truly appreciate you taking the time to meet with me, Dr. Harding," Morganstern said.

Harding smiled and dismissed him with a wave. "The pleasure is all mine, Dr. Morganstern. It's not often that we have the opportunity to receive an aspirant to the fascinating field of surgery."

Morganstern tried to conceal his pride. "Yes, kind words surely, Dr.

Harding, thank you, but I was only recently accepted into the Royal College of Surgeons and am still perfecting my field. Obviously, you received my letter regarding my requirements?"

"Of course, and Bethlem Hospital is eager to assist you."

"That is encouraging news."

Harding sat back in his mahogany chair and twirled a small rock between his gnarled fingertips. The break in conversation allowed a host of tormented sighs to enter the room.

"Did you need me to provide any further information?" Morganstern said, hoping to talk over the cacophony.

"I have a few requirements of my own," Harding said.

"I'd be glad to hear them."

Harding stood and crossed to the window, showing Morganstern his back, the psychiatrist no longer amicable. He folded his hands behind his back, fingering the rock in a circle. "Naturally I would only be able to supply you with cadavers with no known next of kin."

"A perfectly reasonable request."

"And there is the matter of payment, of course."

Morganstern nodded. "To be made by way of anonymous donation to the Bethlem Hospital Trust."

"Excellent. The final requirement is that I would like you to perform your dissections here at Bethlem."

Morganstern gaped. "I thought I explained in my letter that the cadavers were to be transported to St Bartholomew's ... "

Harding turned on his heel to face Morganstern. The psychiatrist's eyes were narrowed, like stab wounds. "I also want to witness the procedure, each and every one."

"I beg your pardon ... "

"Of course, nothing will occur until one of my patients dies."

Morganstern was on his feet, his collar tight around his constricted neck. "Now, see here. Perhaps I can agree to conduct the autopsies here, but I need to conduct them in private."

Harding tilted his head like a schoolteacher to a presumptuous child. "Privacy is a luxury very few of us can expect in these times, Doctor. Still, if you believe you can procure your cadavers more discreetly elsewhere … ?"

Morganstern grit his teeth. Harding was indeed very clever, but then he knew that was to be expected of a psychiatrist. Morganstern replaced his bowler hat and retrieved his briefcase. He turned to head for the door.

"I agree to your terms. Please contact me when a cadaver becomes available."

As Morganstern left, the shrieking sounds of a man wracked with insanity followed him like a wraith.

Morganstern had almost forgotten about Bethlem and its warden when he was visited by one of the staff from the hospital, who informed him of a recent death of one of its patients. The man explained that Dr. Harding had made arrangements for the body to be prepared for Morganstern's arrival. Morganstern replied that he would attend the following day, but that night he was plagued with dreams of stones rolling around inside hollow skulls, producing a plethora of voices. The dream ended with Morganstern extracting one such stone from his own eye socket.

The dream lingered in Morganstern's thoughts for the entire cab ride to Bethlem the next morning. To quell it, he focused on the task to come: the opportunity to work with a fresh cadaver. He checked his surgical instrument kit and suddenly felt a pang of guilt. Who had the dead man been? What so-called treatments had he endured under Harding's harsh instruction? Morganstern harkened back to his first meeting with Harding, particularly the odd stone the psychiatrist continually toyed with. The idea of Harding ogling him while he conducted his work was off-putting to say the least, but it was a sacrifice he was prepared to make. Surgeons relied on flesh for their trade, for the betterment of their profession. To save lives, one needed to venture into the intricacies of death. If such intricacies were

9

only found within the walls of an asylum, watched over by a sardonic, cantankerous upstart, then so be it.

Morganstern was suitably irritable when the cab reached the gates of Bethlem Hospital. Beneath the overcast mid-morning sky, the building appeared hewn from bone. The screams from within crossed the yard to the gate and assaulted Morganstern's ears with the ferocity of a winter gale. The air stank of excrement and pain. It was the very fact Bethlem existed that motivated Morganstern to work harder, to push science and the understanding of human biology to its limits. Humanity deserved better than Bethlem Hospital.

Two of the staff met Morganstern at the entrance and took his bags and coat. At least the hospitality was of the proper standard, he thought. Pity they did not show the patients the same courtesies. But then, what did a surgeon know of the mind, other than how to dissect it? Perhaps spending some time in Bethlem would expand his horizons, teach him something new. Forcing a smile, Morganstern resolved to embrace the opportunity and perhaps find some common ground with Dr. Harding. After all, they were both physicians.

He was escorted through several corridors and down several flights of stairs. Cries for help, cries for death, and cries for blood echoed in Morganstern's ears all the way down, rising in pitch with each successive step. Sunlight diminished the further they descended, with only dirty kerosene lamps to light the way. The surgeon felt the insanity around him with every sense; he saw it pooled in the shadows in the corners, smelled it in the stink of rodent piss, tasted the dirt, but none of the sensations were as strong as the voices. Voices he doubted he would ever forget for as long as he lived.

When they reached the lowest floor, the orderlies walked Morganstern to a door at the end of a short corridor. The surgeon could tell by the damp cold that the room was the mortuary, and the smell of death was strongest here. One of the orderlies opened the door, and in the centre of the room was the corpse of a man laid out on a steel table; beside the body stood the almost regal frame of Dr. Edgar Harding.

"Ah, Doctor Morganstern," Harding said, smiling widely. "So good of you to join us."

"Dr. Harding, thank you for making this possible."

"William here is who you should be thanking," Harding said. "The poor soul kindly donated his body to you."

"Donated?" Morganstern watched as Harding reached out and gently stroked the dead man's hair, almost sensually. The surgeon felt a wave of disgust roil in his stomach. "If it pleases you, Doctor, I'd like to commence the post-mortem."

"Oh, of course, how rude of me." Harding said, stepping back and putting his hands behind his back. "I must say it will be fascinating to observe you."

Morganstern opened his surgical case and raised an eyebrow in Harding's direction. "You've never seen an autopsy?"

"Oh, no," Harding said, shaking his head. He then tapped his temple with a finger. "I believe the human mind is so much more than simple flesh. We wear our thoughts like clothes, Dr. Morganstern; some have but a few layers, while others, like the men and women here in Bethlem, wear them on their sleeves, so to speak."

Morganstern attempted to ignore Harding's meanderings by examining the body. *William* appeared to be in his late forties and fairly emaciated, his closed eyes sunken deep in his skull. The skin of the man's face was rough to the touch, a widespread rash of raised nodules.

"Did this man have syphilis?" Morganstern asked, somewhat aghast.

"Oh, yes, William had been driven mad by it; the fool surrendered to his carnal lusts all too often. He'd been a patient here for twelve years."

Morganstern stood back from the body, chest heaving, and fists clenched. "I was under the impression I would receive untainted cadavers."

Harding frowned, his eyes narrowing to slits once more. "There's no such thing as untainted here in *Bedlam*, Dr. Morganstern. You asked for a body, and I have supplied one."

Morganstern grunted and moved to close up his surgical case. "You've wasted my time, Dr. Harding! Quite frankly, I find your actions rather deceptive."

Harding rested his hand on the dead man's head again. "Dr. Morganstern, here you have in William a chance to examine someone who has suffered the disease for more than a decade. Surely that would be of interest to you. I have seen his suffering from the outside, yet I would be curious to see how it has affected him on the inside."

Morganstern snorted derisively. "There are syphilis cases all over London! It's a scourge upon the city!"

Harding raised a finger. "Ah, yes, but how many of your fellow students have their own corpse to examine with that very affliction?"

Morganstern stared at William. Harding was right, damn him. He couldn't walk away from a once-in-a-lifetime opportunity. He offered the psychiatrist a placatory smile.

"Forgive my impertinence, Doctor. You're right, this is indeed a rarity. I shall proceed." Morganstern reached for his Liston knife and began to open up William's chest cavity.

Hours later, William's corpse was like a red rose in full bloom. The syphilitic's blood shone bronze in the light of Harding's lamp; the psychiatrist gazed in awe of his former's patient's inner workings. Morganstern's forehead was as slick as his apron, his fingers tacky with the dead's man's essence. He was exhausted but also most gratified.

"Marvellous, Dr. Morganstern, simply marvellous," Harding said, patting the surgeon on the back.

Morganstern flinched, his nerves on edge. "My word, I am parched."

"Ah, how indecent of me." Harding turned and poured Morganstern a glass of water from a decanter. The surgeon gulped it down in two swallows. "Feeling better?"

"Mmm, yes, thank you."

Harding's mouth twisted in glee. "Then, shall we continue?"

"Pardon?"

"What about the skull? Aren't you going to open it up? I want to see William's brain."

Morganstern put the glass down on a nearby table. "My good man, I don't think I can go on … "

"Don't be absurd, man! You're at the juncture, standing at the precipice. You must go on. Think of the knowledge you will acquire ahead of your peers. You'd be a fool to throw it all away now."

The surgeon nodded and reached for the Hey saw, a long-handled, axe-shaped saw designed for cranial resections. He willed his tired arm muscles to force the saw into the bone, the sound like a steed's hooves on a floor of granite inside the icy mortuary. After several hard thrusts the skullcap was free and William's every mad thought and dream was revealed in glistening glory. Harding bent to get a closer look, his eyes tracing every curve and groove of his former patient's brain.

"The brain is riddled with lesions," Morganstern said.

"Remarkable. Absolutely remarkable."

Before Morganstern could reply, Harding was on his feet and shaking the surgeon's still bloodied hand.

"Thank you, Dr. Morganstern, for a most fascinating time. I've learned so much, as have you, I imagine."

Morganstern chuckled and grabbed a cloth to wipe his hands. "Indeed, and I thank you."

"My pleasure. Now, naturally, we'll take care of the corpse, but you're welcome to take whatever specimens you require. I trust that you'll want to be contacted should another patient pass on?"

"Yes, yes, of course."

"Good. Well, I'll leave you to it then. Have the orderlies call for a cab when you're ready to leave. Goodnight."

Harding left with a renewed vigour in his step, while Morganstern was utterly spent. He beheld the extent of his efforts splayed out on the table before him. He felt confident in his skill and, if Harding could keep his promise of further bodies, he would indeed be a surgeon of the highest capability. He sat on a chair behind William's exposed skull and stared into its fleshy canyons.

"Poor fool," he said. "Poisoned by London's harlots; vile temptresses all of them."

A rivulet of blood oozed from inside William's brain, spilling to the floor. Before Morganstern's eyes something emerged from one of the canyons in the grey matter. He stood for a closer inspection, watching as an object was birthed from the left hemisphere. It fell to the ground with a clack and rolled to his shoe. He bent and picked the object up and wiped away the blood on his cloth. A stone, just like the one Harding coveted like a diamond. Morganstern's voice caught in his throat:

"What in the name of God is going on in Bethlem Hospital?"

Morganstern secreted the stone from Bethlem, and took it home to study it. In truth, the stone was more of a fascination than William's organs. Away from the prying eyes of his fiancée, Morganstern scrutinised the piece of rock, feeling its odd smoothness. Under the magnifying glass, the surgeon discovered the rock was decorated with markings: intersecting circles of the tiniest detail. As the days went by, the stone was constantly on his mind; almost as if it was *inside* his mind. Often he recalled its birth from William's brain and wondered how it got there. Perhaps he'd thought about it too long. There was only one way to know, only one man who could answer his question: Dr. Edgar Harding.

In the thick of night, unable to sleep, Morganstern gathered his surgical case, cloak, the stone—of course—and left his house for Bethlem Hospital. He ordered the cab driver to ride with haste, that it was an emergency, and in some deep-seated way it was. If indeed Harding was administering some strange treatments to his patients, there was much more than just their sanity at stake.

Bethlem was a temple made from the night, a mingling of darkness. Gas lamps flared golden in the mist, like watchful eyes of some imaginary multi-ocular beast. Morganstern paid the driver and ran for the gate and shook it, rousing a dozing guard.

"I need to see Dr. Harding!" Morganstern said as the guard dragged himself to his feet.

"Uh … Be … begging your pardon, sir, but it's past three in the mornin'," the guard said, checking his fob watch.

"I don't care, man. You need to rouse him. Tell him I have something of his."

"I'm sorry, sir. The patients are resting—"

"You fool!"

"It's all right, Bernard. You can let Dr. Morganstern in."

The surgeon and the guard jumped with a start when Harding emerged from the mist just beyond the front door of the asylum. He strode towards them, still dressed in his suit, arms clasped firmly behind him, no doubt with the blasted stone in his grasp.

"Right you are, Dr. Harding," Bernard said, before opening the gate. Morganstern observed the knowing smile on Harding's face and tried to contain his anger.

"Thank you, Bernard," Harding said, not taking his eyes off the surgeon. "Perhaps we should speak in my office, Dr. Morganstern? Your timing couldn't be more perfect; sadly, another of my patients passed this evening. Poor man, suffered with dementia."

"I'm not interested in performing any further procedures at your hospital, Doctor." He held up the stone between gloved fingers. "I want you to explain to me what this stone is, and how I found it inside William's brain!"

Harding tutted and ushered Morganstern for the door. "Rightly so. Now let's come inside where we can discuss this matter in a more civil setting. It's dreadfully cold out here in the dark."

Two orderlies emerged and accosted Morganstern as soon as Harding closed the door. The men were powerfully strong, wrapping their arms in his. The surgeon struggled, but he was little more than a rag doll in their hands.

"Harding, you fiend! What are you doing?" Morganstern said, writhing in distress.

Harding stepped forward and slapped the surgeon hard across the face. "Contain yourself, man! If I didn't know better, I'd suspect you were suffering from some kind of mania. Perhaps the pressure of your surgical pursuits have taken their toll."

"You … You're a madman!" Morganstern gasped.

"Am I?" Harding plunged his hand into Morganstern's right fist and extracted the stone. "Madness is a lot like patience." He held the stone up to the light, admiring it as if it were a rare jewel. "It needs to be nurtured and understood."

Morganstern thrashed anew. "Let me free!"

Harding held the stone closer to Morganstern's face. "You want to know what madness is? Come, let us go and nurture it."

Morganstern was dragged kicking and screaming into the bowels of Bedlam. His cries awoke the patients, and they joined him in his exclamations. The patients bayed like dying animals, but in between, Morganstern could hear them calling his name; rejoicing his name. The surgeon felt the weight of the walls. In the dark, the shadows seemed to swell like stains through cheesecloth. Tears flooded his eyes as the fear of being locked inside the asylum came closer.

"Harding, please—you cannot do this!" he said as they came to end of the stairs.

The psychiatrist turned down a corridor, and the orderlies dragged Morganstern in his wake. Ahead, the surgeon saw a familiar door at the end. It was the entrance to Bedlam's mortuary, where just days before, Morganstern had dissected one of the hospital's patients. Bile rose in his throat as Harding's intentions became clear.

"No! No!" Morganstern said. "People will look for me! My fiancée!"

Harding stopped at the door to turn and laugh at him. "Oh, Dr. Morganstern. I'm not going to kill you—you're too useful to die."

The door opened and standing in the mortuary was a hunched man contorted in a straitjacket. He was held fast by another orderly, whose head was protected by a crudely-made steel cage. Morganstern was pulled inside and placed side by side with Harding's patient. The man stank of urine, fresh stains spreading across the crotch of the straitjacket.

"Who? Who!" The man said, his breath like curdled milk.

The psychiatrist took the patient's face in his hands with the tenderness of a parent. "Michael, this is Dr. Morganstern. He's a very talented surgeon, and he's here to help us."

Morganstern pulled against his captors. "I'll do nothing for you! You must release me now!"

Harding went to Morganstern, tried to show the surgeon the same tenderness. Morganstern recoiled from his touch. "But you've come so far, Dr. Morganstern, seen so much. You know that you're here seeking answers. They are the same answers I seek." He stepped back and held up the stone Morganstern had extracted from William. "The first time I saw one of these stones was on my first day, more than twenty years ago. The then administrator, Dr. Bartholomew Colton, was continuing a legacy that goes back millennia to Bethlem's very creation."

The psychiatrist approached Michael Demmick once again and pulled him in for an embrace. Morganstern watched wide-eyed as contentment washed over Harding's face, while his patient drooled into the doctor's shoulder.

"It's time to for you to be free, Michael," Harding said. "I've given you back your voice, but now your song is over."

17

Harding moved to Morganstern and smirking, retrieved the surgeon's bag, opened it, and plucked free the long-bladed Liston knife.

"I always believed that madness changes one on the inside, Dr. Morganstern, but it only became truth when you opened the door into William's soul and showed me its song."

He held up the knife in his right hand and the stone in his left. Morganstern watched in horror as the stone moved of its own accord in his palm, then cracked open like an egg. Hair-thin filaments like silken tendrils crawled out from inside, and his medical mind could only translate them to be like the fibrous connections of the human nervous system.

"Dr. Colton told me they'd come from the darkness between the stars, escaped from the cold void of nothing. They can only communicate through song, heard inside our minds. We must take them into ourselves if we are to bond with them, to better understand man's purpose; his existence."

Harding opened his mouth and placed the stone on his tongue, as if it were the consecrated host. He swallowed it down and shivered in gentle ecstasy. Then he opened his eyes and with a flick of his arm, ran the edge of the Liston knife across Demmick's throat. Arterial blood slapped against the wall and rained down Demmick's straitjacket. Within a moment, the patient collapsed to the floor, his blood painting crimson pathways in the cracks between the stones.

"Mother of God!" Morganstern said, fresh tears streaming down his face. "Mother of God, help me!"

Harding, smiling anew, pressed the blade to the surgeon's neck and produced yet another stone from his pocket, his hand as deft as a magician's.

"It's time to take your medicine, Doctor Morganstern."

The orderlies buckled Morganstern at the knees with harsh kicks and dropped him to the floor, now slick with Michael Demmick's blood. Harding straddled the surgeon and pried his mouth open, which only served to enhance the severity of his screams.

"It's time to hear the song of The Bedlam Stones."

19

Dr. Henry Morganstern stared at the eviscerated corpse of Michael Demmick and considered his handiwork. He'd opened the patient like a stage curtain, and in turn he'd opened his eyes onto the beyond. Beyond flesh and blood there was darkness, an endless blank canvas of thought where the truth lurked. In his mind he saw stones numbering as many as the stars in the sky, their fingers reaching out. The stones were singing; calling out for souls to hear. The surgeon felt Dr. Harding's hand on his shoulder, and he turned to his new master.

"You have a gift, Henry," Harding told him. "The stones want you to use it, to spread their seeds, their song, across the city. They agree with you that flesh is weak, that it is nothing more than a distraction. Those who flaunt their flesh should suffer to make way for the truth." Harding turned him back to his surgical tools, flecked with blood. "You have the tools and you have the purpose. Go now and share the song." Finally, he gave him a velvet bag filled with more stones. "Share their song, Henry, and return home here to Bedlam each morning. Do you understand?"

Morganstern nodded, wiped his hands clean and donned his cloak and hat. He clasped his doctor's bag in his hand and made for the door, for the streets of London. The East End, the stones urged him.

Journey to the East End ...

The Book of Last Words

They call convicts on death row the walking dead, wasted souls on the long ride to hell, but after all these years watching the worst of humanity check out on their backs with a needle in their arms, I can't help but envy them.

I've walked the halls of death row for almost a year, escorting inmates to their final moments, and, to me, their deaths come way too easy. What does anyone deserve when their time comes?

I thought I knew.

The first time I noticed the strange man with the book was at the execution of spree killer Adam John Cole. The man was in the small crowd of approved onlookers. Usually people who come to witness an inmate's execution are family members of the victims or journalists who've been cleared by the Governor's Office. This guy was neither. But once the curtain into the viewing room parted, there was no mistaking the demure figure in the darkest corner of the room.

I felt an overwhelming desire to question the man's presence in the viewing room, but I'd always assumed the witnesses had the right to be there or at least permission. Regardless of my misgiving—my suspicion—I had a job to do. I kept my mouth shut and set about helping my partner, Danny, shackle Cole to the gurney. Cole's cockiness, sharply honed after

21

ten years on death row, kept every one of us—prison guard, clergyman, and warden, on task.

"Well, lookie at all the people who came to my farewell shindig," Cole said, like he was at a rodeo.

Warden Reed stepped up to centre stage and unnecessarily straightened his tie. "Adam John Cole, you have been condemned by a jury of your peers to die by lethal injection; sentenced by a judge in good standing in this state. Do you have anything to say before this sentence is carried out?"

I glanced out into the crowd. Half a dozen faces of all creeds, colours, and ages united in sorrow, except the strange little man. Cole's voice pulled me back.

"I … I killed all those people because … " Cole's unshaven throat bobbed as he swallowed. They all embrace their guilt in the end. I prayed he didn't piss or shit on the floor. He took a deep breath and continued. " … I just needed another fix, you know. It was the drugs."

Cole turned to look at me, as if for vindication, and I turned my gaze back to the crowd. I preferred to look at people crying than a last-minute plea for mercy. I noticed the strange man writing very carefully in a large leather-bound book. I didn't hear the warden call my name.

"Officer Holder."

I froze and looked at the warden, whose fuzzy eyebrows were knotted in consternation. Danny flashed me the same grizzled look. Back on track, I helped Danny turn the gurney around so the crowd could see Cole's profile. The injection team pounced like vultures and inserted the IVs in Cole's arm. Cole trembled, his brow slick with sweat. The reverend stepped in and said his prayer, but I knew deep down he hoped the multiple murderer burned in hell.

As the concoction ran up the IV tube to Cole's arm and invaded his blood, I remembered my friend, Alex, being blown to bits by a roadside bomb in Kandahar and how I almost joined him.

Once Cole had closed his eyes for the last time, I looked back to the crowd.

The strange man was gone.

After all was said and done, the crowd dispersed, but I never saw the odd man leave. Later, in the debrief, I was tempted to discuss him with the warden, but the warden had no intention of listening to me.

"What the hell happened out there, Holder?" he said, removing his clip-on tie now that the formalities were done.

"Sorry boss, I lost my focus," was all I could say.

The warden went to sit behind his desk. "You made me look like a damn fool in front of all those people, Holder. Those families came here to see justice done not a goddamn circus."

I nodded, silently knowing the warden could make a fool of himself all on his own. Danny, who stood near the door, eager to get back to the row, let out a sigh, his belly swelling like a drum.

"Sir, it was just a small lapse on Holder's part. It won't happen again."

The warden studied me beneath those ridiculous eyebrows. I could tell he was thinking he shouldn't have hired a veteran to be a guard in his prison.

"Well, I don't want that sort of mishap during one of my executions to occur again. We got another in just two days—and not just anyone. Leon Porter Johnson." He pointed to me. "You understand, Holder?"

"Yes, sir."

I left the office after agreeing with the warden. I quickly learned Danny was starting to get in the same frame of mind. He whirled on me as soon as he closed the warden's door.

"I'm getting tired of covering for you, Holder. You need to get some focus. We're surrounded by killers in here, and I don't want to end up with a shiv in my back."

Shivs were nothing compared to mortar attacks, machine gun fire, miscalculated drone strikes, or roadside bombs. Death row was a walk in the park compared to a stroll across miles of Afghani desert. Still, I humoured him. Danny was a good enough guy, and I needed this job.

"Hey, I'm sorry. I'll get back in line," I said.

The subject of the odd man never passed my lips for the next two days. I got back into the work, walking the row, escorting prisoners to cells, and doing run-throughs with Danny in preparation for Leon Johnson's execution.

Leon Johnson was the main attraction for the year, but to me he was just another con. Tall, but wiry, he didn't look like much, but I guess there was something about his eyes. Johnson kidnapped and butchered seven young women before he was caught in an FBI undercover sting. They found seven severed heads in a chest freezer in his apartment. The media reported he used to sit with them while he watched television. During his trial, Johnson's gaze managed to put the jurors on edge, with many of them requesting to be dismissed. After a short postponement, a new jury found him guilty of all seven killings in less than two hours. The Governor, keen for re-election, put a rush on Johnson's execution, and the other death-row inmates were more than happy to oblige.

The day before his scheduled execution, Danny and I escorted Johnson to his holding cell and questioned him about his last meal and other special requirements. The son-of-a-bitch seemed to take his impending death in his stride.

"Mint chocolate chip ice-cream," he said, running his tongue across his bottom lip.

Danny wrote it down while I stared at the freak, certain he wouldn't last a day in the desert. That's what he deserved.

"That's it?" I said, and I felt Danny elbow me.

Johnson's eyes flicked my way. "I have simple tastes."

"I bet."

"That's enough, Holder."

Johnson smiled at me. "Holder. You're the veteran aren't you? The soldier."

"What of it?"

"I'm told you survived a roadside bomb, but your friend didn't."

I took a step, but Danny gripped my arm tight.

"You shut your mouth, Johnson," Danny said.

The serial killer looked back to me. He hadn't stopped smiling. "I only wanted to know what Holder's last meal would be, that's all."

Danny dragged me out of there before I could drive my fist into Johnson's teeth. Normally, I hated execution days, but after that conversation I couldn't wait for tomorrow. I was tempted to tackle the head of the injection team to the ground and stab the needle into Johnson's arm myself.

That night, I got back into the habit of staring at my gun way too long and dreamed about Alex.

We were on patrol. The desert was the colour of bare flesh. Children played with their dogs amongst the rubble. Alex and I held a conversation without looking at each other. Our eyes had to be locked on everyone and everything. Anyone could be a suicide bomber. It was almost as if we were already dead, and it was only a matter of when.

"My girl hasn't written in four weeks," Alex said.

"So?"

"I think she's had enough of me not being there."

"Maybe she's got her hands full with your kids."

"Yeah ... maybe."

I could hear the self-doubt in his voice. It was hard not to feel helpless in a place like this. I tried to talk sense into him as I watched a tall, thin Afghani man walking towards us.

"Look, man, you gotta stop worrying about it. She's already written you a letter—it just hasn't gotten through to you yet."

"Right."

The Afghani walked on by, and we both took a breath.

"She loves you, man. You're just being paranoid."

"What if I'm not?"

At that moment I wanted to turn and slap him, but the ground suddenly opened up beneath us. Dust and rock sprayed up in my face. My ears squealed. Then there was the rush of pain, a long, hard burn. The wind was knocked out of me, and all I could feel was air. When I finally hit the ground and opened my eyes, everything was painted red.

I crawled through the blood-caked dirt to Alex. His legs were gone, and his guts were looped around his head like sleeping snakes. He took my hand and said something to me, his final words.

But I can't remember them.

I woke screaming to find Danny standing over me.

"Holder, wake up!"

It took me a moment to steel myself, to get my bearings and realise that I was on the row; in the officer's quarters where officers on duty have to spend the night before a scheduled execution. I sat up and pulled the sweat-soaked sheets off my chest.

"You were howling in your sleep," Danny said.

"Sorry."

"Yeah, well forget it. It's time to get up and get ready."

It took me ten minutes to shower, shave, and put on my uniform. I stared at myself in the mirror for some time and saw that I was the spitting image of someone who had survived an explosion. Someone who hadn't slept a full night in more than a year. But I knew the adrenaline burst from the dream—and the impending execution—would keep me going all day.

After a quick breakfast, Danny and I and the three other officers on duty were called to the warden's office. He wore his best, pressed suit and a serious gaze. Beneath all of that so-called authority was a man who'd never gotten close to a single inmate in his entire career, someone who was only interested in getting close to a news camera.

"Now you should all know how important today is," the warden said. "This is Leon Johnson, one of the most notorious murderers this state has ever seen. The community is expecting his execution to be swift and just. There are going to be a lot of people out there on the other side of that glass—the mayor, reporters, victims' families, and they won't want to see any mistakes."

The warden looked at me for emphasis, but I ignored him, instead realising that I'd forgotten something: the strange man at Cole's execution. Would he make an appearance?

"Am I boring you, Holder?"

I looked up to see every eye in the room on me.

"Uh, no sir."

"Well, I damn well hope not. I don't want any screw-ups today from anyone. You got that?"

Johnson's execution was scheduled for 2 p.m. His last meal was to be served at noon. Danny and I were the ones to bring it to him. Why someone who murdered seven young women deserved a bowl of *Ben and Jerry's* mint chocolate chip ice cream was beyond me. The son-of-a-bitch should've been given a bowl of freshly laid shit, as far as I was concerned.

I presented the plastic bowl of ice-cream and matching spoon to Johnson in his holding cell at 12:02 p.m., but at first, he seemed disinterested in his final meal. His attention rested solely with me, his knowing smile a taunt. But I wasn't going to humour him in the slightest.

"As requested, one bowl of mint chocolate chip ice cream," I said.

"Would you like some, Officer Holder?"

I bit my tongue and took a step back. Danny stood behind me at the door. Johnson just kept on smiling.

"It looks delicious," he said, eventually picking up the spoon to taste it. He spoke as he ate, the green-coloured ice-cream swirling around inside his mouth. People who ate with their mouth open really got on my nerves. "Mmm, it's absolutely divine."

He took another scoop and kept his eye on me the entire time. I couldn't wait until this guy's heart stopped. I felt Danny tug on my sleeve as the cue to leave. We locked Johnson in with his final meal then stood guard outside, listening as he savoured every morsel. As the minutes ticked by, Johnson started whistling an unidentifiable tune.

How could someone about to face their death be so calm about it?

At 1 p.m., the warden arrived and spoke to Johnson, to see if he was being treated fairly, or needed to speak with the reverend or any next of kin.

"I've always received the finest of hospitality here, Warden, sir," Johnson said. "As for family, both my parents died a long time ago, and I was their only child."

The warden nodded. "Do you need to speak with the reverend?"

Reverend Dougherty stood in the doorway, not too close and not too far. His knuckles, clutched around his bible, shone white with exertion. When the condemned serial murderer looked his way, the knuckles shone even brighter.

"Perhaps later."

One-thirty p.m. meant it was time to move Johnson from his holding cell to the death chamber. I heard the sound of cars pulling in outside and people talking. Some voices were raised, with a group calling for Johnson's swift death. They only had to wait another thirty minutes.

Procedure meant we were no longer allowed to talk to Johnson, but that didn't mean he had to follow the rules. As we paraded him down death row, past all the other inmates, who declared him a dead man walking, he started whistling again. Silently I prayed the bastard would fall to pieces inside the chamber, that'd he'd scream, and piss and shit as he realised he was about to become the victim.

Some of the inmates told him he was going to get what he deserved, that the girls he'd mutilated were going to get the revenge they deserved: harsh words coming from fellow killers, hard to believe that some of them wouldn't stoop as low as Johnson. All Johnson did was smile—the smile of a man who hadn't a care in the world.

The hall seemed to stretch on forever. I was reminded of how there were no streets in the desert, only dust with mud houses scattered over the surface like headstones. There wasn't one speck of dust on death row, but way too many stains of depravity.

The door to the chamber swelled into view and another guard emerged—Rudy, I think his name was. He halted our procession to attach the harnesses around Johnson's wrists. These harnesses would allow us to strap him to the gurney. Johnson gave Rudy a smile.

"And how are you today, sir?"

Rudy didn't even flinch. He tightened the harnesses and stepped aside to allow us to walk through the chamber door.

The chamber was as silent as a church at midnight, so our shoes echoed inside the space. Through the glass, which was covered by a black curtain, I could hear the hum of human voices. The anxious anticipation of pre-show conversation laced with sadness. For the families of the victims, an execution was like enduring the funerals of their loved ones all over again.

The injection team was already in the room, checking the intravenous tubes and bags of drugs which would send Johnson to hell. They were a well-honed machine, professionals who only had regard for the procedure rather than the person. How many veins had they punctured? How many hearts had they stopped? I'd only seen three lives taken in my time at the prison, but so many more, so far away.

Johnson shuffled to the side of the gurney and offered the new faces a smile, but his tongue was silent this time. Perhaps the inevitability of death was finally getting to him. Two of the other guards took hold of Johnson's shackles and made him sit on the gurney then lie down. The murderer lay back calmly, keeping any emotions in check. He was simply along for the ride. The wrist harnesses were chained to the gurney. Johnson wasn't going anywhere. He let out a slight grunt of discomfort.

"A bit of pleasure in my pain?" he said to the one of the guards.

He was ignored. I would have said something, but the warden entered the room. He had an even sharper-looking suit on today.

"How are we looking?" he asked one of the injection team.

"We're good to go."

"No time like the present," Johnson added.

The curtain slid back to reveal a room full of people. In the front row a dozen witnesses stared at Johnson, who was splayed out for all to see. Behind the front row was the chief of police, the mayor, and a score of reporters. In the back-right corner, somehow obscured in the shadows, was the odd man. I felt the overwhelming urge to speak, to warn everyone, but what could I have said? I wasn't sure anyone else could see him. But he could see me. In fact, he stared me down, his eyes resolute. The warden took the stage before I could do anything.

"Leon Porter Johnson, you have been condemned to die by a jury of your peers by lethal injection, sentenced by a judge in good standing in this state. Do you have anything to say before this sentence is carried out?"

Johnson turned his head to face the crowd. He locked eyes with everyone, and I knew he was savouring their hatred of him. Even behind bars and at the point of death, he wanted power over all who were present. I looked to the odd man, who to my surprise, had his book closed.

"No, I have nothing to say," Johnson replied.

"Let the sentence be carried out," the warden said.

The warden gave the nod, and the injection team moved in, sliding the inch-long needles into Johnson's arms. In minutes, he would be no more.

Time seemed to stand still for a moment, and my heart pounded inside me. I didn't care about Johnson anymore. Instead I gazed at the strange man, waiting for something to happen. Then Johnson's voice pulled me back.

"Wait ... "

Everyone froze. The warden stumbled over his next words.

"You have something you wish to say?"

Johnson blinked. "Yes ... is the reverend here?"

The reverend had been with us the whole time. With much reluctance, he stepped towards the condemned man.

"Reverend?" Johnson's voice was barely a whisper. "I wish to confess my sins."

I quickly looked back to the strange man, who now had his book open and pen poised.

"Yes, my son?" the reverend said, leaning in.

It all happened so fast. The reverend's scream shattered the solemnity, but it was the sight of his blood which spread the screams like a plague. Guards stepped in to pull Johnson's jaw from the reverend's throat, but the damage was already done. The warden tried to maintain order as the reverend fell, blood gushing over his white collar. Johnson writhed in ecstasy against the guards, a chunk of the reverend's neck dangling from his lips.

On the other side of the glass, panic forced the witnesses to flee, but my legs had turned to stone. Inside the chamber, my colleagues piled on top of Johnson in a desperate bid to contain his mania. Behind the fracas, I saw him: the strange man with the book.

In the back of my mind, I heard the roadside bomb again, and it snapped me back into the moment. I ran across the room to the man and

31

grabbed at his book, a page tearing free in my grip. Then he was gone, like a switch had turned him off. I shook off the impossibility and moved to press the button to administer the life-taking serum. The guards were left speechless by Johnson's sudden lack of struggling.

On the floor beside the gurney, his suit slathered in blood, lay the corpse of the reverend. The execution was over, but two men had lost their lives.

And I slipped the torn page into my pocket.

In the hours that followed, every staff member who'd been in the chamber was interviewed about the Leon Johnson incident. As I sat outside his office waiting my turn, the warden screamed that heads would roll, that guards would be fired, that the FBI would launch an investigation. Some of the guards threw threats back—that they would resign or go to the Board of Prisons about the stress the incident had caused.

All I could think about as I sat with my colleagues was the man with the book. How had he gotten inside the room? How did he know what was going to happen? The answers were on the piece of paper, which seemed to burn a hole in my pocket. I was desperate to look at it, but I dared not move. The look on that man's face told me he knew everything that had occurred in that chamber and more.

I contemplated telling the warden when he called me in, but I knew it would bring more heat down on me. Surely the warden knew by the process of elimination that I'd been the one to push the switch. If the other guards hadn't mentioned it, then the video surveillance would surely show it.

I was about to lose my job and possibly my freedom, because of something I thought I'd seen. Defiantly, I stood and slipped my hand into my pocket. Danny and the other guards raised their heads to flash me looks of contempt. Any camaraderie I'd had with Danny was now over. He wouldn't have my back this time. The paper crinkled between my fingers.

What did it matter if I walked away now, if only just to satisfy my curiosity?

My heels scuffed the polished floor as I stepped to one of the windows. Through the mesh and steel bars I saw a media horde of television cameras. The botched execution of Leon Porter Johnson was going to make headlines around the nation. But they had it wrong: the story should have been about how Johnson took one last victim with him before he was put down. Slowly, I slipped the paper from my pocket, taking great care not to let anyone else see what I was doing. I looked down at the torn piece of evidence and gasped.

The words were golden, swirling in great loops across the page, written with a steady hand and the finest pen. *Calligraphy* was the word that came to mind: beautiful calligraphy. I was so hypnotised by the way the words had been scripted that it took me several moments to understand the phrases they made:

> *Tell her I love her.*
> *I'm sorry for hating you.*
> *I killed a man.*
> *Forgive me.*
> *It was the drugs.*
> *I've wasted my life.*

They were the last words of the departing. Goodbyes, heartfelt and heart-wrenching, presented like the word of God. I tilted the page in my trembling hand and watched the fading light of day dance across its surface. A very careful hand had immortalised the final words of every dying person in a book, and it terrified me.

"Officer Holder."

I turned to the voice and scrunched the page in my fist to conceal it, but it wasn't the warden calling to me.

The strange man stood in the centre of the hallway, between my

colleagues, clutching the leather-bound book to his chest. None of the other guards seemed to notice him or even move. Outside, the media crews were frozen, along with the setting sun. The calligrapher stepped towards me.

He was at least two feet shorter than me, dressed in a brown plaid suit. His face was a road map of the ages, but his eyes saw everything. I held out my fist to him.

"I'm sorry I damaged your book," I said.

I opened my fist and the crumpled paper bloomed slowly in my palm. The old man reached up, took the paper, and opened his book to reinsert the missing page. The page mended before my eyes, the tear gone, and every crinkle smoothed in an instant. The gilded script pulsed in satisfaction to be whole again. The calligrapher closed the book and turned to leave.

"I wasn't meant to see you, was I?"

The old man stopped and shook his head carefully. I wanted to walk around and look at his face, but only my voice was free to move.

"So, you write down the last words people say—is that it?"

He nodded.

I swallowed hard and licked my lips. I didn't want to know what Leon Johnson had said to the reverend before he killed him. That wasn't important.

"Do you ... " I began. "In your book ... do you have Alex Cavell's last words in there?"

The old man nodded again. I moved to ask him if I could read my friend's message, but he was already turning around. The book opened on its own, flipping back hundreds of pages with a sound like bird's wings. I stepped to the old man and read the intricate golden whorls of Alex's epitaph:

Don't you die on me, Holder. You live.

The book closed and time returned to the hallway. I stood there like a fool, tears streaming down my cheeks.

"Officer Holder?"

The warden stood impatiently at his door. I walked towards him, ready to embrace my fate.

The Yellow House

The road was a black vein, an unstitched wound.

Night was closing in, but Fred was drawn to the yellow of the headlights. *The yellow sign.* The back and forth of the wipers were like a metronome, but it failed to soothe the one thought inside his head: *that he didn't belong in this world.*

The three men with him in the Chevrolet paid him no heed. They were nothing more than ushers, he knew, ferrymen. The one to his left wore a yellow necktie. Another sign. Everywhere, the yellow sign.

"Please," Fred broke the silence. "Please don't take me to the bughouse."

The car turned, jostling everyone inside. They refused to acknowledge him, but he had to make them listen.

"You can't ... " Fred continued. "You can't let them lock me up ... "

Through the windshield Fred saw the entrance to the State Mental Hospital, the gates open wide to receive him. A hungry mouth. The headlights glinted off the iron, momentarily turning black into liquid yellow gold.

"Yellow," Fred said, as he bit his nails.

The yellow flowers on Betty's dress, her yellow hair.

"Betty wouldn't want this—she wouldn't want to lock me up in here!"

The man with the yellow tie put a hand on his shoulder to quiet him. "That's enough Fred," he said.

"Fred? Fred? Who is Fred? Where is Betty? My yellow Betty?"

The driver shook his head in consternation and braked hard. Through the beams of yellow light, Fred saw the front steps of the hospital.

"Why are the buildings so dark? Why is everything so dark when it should be yellow?"

The engine stopped, and the three men climbed out of the car, their faces and bodies obscured by their heavy coats and wide-brimmed hats. The man with the yellow tie took him carefully by the wrist.

"Come on now, Mr. Clayton."

Fred stared at him wide-eyed. "I'm not Mr. Clayton."

Arms took hold of his and pulled him from the car. The air was biting, a thousand burning knives. This world was dark and cold.

"Why won't you people listen to me?"

Fred tried to wrench his arms free, but he was abruptly weakened by the sight of the old man in the lab coat at the top of the hospital stairs. The lab coat was yellow. The man in the lab coat—a doctor—flashed him a smile of yellow teeth. He beckoned Fred with an outstretched hand, his wrinkled index and middle fingers yellowed from years of cigarette smoke. As Fred was taken up the stairs he got a closer look at the hospital's façade—painted bright yellow. Fred cracked a smile of his own.

"Is this the place?" he said. "The yellow house? Is this the temple?"

The three men escorting Fred exchanged worried glances, but the doctor's voice quickly assuaged their fears.

"Thank you, gentlemen. I'll take it from here."

The doctor took Fred by the elbow and led him towards the front doors.

"Welcome, Mr. Clayton. My name is Dr. Burke. We're going to take good care of you."

The old man's eyes, above his half-moon spectacles, seemed to have a calming effect.

"Is this ... the yellow temple?"

Dr. Burke smirked. "Come on, let's get you inside. There's a great deal to discuss."

They bathed him with yellow soap which smelled like dandelions and dressed him in a yellow shirt and dark overalls. Already Fred felt at home, the yellow signs comforting and orderly. Perhaps he'd been wrong? Perhaps this was the place he'd always meant to be?

A nurse in a yellow hat and uniform took his blood and offered him water from a yellow cup. He hardly felt the needlestick because she reminded him so much of his Betty. Betty all in yellow.

"Is this place the Yellow Temple?"

The nurse looked up briefly from her work, but she didn't reply, only offered him that same knowing smile. What needed to be said? The truth was all around him. He belonged here. With others just like him.

After drawing his blood, the nurse walked Fred from his room down the hall, where Dr. Burke, and other nurses and men in yellow lab coats were seated, patiently waiting for his arrival. The nurse sat Fred at the front of the room, and he stared back at them. Then Dr. Burke stood to speak.

"Good evening, gentlemen. I'd like to introduce you to our newest patient, Mr. Fred Clayton."

Fred tried to smile at the audience, but none of them smiled back. Many of them smoked cigarettes, the haze, which was yellow, hovering thickly above them.

"Mr. Clayton is a 44-year-old married man with no children. He has been an automotive mechanic for 25 years and until recently, was in a good state of mental and physical health. Two nights ago, Mr. Clayton attacked his wife of 12 years. The attack was entirely unprovoked. When Mr. Clayton was arrested, he told the officers that he beat his wife because she'd dyed her hair. Mrs. Clayton is a natural blonde, but she wanted to be a brunette." Burke turned to look at Fred in that moment, but there was no warmth on this occasion, only judgement. "This, in itself, should not have instigated such violence, but according to Mrs. Clayton it was the climax of a series of strange events concerning her husband."

Fred listened to Dr. Burke intensely.

"In the week leading up to this event, Mr. Clayton had begun

39

experiencing what I believe to be the onset of paranoid schizophrenia. A delusion centered on the color yellow. Right now he believes he sees the color yellow, even in the lab coat I am wearing and in the nurses' uniforms."

Burke opened a manilla folder and produced a tattered and yellowed book. Fred gasped at the sight of it, drawing the gazes of the onlookers. Burke waved it near Fred who followed it with slow motions of his head, like a dog would a piece of raw meat.

"As you can see, the book seems to still have some sort of hold over him, as does the color yellow."

"What is the title of the book?" one of the doctor's asked.

"*The King in Yellow*," Burke replied.

Fred smiled as the intonation touched his ears. "Yellow," he said.

Burke continued. "It's believed that Mr. Clayton found this book under the passenger seat of a car he was restoring in his garage. Although Mr. Clayton is not an avid reader, his wife told the judge at the committal hearing that her husband became obsessed with it, reading it repeatedly, morning, noon, and night."

"Dr. Burke?" Another doctor said. "The book—*The King in Yellow*— what is it about?"

Burke shrugged. "I haven't the faintest. But it's a play, not a novel." Burke handed the book to his colleagues, and they began scrutinizing it. "Now, perhaps we can ask Mr. Clayton some questions in an effort to ascertain the extent of his delusion. Would you mind obliging us, Mr. Clayton?"

Fred nodded, but kept his eyes locked on the book as it was passed from one doctor to another.

"Splendid. Mr. Clayton, why do you think you're in hospital?"

The doctors flicked through the pages. *Would they see it too*, he wondered.

"Be ... because this is where I belong. Not out there."

"You feel you belong here?"

Fred looked at Dr. Burke as if for the first time. "Don't you? Isn't that why you wear the yellow coat?" He turned to the others. "Why you all do?"

Burke addressed his staff. "The delusion is so fully formed that Mr. Clayton can actually see it in others. He believes that his wife changed her hair because she was trying to deny herself from some sort of hidden truth. An alternate reality. Right now, he believes that we're all in on the charade. A conspiracy of color if you will."

Some of the doctors chuckled and whispered, their eyes probing Fred with that same look Betty gave him: that he was a fool.

"You … you don't believe me?"

Dr. Burke placed a hand on Fred's shoulder. "We believe that we can help you, Mr. Clayton. That we can release you from these shackles." He took the book back from one of his colleagues. "This book holds no power over you. It is a fiction and nothing more." He flicked through the pages. "There is no King in Yellow, no Carcosa—"

Fred felt himself go rigid as words escaped his mouth all on their own: "*One morning early in May I stood before the steel safe in my bedroom, trying on the golden jewelled crown. The diamonds flashed fire as I turned to the mirror, and the heavy beaten gold burned like a halo about my head. I remembered Camilla's agonized scream and the awful words echoing through the dim streets of Carcosa.*"

Dr. Burke recoiled. "Remarkable. His voice has changed, in tone and inflection. Nurse, I believe we should take Mr. Clayton back to his room at once."

Fred went limp in the nurse's arms, and she had to call for a wheelchair. As they wheeled him away, the room buzzed with chatter, the doctors all mingling around their leader, eager to get another glimpse at the book.

"Gentleman, I believe that our course of treatment for Mr. Clayton is clear—we'll commence insulin shock therapy in the morning."

As the hallway became a blur, Fred realised that the only way Dr. Burke and the others would truly understand was if he showed them.

The next morning there was no shower or breakfast. There was a distinct lack of birdsong. As if they could sense Fred's trepidation. After taking more of his blood, Dr. Burke and six nurses escorted Fred to a room at the end of the hall. It was still dark, and the other patients slept soundly in their beds. In the dark, Fred could barely make out the yellow of the doctor's coat and this troubled him.

"Where are we going?" Fred asked.

At the head of the entourage Dr. Burke strode with the confidence of a soldier on the march. Fred noticed he clutched the yellow book in his right hand.

"My ... my book?" Fred muttered. "You've still got my book."

The good doctor looked back over his shoulder. "I've been reading it, Mr. Clayton, in an attempt to understand your delusion. It's most fascinating."

"Yes ... it is."

The double doors opened onto an operating theatre style room. A stretcher sat in the centre, and the walls and floors were tiled. Yellow tiles framed by grout as black as night. No one but Fred seemed to notice the significance of the yellow tiles. The nurses had him lie on the bed and remain still as they fastened thick leather straps around his wrists, chest, and ankles. Then they pricked his arms with needles. Intravenous tubes dangled about in the air like snakes. The way the nurses moved with such purpose should have given Fred comfort, but he knew not one of them would truly be able to help him until they helped themselves.

"Is the insulin ready, nurse?" Burke said.

"Yes, doctor," she replied.

"Good, then let's begin."

Burke leaned in close to Fred. His breath smelled of cigarettes. "Now, Mr. Clayton we're going to administer the insulin. It will make you feel very sleepy. The injections will provoke seizures, and these seizures will help your mind rail against the delusions you've been experiencing. Do you understand?"

Fred blinked. "Will I be a sacrifice, Doctor?"

Burke turned to one of the nurses. "We'll start with 100 units nurse and increase the dosage by 50 units per hour." Then he placed a hand on Fred's shoulder. "We're here to make you well again, Mr. Clayton. Don't you want to be well?"

"Don't you want to know the truth?" Fred whispered back. "You've already read about it."

Burke turned away and nodded to the nurse who turned a dial on one of the intravenous tubes. Fred shivered as a coldness spread along his arm and over his chest, like he was adrift in an icy sea. He craved warmth, the golden heat of a Carcosan sky.

Instead, darkness claimed him.

Fred was taken into the arms of a golden light. Its caress was like a summer stream, and he was a leaf carried by its current. He laid back, the bed he'd been placed upon in the hospital was gone, at least from this world. Voices called to him, and when he turned to hear them, he found he was not alone.

Dr. Burke and his staff had been replaced by figures in golden robes. The beings had no faces beneath their hoods, only caverns of the deepest, darkest black. Yet Fred knew they could see him, no, could see *into* him.

"Mr. Clayton?" one of them said, but Fred couldn't be sure which.

"I knew it was true," Fred said, smiling with blessed relief.

"Mr. Clayton." This time the voice came from the right, no from *inside* his head.

The gilded shape leaned in, so close that Fred could see that its robes weren't fabric at all, but rather liquid, shifting and twisting to maintain its shape. Over its shoulder, Fred glimpsed twin suns beating down upon a withered city.

43

"Our words are your words, Mr. Clayton."

"Yes," Fred could taste the salt of his tears.

The creature's robe sprouted a tendril, which became an arm and then a hand. In its fingertips sat a crown. The crown slipped onto Fred's head, like the warmth of a lover. The figure spoke one last time:

"Then make them theirs."

Dr. Burke took Fred Clayton's wrist to check his pulse. Alarmingly, it was well over 120 beats a minute. The doctor checked the insulin flow and listened to his patient's heart. The rhythm was normal, only on the verge of being tachycardic. He would have to keep a close eye on this man and be prepared to pull him from his coma quickly if need be. Burke glanced over at the electroshock machine nearby. If the insulin shock therapy didn't take, then he'd have to resort stimulation of a more direct kind.

Burke took a seat next to Clayton and studied the book that had apparently sent the average, everyday motor mechanic on a rapid downward spiral.

The King in Yellow was a strange text—a series of interconnected plays which hinted at another reality. How a work of fiction had altered Mr. Clayton's psychological state he wasn't sure. Perhaps the man already had deep-seated schizophrenic tendencies? These normally presented themselves in the young, but mental illness was, by its very nature, unpredictable. There was still so much that was unknown. Burke puffed on his cigarette. There was a clear irony between the science of psychology and the power of story, as both stemmed from a desire to understand the human mind.

A gentle touch to his shoulder startled him, and he turned to find a nurse at his side.

"Excuse me Doctor, but Mr. Clayton's wife is here. She was hoping to see her husband."

Burke frowned. "Had no one informed her that her husband is currently undergoing treatment?"

"I'm sorry, sir. I tried to explain, but she said if she couldn't see her husband then she wanted to speak with you."

Burke nodded, stubbed out his cigarette, and slipped *The King in Yellow* into his lab coat pocket. For some strange reason, it gave him comfort to know it was there.

The good doctor thought it oddly provocative that Betty Clayton chose to wear a yellow dress, especially given the fact that her husband's violent action was evident on her face.

She held out her hand, and Burke took it, trying his best to offer a reassuring smile.

"Hello, Mrs. Clayton. I apologize, but we weren't expecting you," he said.

Betty teased a lock of yellow hair behind her ear. The hair gleamed against the purple bruises on her face and neck. "I'm sorry, Doctor," she said. "I just really needed to see Fred."

Burke gently patted her hand. "I understand. Unfortunately, Mr. Clayton is in the middle of his treatment."

"The … insulin therapy?"

"Yes, that's right. So, the nurses did explain, then?"

"Mm-hmm. They said he'd be sleeping."

"In a coma … but he is perfectly fine. We're monitoring him constantly."

Betty swallowed. "I thought insulin was for people with diabetes. Wouldn't this be like … poison?"

Burke cleared his throat. "Well, it shocks the system back into normality. Like a reset."

"And it works?"

"The majority of the time, yes. Now, Mrs. Clayton I am very sorry, but I'm afraid your visit falls just outside the normal visiting hours—"

45

"Can I see him?"

"Mrs. Clayton—"

"Please, you said it yourself, he's in a coma. I just … want to tell him I forgive him. It will only take a few minutes."

Burke could see the sincerity in her blackened eyes. Despite everything, she had an inner strength.

"It's rather unorthodox, but … yes, of course. Just a few minutes."

To Dr. Burke, Betty Clayton resembled a widow standing beside her comatose husband. The only thing at odds with the scene was that she was not wearing black. Yet, the manner in which she carried herself gave the psychiatrist pause. She did not seem fearful or anxious. He watched as she took her husband's hand and stroked it.

"Is he in pain?" she said.

Burke stepped closer, careful not to intrude. "No, he would be feeling absolutely nothing."

She stroked Fred's brow with delicate fingers. "I imagine he is dreaming."

"Inducing a coma allows the mind to heal. There's no signs of the normal sleep-wakefulness cycle, so it's highly unlikely Mr. Clayton is dreaming."

The stroking became more insistent, as if she were tracing a shape on his forehead. Dr. Burke frowned.

"Mrs. Clayton, how are you feeling … after the ordeal?"

"I've missed Fred immensely. It's so good to see him again."

"Yes, I suspect it's heartening to see him … in a much calmer state. Especially after what happened."

She smiled and ran her fingers through Fred's hair. "It was meant to be."

Dr. Burke shifted to try and get a better look at her face. There was something off-putting in her gaze. A perverse lust.

"You … must have been in fear of your life."

"Oh, not at all," she said. "It was just a shock to his system."

"What do you mean?"

This time she turned away from Fred to look at him. "The book."

Dr. Burke could feel the weight of it in his lab coat. "The book?"

Betty moved to him and slid her hand into his coat to retrieve it. "This book. I was

reading it to Fred when he finally woke."

Burke's throat tightened. "You? You were ... reading it to him?"

She opened the book and flicked through the pages. "Of course. I was the one who hid it in that car for him to find."

"You told ... the police that he just attacked you ... I ... I don't understand."

Betty smiled, and for the first time Dr. Burke noticed her eyes were golden, like two miniature suns housed inside her skull. She leaned over her husband and whispered in his ear, and immediately the man sat up, breaking his leather straps. His eyes wide open. Burke was paralyzed by confusion and fear. He could only stare as Fred Clayton plucked the insulin catheters from his arms, walked to the electroshock machine, and took hold of the paddles.

"I ... I ... don't understand ... " Burke said again.

Betty stood aside as her husband came at the psychiatrist, the harsh buzz of the device echoing inside the room.

"Oh, don't you worry," she said. "We'll see that you do."

Dr. Burke awoke to the sounds of screams. He tasted blood and wool in his mouth and quickly realized he'd been bound and gagged. As his eyes adjusted, it became evident the screams were coming from his fellow psychiatrists and the nurses. They were all being subjected to horrible violence at the hands of the people who had once depended upon them for care.

The patients ran about the hall, barely clothed, slathered in blood. Several, Dr. Burke saw, were huddled in a corner, urinating on one of the doctors, staining his coat. As he howled the patients chanted the word *yellow* over and over.

A makeshift stage had been assembled with the tables and chairs from the cafeteria and recreational room. Atop it stood Fred and Betty Clayton, hand in hand, smiling down on the melee unfolding below. The pair had fastened crowns made of bed springs around their heads. Betty came forward to address her parishioners. In her left hand she held the book that started it all.

"This is the King in Yellow … " Betty told the gathering.

Fred Clayton's eyes began to exude a blazing light, and Betty praised him with a rousing cry:

"And I am his queen!"

Behind them Dr. Burke beheld the dawn of a new day. Twin suns rising to herald an age of madness. The King and Queen in their Yellow House.

Betty opened the book and began to read from the First Act:

Along the shore the cloud waves break,
The twin suns sink behind the lake,
The shadows lengthen
In Carcosa.

Strange is the night where black stars rise,
And strange moons circle through the skies,
But stranger still is
Lost Carcosa.

Songs that the Hyades shall sing,
Where flap the tatters of the King,
Must die unheard in
Dim Carcosa.

The Yellow House

Song of my soul, my voice is dead,
Die thou, unsung, as tears unshed
Shall dry and die in
Lost Carcosa.

Daughters of the Veil

The autumn leaves fell in time with Sera's tears.

The park was growing cold, the setting sun casting crystalline light across the grass. The colour was being drawn out of the world, like blood from a vein. Sera wiped the tears from her eyes and looked up at the tall, ancient oak tree. Such sombre thoughts, she thought. But who could blame her.

A cackle of laughter pulled her gaze away from the dreaded tree, and she looked to the street to see a group of children in costume run along the curb; goblins, princesses, devils, and aliens in search of candy and fun.

They had no idea what Halloween meant to her.

Sera turned back to the tree and studied the cracks and crevices in the bark. High above, the branches creaked and moaned in the breeze. Some of the twigs seemed to point directly at her, judgemental and knowing. On one branch a ring of bark had been worn away to reveal the fresh brown wood beneath; a ring worn by a coil of rope. The rope was long gone now, but Sera could still see it swinging, as if it were yesterday. She could see herself hanging at the end of it.

"I'm going to see Mom today," Sera said as she watched the golden leaves tumble along the ground.

The tree branches creaked and swayed. Sera pulled her coat tighter around her shivering body.

"It's Halloween, so I'm obliged to visit her." Sera looked back to the spot of bare bark. "Just like I'm obliged to come and see you, Maggie."

Sera wondered whether the bark would ever grow back, but the deepest wounds always took the longest to heal.

"I've always wondered why you chose Halloween to do it, Maggie, and why this tree. I mean you could have just done it at home, spared us the public humiliation." Sera felt the heat in her tears. "But I guess you wanted to get back at Mom for all that crazy shit she did to us." She tried to swallow the rage down. "You were always eager to make a scene weren't you, Maggie? Not like me. Not like quiet, introverted little Sera. We only looked the same."

Sera wiped away her tears and gazed around the park, towards the hill that separated the lines of trees. She noticed the autumn leaves turning the green grass a dull gold. On the crest of the hill she thought she saw someone watching her—a man—but when she blinked the shadow was gone.

The tree's creaking drew her back, and there was a flicker of Maggie suspended amongst the crooked branches. Sera blinked again to block the memory out.

"Why did you do it, Maggie?"

The wind howled through the branches, out of the park, and into the street. It whipped through the children's costumes.

"Why did you leave me all alone?"

The benevolent home entrance was only marginally decorated for Halloween, much to Sera's relief. A few cardboard cut-outs of jack-o'-lanterns carefully placed on a whiteboard titled, "What's On Today?" near the reception counter. Sera knew her mother would not have seen it, which was a good thing. The staff were serving dinner to the residents when Sera walked in. She was greeted by a receptionist, who was wearing a black witch's hat. A small, jack-o'-lantern brooch with blinking, red eyes sat on her lapel.

"Hi!" she said with a wide smile.

"I've come to see my mother, Magda Cameron."

The receptionist's smile faded. "Oh, okay. I'll ... I'll just get Dr. Howles."

"Is something wrong? Did something happen?"

The receptionist turned away, clearly flustered. "Just wait here a moment, and I'll get Dr. Howles." The woman was gone before Sera could utter another word. She stood in the hall watching the residents enjoying their evening meals, happy, content, and safe. The pang of jealousy felt more like the tip of a knife in Sera's heart.

It was obvious that her mother had caused a fuss. It didn't surprise her; Sera knew all too well how Magda's behaviour changed at Halloween. It was, after all, why she was in the benevolent home.

"Miss Cameron?"

Dr. Howles stood behind her. He was carrying his clipboard and a mournful look on his face. Sera's heart sank.

"Is she ... did she..?"

Dr. Howles shook his head. "She's resting right now. But she was extremely unsettled today."

Sera caught her breath. "What happened?"

Howles straightened his glasses. "It started last night. Somehow she managed to get out of her room. She woke most of the other residents in the special care ward."

"Oh, god, what did she do?"

"Just shouting mainly, but two orderlies had to restrain her. She's quite strong for a 76-year-old."

"I'm sorry. I'll talk to her about it."

Dr. Howles sighed. "Miss Cameron, I think it's time we talked about your mother's future care here at the home."

"What do you mean?"

"I'm afraid she's deteriorating and not just mentally. Her kidney function is negligible and her arrhythmia is worsening."

Sera took a deep breath to stave off tears. "I can't talk about this right now," she said. "I just want to speak to my mother. I might be able to keep her calm before nightfall."

Howles frowned. "I understand you want to help, and of course, you have every right to, but I'm not sure that we should be encouraging her Halloween delusion."

Sera scoffed and pushed past him. "I know it's a delusion, but it's not to her."

Magda was lying in bed, breathing so calmly that Sera thought she was dead.

In a way Magda died when Maggie took her own life at the tree, but it was only her body catching up with her mind.

Sera watched her mother sleeping and harked back to when she and Maggie were little girls. Back then Magda was stronger, brimming with a vigorous desire to protect her children. Every day of their young lives was another day closer to Halloween, when their father would come looking for them. Sera and Maggie didn't know their father; all they had of him was the old photograph her mother kept and pulled out whenever a "warning" was deemed necessary. She remembered how handsome he looked in the photo, with his suit and tie and slicked back hair. As adults, Sera and Maggie wondered whether the photo was just a magazine cut-out or a figment of Magda's wild beliefs, but their mother's fear every Halloween told them she believed the threat of his reappearance was real.

Sera remembered how every Halloween their mother would bake them special cakes with trinkets inside; signet rings and chains. Talismans to protect them from evil spirits, Magda would tell them. Then this would be followed by the mirror ritual where the girls would be forced to sit inside a circle of candles and stare into their reflections. Magda would only let them leave the circle once she was certain that nothing else could be seen in the glass, but their own dour faces. Sera and Maggie never understood why Magda did these things, but they had little choice but to honour her wishes. She was their mother, and they were her daughters.

Magda woke with a start, a cry of genuine fright escaping her wrinkled lips. Sera went to her and held her leathery hands. The old woman's eyes were wide, as if they craved the light.

"Mom? Mom, it's me," Sera said.

"Margaret?"

Sera swallowed hard. "No, Mom, it's Sera. Maggie's not here."

Magda's milky eyes flicked from Sera to the room and back again. She could see, but her mind was blind.

"Where? Where's Maggie?" Magda clawed at Sera's sleeve.

"She's gone, Mom, you know that."

"Maggie's not safe ... not safe," Magda's eyes locked on Sera's. "Neither of you are safe. He's coming."

"Mom, Maggie's dead."

"You girls aren't safe. I made a terrible mistake—"

"Maggie's dead."

Magda tried to sit up, and Sera found it hard to hold her still. "My handbag ... the talismans ... get them for you and your sister."

"Mom, Maggie's dead!"

Magda jolted with shock. Sera watched the furrows and wrinkles in her mother's face droop with sadness.

"Margaret's dead?"

Sera smoothed down Magda's white hair. "Yes, Mom. She took her own life. Two years ago."

"No. No."

"Mom, it's okay."

"No, she's not. He took her. Your father ... "

"Mom, stop it, please."

Magda's nails scratched Sera's skin. "He'll come for you. You have to stay safe! You have to go home and protect yourself. What I taught you ... "

Sera pulled herself free. "Mom! No!" She stood, but still Magda reached for her daughter.

"The mirror and the circle—you know what to do!"

Sera turned and fled the room, the sting of anger and her mother's wailing pleas at her back as she ran out of the home to her car. Magda and Maggie were lost, but she wouldn't join them in their madness.

The street milled with trick-or-treaters, forcing Sera to drive slow. She stopped for one menagerie of revellers, a group of boys in matching red devil masks. Their bags bulged with candy, but Sera knew they would never have their fill. They'd go from house to house, begging for "the filth that will rot their insides," as her mother used to tell her and Maggie.

Magda's madness had always been there, a frustrating compulsion, an unnatural obsession with a long dead belief. Sera knew it was a cultural necessity, a part of her mother's own upbringing by a stern eastern European mother and Scottish father, but now, after seeing her at her worst in the home, it was clear her madness had become a cancer.

The red devils crossed the street, and Sera watched them. A car honked behind her, and she checked the rear-view mirror. Her face stared back, but it was stark white, eyes bulging and tongue protruding from the lips. A bright gash of red curled around her neck like a scarf. The life was being choked out of her. Sera screamed and clawed at her throat, but the vision vanished as quickly as it appeared. The driver honked his car again, and Sera put her head out the window to apologise. He was a businessman in a hurry, judging by his sharp suit, yet his face was what captivated Sera the most, because she thought she'd seen it before.

Shaking off the fog of confusion, Sera pushed on the accelerator, sending out a screech of burning rubber. Trick-or-treaters stared, while their parents scowled. She drove away, her heart desperately urging her to get back home.

Sera lived alone in her mother's home, a one-storey gable that had long been neglected. The once-pristine, beige exterior was cracked and peeling, the windows dark and grimy. At night the house was anything but inviting, but there was only so much Sera could do to maintain it, with her job as a freelance graphic artist. With Maggie's death however had come a loss of enthusiasm, and she knew her work was suffering for it. She wanted things to return to normal, but her sister's suicide and her mother's decline kept her in the depths of despair.

The kitchen and living room had become her studio, with Sera's iMac and Cintiq drawing tablet taking the place of the television. In between Magda's rituals of protection from an omnipresent force that would never come, she did foster in her daughters a sense of creativity. Expression through art was vital, she told them. To understand the world and all its secrets was to have control of one's destiny.

Sera put on some coffee and walked up the hall to the bathroom. At the far end of the house was her mother's bedroom, which Sera had sealed up when she sent Magda to the benevolent home. Opposite was her sister's old room. Sera left this room open, and she stopped at Maggie's door to admire her past. The simple wood-frame bed with matching bedside table and bookcase Sera thought had always been an odd choice for someone so extroverted. Maggie: a beautiful soul who expressed an outward joy in order to keep her dark past from getting out. Sadly, she'd failed.

Wiping away fresh tears, Sera went into the bathroom and looked at her weary complexion in the mirror. The vision she'd experienced in the car had rattled her, but she put it down to the meeting with Magda. Even as a little girl Magda's warnings of spirits lurking and making themselves known in the everyday world, could produce horrible nightmares. A nightmare is a one-way conversation with the dead, she'd tell them. All you need is a translator. Sera leaned in to the glass and sighed at the grey pools of skin around her eyes. She needed to go to bed.

Sera blinked, and a black skin passed over her eyes, like a nictitating membrane. She recoiled in horror and fell back into the shower curtain. The fabric slid along the rail with a shriek of metal and revealed a naked woman hanging on a rope from the shower head. Sera fell to the bathroom floor and screamed.

She squeezed her eyes shut, and listened to her frantic breaths. Maggie's corpse is not hanging from the shower. It's not a ghost. It's your mother's fucked-up imagination getting the better of you! When she opened her eyes, the shower was just a shower. Sera stood on shaking legs and caught her reflection in the mirror once more. An exhausted, terrified young woman looked back at her, and she would have been lost in her eyes if not for a knock at the door.

"Trick 'r treat!"

Sera walked to the front door in a daze, the corners of her eyes now aware of every shadow and movement in the old house. The knock came again, more incessantly, along with the cry to trick or treat. She opened the door to find a boy and a girl and their parents dressed in matching princess and Spider-Man outfits.

"Trick 'r treat!' they all intoned.

Sera pressed a hand to her forehead. "Hi, look, I'm sorry, but I don't have any candy."

"No candy?" the spider-boy said through his mask.

"Oh, that's okay," Mother Princess said. "We'll try next door."

Behind them, at the end of the path, Sera glimpsed a figure standing near the tree on the curb. It was her mother. The old woman was screaming, but only Sera could hear.

"The talismans! The talismans!"

Magda's nightgown was flecked with blood and urine. It clung to her stooped frame like a death shroud. The old woman turned to point her crooked hand into the street, where on the other side, stood a man in a suit, dappled in the shadow of a leaning willow tree. Sera saw the man and the terror on her mother's face and shivered.

"The talismans!" her mother said again.

Sera's voice caught in her throat. "Get ... Get away!"

The trick-or-treaters gasped.

"There's no need to speak to us like that," Spider-dad said, pulling down his mask.

Sera looked at the man's appalled face and back to the spot where her mother had stood. She was gone. Before another word could be spoken, Sera slammed the door in their faces and fled into the house. As she passed the phone, it rang. Gingerly, she answered it.

"Hello?"

"She's dead."

Sera's heart echoed in her skull. "Who ... who is this?"

"Mom's dead, Sera."

The voice warbled in Sera's ear, from high pitch to low, a female tone overlapping with a male. It was her voice, tainted with darkness.

"Maggie?"

"She's dead, Sera," the voice said with a definite baritone. "Maggie's dead, Magda's dead—and you're next."

Her mother's room was stale and caked in dust when Sera entered it.

She ran to Magda's cupboard and pulled out the boxes of clothes she'd been meaning to drop at the thrift shop since her mother had gone to the home. Waves of dust curled into the air as Sera stacked the clothes on the floor. What she needed wouldn't be in those boxes, but in another, much older box. It was at the back on the bottom of the cupboard; a wooden chest, with a brass lock. Sera pulled it free and tried to open it, only to find it locked.

"God damn it!" she said.

With shaking hands, Sera tried to pry open the lid, but without the key there was no way she'd get inside. She picked up the box and threw it against the cupboard. It fell to the floor with a thud. The intricate coiled carvings in the wood looked like mocking eyes.

"God damn it, Mom!"

Sera slumped to the floor, as tears flooded her eyes. The phone call had left her weak and afraid. She didn't know if it had been real, but she knew there was only one way to find out. Sera grabbed her cell phone from her coat and called up the phone number for the benevolent home. She had to know.

The same receptionist picked up at the other end.

"This is Sera Cameron. I'm calling about my mother."

"Oh … I … can you please hold?"

Sera stared at her mother's old box; she prayed she wouldn't have to open it.

"Miss Cameron? Did … did someone call you?" It was Dr. Howles.

"My mother … "

"Miss Cameron … I think you should come in."

Sera ended the call and threw the phone away. Sobbing, she crawled across the floor to the box and dug at the lid with her nails. She lifted it high and smashed it on the floor, over and over. Sera bit through the pain in her hands, only finding release when the box finally cracked apart. Candles, jewellery, necklaces, and an assortment of bowls and books all spilled out. At the very bottom of the box, wrapped in a piece of black cloth, was a photo frame. It contained the photo of the man Magda said was her father. Sera studied the man's face and suit with much older eyes. There was aloofness in the way he refused to look directly into the camera, but Sera could sense the coldness in his eyes, even malevolence. Was it the same face she'd seen in the street? Had her father finally come?

Sera quickly wrapped the photo and put it back in what was left of the box. She picked up the rest of the contents in her arms and then turned to look at the drape-covered mirror by her mother's bed.

She was about to look evil in the face.

The oblong mirror was as tall as Sera, an ornate frame of polished, red teak around a stained ellipse of dark glass.

Sera's form appeared trapped inside it. Shivering with fear, she sat down in the circle of candles opposite the mirror and slipped a silver amulet over her head and several silver charm bracelets on her wrists. The talismans glinted in the candlelight.

She kept her eyes on her reflection and thought back to her mother's rituals when they were children. The veil between worlds was at its weakest on All Hallows' Eve, she'd told them. Like a door left ajar. Communication with the dead was possible, and ghosts and other entities could roam the world of the living. Sera thought her mother's rituals were nothing more than an antiquated obsession, but now she didn't know what to believe. What she was about to do—was it disproving her fears or embracing them?

In the old days, Magda used to tell her daughters, women would sit in front of a mirror on Halloween and gaze into the glass and ask to see their future betrothed. It was a gimmick splashed across vintage postcards. Magda said what they should have been looking for was the reflection of their very own predatory spirit; the antithesis of the guardian angel.

"Show me," Sera said into the mirror.

The glass only reflected back her tear-slickened face.

"Show me the spirit which haunts me."

The tongues of candle flame froze inside the confines of the mirror. Seven jewels of fire. Sera waved her hand in front of her, but her reflection remained motionless. A hand emerged from the shadows around her reflection and squeezed her shoulder. Sera shrieked, but still her reflection was unable to waver.

"I'm sorry," the voice said from the mirror.

"M-Mom?"

Magda emerged from the blackness, not as an old woman, but as the glowing confident woman from Sera's childhood.

"There's so much I left unsaid. About who I was. About who you are."

Sera reached up to touch her mother's hand, but all she felt was her coat. "Mom, why did you leave me?"

Magda stroked her daughter's hair, but Sera felt no contact. "I've put you in danger. Just like your sister. And I'm sorry. I should have protected you both better."

"Mom, what's happening? I keep seeing Maggie. And … a man. Is it my father?"

"He is my bane and yours too. I should never have summoned him. I should never have been so wanton and selfish." Magda retrieved something shining from inside her robes and placed it in the front pocket of Sera's mirror image coat. "This is all I can give you. I hope it can help you." Magda pulled back into the darkness. "I cannot stay. Be strong child."

"Mother, wait!" Sera reached out for Magda, knocking over one of the candles.

The reflection shifted, like ripples in a pond, and Sera could see herself moving desperately to relight the candle—to repair the circle. But she knew it was too late. Her reflection vanished from the glass and reappeared from fog in the doorway to her mother's bedroom: Sera's mirror image, naked and hateful.

"Is it you, Maggie?" Sera said.

The naked reflection's eyes were cold and unblinking.

Sera grabbed and picked up one of the lit candles. She held it out in front of her, and the orange light revealed the tell-tale redness of hanging around Maggie's neck. Her dead sister's hair dangled around it like strips of ancient spider-web.

"You need to go back, Maggie. You're not welcome here."

Maggie sneered, but then craned her neck back. Her body contorted, as if in some invisible ecstasy. Strong hands appeared from behind Maggie and within. The arms, draped in a grey, silk suit wrapped around her hips and chest, hungry for her flesh. Then Sera saw his face. The face of the man her mother had been trying to protect them from since they were children. Up close, he looked like James Dean or a young Frank Sinatra. He tongued at Maggie's neck, but locked his cold eyes on Sera.

"Did she tell you I am your father?"

Hot candle wax seared Sera's fingers, but she refused to let her only light go. She watched horrified as her father caressed Maggie's flesh.

"Your mother? Did she warn you that Daddy was coming?"

"You stay away from me," Sera said.

"But I've already got you." He wrenched Maggie's head back and kissed her deeply. Maggie's body withered, the skin tightening, losing its thickness. Undulating rib bones rose to the surface. Blood oozed from both their lips. He pulled away and licked the blood from his mouth. "Both of you were promised to me—a long, long time ago."

"What are you talking about? Who are you?"

He threw Maggie to the ground, and she lay there, gasping for breath, but still in the throes of arousal. The man straightened his narrow tie and smoothed down his suit. Sera couldn't help her sister; she was lost when she hanged herself in the tree.

"You see, this is the thing," he said. "How can your mother love you, if she doesn't tell you the truth?"

"She did love me ... She was protecting me—protecting us!"

He looked down at Maggie, who was now just skin and bone. "And what a great job Magda did."

Watching Maggie decay was like seeing the future. "Shut up! It was you! You made Maggie kill herself, and you killed my mother!"

He waggled a finger. "Oh, no, your mother died from guilt, nothing more. If she'd taken her own life, I'd have her already. But that's fine. I'll take you now, and I'll have two maidens for the price of one, just like we agreed."

He stepped closer and Sera backed away. "What do you mean?"

"Oh, come on, Sera, you're a smart girl. Think it through. I've known

63

your mother for a very long time. She sought children. I sought children. We helped each other out."

"You're lying!"

"Am I? Your mother was barren, a white witch without a womb, and after years of spells and potions, she finally caved and sought me out one Halloween."

Sera swallowed hard. "She … she gave herself to … what, a demon? Just so she could have children?"

The demon sneered. "That was the deal." He looked at Sera lasciviously. "And I still require more offspring."

Bile rose in Sera's throat. "You can't touch me."

He waved his hand dismissively. "Your circle is broken and your trinkets are nothing. And this is Halloween. Everything is in a state of flux."

He whipped out his hand lightning fast and caught Sera's wrist. The candle fell and, as Sera tried to pull free from the demon's grip, more flames were snuffed out. Darkness swarmed. She cried out and pulled and writhed, but he exuded power. Yet Sera refused to relent, pulling and clawing at the creature's hand and arm. He only laughed.

"You're wasting your time. You belong to me. You'll be my maiden, just like your mother agreed. That was the catch you see: Magda got to be a mommy for you and little Margaret, but your days were always numbered. It was a bit of a shock for Maggie when I turned up on your doorstep two years ago. When I told her who I really was, she fashioned the noose all on her own. I just showed her the tree."

Her demonic father's laugh was smug and grating.

"Fuck you!" She twisted and felt something thud against her breast.

A forked tongue oozed from the demon's lips. "Oh, you will."

Sera remembered her mother's apparition placing something in her coat. She tried one last time to pull free and managed to drag herself into the mirror. She looked over her shoulder into the glass and saw a shape mingling behind her.

"What are you doing, you stupid cur?"

"Use it, Sera!"

Sera heard her mother's voice resonate from the mirror. The demon did too; he looked past Sera at the reflection.

"Who's that?" he said.

"Now, Margaret!"

Sera slipped her free hand into her coat pocket and looked down to see Maggie wrap her bony arms around the demon's legs. The creature hissed at her.

"Get off me, you bitch!"

"Use it, Sera! Use it now!"

Sera pulled the knife free from her coat, its ancient iron blade, finding the smallest hint of light. Sera knew iron was the most potent protective alloy; her mother had told her so. She yanked the demon's tie and stabbed him in the heart.

Her vile father recoiled and screamed at the knife protruding from his chest. Maggie still held on with impossible strength as the demon staggered around the room. The wound sparked with an inner fire, like flaring coals and spread across his shirt and jacket. Sera shared a look with her long dead sister. There was a smile on her haggard spectral face.

The demon ignited with a bright whoosh of orange light. Liquid fire spilled onto the floor, onto Maggie, and they were both quickly engulfed.

"Maggie!"

Sera moved to help her sister, but two arms from within the mirror held her back.

"No, Sera, don't. It has to be this way," Magda told her.

The demon's howl reached its zenith, forcing Sera to cover her ears. Her father and sister turned to ash in an instant, the embers falling and fading before they reached the floor. The only thing that touched the surface was the iron knife, which clattered and spun, its task done.

Sera turned and saw her mother and sister inside the mirror. Restored and radiant.

"You did it, sis," Maggie said.

Sera sobbed with happiness at the sight of her sister's soul alongside their mother. "Maggie."

"I always believed in you," Magda said. "You were both the best part of me."

Sera dropped to her knees. "I ... I can't believe you're gone."

"We'll see you again in time."

"What?"

"You have to destroy the mirror, Sera," Maggie said.

"Why?"

"If you don't he'll have a door to get back to you," Magda said. "Burn everything, even his photo. I should have done it a long time ago."

"But—

"Take up the knife child and break the mirror."

Maggie offered her a reassuring smile. "You'll see me again, sis," she said. "Whenever you look in a mirror; it just can't be this one."

Sera blinked away the tears, and picked up the knife from the floor.

"We'll see you again," Magda said.

"I love you," Sera said. "Both."

She raised the knife and slammed it against the glass. The crack was like thunder, like a door slamming. It split the veil from top to bottom. When the sound faded, Sera realised dawn was breaking.

Light was pushing away the darkness, and Halloween was no longer something to fear.

Dura Mater

A red door.

Red with the blood of past sacrifices.

Naked men contorted in rigour, lay in heaps around him; evidence of the failures that had come before. Their eyes—and they were his eyes—stared at him, devoid of life, yet watching and waiting. It was his turn now, his time to cross the threshold. He was their last hope.

A distorted voice crackled through a speaker in the corner of the room. "Are you ready?"

He glanced to his right, at the two-way, mirrored window inside the small room. The bodies were so close their cold skin touched his, and their decay invaded his nostrils. He sat on his knees in a bid to make his naked form more comfortable and inadvertently knocked against one of the corpses. It flopped onto its side, exposing its face, and revealing a cavernous hole in the centre of its forehead.

He ignored the sight, closed his eyes, inhaled and nodded.

The thrum of the steel bolt unlocking the door made him reopen his eyes.

A man in a grey suit stepped gingerly between the corpses toward him, briefcase in one hand, handkerchief clutched to his face with the other. He opened the briefcase and unveiled a long silver trephine, the sharp end gleaming in the overhead lights.

"Number 223, it's time to open the door," the suited man said through the handkerchief.

Number 223 took the trephine from the briefcase and felt the weight of it in his hand, the weight of responsibility.

"What if I can't open it?"

The suited man withdrew his handkerchief for a moment. "Think of your brothers," he gestured to the dead. "How much they sacrificed."

Number 223 considered his clones and the holes in their heads. The trephine was cold in his palm. The suited man crouched to meet his gaze.

"Think of the people counting on you to make contact."

He thought of his dead brethren "Why would it turn out any differently than before?"

The suited man rested a warm hand on Number 223's shoulder. "I know this is daunting. But you need to have courage. You're not the first to have taken this step. Think of all those who came before you, before all these others. The first explorers who tried to touch the great beyond: the heroes of Project Bluebird and Project Artichoke."

Number 223 looked up at him. "What if there's nothing? What if it's just … darkness."

"You must have faith. We know there must be something on the other side."

"Why is this the way?"

"Shh, take it easy."

Number 223's heart pounded against his ribs. The trephine like a stone. The bodies swelling with each passing second. "Why do they all look like me?"

The suited man glanced at the mirror and back to him. "Just take a breath, okay. You're ready for this. Think back on your training."

The speaker crackled again. "Commence the experiment."

The suited man nodded and withdrew, almost skulking out of the room. The bolt slid back in the door, and Number 223 was left alone with his lifeless selves. He had to ignore the panic and make their losses worthwhile. There was a message coming from the great beyond, and he had to be the one to hear it.

He lifted the trephine to his eye-line and stared at its brilliant apex. Would it feel cold when it went in? Would he feel anything? How deep would he have to go? All he had to do was open the door.

"Commence the experiment," the disembodied voice said again.

Number 223 gripped the trephine, balancing it above his eyes. He pulled back and …

"Commence the experiment."

He stood, fingers wrapped tight around the trephine, the key to the truth. He staggered through his own corpses for the red door. An alarm sounded. The space filled with crimson light. He stabbed the trephine into the lock, and it opened with a sliding crash.

Number 223 was going to show them darkness.

Hell-O-Ween

Hell is always at its brightest in October.

A deep orange glow, powered by a billion, billion candlelit human skulls, is a sight to behold. The light seems to seep into the rock tunnels and brighten flames in even the darkest pits of the Underworld.

Demon children can't help but be excited by the festivities and their contemplation of All Hallow's Eve. Halloween is infectious. Therefore, October 31 is celebrated with much spectacle. Like those children in the living world, the demon children take to the pastime of "Trick or Treating" with equal gusto. They don their traditional vampire and mummy costumes and head out to knock on the doors of the neighbourhood.

The "neighbourhood" in Hell, however, is well beyond the norm. Streets can disappear into shadow, houses don't necessarily have walls, and the people who greet you at the door can be quite temperamental.

Such was the case when four young demons set out to Trick or Treat the bowels of Hell one particular Halloween.

Xek, a rather rambunctious little fellow, was considered the leader by his friends: Glod, Sysk, and Sannastasia. Xek, dressed in the cliché-worn Dracula costume, complete with pointed fangs and real blood on his chin, was the poster boy for the celebration. Glod's approach to costuming was minimal; an executioner's hood with the eyeholes cut out and a tomahawk. Sysk wanted to go as a werewolf, but due to a mishap involving him standing too close to a pit of flames, he had to go as a mummy instead. Sannastasia looked adorable in a Lizzie Borden costume, complete with an axe of which Glod was most envious.

The quartet set off down Blood Brick Road, determined to make this particular Halloween the best ever.

"Where are we going first?" Sysk said with a voice slightly muffled by his blood-soaked facial bandages.

"Machecoul Castle," Xek replied, a wide smile on his unnaturally white face, courtesy of an acid bath from his mother.

"I thought we were going to check out Amityville?" Sannastasia complained, her axe dragging along the ground.

"No, not this year," Xek told her. "I've got it all planned out. We're gonna see some real sights tonight."

They followed the Blood Brick Road for about half a mile and passed other demon children screaming in fear as one of Cerebus's pups gave chase. They saw other children knocking on the Black Gates only to lose their hands to some huge shape on the other side. The sight brought raucous laughter from the foursome.

Eventually the children came to the ruins of the Castle of Machecoul. Hell isn't all just fire and brimstone; it is also the graveyard for the living world's most evil locales. The Castle was a pile of stones and dust, blackened by Hell's flaying heat. The children tried to find the front doors.

"Maybe it doesn't have a front door," Glod surmised, scratching his hooded head with the edge of his tomahawk.

"Of course, it has a front door," Xek reprimanded him.

"*Had* a front door," Sannastasia said, somewhat annoyed. "Can't we just go onto the next house? There's no one here."

A voice suddenly rose out of the shadows, thick and French. A man, long dead, dressed in rusting knight's armor fused to his skin, stumbled towards them, his neck crooked from being hanged.

"Children! Children!" he said. "Please don't fight on my account. I am here now."

"Who are you?" Sysk said, trembling beneath his bandages.

"Gilles de Rais, at your service," he said with a bow that looked awkward because of his neck.

"Is this your house?" Glod asked.

Gilles de Rais looked around him. "It was once, yes. But it was knocked down a long time ago."

"By who?"

"You mean, 'by whom'," de Rais corrected him. "My enemies knocked it down."

"Why?" Sannastasia asked, curling the hair of her lice-infested wig.

Gilles stepped towards her, his steel shoes clinking on the rocky ground. His gaze was menacing.

"They hated me. They hanged me, and then they burned down my castle."

"They hanged you? Cool!" Xek exclaimed. "You must have been pretty mean when you were alive, *Mr. Deranged.*"

Gilles snapped. "de Rais! Gilles de Rais, you insolent little cretin!"

Xek and the other children withdrew, heading for the Blood Brick Road. De Rais kept after them, his armored body creaking and bleeding.

"Wait! Don't go! You can come inside and play! I promise I won't hurt you!"

"No thanks, Mister," Glod told him, shaking his hooded head.

"Treats!" de Rais continued. "I have treats inside! Come and play with me!"

But the children were gone, leaving the decrepit knight and his filthy home behind. They ran together holding hands, all keeping a watchful eye on the madman who fell to the ground to cry into his skeletal hands.

"Who was that guy?" Sysk asked.

"Some looney," Xek told him. "There are so many of them on this road."

"Then why did we come here?" Sannastasia whined. "How are we going to get any treats if we don't knock on any doors?"

"Okay, just settle down," Xek ordered her. "It's not much further to the next house."

The next house they found was just around the corner. But it wasn't a house, it was more like a small city. Gas lanterns burned in the boiling air, and the brick walls seemed to sweat in response. The demon children huddled together in fear as a thick darkness crept towards them. More corners appeared, leading to alleyways, where, at the end, was a half-naked, eviscerated woman.

"I don't like this place," Sannastasia said.

"What are you kidding? It's fantastic," Xek replied, barely able to contain his excitement. "We'll get treats here for sure."

"But I don't see any doors. There are only walls and alleyways," Sysk said, worriedly looking over his shoulder.

"We have to keep going," Xek reminded them. "We can't go home yet."

So they walked hand in hand, trying not to look down the alleys, but they were everywhere, as if they were sprouting from the shadows. There seemed to be more and more with each step, and the women's bodies got bloodier and bloodier.

Abruptly a shadow in a top hat and coat burst from the cobblestones at their feet. The children screamed and howled like a pack of wolves.

"Hello, children," the shadow said. "What are you doing here?"

"Trick or Treating," Xek replied, putting on his bravest Dracula grimace.

The shadow gasped. "Truly? Is it that time of year already? Although it's not really celebrated where I come from. It's more of an American pastime."

"But it's about witches, and they came from Europe," Sannastasia pointed out.

The shadow produced a shadow-gloved hand, which held a very long and very sharp knife, fresh with blood. The children shrunk back.

"That's true, my dear girl, but by tradition, the New World is the one pagan nation. Yet we are far too civilised for such things. We have order here. Everyone knows their place. The Queen sits upon the throne and her subjects give their lives for her."

The shadow, like a stage performer, turned his hand deftly to show the children the end of an alleyway. There, in the corner, was a woman holding her entrails in her skirts.

"Mary here gave her life for the Empire, as have all the other girls. It's only fitting that I take care of them."

Xek tried not to look but couldn't turn away. The other children all had their eyes squeezed tight shut.

"Do you ... have any treats, Mister?" Xek asked.

"Please, call me Jack. Everyone else does."

"Jack ... do you have any treats?"

Jack reached into his black cloak and produced a leather apron, dripping with blood. He handed it to Xek.

"This is all I have, I'm afraid."

Xek snatched it and turned to his friends. "Run!"

They ran, almost tripping over each other to get back to the Blood Brick Road. Jack waved them goodbye, but seconds later he was stalking another woman down another alley. She looked just like all the others the children were forced to see. They breathed a lot easier when their little, clawed feet felt the familiar pulse of the Road.

"Who was that?" Glod exclaimed.

"I don't know, but I don't ever want to see him again," Sysk said.

Xek stepped forward and waved the bloody apron in the air triumphantly.

"Yeah, he was weird, but check out the treat he gave us."

The children mingled to get a better look at the apron. The only thing remarkable about it was the fact it appeared to be bleeding, not just soaked in blood.

"That is so cool," Xek whistled.

"How are we going to share that?" Sannastasia said.

"Gee, I don't know," Xek said. "What, do you expect me to cut it up into four pieces?"

Sannastasia's gaze could have turned him to stone. She turned and started to head up the Blood Brick Road.

"I'm going home," she squealed. "This is the worst Halloween ever! I should never have come with you!"

"Fine! Go home then! See if I care!" Xek shouted back.

Sysk tugged at his bandages. "I don't want to go if she doesn't."

"What are you a bunch of wussies? We can't give up now. We've already got one treat."

Glod looked at the ground. "I thought we would get a bag of maggots or some eyeballs. I don't want a yucky leather apron."

Xek wrapped his arms around his friends. "Come on guys! This is Halloween. There's a few more houses this way."

Reluctantly, Sysk and Glod followed Xek along the Road. They were all quiet for some time. Great hungry bats screeched overhead, running circuits around them. They came to the crest of a hill and found a man sitting in a battered old Volkswagen. He was dressed in a dirty, blood-stained suit. He gave the boys a wry smile.

"Hey, fellas," the man said. "Aw, are you guys trick or treating?"

Xek was enthused to run into someone else, but he frowned when he saw the man was strapped to the driver's seat by a plethora of cables and wires. On top of his neatly parted hair was a metal cap.

"Yes, sir," Xek replied. "Do you have any treats?"

"What's your name kid?"

"Xek."

"Mine's Ted. Hey, if you help me out of the car, I can help you look for treats."

Sysk and Glod, who were standing back aways from Xek and his new friend, whimpered. Xek turned to them and saw they were both shaking their heads.

"You're not scared of me are you, Xek?" Ted said.

Xek gulped. "No, sir."

"Well, why don't you help me out?"

Ted smiled even wider and winked at Xek.

"Why are you tied up in your car?" Xek inquired.

"I did some bad things, and I'm being punished."

"Oh, okay, that makes sense," Xek replied, but then he thought for a second. "What bad things?"

Ted sighed and put his head back. He seemed very tired.

"I couldn't control myself around women," Ted said. "I liked to get my rocks off with them whether they liked it or not. Usually it ended in them being dead."

He ended the last sentence with another smile, a smug bastard smile.

"Why?" Xek.

"Geez, kid, you ask a lot of questions. Tell ya what, you let me out, and I'll answer all the goddamn questions you want. Okay?"

Xek stared at Ted for a long time, contemplating. Then he said: "Give me the treats first."

"What?"

"You tell me where your treats are, and I'll let you out."

Ted laughed heartily.

"You got some balls kid. They're in the trunk."

With Sysk and Glod's help, Xek cracked open the trunk. Inside was a duffle bag. They opened it and inside were ropes, gloves, a balaclava, handcuffs, an ice pick, a box of trash bags, a flashlight and a crow bar.

"Awesome!" Xek said.

Sysk and Glod sighed miserably.

Xek bundled the duffle bag in his arms and ran back to Ted.

"Thanks, Mister!"

"You're welcome, kid. Now what you've got to do to get me out is—"

But it was too late. Xek had pulled the door handle, and a series of electric sparks cascaded over the car. Inside Ted writhed and screamed and spat as tens of thousands of volts riddled his body. The energy was so fierce the car's cabin burst into flames. Ted was fried.

The boys ran and ran all the way along the Blood Brick Road to escape the ensuing fireball.

"I can't do this anymore!" Sysk said. "I want to go home!"

"All the more for me then," Xek said, excited by his second lot of treats. "Man that guy just exploded! Lucky I got his stuff out of the trunk."

Xek stopped and looked for his friends. They were some distance back, running for the hills.

"Wimps!" Xek yelled after them.

The little, Dracula demon hefted his duffle bag and tucked the piece of leather apron into his shirt pocket. He began to chuckle at how much luck he'd had. He couldn't wait to see what was around the corner.

Over another craggy hill was a large house swarming with crows and flies. Xek fought his way through them to the door. He knocked and a short, fat man, dressed in a tattered, but colourful, clown outfit greeted him. The make-up made his face look like a skull.

"Hey there," the clown said.

"Hi," Xek said. "Trick or treat."

"How old are you?" the clown asked.

"1400."

"Fourteen-hundred?" the clown suddenly looked anxious and licked his lips, the make-up coming away.

"Yes, sir. Do you have any treats?"

"Why don't you come inside, and we'll have a look?"

Xek looked past the clown and saw many corpses rotting away in the living room. He cringed, but more at the thought of the smell than anything else. He'd seen worse.

"No, thanks!"

The clown sniffed and feigned a smile. He didn't know what else to say.

"I like your costume," Xek told him.

The clown looked at what he was wearing. "It's all I have." He considered Xek's Dracula costume. "Yours is nice too."

"Would you like to swap?"

The clown mulled it over for a while. Occasionally, he turned to observe the mass decomposition occurring in his home. Then he took off his clown hat and kicked off his clown shoes, and then finally the whole costume fell to the floor. Xek undressed and gave the clown the Dracula costume. It looked way too small on the fat man. Xek was over the moon with his new costume.

"Thanks Mister," he said.

"That's okay. I have to go now. I have to put all this … " he indicated the bodies " … away."

With that, the clown closed the door and Xek, dressed in his new costume, and carrying his new treats set off down the Blood Brick Road. He thought about heading south onto the next house, but abruptly he heard laughter and thoughts of catching up with his friends and making them feel sorry for leaving him to haul all the treats came to him.

As the Halloween fires raged on, Xek smiled and headed north after them.

This Sublime Darkness

Valerie's mother died on our wedding day.

What should have been a day of commitment and love became a spiralling descent into mourning. The light inside my Valerie faded, her eyes grey pools of despair and longing. She was inconsolable, and of course our plans for marriage were put aside to make way for a funeral.

I'd only met Valerie's mother, Ita Karga, on a few occasions, the last time being when I'd asked for her daughter's hand in marriage—being a widow, she assumed the duty. She was a quiet soul, yet refined. Behind those eyes was a wisdom that only came from experience, and at 79 years, she'd seen more than her fair share of hardships. I recall how, after my question, she told me what marriage was meant to be.

"Sacrifice," she said, sitting in her chair as if it were a throne; as if she were Queen Victoria herself. "The man must serve his woman."

Sadly, her husband didn't live long enough to play that part, only long enough to provide his wife with a daughter. The task of raising Valerie had become a solitary one, but despite the lines on her face, her core remained strong.

"You do my Valerie right," she said after accepting my request. "You give her a child and make a woman out of her."

Valerie had been so happy, like a summer rose all-a-bloom when I proposed. She was overwhelmed by her mother's acceptance of me. Our courtship had been well-received by all, the two families matched in status. Her friends admired me and were always there to ensure Valerie's best interests were at heart. Greetings at luncheons led to walks in the gardens around my father's house, and I very quickly found the courage to write Valerie and express my feelings. Rather brash of me I know, but I truly felt she had stolen my heart. I was gladdened by the fact that her mother approved of the letter and our pairing.

I owed Ita that much. I was at my fiancée's side during the funeral. Of course, I felt a sliver of sadness at the loss of the matriarch, but Valerie's grieving took a strange turn the moment the service concluded and her mother's coffin was covered by six feet of earth. I remember the hollowness of Valerie's eyes through the black lace of her veil. I couldn't help but imagine the veil had been weaved by some hideous spider, or that it wasn't lace at all, but rather scars from where Valerie had inflicted the loss upon herself.

"Mother left the house to me—to us. It was her wedding gift, Eddie," she told me afterwards.

The image of Valerie's family home bled into my mind: imposing, the colour of a storm, neglected. It chilled me more than winter's fingers ever could.

"Of course, my love," I told her. "If that is her wish then I must honour it—if I am to serve you."

This brought a smile to Valerie's face, a fleeting smile without any semblance of warmth, one that I hoped to never see again.

We were married a week later at St Paul's. What should have been a clear spring day turned sour in the afternoon, the storm clouds like grey beasts from hell's mouth itself. I tried so hard to keep my disappointment concealed for Valerie's sake. She was a radiant bride, her ivory-tinted gown evoked so much in me; I truly believed I was marrying a princess of beauty and grace.

Yet, my bride seemed pre-occupied throughout the ceremony. She faltered while reciting her vows. Once she had to compose herself from a well of tears. While I slipped the ring on her finger, she seemed to fade, and I had to hold her upright out of fear she would faint. Grief had taken its toll, but God bless her, it had not shaken her resolve. She even ordered the minister to finish the ceremony!

We embarked in the bridal carriage for her mother's estate, and after sharing the briefest of kisses, my Valerie fell into the deepest of sleeps, her head on my shoulder. Despite her beauty, I was astounded to see her face tainted by fresh tears. I told myself that these were tears of joy, and that the grief was gone. Our new life together was about to begin.

But behind Valerie's bridal gown dragged a train of darkness.

Valerie wore her melancholy like a second skin.

By day, she slept in her room, cocooned inside the curtains of her four-poster bed. The windows she had covered with thick curtains, shutting out all sources of light, shutting out the world, including me. The bedroom was locked from the inside, and there was no skeleton key to be found in this monstrous house. Her mother's ancient three-storey gable was held together as if only by the breath of those who resided within.

The tragedy of the old woman's death was a dagger in her daughter's heart, so agonising that not even my love could quell it. Valerie's mourning had grown in strength with each passing day. The prolonged periods of sleep, the starvation, the avoidance: all these things culminated in her locking herself away in her room and planting a seed of sadness in my own heart.

Her nocturnal wanderings began after we moved into the house. I'd been knocking on the bedroom door, begging to come in (or for her to come out) for days. The plates of food I had left outside her door were left untouched, my tears and declarations of love unanswered. She finally spoke when I asked the right question.

"Why do you love your grief so?" I asked through trembling lips.

My wife's shadow passed across the threshold, and I bent to peer beneath the door. I wanted to see her, I needed to. Valerie had crouched against the door, and I glimpsed her bare knees in the golden glow of the full moon that streamed in from outside.

"It's all I feel," she said so matter-of-factly that I shivered.

Desperate to connect with her, I lay down and slipped my fingers through the gap. "Let me comfort you, my love."

The door opened with an inward gust. Before I could move Valerie jumped past me and alighted down the hall. I got to my feet to give chase and gasped at her naked form dashing down the staircase. I called for her to stop, but there was no weakness in her as she flung open the front doors and escaped into the night.

The frigid air halted me at the staircase. My eyes struggled to adjust to the dark, to see beyond the moonlit edges of the fir trees and brushes surrounding the estate. An owl screeched in the distance as if mocking me. I called out to my wife, urging her to come inside. I stepped out into the yard, embraced myself against the cold, and called for Valerie once more. A piercing shriek almost stopped my heart, and I turned as a gust of wind slapped against my shoulder. My rattled mind took several moments to realise it was an owl. It flew past me, gliding low towards the greenhouse at the southern end of the yard.

It was there, outside the greenhouse door, that I glimpsed the stark white shape of Valerie beckoning me to follow.

I ran through the brushes and past the silent fountain. The ends of thorns reached for me and left their marks on my skin, but their stings were nothing compared to the ache I felt for my wife. Through the grimy glass of the greenhouse door I saw Valerie lying spread-eagled in the soil.

This was the first time I'd seen her in days. My eyes traced her milky skin in the moonlight, the curve of her breasts, the arc of her pelvis. Eyes like pearls of night. Blood rushed through my body, and the ache fixed me to the spot, turning my legs to stone and pushing all my senses to their limit. My wife's voice shook me.

"Come here, Eddie," she said.

Valerie had never been so wanton, so sensual. Yet the man in me wanted to betray my confusion and give in to her. I stepped towards her, my gaze lingering as she explored her body with eager hands.

"Come inside, my love," I said. "Please."

"Yes," she said, but the voice wasn't her own and it echoed inside the greenhouse. The bromeliads and cycads were dead in their pots.

I reached out my hand to her. "Valerie ... please, you will freeze to death. Come with me inside."

Her face contorted into a grimace.

"Come inside!"

For a moment she was lost to me, her smooth face becoming like sackcloth.

I pulled off my nightgown and threw it over her. Valerie shrieked and writhed when I lifted her off the ground. She was bones wrapped in skin, thrashing in my grip. Her hands slapped at my face, but I held firm and carried her back into the house. I laid her in our marriage bed alone and sat with her until she fell into a deep sleep, telling myself that I would summon a doctor in the morning.

I awoke in the middle of the night to find Valerie clawing at my lap.

She was so forceful in her advances that I fell from my chair to the floor. Dazed, she overpowered me, pinning me down between her slender legs.

"Consummation!" she said, and that growl had returned to her voice.

I made to speak, but she pressed her lips to mine. They were cold, and her tongue probed mine like a worm in the mud; like a dog licking its master. I pushed her aside and clambered onto the bed to put some distance between us. She climbed after me like a cat and pulled at the nightgown I'd managed to dress her in just hours before.

"You do not want this body?"

"Oh, Valerie, what has happened to you?"

"You are my husband!" Her mouth was a cavern of darkness, and tears ran down her gaunt cheeks. "This is our wedding night!"

I dropped to my knees and reached for the woman I'd known before; the sweet, chaste woman I'd fallen in love with. I did want to embrace her and consummate our marriage, but it was meant to be a night of love and passion, not animalistic lust.

"Valerie, you're not well. Can't you see that?"

Valerie wailed and pulled at her clothing as if she was in a foreign place. She grabbed at the items on the bedside table, casting them across the room in a rage. She pulled at the curtains, tearing them with preternatural strength. I tried to constrain her, but she pushed me aside. There was such fury in her eyes as she gnashed at me with bloodied teeth. She bent to pick up a silver hand-mirror and smashed it against one of the bed posters. Shards of glass rained down and she scooped one up between trembling fingers.

"Put that down, my love—please! Before you hurt yourself!"

She swiped at me with the makeshift knife, and drops from her own bloodied hand spattered against my shirt. I could take this insanity no more. Ignoring my safety, I lunged at her and gripped her wrist. Valerie screamed and tried to claw at me with her other hand. I gritted my teeth and, swallowing the guilt, struck her across the face. She collapsed unconscious onto the bed.

And through the night I wept.

While Valerie slept, I was alone with the shadows of the past. The entire house seemed devoid of light and I wondered if it was contributing to my wife's sickness. There was no doubt she was experiencing more than grief; her entire body had been infected by her mother's passing. My parents were still alive, so it was difficult for me to comprehend the pain, but Valerie and her mother clearly had a strong connection.

I wandered the halls, checking the oil in all the lamps. They were full, yet the light seemed unable to push back the dark. Outside, the night howled; tree branches tapped the windows, demanding entry, and the fearsome owl seemed to call my name. My meanderings led me back to the sitting room where I proceeded to stoke the fire in silence, praying for my Valerie to return to me.

On the mantle rested several photographs of my wife as a child, her refined looks already evident at such a tender age. Another, of her as a teenager standing beside her mother who was seated in her chair, caught my attention. Their eyes were almost identical, although the brightness in Valerie's was significantly more evident. Her mother's simply stared, and I couldn't help but feel she was looking right at me. Into me.

Oddly, I could find no photographs of Valerie's father on the mantle. Perhaps the unexpected loss still lingered in Mrs. Karga. Could the effect of grief be passed down through the generations? I thought of Valerie's depressive, manic state and considered summoning the family doctor. These thoughts plagued me, heightening my fears and sleeplessness. I left the sitting room and went to the drawing room. The space carried no sign of its master, but the matriarch's empty ornate chair still managed to dominate and intimidate me. Ita Karga might as well have been sitting there, studying me.

The sensation forced me out of the room, and I traversed the staircase to the upper floor. I checked on Valerie and, finding her asleep, gently closed the door. At the end of the hall I saw the small flight of steps leading to the attic. Lamp in hand, I surrendered to explore the house further. To my astonishment, the key was already in the lock.

I opened the door and was assaulted by a miasma of decay. Dust motes swarmed like flies, illuminated by a sliver of moonlight reflected through an oculus window high on the far wall. Through the haze, I could discern many large crates and chests. My heart leapt in my throat when I made out a face in one of the dark corners. I cast the lamplight ahead of me and breathed a sigh of relief when I realised it was only a framed portrait of Mr. Karga. The man looked in his prime, regal. Pity filled my heart; the master of the house relegated to the attic.

Turning on my heels, I took in the rest of the room. Volumes of unknown texts were stacked against the walls, damp infiltrating their pages. Some of the tomes appeared ancient, with faint traces of gold leaf on the spines. Other items were even more perplexing: iron rings and keys, grime-covered mirrors, and large silver coins etched with inscriptions I recognised as Latin on one side and a crowned king on the other. They looked medieval. A dark stain curved around the edge of one coin. None of this made sense to me. I was overwhelmed by the oppressive nature of the walls.

I made for the door, only to be greeted by my wife.

"Valerie?" I rejoiced and took her in my arms.

Her arms wrapped tightly around me. "Oh, Eddie, I'm so sorry. I don't know what came over me."

I took her face in my hands and wiped away the tears. "You were grief-stricken, my love."

"But ... I tried to hurt you."

"It's all in the past, darling. You're here now, well again."

"Yes ... "

Valerie leant into me once more, her lips brushing against my cheek. The warmth between us swelled, and I turned inward to return her kiss. Our lips met and we collapsed into each other's desire. We kissed deeply and whether from relief or passion, I cannot be certain, we found ourselves on the floor of the attic. Valerie's hands pulled at my clothes, her breath heaving in my ears. We became husband and wife in that moment, our love a singular purpose that pushed back the dark.

Now I know that I had deceived myself, for that same darkness had taken up residence inside my Valerie. I saw it in her eyes: a dark glee. Satisfaction that was far more sinister than sensual. She was no longer my

Valerie. I believed she'd ceased to be at the very moment her mother had died.

Dear daughter, if you find this, if you are reading this, then my part has been played. If you are reading this then I am lost, and you are as well. Please my child, fight your mother, fight her with all your soul. Break the line of evil that plagues this family, and cast that witch back to hell.

Godspeed, my child.

I love you.

Light House, Dark House

O n first glance, Barry thought the St. Christopher Lighthouse had been poorly named.

Even in the stark light of late-morning, the towering structure seemed obscured by shadow. Gulls flew around it, but never landed, as if they were more like vultures waiting for some creature to die within. The waves rolled in and crashed against the lighthouse's craggy foundations, but never quite eclipsed its dark stature. To Barry, St. Christopher's Lighthouse was not a beacon, but a warning to stay away.

He retrieved his NIKON camera from its case to get a closer look. Through the long lens, Barry discovered the lighthouse's surface was caked with what appeared to be black scales, or mould, he couldn't be sure. When one pictured a lighthouse, they thought of a grand white tower, its cone of light piercing the darkness and offering safety to those lost at sea. This lighthouse was the complete opposite; weathered, run-down, almost decaying. The building had been neglected for many years, possibly decades. Still, St. Christopher's Lighthouse would make an interesting point of difference for his book, a chronicle of the country's lighthouses. He took a few shots, the lighthouse disappearing into darkness with each frame, night to day, then night again. The images he captured piqued his interest. All he needed now was a local to tell him about the building's history.

He shifted the lens zoom to examine the lighthouse in its entirety. The light room at its apex was as decrepit as the whole, the windows grey

with grime and caked sea salt. He imagined the light inside was long dead. He thought of the danger the lighthouse posed; weren't they meant to be maintained so ships could pass by safely? Where was the lighthouse's caretaker? Eager to answer his questions, Barry scanned the lighthouse's base for any sign of life and found a small house at the front; a cabin, caught in the lighthouse's shadow.

Barry scanned the hill around him for signs of passers-by. The area seemed deserted, not even any tourists around taking pictures. The sea breeze intensified in a wild gust, and Barry had to steady himself against the hood of his car; even the weather was freakish. Barry barely managed to hear the ring of his cell phone over the howling air. He looked at the screen and saw it was his daughter, Meredith.

"Merry! I was hoping you'd call," he said.

"Hi … "

Meredith's voice was distant, even with the added nuisance of the wind. It had been almost a month since he'd last spoken to his daughter, since the separation. With Meredith away at college, informing her of the divorce seemed like an even greater betrayal.

"How are you?" he said. "I've missed you." Again the spiteful silence. "Merry?" Meredith's reply was torn apart by the wind. Barry put his back to the breeze so he could hear, but it came from all sides. "Merry? I can't hear you! Are you there?"

He heard his daughter's voice as static. "Where … you?"

"Honey, listen, I'm down on the coast for work. The wind is really bad. I'll have to call you back, okay?"

The wind abated long enough for Barry to hear the engaged signal. Whether Meredith had ended the call or the reception failed, he couldn't be certain, but he hoped it was the latter. His relationship with Meredith—and his wife, Laura—had always been rocky. As a freelance photographer he was constantly on the road. Bitterness swelled inside him as thoughts of the divorce raged in his mind. He resented his wife for not talking to him about her concerns. Worse still he resented her for not seeing that his absences weren't voluntary. He was only doing his job and putting food on the table.

Guilt twisted its fierce barb into Barry's heart as he thought of the moments he'd missed in his daughter's life—the school recitals, her school awards, and others he couldn't recall because he'd been halfway around the world photographing war zones or government upheavals. His wife had reminded him of every one of his "failures," but he'd chosen to ignore her warnings out of spite and pride. Yet since becoming a freelancer, he'd strived to spend more time with Meredith but found that being freelance meant he had to be even more in demand if he was to feed himself.

Barry tried to call his daughter back; he knew she'd be waiting for him to call. Her grades had slipped since the divorce, and she'd become distant. Meredith had always been a placid girl, cautious, yet very self-aware. Things could get the better of her, if she didn't stay in control, and weeks would go by when he wouldn't hear from her. If there was ever a time she needed him, it was now. Barry swore when the call went through to voicemail, but he made a point of leaving a message.

"Merry, honey, it's Dad. Call me back when you get this, I really want to talk to you."

Barry got back into his car to escape the wind. He sat in the driver's seat, staring at the screen of his phone, begging for it to ring and his daughter to be on the other end. Minutes passed. He called Meredith again and left another message. Despair broiled inside him, and he found himself drawn to the lighthouse. The sun had begun to reach its zenith, yet the lighthouse remained immune to its light.

"She'll call back," he told himself before stepping out of the car. The wind had all but died off, and the ocean had become an ebb, the waves caressing the rocky shore. He started walking towards the lighthouse, eager to ease his worried mind.

As Barry came closer to the lighthouse, he was astounded by how it seemed to dominate the skyline. It was much taller than it looked. The house at its base truly was a ramshackle. He took several photographs of the façade, the wood so cracked and worn it looked like a scabbed-over wound.

He reached up with a shaky hand and knocked on the door. Flecks of ancient paint fell like dust beneath his rapping, and he wiped his hand on his jeans. When there was no answer, he peered through the cobwebbed windows, careful not to make contact with the glass. He could make out a table and chair inside and a collection of old pots and pans hanging from the ceiling. He felt the urge to go inside, to answer the call of the artist. He ignored the lingering doubt in the back of his mind and turned the doorknob, surprised to find it unlocked.

The stench of offal and salt assailed his senses, but he saw nothing in the room that could cause such a stink. Thick layers of dust and insect carapaces covered the room. Daddy long-legs spiders hovered in ceiling corners, their narrow legs arcing at the newcomer. Barry stepped inside, his boots crunching on sand and seashells. The cabin, just like the lighthouse, was unattended.

Barry took out his camera and took some photos of the room, the rusting pans, the spiders, the razor sharp shadows in every corner. He took careful steps, eager not to make a noise, which was foolish, given the fact there was no one around. Still, he couldn't shake the feeling there was a presence, a sensation, tingling at the edge of his vision. As Barry bent to take a photo of the chair, which had clearly been pushed in under the table by someone, a fresh wave of wind flooded the room. The pans rattled and swayed under its power, the steel clanking together in a shrill chorus, but it was the long sigh of old door hinges which made Barry jump with a start.

The old man was standing in the doorway. He was at least a foot shorter than Barry, his heavily bearded face crowned with a tatty sailor's cap. Pale, deep-set eyes examined the photographer but seemed unperturbed by his presence in the shack.

"Oh, I'm sorry, I didn't think anyone was here," Barry said.

Barry flinched when the old man slipped a hand into the pocket of his long, weatherproof coat, only to feel like a fool when he produced a pipe.

The old sea dog proceeded to light the pipe, puffing out blue smoke, but offering no words. Barry swallowed hard at the man's indifference.

"This lighthouse has to be one of the oldest I've ever seen," Barry said. "How long have you been lighthouse keeper?"

The sailor puffed his pipe. "Many a year," he replied.

Barry offered a nervous smile and tried to ignore the foul aroma of the pipe. He held up his camera. "Oh, that's great. I should introduce myself. My name's Barry Levin. I'm a photographer, as you might have guessed. I'm travelling the country taking photos of lighthouses. I'm putting a book together. Would you mind if I took some photos of your lighthouse?"

The sea dog pulled the pipe out his mouth to lick at his lips thoughtfully. "Makes no difference to me," he said.

"Uh, okay … I might start outside then and maybe, if you're interested, I could get a photo of you in your shack?"

The old man took another puff and then tamped the pipe into the palm of his hand, rubbing the burned tobacco remnants between his wrinkled fingers. Barry took his silence as acquiescence and turned to head out the door. The caretaker's voice drew him back.

"There's a lot more to see in the light room," the old man said.

"Excuse me?" Barry said, hesitating on the threshold.

"The light room," the sea dog said. "You should start there."

Barry scratched at his hair nervously, the old man's blank stare crawling into his skull and planting a seed of fear. The photographer tried to ignore the bad sensations and act professional.

"You'll take me on a tour? That'd be fantastic. How old is this lighthouse, if you don't mind me asking?" he said.

The sea dog's eyes narrowed. "It's seen many days and nights. It's one of the oldest light'ouses there is."

"How long have you been its caretaker?"

"I've been here many days and nights, watching and waiting."

Barry smiled. "I bet you've got some stories to tell. I'd love to hear a few."

"There'd nought be enough time in the world for my tales of woe. I've heard so many over the years, and they all sound very much the same. I see the same souls day after day, hour after hour."

Barry wasn't sure what the caretaker meant; he found the old man's words confusing and archaic, but then he realised he could be talking to someone who was more than one hundred years old.

"Well, I'd love to see your lighthouse, if you're happy to show me around."

The old man didn't answer, just turned his back on Barry and vanished into the doorway from whence he'd first appeared. Barry heard his shoes ascending the stairs; an open invitation for the photographer to follow. Taking a deep breath, Barry walked through the shack and through the door to the stairs. The staircase spiralled up like a twisted backbone. The old man climbed the steps effortlessly and only once looked back over his shoulder to see if Barry was following.

"How rude of me," Barry said, trying to catch his breath. "I meant to ask your name."

"Leopold," the old man said, his voice bouncing off the staircase walls.

"Well, thank you for letting me take a look around your lighthouse, Leopold."

Leopold made no response, only finished ascending the stairs and bent to unlock the door to the light room with a large brass key jangling amongst dozens more from his hand. The door opened, and Barry gasped in fright.

In the centre of the light room shone a blazing glow, a dazzling orb, shifting, spinning—and screaming. Barry's instinct was to shield his eyes from the sun-like light, yet he was desperate to understand it. He could see eyes and mouths, all agape and crying out for mercy within the shimmering sphere. Human faces seemingly trapped inside some beautiful horror.

"Oh, my God. What is this!?" Barry said.

Leopold harrumphed and retrieved his pipe to relight it. "There's no brighter light than the human soul," he said. "That's what that is."

Barry stared at the orb, trying to determine whether the sea dog was mad or if he himself was. The impossible light spun in the air, a nightmare carousel of suffering. He heard the souls' screams for release. The light also gave off a fierce heat, like they were burning.

"This can't be real!"

"Aye, but it is," Leopold said, puffing on his pipe. "They power this lighthouse, these lost souls."

"Lost ... lost souls?"

Leopold stepped closer to the glow, basking in its light. "There 'ain't no sanctuary here, no light to lead you to safety."

"What the hell are you talking about!?"

The orb's shrieks rose inside the room as Leopold pointed out some of the faces in the crowd with his pipe. "Free will brought them here, but my will keeps them here." He looked upon Barry. "Their light feeds my darkness."

Barry clawed at his hair. Madness gripped him, his chest tightening, sweat running down his back. He dropped his camera on the floor, and its flash fired, setting off a fresh cacophony of screams from within the ball of light. Amongst the screams for help he heard a soul call for its father.

DAD!

The photographer knew the voice; he'd heard it not long ago, broken and desperate for connection. His daughter. Meredith's face suddenly pushed through the others inside the light to shriek for him.

DAD!

"Merry!? Oh, sweet Jesus!"

He saw her anguished face, mouth contorted in agony. She reached out from the light to her father, wrists bearing vertical slashes. At the sight Barry's voice joined in his daughter's sickening chorus.

"Merry!"

Leopold smiled and puffed. "She called to say goodbye you know," he said. "Before, when she rang you outside; she wanted you to know how alone she was. How you'd left her all alone. She killed herself because you forgot about her. I'll say it's not much of an excuse for taking one's life, but it's suicide nonetheless."

Barry fell to his knees, the intensifying light burning his eyes, the sound of his daughter calling tearing at his heart.

"No!"

"Oh aye," the old sea dog said. "You made her do it, but don't you fret now, Barry. I'll take good care of her."

DADDY!

Barry scrambled to his feet out the door and ran down the stairs. His legs descended step after step, heels clacking on stone, the scream of his daughter's lost soul in tow. The staircase twisted inwards and around, disorienting Barry's vision, a blurred spiral that infected his mind. All he could think of was reaching his phone and calling his daughter. As he stumbled down, he pulled his phone free and dialled Merry's number. It answered on the first ring with a high pitched squealing through the earpiece.

DAAAAADDDDDDDYYYYYY!

Barry dropped the phone in shock and watched it tumble over and over down the stairs and, he found himself bending to catch it. How could she be dead, he asked himself. She can't be. The stairs spun around and around, the never-ending steps sapping him of strength until Barry's legs folded beneath him. He rolled head over heels, the steps slamming into his back and ribs, knees buckling.

He came to a sudden halt, slamming against a wooden door. He rolled on to his back and opened tear-soaked eyes to see the old sea dog Leopold peering down at him. Blue smoke oozed from his nostrils, but there was no pipe, only an everlasting fire from within. He pulled Barry to his feet and opened the black door for the photographer to see inside.

A panorama of blood and flesh and fire spread out before Barry in every direction; human vessels contorted and torn, but still experiencing some level of consciousness. In contrast to the light room, the screams in the dark room at the bottom of the lighthouse were silent, the victims' mouths stretched, yet muted.

Leopold whispered in Barry's ear. "My light'ouse goes deep down," he said. "The light of the lost up there feeds the darkness down here, the darkness of those who lead the lost down the wrong path. People like you."

"No! I loved my daughter!" Barry pleaded.

"I'm sure you can find a way to prove that to her."

Barry felt Leopold push him through the door, heard it slam behind him, and St Christopher's Lighthouse became his hell.

The Darkness at the End of the Tunnel

The train carriage was a coffin, full of lifeless people.

The thought occurred to Wayne Lovell as he glanced around at the other passengers; he was riding on a death train. No one talked to each other. They just swiped at their smart phones, or read a book, their eyes looking south, always south.

The carriage was scarcely occupied (Wayne had deliberately avoided the rush hour crush), but seeing these zombies jostling from side to side in their seats, without a care in the world, made him wish he was dying too.

There was one passenger who glanced his way, a short elderly man sitting in the seat just near the doors. There was no smile on his wrinkled face, just a nod of acknowledgement; a fleeting gesture. Wayne accepted it in silence and went back to watching the city blur by.

Death was on his mind. Not random morbid thoughts, but precise thinking about his wife Judy, and the inevitability of time.

Wayne looked at the passengers again, counted five of them. He was riding the death train with five passengers—and the shadow of his weary soul.

Judy's ragged breaths frosted the oxygen mask which obscured half her face, yet still managed to emphasise the weakness in her hazel eyes.

"Seven months," the oncologist said.

Wayne watched a tear run from his wife's eye and vanish beneath the mask.

"Seven?" Wayne said and clutched Judy's hand. She couldn't squeeze it back.

"I'm very sorry, but the cancer has metastasized," the doctor said. He turned to Judy. "It's gone into the spine and left lung. That's why you went into respiratory arrest last week."

"You told us you got it all," Wayne said. "A year ago you said you got it all."

Judy squeezed his finger, but he barely registered it. He looked at his wife and she was shaking her head at him.

The oncologist referred to his chart and Wayne imagined a series of pre-prepared responses typed on a piece of paper that doctors could use when they had to break the bad news to the husbands of their cancer-riddled wives.

"Uterine cancer is a very aggressive type of cancer. Even if you remove the reproductive organs it doesn't always guarantee—"

Wayne got to his feet, and the oncologist straightened.

"Just tell me what our options are," Wayne said.

"I can have one of the palliative care team meet with you."

Wayne saw Judy nodding; had she already given up?

"Is that it then? Judy just lies in bed and dies?" He slipped out of her feeble grip.

"Mr. Lovell—"

"Don't!" he said. "Just don't!"

"Mr. Lovell, I'm sorry, but we've exhausted all the options. But please rest assured we'll do everything we can to make your wife comfortable. "

Wayne looked at all the wires and tubes hanging out of Judy. Beneath her robe, he knew there was a 20-centimetre scar across her abdomen: the mark of death. "Make her comfortable?" he said. "You've all failed her. No, I'm going to take her home. If she's going to die, she won't be dying here."

The Darkness at the End of the Tunnel

Wayne rode the subway at the back of the carriage with his head in his hands. All he saw were tears.

His wife was going to die, and selfishly, he was the one who'd decided how she'd pass on. He gripped the handles of the chair in front of him and shook it. He wanted to scream, hear the echo of his anguish bouncing off the steel walls, but he knew it would startle the other passengers, make them stare. Wayne didn't want to look at anyone ever again, no doctors, or nurses; he didn't even know if he could look into Judy's pleading eyes anymore.

How was he going to arrange palliative care in their cramped two-bedroom apartment? Did he have the strength to bathe her and clean her, to hear her desperate gasps for breath in the pit of night, to watch her die? It wasn't meant to be this way. They were supposed to be happy; they were supposed to be parents, revelling in the joy of a child's wonder at the world.

"It's not meant to be this way … " Wayne said through gritted teeth.

"Life rarely turns out the way we planned," someone said.

Wayne looked up and wiped his nose on the back of his hand. A small, old man peered at Wayne from across the narrow aisle. The automated train message system announced the city stop was two minutes away. The old man stared, unblinking.

"Excuse me?" Wayne said.

"I couldn't help overhear," the passenger said. "Are you alright?"

Wayne blinked the tears from his eyes. He thought about moving away, farther up the carriage, then realised he was looking at the man who'd acknowledged him just hours before. Wayne sniffed.

"I … I'm fine."

The old man's bushy eyebrows lifted, furrowing his brow. "Are you sure? If you need a friendly ear?"

Wayne frowned. "I don't even know you."

The passenger held out his hand. The knuckles bulged beneath the skin. "Ed. The name's Ed."

Wayne slid back in his seat as the train came to a stop. A dozen other strangers stepped inside and took their seats. The old man put his hand back in his jacket, but never took his eyes off Wayne. They stared as the train restarted down the line. A moment later the old man started talking again.

"I used to drive a train like this one, oh, nearly twenty years ago." Ed glanced around the interior. "They're a lot more high-tech these days. But I guess you can't stop time, can you?"

Wayne made to move out of the seat. "Look, mate, I don't feel like a friendly chat, okay?"

The old man stood and moved to sit in the chair in front of Wayne. Wayne backed up. He scanned for a security a guard, but there was none in sight.

"You're upset, I know," Ed continued over his shoulder. "I want to help you get back on track."

Jesus, I've been befriended by a fucking crazy person. Wayne swallowed hard; he didn't want to provoke him.

"Can you please move away from me?" he said, as quietly, but directly as possible.

"You're in pain, because someone else is in pain, I know," Ed said.

Wayne felt hot tears on his cheeks again. He clenched his fists, fighting the urge to let the old man feel the brunt of his frustrations.

"Why the hell is it any of your business? Please go away, or I'll call for security."

The train entered a tunnel and the overhead lights snapped off, plunging the carriage into shadow. The old man's reflection played on the window beside him and Wayne could see every line of his face. None of the other passengers seemed to notice their strange conversation.

"I sense other people's pain because I used to be in pain myself," Ed said. "I had cancer. Too many cigarettes." Ed turned around and lifted his shirt to show Wayne a long pinkish scar that ran from his armpit to his hip. He dropped the shirt just as the train emerged from the other side of the tunnel and the harsh lights came back on. "Not long after I was diagnosed I was told about a train, a ghost train that only a few know about."

Wayne felt his heart thrumming in his ears in time with the train's wheels on the tracks beneath them.

"You're fucking crazy."

Ed smiled, revealing perfect dentures. "That's what I told the guy who told me, until he showed me his scars." He looked towards the sign near the doors which showed the train routes through the city. "If you want to help your wife, go to the tracks between Shipton and Annandale stations. There's a tunnel there, an abandoned route. That's where you'll find the cure to what ails her."

Before Wayne could scream at the old man to explain the madness he was speaking, Ed stood and walked out of the carriage. Wayne tried to follow him, but the next car was so full of people that Ed was lost. The train stopped at the next station, and Wayne watched the people file off, but the old man wasn't among them. He spent the next twenty minutes fruitlessly searching every other car. It was almost as if the stranger had never existed at all.

At the apartment, Wayne spent the next few hours on the phone with local hospices and palliative care services. Their grim frankness got the better of him, so much so that he hung up on the fifth call. Every thought was infiltrated by images of Judy suffering and dying. He didn't want her to suffer; he didn't want to lose her. The hole in his heart was swallowing him from the inside out, and he didn't know what to do.

He went to the fridge and took out a beer. The bottle was cool against his forehead, but it did little to quench the rage. He took a long drink, and he realised everything tasted stale. Through the kitchen window he saw the lines of traffic in the distance; people living their lives. He wondered how many of them had cancer.

Wayne threw the beer bottle at the dishes piled high in the kitchen sink. Shards of glass, plates, and beer exploded onto the tiles. He screamed at the chaos he'd created. Everything was breaking apart; his entire fucking life.

He remembered his wife smiling with the pregnancy strip in her hand; the blue cross symbol revealing how their lives were about to change. First there'd been joy, then the sorrow of a miscarriage, then the unparalleled fear of cancer, and Judy having all chance of motherhood cut from her. Now, the thing that took her flesh was going to take her life.

If you want to help your wife, go to the tracks between Shipton and Annandale stations. There's a tunnel there, an abandoned route. That's where you'll find the cure to what ails her.

The old man, Ed, spoke to Wayne's soul. He didn't know if the man on the train was lying, but there was one common truth he was willing to accept: Ed and Judy both bore the scars of cancer.

Wayne waited until midnight before driving to the car park at Shipton station in the eastern part of the city.

The parked cars were like graves, hollow and devoid of colour despite the neon glow of the overhead lights. Wayne parked and walked towards the station entrance, scanned his rail pass and slipped through the turnstile. The buzz of the power lines over the platform made his skin hum. Half a dozen people waited for the next train, young men laughing and egging each other on for a night of drinking, an elderly couple with large suitcases, obsessing over their tickets; ordinary people taking ordinary journeys. Wayne hoped to catch a different train.

He sat and watched the minutes tick by on the train schedule screens. He wasn't going into the city. Annandale was the next stop up from Shipton, but he didn't intend on going there either.

Go to the tracks between Shipton and Annandale stations …

The Darkness at the End of the Tunnel

The automated voiceover announced the City train's arrival moments before it pulled into the station. The young men clambered on board. The elderly couple followed, fussing with their suitcases just outside the train doors. When one of the rail staff came to their aid, Wayne got up from his seat and walked towards the rear carriage. When Wayne was certain that the porter was occupied and that no other trains were coming, he jumped down from the platform onto the tracks below and bolted into the dark.

There was no doubting the thrill of doing something forbidden. His feet crunched on the gravel as he ran, sucking in the cool air and letting himself smile, for the first time in what felt like an age. He knew there were security cameras so he stayed out of the light as much as he could. He didn't care if he was caught; all he cared about was helping Judy, even if it meant running around a rail yard in the middle of the night in search of a ghost train.

Wayne was careful not to trip on the rail lines; he couldn't afford a sprain, or worse, a fracture when Judy needed him. The tracks curved in all directions, gleaming and glinting in the half-light like flattened sabres. Behind him he heard the blare of the train horn. Were they onto him? He had to act fast. He looked about for a tunnel, mindful of his feet, keeping out of the light, watching for other trains. How was he going to know where the spot between Shipton and Annandale stations was?

He stopped to lean against a signal pylon and catch his breath. He felt ridiculous running around in search of something that probably didn't exist. He spat on the tracks, cursing the old man, and his own foolishness. Wayne decided then and there to give up his wild goose chase and head back to Shipton station where the authorities would no doubt be waiting.

As he placed his boot on one of the rail lines, a tremor pulsed through his body. It was a deepening rattle that rose from beneath the very ground. He turned to look over his shoulder, and in the distance some hundred feet away, an archway of night bloomed before him. The concrete edges of the rail yard and even the tracks seemed to disappear into it. He couldn't recall seeing it before. As he stared into the darkness a spark of light appeared, like that first strike of flint. The spark intensified, swelling in time with the rumbling earth. The great shriek of a train whistle cut the silence, so loud that Wayne had to cover his ears. The train emerged from the pitch, a gargantuan hulk of blue-black steel and steam. Wayne jumped out its path just as it passed in a chorus of grinding brakes. He rolled onto his back and gazed open-mouthed as the ghost train slowed to a stop on an abandoned piece of track between Shipton and Annandale stations.

The crazy old man had been telling the truth.

Wayne stood at his wife's hospital bed and reached out to stroke her hair. She flinched awake.

"Shhh, Judy, it's me," he said, offering her a grin.

"Wayne?" Judy looked from him to the window and frowned when she saw it was still dark outside. She pulled down her oxygen mask. "What are you doing here? What time is it?"

He took her hand and kept his voice low. "Babe, I'm going to take you somewhere where you can get some real help."

"What are you talking about?"

Wayne glanced over his shoulder and then leaned in close. "I met this guy on the train and he told me about this place ... a special place where you can get treatment."

He saw a sliver of doubt pass over her face. "Wayne ... please ... this isn't right. I already met with one of the palliative care nurses. We talked about the next step. I was going to tell you this morning—"

Wayne shook his head. "Don't worry about all that. After this trip you won't need palliative care. You'll be cured." He pulled gently on her arm, trying to get her out of the bed. "Come on. We have to go before one of the night nurses comes around."

"Wayne ... stop," Judy pulled away.

"Babe, you have to trust me."

"Trust you?" She took a sharp breath, her voice straining under the pressure. "You come here in the middle of the night to tell me some old man told you about a cure? You look … I don't know … wild. We need to stop looking for a cure and accept what's going to happen." She pulled the mask back over her face.

Wayne dropped to his knees. "Babe, you can't just give in," he said. "There's a chance here, a real chance that I can save you."

She put her cold fingers on the sides of his face. "Wayne … I know you love me … but you can't save me from this."

Wayne's eyes narrowed. He felt hot tears. "You have to let me try, Judy," he said. "You're my wife. Just let me take you to the train. Let me show you."

He watched her run a hand through her thinning auburn hair, shake her head. "Take me to a train … what? Do you hear yourself..? Wayne … just stop."

Judy gasped and slumped back on the bed. Wayne felt the twist of anguish in his gut. He never wanted to upset her; he only wanted her to be safe. He smoothed her hair and watched her breathing normalise. She was so weak, the exhaustion of their argument causing her to pass out.

"You have to let me try, babe."

Wayne looked out into the hall and saw a wheelchair abandoned near a storage cupboard. At the far end he saw the nurses' station, where two nurses were distracted in conversation. He stepped across the hall, grabbed the wheelchair, took it to his wife's room, then scooped her off the bed and into the seat. He wheeled her out of the room to the elevator, and it was an uninterrupted ride all the way to the ground floor. When the doors opened onto a security guard near the main entrance, Wayne tried to remain calm. The burly man scrutinised him with his dark eyes; it was an odd hour to be going for a trip around the hospital.

"Everything alright sir?" the guard said.

Wayne nodded to his wife. "She ah … wanted to see the stars."

The guard looked at Judy slumped in the chair. "She looks like she should be in bed."

"That's what I said, but um … she got some bad news today and needs some air."

The guard's expression softened. "Very sorry to hear that," he said. "It's a clear sky tonight, but I wouldn't be out there too long. It's a bit nippy."

Wayne managed a slight smile. "Thanks, mate. Have a good night."

He wheeled Judy through the doors and didn't stop until he reached the car park.

If he didn't hurry, they were going to miss their train.

Judy came to as he carried her across the rail yard.

"Wayne? What are you doing?"

Even though she weighed nothing in his arms, she was heavy with fear.

"It's okay Judy," he said. "We're going for a ride."

She clawed at his jacket. "Wayne … " she said, her voice wracked by tears. "You're … scaring me."

He stopped between the train tracks and held her close. "There's no need to be afraid. The train is coming, and you're going to be okay." He kissed the tears on her cheek.

"I don't understand … "

"There's a train. I've seen it Judy. It's … not of this world. There are … people on board who have offered to take your pain away. You only have to choose."

Judy's eyes revealed that she'd lost her faith in him, but he had to be strong and have faith in himself. Wayne carried her over another line of tracks towards the spot where the tunnel had last appeared. He stared at the spot, willing the train to come into existence. Judy shivered in his arms.

"Wayne … please take me back to the hospital."

"Shhh, babe. Just listen!"

The train's whistle echoed from out of the dark. Wayne watched the realisation pass over his wife's face as the tunnel formed about them.

Vibrations rose along Wayne's legs and into his wife's frail body. The sensation quickened her. The clickety-clack of the wheels was the heartbeat of the night, pounding so fiercely it took control of them and set their own hearts into a new rhythm of anticipation. The train emerged from the tunnel as if it were hewn from it. The chimney hissed and spurted ethereal steam, driving pistons and crankshafts which looked more like blackened bone than steel. Wayne was in absolute awe of it, but Judy was terrified.

"Oh my god!" she said, trying to get out of his arms.

"Judy, it's okay. It's okay!"

He let her stand, but her grip on him was more desperate. "What is this?" she cried. "What are you trying to do?"

A twirl of steam slipped from the cab window and took up the shape of a man—the train driver, slick with sweat and soot, a grubby handkerchief tied around his neck. He offered her a polite tip of his cap.

"Ma'am," the driver said.

Wayne felt his wife's frantic heart through the weave of his jacket. "Judy, this is Bill. He's going to take us on our ride."

"What? No! I'm not getting on that thing!" she said.

Bill looked at Wayne as if his time was being wasted. Wayne took a gentle hold his wife's shoulders.

"Judy, it's just a short ride. They promised me that you will be safe." There was still so much fear in her eyes. He had to take it away. "Judy, the man I met on the subway had cancer too, and he said this train saved his life. I saw his scar Judy, and he was alive!" Wayne moved to the steps leading to the first carriage. "Come on, babe."

Judy reached for him. "Wayne, don't!"

"It's okay. Just come with me. I've already been on a ride, and it's amazing. I promise."

Judy looked over the black train and the driver. There was so much uncertainty in her eyes. "I'm sorry ... I can't."

"Okay," Wayne said. "Look, just come for a ride. That's all I'm asking. I know you'll enjoy it." He held out his hand and after several moments of hesitation, she took it. He led her up the steps into the carriage.

The inside of the train was in complete contrast to the carapace-like exterior; the walls were freshly varnished timber, the booth style seats furnished with red velvet. Gas lamps cast everything in a golden glow. Wayne shed tears of joy as Judy stared at the train, as wistful as a little girl.

"I told you," he said, urging her to sit down with him. The train jerked forward on the tracks and Judy fell into Wayne's lap. They hadn't laughed together in so long. Outside the sky was blooming with a new day.

"How is this possible?" Judy said. "How can no one see us?"

Wayne shook his head, but he was still smiling. "It must be magic."

The train rolled along an invisible track through an impossible rift in reality. The city was a never-ending, moving landscape. For the first time, Wayne felt hope in his heart. His wife was already looking brighter, more alive. Perhaps the train ride would be enough. He turned her face to look at him, and they shared a long, deep kiss.

Before them stood a waiter, tall and broad shouldered, with neatly parted hair and dressed in a bright, red jacket with brass buttons.

"Uh, hi," Wayne said. He looked to his wife. "Judy, this is Jack."

Jack nodded at Judy. "Hello madam. I hope you are enjoying the ride?"

Judy giggled. "Um, yes ... thank you."

"Wonderful," Jack said, before looking Wayne's way. "Perhaps it's time to discuss the arrangement?"

Judy's expression shifted to apprehension. "Arrangement?"

Wayne squeezed her hand. "Remember, I said they can help you? You only need to choose."

Judy studied Jack carefully. "You ... you've helped people before, people with cancer?"

Jack smiled. "Oh, many people. We've had many poor souls on this train over the centuries and offered them hope."

"How do you help them?"

The waiter straightened. "Entering the train is only one part of the journey. In fact it's just another station, another stop in life. On this train you have the chance to diverge, to change tracks, so to speak. Your life is at a crossroads, Mrs. Lovell, and it's up to you where you want the journey to go."

Judy looked to her husband and then to Jack. "You mean, I can choose whether … the cancer kills me or not, just like that?"

Jack chuckled. "It's a bit more complicated than that. Let me put it this way: right now, your cancer is in control of your body, like the driver of this train. It wants to take you on a very dark journey."

Judy and Wayne held each other. Jack leaned in, the smile still on his face.

"So here is the choice," he said. "Let us take control. Let us steer you on a new path."

Judy's frown deepened. "What do you mean?"

Wayne slipped down from the seat to kneel before her. "Babe, you've seen the train and what it can do. Jack is, well, for want of a better word, a spirit guide. He told me he'll give you—and me—a new path where there's no cancer."

She considered the waiter and the train. "How?"

Jack, still all smiles, produced a silver platter from behind his back. On top were two glasses of champagne.

"All you need do is take a sip of this."

"Champagne?"

"It's more of an elixir," Jack said.

Judy stood and backed away. "Sorry, but this is all just a little bit too fairy tale for me," she said. "How do I know that it's not poison?"

Wayne got up and grabbed one of the glasses. He took a mouthful. "See, it's perfectly fine. Babe, it's time to let go of the fear. It's ruled our lives for too long."

Gingerly, Judy took her glass from the platter. As she put it to her lips and drew in the champagne, Wayne felt his knees weaken. At first he thought it was the rocking of the train, until he looked at the contents of the glass. Black particles of soot floated in the liquid. Panic striking in his chest, he looked at the same particles pass into his wife's mouth.

"Judy, wait—

The train jerked on the tracks, and Judy staggered to the left, dropping the glass to clutch her abdomen. Her scream pierced the carriage walls. Wayne tried to go to her, but his head swam with dizziness. Around them, the lacquered walls began to crack and scorch, spewing black smoke and steam into the carriage. The wisps coiled in Judy's direction and seeped into her mouth and nose. When Wayne heard Jack laughing he grabbed the waiter by his pristine lapels.

"You lying bastards! You promised me you'd save her!"

Judy buckled as the black smoke tore at her insides. Blood ran from her lips onto the floor, her face a mask of anguish and betrayal.

Jack gripped Wayne back. "Oh, we'll save her. We'll take all that pain away—by taking her soul!"

Jack dragged Wayne to the carriage door and kicked it wide. The train rocketed along the impossible tracks atop an all-encompassing darkness.

"This is a ghost train, after all," he said.

Wayne felt the cold caress of the dark as he was flung from the train. His head, clouded with the train's poison, left him like a puppet with cut strings. He heard his wife's scream fade into nothing before the real world came up to meet him with a crash of dusty gravel.

When he opened his eyes in the rail yard, the train, and his wife, were gone.

Wayne tried to find the train the following day and night, but after many hours of skulking about the rail yard, he realised the spirits had what they wanted, a fresh soul to torment. There was no telling when—or if—they would return.

When the sun rose and the tears had dried in his stubble, Wayne's mind pushed down the self-pity to give him another possibility—the one face that had started it all. He started to leave the rail yard to find that face when he heard the crunch of shoes on gravel.

"Hey!"

Wayne turned and saw the distinctive glow of a high-visibility vest, a rail employee. Wayne burst into a run, his legs stiff and aching as he bounded over the lines of track. He could hear the employee giving chase, but that desperation which had driven Wayne to foolishly condemn his wife was reignited; there was still a chance to undo all his wrongs. He leapt up on to the platform, startling the handful of commuters waiting for the train. No one approached him as he slipped out of the station and back to the car park, but he sensed the police would be on their way. He ran to his car, started the engine and sped out of the car park, headed for the train station where he'd lost his way.

In the frantic drive through the dawn traffic, Wayne heard on the radio that the authorities were looking for a man who took his terminally ill wife from the hospital. He knew then that there was no turning back.

Wayne ran through the city station, shouldering commuters out of his way on the escalator to reach platform one. He knew there was little chance that the old man would be on any of the trains, but there was nothing else he could think to do.

The old man, "Ed" was obviously in on the act, riding the real trains to find people at the edge of despair or facing the end of their lives. It was a cunning system to find lost souls and offer them tickets to a train that only really offered them a one-way journey to hell.

The thought of Judy trapped on the shadow train terrified and angered him. He stared at the display screen and paced the platform; the first morning train which stopped at the hospital was imminent.

"You'll be on that train, won't you, you bastard," he thought he said under his breath, until a young woman eyed him warily. When he glared at her she backed away. He imagined he looked dishevelled and crazed, a man at the end of his tether.

Wayne heard the train's approach and licked his lips in anticipation as it rolled slowly towards the platform.

"Hurry up, for Christ's sake!"

The people on the platform frowned at him.

"What the hell are you looking at?"

"Sir, could you come with me please?"

Wayne turned to see two police officers approaching him. He knew when he looked in their eyes that they knew him; they'd been searching for him. His face would have shown up on several security cameras by now.

He waited until the train stopped and the passengers started to walk into the carriages before he jumped down onto the tracks and ran for it. He couldn't let them catch him; if they caught him, Judy would be lost forever. He weaved between signal posts, ignoring the pleas of the police and the frightened screams of the other passengers. He'd keep running and would never stop until he was with Judy again.

Wayne tripped and came down hard onto a line of track. He felt blood dripping into his eye and the cold touch of steel. As he tried to shake the dizziness from his head and stand, he heard that train whistle, high and long. It wavered through his very soul. He stood as the great black train appeared from a void of darkness. Yet his eyes betrayed him, the sight flickering from the antique ghost train to a modern city train and back again. In the driver's seat he saw the old man, Ed, one hand controlling the train, the other around his wife's gaping mouth.

"Judy!" Wayne cried.

Ed's face shifted to Bill, and then to Jack, but always bearing that same smile. Judy's face was sheer terror.

Wayne understood he was never going to save her or himself from fate. But at least they would take their last journey together.

And with outstretched arms, Wayne let the shadow train take him away.

Happiness on Cemetery Street

Mummy said we have to start letting people bury their dead in the backyard so we can have enough money to buy food and clothes.

Everybody in our street is doing it; there are so many dead people, but no more graveyards to put them in, Mummy said. It was an idea all the governments had before I was born. The cities are all too big with too many buildings and too many people. On the TV they say there's not enough food and water and land. Mummy said it would be easier if everybody was turned into ashes, but some churches are against that. So now, people pay to have funerals at stranger's houses. They're called Cemetery Streets. The name sounds funny, like *Sesame Street*. Mummy said it's a good idea, but there are only so many backyards, and we might have to start burying people in the desert.

We've had two funerals at our house: one with a man from a country called Iran and another of a little boy, whose mummy and daddy come from a place near Russia. I asked Mummy why there are so many different types of funerals, and she said it's because we live in a multi-cultural society.

It's funny how some funerals are like parties not just people crying, but there was some crying at the man from Iran's funeral. He was brought in with a big white sheet wrapped around him, and all his family, who were dressed in black, stood around him, and there was a man who sang songs in a different language. I didn't know the words, but it sounded beautiful. He sang the word "Allah" a lot, and Mummy said that was their name for God. After the singing was over they took him outside and placed him on the ground near the grave under the big mango tree. Mummy said we had to be respectful and stay inside the house. I looked through the window as they lifted the man's body up four times and then placed him in the hole. Mummy said too that the man's family would come back to visit him sometimes, but they only had to pay once.

I saw my first ghost a few days after the Iran man's funeral.

His crying woke me up in the middle of the night. I went to wake Mummy to try and tell her, but she was too asleep. The man was standing in the backyard, crying and singing, but his singing sounded a lot like moaning. I heard the word Allah again and wondered if he wanted his God. My body was all shaky as I watched him through my bedroom window. He wasn't see-through like ghosts on TV; he was wrapped in his white sheet. His grave was the same so he couldn't have dug his way out, which meant he was definitely a ghost. I let out a squeal when he turned to look at me. His tears were all shining in the moonlight.

"Where am I?" he said.

He just kept saying it over and over. I jumped into bed and covered my ears. I must have been crying out for Mummy, because all of sudden she was next to me, asking me what was wrong. She didn't believe me when I told her there was a ghost outside. I begged her not to let any more funerals happen in our backyard, but she got really cross and told me to go to sleep. Only after Mummy left and the man was gone did I finally close my eyes.

The boy from near Russia was buried two weeks later. His family was much bigger than the Iran man's, but the funeral was a lot like how Mummy said she remembered funerals. Later, Mummy brought out some tea and cakes, and while I sat in the kitchen eating a piece of cake, the boy's grandma came in looking for the toilet. Mummy showed her where it was, but the old lady kept staring at me. I was finishing my cake when the lady stopped to talk to me.

"You look just like my daughter—when she was younger."

I looked to Mummy, and she gave me that face she uses when we need to be nice to the people who come to our house for the funerals.

"I'm sorry about the little boy," I said.

She reached out and patted my head. "Petro was his name. He was a good boy."

"Was he sick?" I asked.

Mummy gasped.

"Is okay," the old lady said. "He had the cancer."

"I'm sorry," I said. I felt sad because so many people were dying of cancer.

The old lady smiled at me and decided to sit next to me at the table. Mummy nodded that it was okay. The old lady reached out and took my hand.

"Are you afraid of dying, child?" She smiled, her wrinkled lips smoothing out.

I looked at the floor, the Iran man's ghost in my mind; I didn't want anyone to know about him. "I don't know."

She rubbed my hands gently. "Is okay, is okay." Her smile widened, and I saw she was missing some of her teeth. "When I was young like you, long time ago, I remember funeral of my uncle. In those days people afraid of death; that their loved ones would come back. So they would have big celebration in their memory and give away their things to strangers."

"Why?" I asked.

"To make sure the dead were happy when they went to heaven. I remember how my great uncle's body was wrapped up and placed under a window in our house. It was a small house, and we were a big family. We had to make sure his feet faced the door." She squeezed my hands. "On day of funeral his coffin was carried feet in front to the grave, and we lined up behind him, so he could not see us."

I frowned. "He could he see you?"

"People thought the dead could still see. The coffin was put on the ground at the door and tapped three times … " she tapped her old shoes on the floor. "That was to tell him it was time to go, to say goodbye." She raised an eyebrow. "Did I say his coffin was full of feathers?"

I shook my head.

"Well, it was—full of duck feathers. That was so he had comfort—'May the earth be like feathers for him,' my momma and poppa said. Then he was placed in the earth, facing the sunrise. That way when he woke up in the other life it was his first day in heaven. Afterwards anyone who touched my great uncle had to wash their hands before the feast."

The grandmother's story was so strange, but all I could think of was their worry that the dead man would come back.

"Did your great uncle come back?"

My mother sighed, but the old lady waved her hand in the air and laughed.

"Is okay, is okay," she said. "No, my child, he slept in the ground, and he has ever since."

She stood up to leave, but I had one more question.

"Has anyone ever come back?"

"Sissy," my mother said. "That's enough now."

The old lady frowned. "You mean, like ghost?"

I nodded and licked my lips.

She reached out and touched the top of my head, smoothing down my hair. "I have never seen one, and I have lived a long time."

After she and her family left Mummy put me to bed and told me that ghosts were not real. She said it was best that we didn't have any more funerals at our house for a while. When I asked what Daddy's funeral was like Mummy began to cry and said goodnight without giving me a kiss. She was really sad. I didn't mean to make her sad; I only wanted to know about Daddy's funeral. I went to sleep praying that if I ever did see a ghost again it would be Daddy's.

It was the middle of the night when the dead boy woke me.

He stood crying at the side of my bed, and I really fought hard not to scream. I put my hand over my mouth and stared at him. His skin was white and his lips were all bloody. I curled up in my bed and pulled the blankets over my face. I wanted to cry out for Mummy, but I knew she wouldn't see him; I was the only one who could see the ghosts.

"Hello?" the dead boy said.

I tried to pretend I was asleep.

"Hello?" the boy said again.

I wanted him to go away, but I could feel him through my blankets; he was so cold. My heart was beating so fast, and it was hard to breathe. I prayed he wouldn't be there when I looked out from under the blankets, but God must not have heard me.

"Hello?" the boy said one more time. He stood there in his suit and looked at me with black eyes.

"Hello," I said back.

"Where am I?" he said.

"You're dead."

The boy frowned, but he didn't seem scared like me.

"I was sick."

"I know. Your grandma said you had cancer."

"I don't remember dying; only going to sleep."

"That's a good way to die, I guess."

He glanced around the room and then back at me. "Is this your room?"

"Yes, my name's Sissy. You're Petro, right?"

He nodded. His mouth curled up at one corner. "Why am I in your house?"

"You're buried here, in our backyard."

119

Petro's eyebrows arched. "Why?"

"Because there are no more graveyards and your parents paid my Mummy to bury you here."

"Oh."

"I think you should go now."

"Where?"

He had so many questions, and I just wanted him to go away. "Back to your grave."

"How?"

"I don't know." I lay back down and pulled the blankets tight over my head.

"Why can you see me?" I heard Petro ask.

"Get out of my room."

I heard nothing. When I slowly pulled back the covers to look, Petro was gone.

*

The next morning Mummy cooked me my favourite breakfast of pancakes and golden syrup. For a while she looked happy-sad, but I guess I must have looked sleepy because she suddenly got all worried.

"Are you still not sleeping sweetheart?" Mummy said.

I pushed a piece of pancake around my plate. I didn't want to look Mummy in the eyes.

"Are you upset with me?" She lifted my chin up with her hand. I shook my head. Mummy's eyes were shiny with tears. "Is it because I yelled at you about Daddy?"

"No, Mummy," I said.

She rubbed my cheek. "Your Daddy loved you very much—that's all you need to know."

I looked over to the shelf above the TV, at the picture of Daddy and Mummy smiling. It was next to the one where he was dressed as an army man.

"What happened to him?" I said.

Mummy's lips trembled. "Oh, Sissy … don't," she said.

I felt hot in my chest, and I pushed the plate away. "Why won't you say what happened to Daddy, or what his funeral was like?"

"Sissy! Now stop it!"

"It's not fair! Why does everyone come here for funerals, but I'm not allowed to know how my Daddy died?"

Mummy stood so fast she bumped the table, and my glass of orange juice fell to the floor with a big smash.

"Because he was killed in that bloody war!"

Tears ran down Mummy's cheeks, and I started to cry with her. I didn't know what a war was, but I knew what killed meant. Mummy bent down and started to pick up the bits of broken glass. She wouldn't look at me; she didn't want me to see her crying. The pancakes felt heavy in my stomach as I thought of Daddy being killed.

"What … what happened to him Mummy?"

Mummy sniffled as she put the pieces of glass in her other hand. "I don't want to talk about it, Sissy."

I got on the floor and tried to help Mummy pick up the glass. The juice spread under the table in a big pool of orange.

"Don't," she said. "You'll cut yourself."

"I want to help, Mummy."

She looked up at me. There were so many tears on her face. "I know sweetheart," she said. "You go to your room, and I'll clean it up, okay?"

I waited in my room, staring at the places where I'd seen the ghosts; near my bed and outside under the mango tree. I hadn't seen Petro or the man from Iran for a few days. It was really quiet. I sat on my bed thinking about why Mummy was sad. I thought she seemed happier when there was a funeral at our house, so when Mummy came in to my room, I decided I would tell her I wanted to do something special to make her happy again.

"I'm sorry I yelled at you, Sissy," Mummy said as she sat next to me on the bed.

"It's okay, Mummy."

She took my hands in hers. "It's just that I get so upset when I think about Daddy. He went off to the war and never came back."

"Did you have a funeral for Daddy?"

Mummy shook her head. "They never found Daddy's body."

"So, how could they know he went to heaven?"

"There was an explosion sweetheart—a bomb."

My throat got all tight again. I wanted to cry, but I took a deep breath.

"Mummy, what if … we had a funeral for Daddy?"

Mummy's eyes widened, but not because she was angry, more like surprised.

"Sissy, I don't know … "

"We have funerals here for people we don't know. We should have one for Daddy."

Mummy's eyes filled with tears again, but they looked more like happy tears. "You really want to?"

"Oh, yes. It wouldn't have to be like the other funerals—we could just say some prayers and maybe put a cross under the tree?"

Mummy reached over and gave me the biggest hug ever. Then she took my hand and we went around the house grabbing things that reminded us of Daddy: there was a photo of him holding me when I was a tiny baby, a photo of him on his wedding day with Mummy, and a shiny medal that he wore when he was a soldier. The rest of the day we planned for Daddy's funeral, and we made a chocolate cake to have after. I'd never seen Mummy so happy. Mummy let me sleep with her that night which was good because no ghosts came to visit me. It wasn't that I was scared; I was just worried that Mummy might see them and not understand. But I hoped everything made sense tomorrow.

When I woke up I heard so many birds singing and the big sun shone brightly on our house. Mummy came in and gave me breakfast in bed. While I ate my toast and vegemite, she showed me the dress she was going to wear to Daddy's funeral. It was a long, yellow dress, with little silvery beads on the skirt. Then she showed me another dress from the cupboard—the most beautiful dress I'd ever seen. It was all pinks and purples and blue flowers, and the skirt was all wide at the bottom. It was my size.

"Is that for me, Mummy?"

Mummy's smile was even prettier than my dress.

At 10 o'clock Mummy and I laid out the chocolate cake on the table, and we put our memories of Daddy inside a box that Mummy had kept her jewellery in.

"What happens now, Sissy?" Mummy asked.

I thought about all the funerals we had at our house and decided that Daddy's funeral should be just as special.

"Let's line up. I'll carry the box, and we'll walk outside."

Mummy nodded and I picked up the box of Daddy's memories and walked toward the door. I looked down at the photo of Daddy holding me when I was a baby. He had such a big smile on his face. The smile was the same in the photo with Mummy on their wedding day.

We walked out into the sunlight. The mango tree was big and green, and the shadow under it was cool. The Iran man's and Petro's graves were big lumps in the ground. I walked around the other side of the tree and knelt down.

"Mummy, will you help me dig?"

Mummy was crying happy tears, but she came down beside me, and we dug a small hole with a one of Mummy's gardening tools. I placed the jewellery box inside the hole.

"I wish that I'd got to meet you Daddy," I said. "But I want you to be happy in heaven, so I'd like to give you these memories. Like Petro's grandma said, it's important that you're happy when you go to heaven."

Mummy put her arm around me and started to cry.

"Every funeral is different, but they're all the same too, because everyone remembers the times when the person was happiest."

We covered up the hole with dirt, and I placed a small white cross on top. Mummy hugged me and said she loved me very much and Daddy too.

When I looked up from the grave I saw the Iran man's and Petro's ghosts standing under the tree with us. They were smiling at me. Another man appeared behind them. He smiled too, just like Daddy.

And I smiled back.

The Droste Effect

Chris clutched the photograph of his dead wife and son and spoke tremulously into the phone.

"I don't know when I'll be coming back to work," he said.

"It's okay, Chris, you take all the time you need, mate," his colleague Matt Hoffman said, and the man's words grated because Chris wanted him to be inconsolable too.

"No ... I don't think I can ever come back."

"Chris, I know this is hard. Christ, it would be impossible not to feel like chucking it in, but things will get better with time."

Marissa and Daniel smiled at him from the photograph, the snow-capped slopes of Mount Ruapehu looming and glinting in the midday sun. Their smiling faces made him shiver with a wave of nausea. Chris had taken the photo on their last family trip together, three months before they'd died.

"No, no it won't." Chris said.

"Chris, listen mate. You need to take a break, get away and relax. Go back and see your folks in New Zealand. We can deal with all your patients while you're gone."

Chris's patients were complete strangers in need of psychiatric help to kick their addictions, like smoking and self-harm. He'd moved across the Tasman to Melbourne two years ago to work in a special clinic with Matt and their other partner, Alexis. He used hypnotherapy to help people to quit, and the majority of the time, it worked. He hadn't thought about any of his patients in a long time.

"Chris?" Matt said.

"I can't go back home, Matt. Not now … "

"Well, go anywhere, mate. Take a drive. Get some fresh air." Matt sounded like he was trying to treat him. Chris knew Matt meant well, but sometimes the guy couldn't stop playing doctor.

"I've got to go."

Chris tossed his mobile phone on the couch where he'd spent every day since his family was killed in the car accident. Marissa and Daniel had been driving along Toorak Road in South Yarra when a cyclist came off his bike right in front of them. Marissa panicked and veered into the path of a cement truck. She died instantly, while Daniel died a day later from irreparable chest injuries. Chris had been at the surgery, putting one of his patients under when it happened.

After he put his loved ones in the ground, Chris had wanted to be with them; so much so that every day he played and replayed in his mind the last words he'd spoken to his wife and son—and what they'd said back. The couch and living room was a patchwork of pain, photographs of every milestone, big or small, splayed out like the dead in a mass grave. He wanted to relive each moment, just so he could have them back.

He went to the kitchen and grabbed a dirty glass to pour another hit of mind-numbing scotch, only to change his mind. The effectiveness of the alcohol was wearing off, and now even sleep eluded him. Maybe Matt was right, maybe he needed to leave town to clear his head. But he couldn't face his parents or Marissa's; there was too much worry in their prying gazes and words.

He slumped to the couch and stared at the piles of recollections on the floor: Daniel's first day at school; Marissa in the maternity ward; Marissa holding Daniel for the first time; Daniel and Marissa chasing each other in the backyard; Daniel's first birthday; their first visit to Old Melbourne Gaol and Luna Park. He wanted to dive into each one and disappear.

He knew he was poisoning his mind and body with grief, but he didn't know how to let go. He felt tears stinging his cheeks, but there was irony too. He realised he was telling himself the same thing he told his patients:

Grief is no more than an addiction you have to let go of.

Chris closed his eyes, forcing himself not to obsess on the images at his feet. He took a deep breath and tried to focus his mind, the words he so often spoke in his surgery surfacing in his subconscious.

Imagine the smoke from a cigarette is the exhaust fumes from a truck.

Chris conjured an image of a truck exhaust. The image panned wider and revealed the exhaust belonged to the cement truck as it slammed into his wife's SUV.

He opened his eyes and gasped for breath. His wife and son smiled up at him from the floor, a sea of sorrow. His head and body ached, pounding with need. He raced to the bathroom to retch into the toilet. In the bile-tinged water he saw his reflection, devoid of light. The mirror on the wall was vicious in its clarity. *FLASH*—he saw his wife standing in the same spot draped in a towel, the beads of water on her shoulders like precious gems. *FLASH*—he saw his son pulling out his first tooth, the blood so bright with life.

Forcing his eyes shut to halt the memories, he staggered out of the bathroom like a blind man, arms outstretched, to feel his way to the main bedroom. When he reopened his eyes they were blurry with tears. Still he could make out cruel details in the dozens of photo albums he'd left on the bed to torment himself with. Before, they comforted him, but now he wanted to throw them in the trash and set fire to them.

Imagine the photos are a window to escape from your grief.

The pure white edges around the photos seemed to capture his wife and son in a void. Shards of life floating beyond the pain he was feeling. If he could find a way to be where they were, he could feel whole again.

Imagine yourself climbing through the window to be with Marissa and Daniel.

He told himself he had to close the albums and put them away.

His body refused to comply.

Can you see yourself climbing through the window, Chris?

He took a long breath and exhaled, but although it served to slow his heart, the ache infecting it never wavered. The photographs gathered around him like flotsam. Each print was a spinning top. No, it was a more familiar sensation. He harked back to the first time he'd been hypnotised, how susceptible he'd been. He and Matt had hypnotised each other during their studies, and Chris had found his friend's voice soothing and convincing. The veil had been lifted easily, and Chris was able to travel back through the pages of his life in just a few minutes. It took him a few more years to master the power of suggestion himself, but once he did he'd made a living from it.

Perhaps he could conjure life itself with it?

Through the night, Chris decorated the bathroom mirror with photographs of his dead wife and child. The display comprised a montage of memories which framed his gaunt features, sparkling colour against blanched and tired flesh.

He was numb to the outside world. There were only the photographs. He reached out and pulled the image of Daniel and Marissa standing in front of Mount Ruapehu and held it so it faced the mirror. With his other hand, he took a photo on his phone of the reflection. Then very delicately, he put the photo of his family back in its resting place on the mirror. For several minutes he gazed at the new image of himself on the screen of his phone. His wife and child floated in space over his chest, over his heart. Tears streaming down his face, Chris turned the phone screen back to face the mirror and focussed on its image on the glass.

Chris felt like he was holding his own grief-stricken soul in his hand. A moment in time trapped in the same moment. Within the reflection, the image became a vortex in his mind, a doorway to the loves of his past. The photo twisted and curved in on itself, receding down and down—but within. A vortex into unreality.

He'd read about the phenomena in a book once. It was called the Droste Effect, and it was real.

Imagine you're with them again, Chris.

Count backwards from five …

… four

… three

… two

The sun warmed Chris' back, and the wintry air burned slightly in his nostrils when he breathed. Through the camera in his hands he could see Marissa and Daniel smiling. Mount Ruapehu dwarfed his family and the hundreds of skiers sliding, falling, and laughing in the sea of snow. The mountain was a white diamond glinting in the sun.

"Hurry up and take the picture, Dad. I want to go skiing," Daniel said.

Chris dropped his hands to his sides and stared open-mouthed at his wife and son.

"You … you're here … " Chris said.

Marissa frowned slightly. "Of course, we're here. Are you going to take the photo?"

Chris's throat tightened with grief, but on the outside he was smiling. "Oh, God, you're alive."

He moved to hold them again, but his wife pushed him back. "Chris, you need to wake up!"

Screams rose around them, and Chris turned to see tourists scattering in all directions. Somehow a cement truck had found its way onto the ski fields. Its headlights burned his eyes. He felt a force against his back, and he fell face-first into the snow. A column of wind buffeted him as the truck went past and careened into his family. Chris lifted his head and cried out as Daniel was crushed beneath one of the truck's wheels. The impact knocked his wife twenty feet into the air, and she came down on a small outcrop of rocks with a crescendo of cracking bones.

The snow turned red with their blood.

Chris opened his eyes. He saw his wife standing on the shores of Denarau Island in Fiji. The setting sun wrapped her skin with fire, as if she was made from it. The resort was deserted and the sand cut at the soles of Chris' feet; even the water was dead, black like oil. Chris remembered that this was his and Marissa's first wedding anniversary—and the night Daniel was conceived, but this memory was tainted, just like all the rest. Marissa stared at him as she toyed with the string of her bikini top.

"You need to wake up, baby," she said.

Chris raised the camera and took her picture. "I … I don't want to."

Marissa slipped the bikini top off and let it sail to the sand. "You're torturing yourself."

Chris slipped his arms around her waist. His wife's skin had no elasticity, like raw dough. "Please … stay with me."

Marissa kissed him, and he felt her tongue inside his mouth. It was cold and tasted like metal. Chris pulled away and gasped at the sight of blood running from his wife's lips, down her bare breasts. Marissa stood hands on hips, unimpressed. Her body was ravaged with black bruises and torn flesh from the collision with the cement truck. Two ribs protruded like tusks from her abdomen and her jaw hung slack in her face.

"You need to stop, Chris," she said, trying to create a smile with her shattered maxilla. "I'm dead."

The camera thudded to the sand and brushed against Chris' foot. He glanced down and saw a new image on the camera's display screen. His legs bent beneath him, and he fell hard into the image, like a stone into a pool.

When he surfaced, he was in the backyard of their Melbourne home with Daniel. Moments earlier, they'd finished burying their German shepherd puppy, Butch, under the Weeping Myrtle tree. Chris remembered Butch had chased a tennis ball which Daniel had thrown out onto the road, and the dog had run straight underneath a provisional driver's souped-up Subaru. The teenager behind the wheel had been more concerned about any damage to the paintwork on his car rather than the tears in Daniel's eyes.

Chris looked at his son, the smell of the burial mound still thick in the air. Six-year-old Daniel stood clutching a photo Marissa had taken of the boy and his dog cuddling on the back landing. Chris felt the irony of the moment like a cold dagger in his chest all over again.

"Why do things die, Daddy?" Daniel said, and his teardrops slapped against the photo of his dead best friend.

Chris couldn't remember what he'd said to Daniel then; at the time it was just a dog that had died. Chris had never wanted the dog in the first place, but Marissa didn't want her son to be lonely. Chris turned on his feet, wondering why she wasn't there with them in this memory. Why had she left them all alone this time? Maybe she was still at the beach waiting for him to wake up, slowly rotting into the rising tide?

Daniel's voice pulled him back, and Chris saw his son's eyes narrow with anger. "Why do things have to die, Daddy? Why did Butch get run over?"

"I ... I'm sorry, Danny," he said, and reached for his son, eager to never let him go, to not let him rot too.

Daniel pulled away from his father and ran, crying and screaming. Chris gave chase up the side of the house. The six-year-old was so light on his feet, and he reached the side gate so easily that he had it open before Chris could stop him. The boy kept running and running, across the front yard and out onto the road.

It was almost as if the cement truck had been there waiting for Daniel. It struck the little boy with such force that his head split open with an audible crack on the bitumen. Chris cried out for his boy, for help, for the truck to stop, but it kept roaring on, down the street, disappearing into the foggy boundaries of Chris' memories. Memories now corrupted by a never-ending slideshow of death.

When Chris dropped to his knees and scooped up his son's corpse, he found a multitude of photographs and not blood oozing from the boy's open skull; pictures of Chris, Marissa, Butch, his grandparents, and kindergarten friends popping out like Polaroids. *We're all just snapshots*, Chris thought, *filing cabinets full of fucking images—and when we die the photos fade away to nothing.*

Chris! Chris!

Jesus Christ! Wake up!

Chris let go of his son and turned towards the voice. It was Matt calling to him from the other side.

"Matt?" Chris said into the fog.

Chris, what have you done?

"I had to see them again. I just can't go on without them."

You have to come back to us, Chris!

"No."

Chris listen to me! Listen to my voice: if you can hear me squeeze my hand.

Chris backed away from the edge of the fog, but it was closing in fast to swallow his world of shattered memories. He frantically searched his pockets for another photograph; another door to Daniel and Marissa, but they were gone. Even his camera was lost to the sea of grief.

I'm going to get you back from this, Chris. You're going to come back. Do you hear me?

Chris felt the icy caress of the fog on his face and arms. He wouldn't wake up; he'd find a way to get stay in his memory-made world.

... ten

... nine

He curled up on the ground and put his hands over his ears to block Matt's voice. He tried to find a memory inside himself, anything to escape, but without a photo, there was no key, no path.

   ... *eight*

   ... *seven*

   ... *six*

Then he opened his eyes, a realisation coming to him. If he woke up he could simply climb back inside one of the photos later; Matt would never know. "Matt, I can hear you. I'm coming back!" he cried into the fog.

   ... *five*

   ... *four*

   ... *three*

   ... *two*

"One, two, three, four, five six, seven, eight, nine, ten!"

Chris opened his eyes to see his friend, Matt, pushing down on his chest. Chris wondered why his friend looked so stressed and why the tiles on the floor beneath him were cold and sticky on his back. On the walls and mirror behind Matt were dozens of photos of Marissa and Daniel smiling down on him.

"Don't you fucking die on me, Chris!" Matt said through gritted teeth.

The smell of blood was undeniable. Chris didn't know what he'd done to himself, but he knew the blood was his own. He felt Matt's hands on his chest and then his lips on his own, but he knew his friend was fighting a losing battle. Chris knew he'd been weak, too weak to assuage the guilt and beat his addiction. As he lay dying, he wondered whether he'd stepped inside his own memories after all.

He moved his eyes back to the mirror where his photo montage sat like a shrine. In the centre was his phone, duct-taped to the glass. On the screen was the photo he'd taken of himself holding his wife and son as they stood before Mount Ruapehu. In the photo he could see fresh rivulets of blood running down his forearms.

He hadn't hypnotised himself to remember at all; he'd hypnotised himself to die.

Chris closed his eyes and listened to Matt's voice counting the numbers between compressions.

" ... one

... two

... three"

Matt's panic felt strangely calming to Chris and he easily imagined himself as one of his patients lying on the couch, listening to Matt's words.

Listen to my voice.

Imagine you're lying in a fog.

That your blood and all the grief it contains is slowly running out of you. When I count to ten, your pain will be no more.

... one

... two

... three

... four

... five

... six

... seven

... eight

Schism

The veil between day and night was turning blood red when Elle doubted if she loved Steven anymore.

She stared out the passenger side window at the trees blurring past, to the black road winding before them like a stitched wound. Yet, the outside world offered nothing and only served to accentuate the rift of silence.

How the bleak English countryside fascinated Steven, Elle didn't know. Why he loved the past more than the present was one of the many aspects of his personality she failed to understand. They'd been driving aimlessly through Dover for almost a week, whetting Steven's appetite for all things historical. But their so-called adventure had only left a sour taste in Elle's mouth. *Is this what the future holds, after only five years of marriage*, she wondered. Colourless, empty silences? How could she tell him it wasn't the future she craved?

She opened her phone and started doom-scrolling, the app's algorithm offering her adverts of women who looked far happier. She promptly closed the app and went back to looking out the window. Steven cleared his throat, and she knew he was about to speak to her.

"About another ten miles before we reach the homestead," he said.

The setting sun slowly turned the surrounding woods into shadow.

The road curved off to the right, and their SUV seemed to veer sharply. Elle's body stiffened in response.

"Do you think you could slow down?" she said.

"Sorry, I guess I'm eager to get there."

"Oh, I know you are." Elle immediately recognized her demeaning tone and sighed.

"What's that supposed to mean?" Steve countered.

She glanced his way and watched him look from her to the road and back again. "Nothing."

"Well, it sounds like you want to get something off your chest."

"No."

"You've barely said a word to me since we left the B&B this morning."

"I'm just tired. It's a long drive."

"Like I said, we'll be there soon. And you'll love the place, Elle. I promise."

The trees darkened against the light, which shifted from ochre into velvet with each passing second.

"Oh, I will, will I?"

"Elle, what's going on? Did I do something to upset you?"

Silence, then: "No."

"Really? Because it seems like you're angry with me."

Elle faced him. "Do you ever think that maybe I'm not interested in gallivanting around the countryside looking for coins, or rocks, or whatever the hell it is you're looking for with your bloody metal detector?"

"Elle—"

She turned away to avoid seeing the dismay on his face. Outside she noticed the trees were thinning out as they went along, the branches exposed and gnarled like fingers caught in the throes of rigor.

"Can we just not, Steven?"

"Not what?"

Elle pressed a hand to her temple and focused on the stretching landscape, the bleeding in of the night. *Were the trees losing their leaves? Were they dying?*

"Are we … ?" she whispered.

"Are we what?" Steven's voice rose in desperation.

"Are we almost there?"

Steven flicked on the headlights, and in that instant, the empty road was no longer empty. A shape rushed in from the right, a smudge against the twilight. Elle screamed as the object came out into the path of their vehicle. Steven slammed on the brakes, and everything lurched, coffee cups, phones, and luggage wrenched from their resting places to the floor. Once the car finally came to a halt, Elle acknowledged the tight burn of the seatbelt across her breast. Still, it was the sight of the shape lying in the middle of the road that made her gasp, and before she could stop herself, she was opening the door to step out into the frigid dark.

"Elle, what are you doing?" Steven called.

She ignored him, her eyes locked on the thing lying on the asphalt, something hidden beneath a thick, crimson blanket. She approached the bundle, heartbeat ringing in her ears. Beyond that sound, there was nothing but the idling of the car engine. No wind, no rustling of leaves, only her frantic heart. Until she heard Steven behind her back.

"Jesus, Elle! Stop!"

Again, she ignored him, watching the mound at her feet. "I think it's a person."

"What?"

The shape shifted and released a low moan.

"Oh, my God!" Elle dropped to her knees beside it.

"Elle, wait—don't!"

She whirled on her husband. "For god's sake, get the first aid kit!"

Something cold and slick touched Elle's hand, and she stifled a scream. She looked down and saw a contorted face, mouth wide in agony. A man, pale skin streaked with blood. He clutched her wrist, pleading with wild eyes.

"R-Run ... " the words barely passed his lips, but his eyes said so much more.

"Sir?" Elle said. "Sir, what happened to you?"

His groping hands found purchase on her jacket, pulling her close. "Have to ... get away ... please ... "

He was trembling beneath the robe, which, to Elle, looked like something a monk would wear. The fabric was thick and coarse, and the man himself was at least twenty years her senior. Questions of who he was and what he was doing in the middle of the woods—covered in blood— raced through Elle's mind.

"Sir, can you tell me what happened to you? Did someone hurt you?"

Steven returned to her side with the first aid kit. "There's, like, one bandage in here and some iodine. That's it."

"I think we need to get him to a hospital," Elle said.

Steven reached for his phone. "Or call an ambulance. Ah, damn it, there's no bloody reception out here."

Elle squeezed the man's hand. "Sir? It's going to be alright. We're going to get some help, okay?"

The stranger shook his head. His face glistened with sweat. "No … no … just go … get … away."

"Shh, you're going to be okay." She looked at Steven. "I think you should drive to the homestead. See if they can get help."

He frowned. "What if we try and get him into the car?"

"I think he's in too much pain to move. You go and find the homestead. They'll have a phone, and you can call for help."

He shook his head. "I'm not going to leave you here in the dark, Elle—"

Elle observed the pain in the stranger's eyes and his blood, and a wave of anger boiled up inside her.

"Just go will you! Go and find help, for Christ's sake!"

A different wave of misery washed over her husband's features, a hurt she'd never seen before. But she needed him gone. After a moment, Steven stood and walked to the car. She kept her eyes on the injured man as her husband eventually drove off down the road. The relief she felt was palpable. The robed man looked up at her and gnashed his teeth.

"You … should have gone with him … "

She held his hand. "No, it's alright. Now what's your name? Mine's Elle."

He swallowed hard, the moonlight catching the bob of his throat. "Go … "

"I'm not leaving you."

He thrust her hands away, and she flinched in shock.

"I'm only trying to help you—"

The man screamed and buckled where he lay, a fresh jolt of torment passing through his body. Elle recoiled and stared as the stranger went rigid, back arched, hands clawing at the air for help.

"Get … away from me!"

His scream deepened, and became guttural, like that of a beast. Elle heard something tear. Was it the robe or something beneath? She couldn't know. She scrambled to her feet as the man continued to writhe, his arms and legs swelling and contorting before her eyes. The noise emanating from his mouth was anything but human, the low-pitched whine of an animal in a trap. Then, his agony ceased, as if whatever change he was undergoing was complete. Elle glimpsed thick fur protruding beneath the red robe and heard the steady rise and fall of deep, guttural breaths. Then, his body ceased, giving way to silence. Shaking with terror, Elle remembered the man's last warning:

Get away.

She ran from the road into the stalagmite woods, unknowingly crossing into a threshold of even darker silence.

Steven almost lost control of the car on a bend, he was going so fast.

His wife's last words to him were still swirling in his head, a dangerous distraction. He tapped the brake, forcing himself to slow down, to catch his breath. He didn't understand what was going on with his wife or the man who ran out into the path of their car. His adventure was turning into a nightmare. Why was Elle treating him like she didn't want him around? He wasn't blind to the fact that they had been arguing more lately, but the way she spoke to him had become more spiteful. Like his very presence was irritating to her.

He sighed and steered the car along a right-hand turn, trying instead to concentrate on making it to the homestead.

"Where the hell is it?" he muttered to himself.

The trees were strangely thinning out. *Were they long dead? Suffering from some sort of blight?* In the light of the full moon, they resembled watchful creatures. Waiting. Through the gaps in the branches, Steven saw a wide field beyond, but the landscape appeared bleached, lifeless. Then, a glint of light, like oil on water, gleamed on the horizon. Only for a second, like the turn of a lighthouse beacon.

Steven brought the car to a stop along the edge of the road and opened the door. The urge to walk to the light was undeniable. He left the car and stepped onto the field, the sound of desiccated grass grinding beneath his shoes a macabre drumbeat. He marched on for the crystalline light.

Was it the homestead?

He prayed that it was. He couldn't stand the thought of Elle alone on that road with the bleeding man.

The light swung around again, casting the field in hues of vermillion, emerald, and cerulean all at once, like an exploding nebula. Steven quickened his pace and, over the hill, the silhouette of a structure began to emerge, a black shadow against the otherworldly illumination. The edges of the building became sharper with each step, yet faded at the same time. An ever-shifting, shimmering mirage. Steven squinted. *Was it a house, or not?* Whatever it was, he had to reach it. The sooner he did, the sooner he could return to Elle.

The thing was at Elle's heels.

It had once been human—the poor man on the road she'd tried to save, but now it was malevolent and hungry. Elle pushed through the tree

branches as the thing's snarls echoed around her. She dared not scream, desperate not to expose herself to the creature she knew wanted her flesh and blood. What was it that wanted her so? What hell had she fallen into? *Will I ever see Steven again?*

Will I ever have the chance to tell him, I'm sorry?

The branches clawed at her jacket and hair. Again she wanted to cry out for help, but she knew she'd be dead if she did. She shoved the branches aside, eyes eager for escape. Then the trees receded, giving way to a field. Pale grass stretching off to a vast horizon. Panicked that she now had nowhere to hide, she glanced over her shoulder. Back through the trees, the thing followed, hunched and lumbering on all fours, red robe flapping in its wake. She had no choice but to cross the field.

Ahead, on the edge of the horizon, Elle beheld a brilliant glow, iridescent and pulsing.

She ran in its direction.

The structure shifted before Steven's unbelieving eyes.

In one breath, it was a gargantuan gothic house, in another, a scattered ruin of pock-marked obelisks. Steven took a step closer and it shifted again, turning back millennia to take on the appearance of an ancient stone hut. When he blinked it flickered back to the house, to the ruins, and the hut again. Time jolting back and forth like lightning breaks the sky.

Is my mind playing tricks on me?

Is it shock?

The knife-edge of Elle's last words bleeding him dry?

Steven put one foot in front of the other, registering all at once how quiet it was. How silent.

He stepped closer to the domicile again.

One step further away from his Elle.

Elle saw a building on the horizon.

Thank God, it's the homestead!

Gasping from exertion and fuelled by adrenalin, she urged herself through the now knee-high grass. The beast's growls seemed further away, and a new sense of relief and hope drove her forward. But the closer she got to the place, the less defined it became. The soft kaleidoscope of colour in the sky somehow obscured it. She didn't know what the light was, but she knew it wasn't the moon, which was much higher. Still, she kept on, certain Steven was inside. She realized now what a mistake she'd made, that anger wasn't going to change—

The building wasn't a homestead, but an old Victorian house.

Or was it?

She stopped and tried to make sense of what she was seeing.

It was a house, but also a burial mound.

Or a temple?

Or a huge, lifeless, oak tree?

When she blinked it transformed again.

It was an altar.

And her husband was walking towards it.

Steven held the metal detector in his hand.

I don't even remember getting it out of the car.

Regardless, he swept it over the ground where he thought the house once stood.

Was it a house?

Or ruins?

He couldn't recall.

The light swelled in time with his heart.

Schism

I'll find it, and when I do, it will be the greatest discovery of all time.

He swept the detector in a wide arc, and the machine started to sound out a frenetic tone.

There was something under the earth.

Something silent and waiting.

Waiting for him.

Steven joined three robed men who stood watch around the altar.

Elle called out to him, to warn him, but her voice was silent, like she was mute to begin with.

Everything was silent and waiting.

Waiting for them both.

The ground opened up beneath Steven's feet.

A chasm.

No, a schism.

From which the old house had grown.

Where time and space dwelled.

Steven bent to peer into the schism and there, through the carpet of stars and cosmic gasses, he found his Elle in the forever sleep.

Smiling, he fell in to join her.

Elle shrieked without sound as the altar cracked and swallowed her husband and the robed men. The hole became a chasm, a rift of silence that spread across the field in a wave.

She turned to run, but the robed man from the road, face covered with thick bristles and spread with a rotting tusk-filled smile, had been waiting in silence.

Waiting for her.

The schism spread across the world.

Consuming all.

Putting out the light.

Chiaroscuro

He toils within the darkness of his own soul.

Paper is his flesh, the brushes a supernumerary limb. Ink and blood pulse in his veins. His eyes see beyond the feeble existence of reality to where the penumbra reside. The compulsion to bring the shadows to life is more than an urge or addiction. It is the same as breathing.

The practice of creating is an act he's always performed since he was a child. A gift, passed down from generations lost. Crude figures on discarded remnants of tissue paper, depictions of people brimming with hope and courage. Yet, as the years went by, he noticed a change.

At first he believed it was the bleakness of the world reflected back, but often he would find himself standing in his studio, hands almost black with charcoal, vile faces peering up at him from the paper. Contorted skulls or fang-filled maws, over and over. Sheafs of paper splayed at his feet, with no memory of having created on them.

Now, as he rubbed the powdery charcoal between his fingers, she entered the room: the woman who once loved the man he used to be. Before he fell into the gloom. Her voice pulled him back from the precipice of his thoughts if only for a moment. She told him she was going, and he looked at her as if for the very first time. He took one step in her direction, only for one of his still fresh artworks to adhere to the sole of his foot. He peeled it off and let it sail down to join the other horrid faces he'd birthed seemingly from nothing.

Where, he said.

Going, just going, was all she said, back. Her face resembled one of his scattered creations. If only for a moment.

He opened up to her then, bared his soul after many years.

There's something ... something growing inside me.

She shook her head, held back tears. No regret.

It's beyond imagination, he told her. It's not just dark thoughts. It's like ... like I'm not in control anymore.

She adjusted the strap of the bag on her shoulder. I know, she said.

He didn't hear the door close behind her. There was no sadness, no realisation of the meaning of her last words, only its need. The silent, cloying thing inside him that wanted out. The shadow, in black, white, and red. He couldn't feel it, smell or taste it. It was simply there, taking over his body, mind, and soul.

The day slid into night so effortlessly, and the pages drifted from his desk like snow. Droplets of ink, spilling, staining every part of his home. He tried to wash the ink away, scrubbing until his fingers were raw. Until he realised the ink was dripping from his fingertips. Had been for some time. He glanced from his oozing hand to the kitchen window. The ink was the same shade as the night outside.

How long had he been standing here, pouring himself down the drain?

Metamorphosing in the murk?

He slipped away from the chance of escape, back into the hollow of the house, to paper, paint and the multitude of brushes caked with his ichor. There was nothing else, only creation. Transformation.

The sun reached its aphelion and then fell, the process repeating in timeless succession while he worked. Day and night. Night and day. He bled black onto the paper, spatter-patterns of the enigma lurking and crying out for release. In the moonlight his skin faded with each finger-painting, until there was no discerning paper from flesh.

He took a breath, the first in an age and beheld the hundreds of still-lifes he—no, it—had conjured. Twisted spines, headstone houses, eyeless, mouthless torments. Why he was painting them was to pay homage to his companion. To worship his own demise. To give praise to the thing that was leeching his marrow and bile and providing a turgid mass of exquisite horror for all to see.

His phone rang, a shriek from the other side of his temple. He answered it, if only to end the distraction from his vital labour. It was his agent, informing him that he'd sold another painting.

The thing inside answered on his behalf: Good.

Then he threw the phone away, beckoned once more by the demon's call.

Phalanges protruded from his fingers, the tips scratching over the rough surface of the paper. He shivered in the chiaroscuro, skin taut around his ribcage, heart barely beating, sustained only by the muse deep in the viscera of his gut.

Set. Me. Free.

Page after page, falling.

The bones of his hands crumbling to dust.

Sun rising and descending.

Ink pooling.

Spiteful eyes staring back.

He could no longer feel his arms or legs. The ragged clothes sloughing down to join the art.

He was nothing more than a tool, guided by malignant melancholy.

And with one final, single thought, he smeared himself across the last page.

Hell in Her Wake

This is a work of horror and all that entails. It contains themes of familial abuse and trauma and ritualistic violence

PROLOGUE
1997

The dogs of hell snapped at the girl's heels.

She sprinted barefoot through the woods, branches whipping at her face from the shadows, her heart slamming against her chest.

Her soul was on the line.

Her name echoed through the trees, cries for her to come back. Cries of warning. Threat-home was a place of blood and terror she did not want to be a part of. Despite the risk and pain, Selena fled the darkness—both inside and out.

She scrambled behind a broad oak and gasped in the cold dawn air. Despite her pounding heart and its insistence to keep moving, she pushed away her sweat-slick hair and reached into the pocket of her night gown to retrieve the amulet.

The wooden object felt smooth against her fingers, a secret crafted over many years, its weight comforting. She slipped the bracelet over her wrist, the weathered string of her baby teeth rolling and clinking softly against one another. It was a simple device, so she feared it might not be enough to protect her.

"SELENA!"

The girl flinched as her name soared through the woods again. A stab of cold tightened in her chest, her mouth suddenly dry. The dogs were close, their unearthly barks set her heart pounding. She could taste their rage. If they found her, they'd tear her to pieces.

Low, guttural, reverberating growls sounded from her left and she froze. They'd had found her. Three rottweilers, mangy and rotten, circling. Long-dead muscle draped from their bones, which creaked with each movement of their hind legs, each crane of their necks. Their eyes glowed red, hunger and rage burning like embers caught in a sliver of time. Bloody drool dripped from their rotted lips, their bodies a second away from attacking, shaking from maintaining their urge to kill.

But they'd only been sent to find her. They would leave her punishment to their master—Selena's mother. She would be the one to devour Selena for her disobedience.

Her gorge rising in her throat, Selena kept her eyes locked on the hounds and whispered the spell she'd memorized:

"Parum luceat."

Her fingers worried the teeth on their strap, clumsy and frantic, but the sudden warmth burst into her fingertips. Encouraged, she tried again.

"Parum luceat: it does not shine."

Warmth spread to her chest, as if she stood before an open oven door. In an instant, her entire body was enveloped in a comforting glow. She watched the undead dogs' heads swivel as they darted about, sniffing the ground. Selena took a breath.

They've lost me. It worked!

As Selena ran, her footsteps falling silently on the damp leaves, her mother's howl of frustration shocked birds from their trees to scatter into the night. The spell would be enough to keep the dogs away, but if she ever stopped running, the coven—and her mother's fury—would drag her back to Hell.

1
PRESENT DAY

Hands and voices grabbed at Selena in the haze of wakefulness. Cries for her return merged with vicious barks. Flashes of a shadow chasing her in the woods. She thrashed against the vision, but the shadow came closer, gripping with fingers so cold she was wrenched screaming into the real world. The nightmare faded once her eyes opened onto her husband and daughter. They held her still, expressions of concern etched on their faces.

"Jesus, Steph, are you alright?"

The space inside their tent was thick with the smell of her fear-tinged sweat. She wiped her brow.

"Sorry about that, guys."

"You had another nightmare, Mom."

Selena reached out and pulled Gemma close. "It's nothing to worry about, honey."

Luke laid a hand on Selena's back. "That's the third night in a row."

She looked into his pale blue eyes. "I said it's nothing." She inched away from them both and pulled on a sweater. "It's just being in the outdoors—not in my own bed."

"Steph, you were calling out in your sleep."

Selena smoothed down Gemma's ebony hair and avoided her husband's prying gaze and questions. "It was just a bad dream."

"You were screaming that dogs were chasing you," Gemma told her. "You scared me."

Selena stood and unzipped the tent to step outside. "Well, I don't remember any of it, so just drop it."

They'd camped beside a wide stream, flanked by thick brush and lines of Ash trees. The lush greenery and steady flow of water should have calmed

151

Selena, but she knew the dreams—the nightmares—were more than just visions from her past.

Something was trying to get inside her head.

Selena studied the tree line on the other side of the stream. The spaces between the trees and their lengthening shadows unnerved her.

Have they found me, after all this time?

She reached inside her pocket and touched the familiar, comforting shape of the amulet she'd crafted thirty years before. The teeth were tiny in her fingers. *Had they lost their protective power?* For her sake—and her family's—she prayed not.

It had been so long since she'd performed any ritual, perhaps it was time to reinforce her protections. Luke had kept her safe, and after they'd married, she no longer made specific protections. She'd left the cold dark of her past behind.

Hadn't she?

The crack of a snapping twig made Selena cry out. Luke stood right behind her, holding his fishing rod like a deer in the headlights, as she spun around to face him.

"Shit, sorry, Steph. I didn't mean to startle you." He moved to her, frowning in concern. "Is everything okay? You seem on edge."

Selena kissed him. *Does he know he's kissing a liar—a deceiver?* "I'm fine, really."

"Are you sure?"

She'd always found strength and comfort in his gaze, but now she feared he might see through her hidden truth. *Should she just tell him? No, that would be foolish. The betrayal would bring it all to an end—and endanger them all.* She kissed him again, longer, but more gently. She couldn't lose him.

"I'm okay Luke."

Luke smiled and adjusted his cap. "They're just dreams?"

"Just dreams."

"You don't want to tell me about them?"

Selena shook her head. "You doing some more fishing?"

He shifted his fishing rod to his other hand. "Well, you want some breakfast, don't you?"

"Big, strong man's gonna catch me a fish?"

He walked past and playfully slapped her butt. "Well, we're miles from the nearest McDonald's so yeah, big, strong man's gonna catch you a fish."

"I think Gemma's getting tired of fish."

"Well, she'd better start walking to McDonald's then."

"Okay, Big Man. Speaking of Gemma: is she getting dressed?"

"Not even outta bed, yet. She seems a bit freaked out by your dreams."

The sight of Gemma holding her knees and staring blankly at a corner of the tent was one of the most terrifying sights Selena had ever seen.

"Hey, you doing okay, baby?"

The girl kept staring into nothing, until Selena took her hand. The contact seemed to bring her daughter out of the trance.

"You said dogs in your dreams?" Gemma said.

She frowned and studied Gemma's face. Even at thirteen, the girl reminded her so much of herself. Selena might as well have been looking in a mirror. They both had the same black hair and emerald eyes. She cradled her daughter's face and gazed into those same eyes.

"It was just a dream, Gemma."

"Was it though?"

"Yes. It was nothing."

Gemma's eyes filled with tears. Selena tried to hold her, but she recoiled, shifting from confusion to anger. "Why are you lying?"

"What? I'm not lying." Selena's heart pounded. "You need to stop this. You and your father."

She stood, her brow fierce, bottom lip trembling. "Why are you still lying?"

"I'm not. Now stop it!"

"You know how I know you're lying?" she whispered through thin, white lips.

A weight fell through Selena's core, Gemma's defiance leaving her numb. The girl's determination was palpable.

"Because dogs were chasing me in my dreams too."

Selena followed Gemma out of the tent into the woods, anxiety twisting knots in her stomach. The girl was running to her father—even on the cusp of womanhood there was still a strong connection between them. She felt safe and certain in his arms. But now Selena feared what Gemma might say to him could tear them all apart.

Selena found them at the edge of the stream. Luke held Gemma in a tight embrace. He flashed his wife a glance of concern before turning back to his child.

"What's wrong, Gemm?"

"We were just talking," Selena said.

Gemma pulled away from her father. "Mom doesn't want to talk to me about her dreams."

Luke put his fishing rod down. "Hey, she said it was nothing to worry about."

She frowned at him. "Oh, come on, Dad. I know you're wondering what's going on with her too."

A cold pang of regret rose in Selena's gut. She had to bring this discussion to an end. "I don't know why you're both making such an issue out of this. People have dreams."

Tears streamed down Gemma's face. "Then why did I dream about dogs last night too?"

Luke frowned. "What? You dreamt about dogs?"

Selena raised her hands. "Luke, it's nothing, honestly."

He looked at Selena and for the first time, she saw disappointment behind his eyes.

"Sweetie, look you probably just heard mom's cries when you were sleeping beside her and unconsciously picked up on it. It can happen, but it's nothing to worry yourself about."

Gemma held him, but kept her eyes locked on Selena. She held the contact, her mouth a thin judgement, then withdrew and walked to the shoreline.

"Wow. You don't believe me and, as usual, you're taking her side. Thanks for having my back, Dad."

The girl's barb landed true in Selena's heart. Even if she protected her daughter, she could still lose her. Once Gemma was out of earshot, Luke turned to his wife and released a long sigh.

"Steph, start talking."

2

Selena and Luke sat on the grassy bank beside the stream, a space between them. For a few moments, they watched their daughter sitting at the water's edge, throwing rocks into the current. A rift was emerging, one she worried was about to become a wound.

"So, what's really going on with you, Steph?"

Gemma hurled another rock. There was so much frustration behind the throw.

"I keep telling you they're just dreams."

"I sleep beside you, and you've never had nightmares before."

"You've never had a recurring nightmare?"

"Sure, I have, but I don't wake up screaming like someone's trying to kill me. It's like you're having a night terror or something."

She picked at her fingernails. "Okay, so they're vivid."

"Why dogs, though? You have a fear of dogs or something?"

A flash from thirty years ago ricocheted in her mind. "When I was a

kid … I was chased by a pack of dogs … when I was, uh, riding my bike one day."

Luke removed his cap and ran a hand through his hair. "Did they attack you?"

"They almost did."

"Must have been pretty traumatic, then, if you still dreaming about them all these years later?"

"Yeah, I guess."

He put an arm around her. "Why haven't you told me about this before?"

"I didn't think it was important."

"Of course it is. You're important to me. You and Gemma."

They kissed, and everything inside Selena ached with guilt. He took her face in his hands.

"Look, I know there's some things in your past you don't want to talk about. I respect that. You wanted to start a new life, and we have one together, and it's great. I just don't want that past—whatever it is—to jeopardize our future."

"I don't either. I'm sorry, babe. The dreams are just dreams. I promise."

"Okay, okay. But listen, you're gonna need to go and have a heart-to-heart with our girl, too. Explain it to her."

The thought of spreading the lie twisted in Selena like a knife, but the walls had to go back up.

"Okay."

Selena rose to make her way to the shore when Gemma's scream shattered their moment. Her daughter stumbled back from the water's edge, her eyeline directed at the other side of the stream.

Two rottweilers stood watching them.

The same dogs that had chased her all those years ago and tormented her all her life. Her mother's hounds of Hell.

"What the fuck?" Luke turned to his wife, seeking an explanation. "What the hell is this?"

157

Before she could answer, the dogs barked, deep, unnatural, grating barks that shuddered her to the core.

"Gemma!" Luke ran toward the shore.

"Luke, no, stay back!" she reached for him, but he was gone. Instinctively, she grabbed her teeth bracelet. The amulet could protect her, but she had nothing to protect her family.

He reached Gemma and took her arm. The dogs' barks became growls as they stepped into the stream.

"Jesus Christ! What are they?" Luke said.

Even from a distance, Selena recognized the dogs' rotten nature: the flesh sloughing off their bones, ribcages protruding, muzzles deformed, and broken fangs bared.

How did they find me? After all these years? How had Mother found me?

"Luke! Gemma! Please, get back up here!"

The hounds' hollow gazes shifted to the sound of Selena's voice, and, in seconds, they bounded across the water.

"No! No!" She had to do something. They would be on her family in moments.

The water!

Visions of her days in the old woods surfaced. The cabin where she had shared her life with darkness. The dark arts would always be there in her subconscious, her blood. With tears in her eyes, she remembered one of the many things her mother had taught her. The elemental force of water. How if you were strong enough, it could be bent to your will.

As her husband and daughter scrambled up the hill away from the creatures, she raised a hand and focused on the rushing stream. In her mind, she recalled her mother coiling water like a snake in the stagnant pond behind their cabin.

Gemma's screams pushed Selena on. She imagined the blood in her hand, racing to her fingertips, synchronizing with the pace of the water. Blood and water. Within and without. One and the same. Selena curled her hand, and the currents swirled, spinning into a whirlpool beneath the dog's ragged legs. The hounds struggled in the flow, yelping and whining in despair. It was enough to allow Luke and Gemma time to get to safety.

"Mom, what is going on?" Gemma asked as she reached her side.

"Please, Gemma, I have to focus!"

From the corner of her eye, she saw Luke watching in terror and confusion. She could tell he no longer understood what he saw. He no longer knew his wife.

"Steph ... ?"

Selena twisted her hand further, forcing the water to pull the dogs down. They thrashed against her will, driven by one much more powerful, many miles away. Their master.

"Please ... " she said, not taking her eyes off the task at hand. "Luke, you have to get Gemma away from here."

His expression was torn between helping his wife and fleeing.

"Please!" Selena said.

He stared at the dogs, chest heaving in panic. "You lied to me!"

"I'm sorry. Please, you need get Gemma to safety!" Regret got the better of her, and she lost her grip on the spell.

The whirlpool receded in strength, and before she could recover it, the hounds wrenched themselves free and bolted for the shore.

"Luke, *please!*"

He stepped between the path of the dogs and his family. He threw his cap to the ground and dug in his heels as the slavering mongrels charged toward them.

"Get out of here, Steph!"

"Luke, no!"

Gemma tried to go to her father, but Selena kept her back.

"Dad!"

He charged, facing the monsters head on. "Go! Go now!"

The dogs set upon Luke, knocking him to the ground. Selena and Gemma watched in horror as he fought hard against the savage snaps of their teeth and tearing claws. Gemma screamed like it was she who was being mauled to death.

Selena dragged the girl away, pulling her with all the strength she had left as Luke's cries of agony echoed in their ears.

✶

Selena led Gemma through the long grass. The air in her chest burned, but she pressed on, desperate to get them both to safety. Luke's screams had gone silent. He was gone, and no doubt the dogs wouldn't be far behind. The blades of grass sliced at her hands, but she was immune to their sting. There was only the will to escape the threat. To save herself and her daughter.

In a blind panic, they'd run from the campsite and Luke's truck. But even if Selena had thought of it, the keys were in his jacket, back with his body. There was no choice but to keep running.

Ethereal howls brought them both to a standstill.

"Mom, we have to go back for Dad!"

"Shh. Get down."

They crouched behind the tall grass. Selena listened and thought. She wished she could make a circle of protection, but she had no salt, no flame, no blood. Besides, the blood would only help the dogs find them. Gemma pulled at her sleeve.

"Mom … they're the dogs from my dream."

The sheer terror on Gemma's face almost broke her.

"You saw *those* dogs in your dream?"

"Yes! Mom, what's going on? How can they be real?" She sobbed. "What did they do to Dad?"

"Listen to me. We need to stay quiet, but we also can't stay here."

Gemma reached into her hoodie and retrieved her phone. "We need to call the cops. They can come and shoot these damned dogs."

"Your phone isn't gonna get any service out here. All we can do is get to higher ground."

"But what about Dad?"

160

We can't help him. We can only help ourselves. Now, look, do you see those trees on the other side of this grass?"

Sniffling, she looked over her mother's shoulder.

"Yeah … "

"If we move to them and climb to the top, the dogs won't be able to reach us." She took Gemma's hand. "I know you have a lot of questions, and I swear I will tell you everything, but now we have to escape, okay? Are you ready?"

The girl nodded, but still, the tears came. "Are we going to be okay?"

"Yes, sweetheart. Everything's going to be okay. Whatever happens, I love you."

They embraced, and Selena gasped as a rustling startled them. The dogs burst through the grass in their direction, their red eyes and blood-streaked maws snarling.

"Run!" Selena cried.

She grabbed Gemma and bolted for the trees. Hellish barks followed and mingled with their screams. All Selena could focus on were the trees ahead, which seemed impossibly far away. Then, she lost her grip on the girl. She stopped and scanned the sea of grass and trees. Gemma was nowhere to be seen, but her screams arose anew.

"Mom!"

"Gemma, where are you?!"

Something slammed into Selena's back, and she tumbled over. When she turned, she was met by the vile visage of one of her mother's demonic pets. Its snarl could have been mistaken for a smile.

"Mom, help me!"

Growls sounded on Selena's right. The second dog must have had Gemma cornered. She addressed the dog facing her.

"You mongrels keep away from my daughter."

The canine threat padded closer, and the stench of rotting flesh crawled into the back of her throat. The thing was biding its time, allowing its twin time to capture Gemma.

"If you hurt her … " she told the beast before her, "I'll fucking kill you."

"Mom!"

Her one chance lay in her pocket. If she could obscure herself, move unseen to Gemma's location, and help her escape. She slipped the bracelet over her wrist and uttered words she hadn't spoken for thirty years:

"Parum—"

A blaze of light erupted over the field, a circular portal comprised of ash and flame. The force of the opening parted the grass like the Red Sea, giving Selena a front row seat to the sight of the other dog dragging Gemma by her heels toward it.

"No! Noooo!"

The other zombie dog put itself between her and any attempt to aid Gemma. She realised, then, that they were never sent to get her and before Selena could act, the demon hounds pulled her daughter into the portal, and it swirled shut.

Selena's scream came from her very soul.

3

The clouds were singed black by the time Selena summoned the strength to go to Luke's body.

The oncoming storm closed in around her, trembling the ground, and with every step she took she thought she'd fall. The more she stumbled through the dark, the more helpless she felt. Not even the force of the wind or the cascade of lightning registered. There was only emptiness.

It rained steady sheets that pushed back the grey light. Instinctively, Selena knew the way to him, she just didn't want to walk the path.

The sight of Gemma being dragged away in the clutches of the hellhounds tore at Selena. It was the moment her heart—the heart she'd grown with Luke—finally split in two. She thought she'd left her mother and vile kin behind. She thought they'd forgotten about her. How foolish she'd been.

How stupid.

Lightning cracked, turning the stream to glass and emphasizing the silhouette near the shore. Luke's body. The wind pushed at her, urged her to take those final mortifying steps. Moments passed and, strangely, before she realised, she stood over her husband's lifeless form. It had been a very long time since she'd seen someone dead or that much blood. So long that it should have shocked her. It didn't.

Lightning flashed again and unveiled the dogs' work. Luke's blank eyes stared at the sky, his mouth caught in the moment of his final breath. Yet, she couldn't tell where his mouth stopped and his throat began. What was once beautiful to her was now a ragged, bloody hole. She used to kiss that throat, those lips. Now, he was dead. She'd brought his death upon him. All because of her lies.

Thunder boomed, and she sobbed. "I'm sorry."

The lightning thrust back the grey for an instant, and Selena thought she saw him blink.

"I never wanted this to happen to you," she continued. "I should have told you everything."

Falling to her knees, she cradled his hand, carefully sliding the wedding band off his finger.

"You were too good to me. I thought if I told you the truth about my life you'd think I was crazy. That you'd leave." She slipped the ring over her thumb. "I was selfish, and I'm sorry. You loved me with everything you had, and that was something I'd never known. So, I'm sorry."

She leaned down to kiss him, tasted his blood. The rain made it run anew. She drew him to her.

"I want you to know that you saved me. I want you to know that I'll get her back."

She reached down and clawed at the saturated earth.

"I will save her."

Her hands scraped at the mud. Rage and sorrow came to the surface, from her heart down to her fingertips, and sent her into a frenzy. She clawed deeper and deeper, past razor-sharp rocks and gnarled roots, digging into herself as well as the ground. The storm raged along with her, the rain serving to soften the grave she created.

Selena left her body, disassociating from her broken fingernails and lacerated palms, sadness welling up inside. She was burying her pain as much as she was burying him. It was as undeniable as the fact that, in time, the storm would pass.

With bleeding hands, she pulled Luke into the hole and laid down beside him. For a moment, she contemplated covering them both in the blanket of dirt, but she couldn't dishonour him anymore. She'd made him a promise. Caked in mud, she rose from the grave and looked upon her love one last time.

"I'm going to get her back ... "

With aching hands, Selena pushed the earth over him until he was gone, her heart—the one he'd helped her grow—gone with him.

" ... and I'm going to make them all fucking pay."

The freezing rain washed away the mud, blood, and guilt. Selena knew the storm had gathered for her, manifesting her grief and baring her soul to the world.

Storm-calling was one of the first rituals Mother taught her as a little girl. Selena had performed it so many times it had become second nature. A thought. Now, she'd willed it into being without any thought at all.

She peeled off her sopping wet sweater and let the rain caress her bare skin. She drew the droplets in, through her shoulders and eyelids, letting the water swirl alongside the force of her tears—and Luke's blood. She gathered power, gathered strength for the pilgrimage to come.

Yet, as inherent as her gifts were, she needed help to turn the darkness on again. If she was to destroy her mother, she'd need all the help she could get. Turning her gaze to the sky, the rain stopped in an instant. She tied back her hair and retrieved Luke's filleting knife from the edge of the stream with Luke's fishing gear. The steel gleamed like a full moon.

The keen edge hovered over her palm. Her conscience begged her to put the blade down, to run to Luke's truck and drive away. She pushed the thought down and squeezed the handle tighter, guiding the blade across her flesh. Blood oozed in a dark line, spilling onto the dirt. She watched the soil drink it up and said:

"Azamir veni ad me. Azamir, come to me."

The soil shifted, softly collapsing into a depression as if something beneath had woken from its slumber.

"Azamir veni ad me."

Earth crumbled. The sound of every pebble and rock beneath Selena's feet rang in her ears. Petrichor invaded her nostrils and rested on the back of her tongue, musty and sour.

Summoning rituals were as much internal as external. Within and without.

"Azamir veni ad me."

It had been many years since she had uttered his name. Many of his years had been waiting to be recalled up from the depths. *Would he remember my voice?* She realised at that moment she should have drawn a protective circle. *No, I have nothing to fear.*

The ground cracked open before her, spewing foul breath. Tendrils of brimstone coiled around her, but she stood firm, daring herself to not move.

"Azamir veni ad me!"

Her voice was thunder, her blood lightning. The crack grew wider, a cavernous maw. Hell, spewed forth one of its own. A long, black appendage, bristled and tapered, emerged, and another, and another, five, six, seven, eight. A gargantuan orb-like abdomen, glistening black. Eight smaller black orbs across its face atop a mouth full of fangs.

"Azamir est dominus tuus."

Azamir, it is your master.

The demon crawled out of the hole ever so slowly. The thing was five times Selena's size. She held out her bleeding hand to it.

"Venire gustere dominum tuum."

Come and taste your master.

The great arachnid shuffled forward, one leg after the other, cautiously, deliberately. Its fangs rubbed against each other in contemplation. She urged it closer.

"Sanguis meus est sanguis tuus."

My blood is your blood.

Azamir skittered forward then in a flash and coiled its legs around her. It was so close she saw her trepidation in its many eyes.

"Est me, Selena."

It's me, Selena.

It lifted its fangs, revealing the mandibles beneath. Very carefully, it reached out to taste her blood. Immediately, recognition flashed in its gaze. It shivered and shrank before her eyes, down and down to the size of a small cat. She scooped it up and let it suckle at her hand.

"It's good to see you, Azamir. I missed you."

The spider-demon scaled her shoulders and spine, circling around and back down to her warm embrace like a kitten trying to get comfortable.

"You're a good boy. But your master needs help."

Azamir craned his head up in attention.

"I need you to help me find the other covens in the city."

Azamir pulled his legs in and moved his mouthparts as if in reply. Selena sighed.

"We can't really talk like this. I need you to shed so I can explain. Can you do that for me?"

It considered her request, running a leg gently between its mandibles. Then, it jumped to the ground. After a moment, Azamir quivered as if in the throes of a seizure. It grew again, writhing and twisting, harsh rasping breaths passing from its mouth. The legs drew in, fusing together, the black leeching from its skin.

Seconds passed with Azamir's cries deepening until they resembled something human. Legs filled with meat and bone. The abdomen reduced.

Eight eyes became two. Mandibles morphed into a human mouth. Until Azamir, the man, stood naked in the mud, staring at his two plain arms and legs in mute disappointment.

"Cover yourself," Selena said.

Azamir heard the command and grew thick black bristles all over his body.

"No. I can't have you walking around the city looking like that. Put on some clothes."

He thought again, and a ripple of invisible energy washed over him from head to toe. The bristles were wiped away and replaced by a heavy black overcoat, trousers, and shirt.

Demons like Azamir had considerable power but could only use it if their master allowed it. Selena thought he looked like a character from *The Matrix*, but at least he was no longer a gigantic spider.

"Good. Can you talk?"

"Yes."

"Good. I need you to help me destroy my family."

Azamir blinked. She knew he understood what she'd said, the gravity of it. She strode up to him.

"They sent their dogs after me. Killed my husband and took my daughter. I need to get her back."

He looked her up and down and locked onto her eyes. He may have only had two, but Selena knew his hunting gaze well. Still, his answer shocked her.

"I will help you find the girl but nothing more."

She grimaced and took him by the lapels of his coat. "You'll do as I tell you."

"They'll destroy you," he said.

Selena pulled him closer. "They'll die trying."

4

The sting of woodsmoke assaulted Gemma's senses the moment she opened her eyes and discovered she was trapped in a waking nightmare.

Panic set her heart racing. She tried to move, only to realise she was bound to a chair. Heat blazed at her back, and when she looked over her shoulder, she saw it came from an old fireplace. Something bubbled over the flames in a cast iron pot. It smelled like soup or broth. Her stomach growled in response. She hadn't eaten in hours, but the sense of foreboding she experienced pushed all hunger aside. Her mind told her she was in terrible danger.

She scanned the room, a log-style cabin. Old, very old. Candles barely illuminated the space, and molten wax pooled in the corners and on windowsills. There was a table and chairs in the centre, and a fraying rug on the floor. Simple accoutrements for someone who appeared to be living a simple life.

Tattered lace curtains moved softly over the windows on either side of the front door, which strangely, was wide open. The sound of a hooting owl washed into the house, an eerie call which accentuated the fact that whoever owned the cabin had a teenage girl tied up inside.

Soft clinking sounds attracted her attention back to the front door. Beyond, on the porch, she glimpsed the source of the noise. Wind chimes made from very long pieces of wood. No, not wood—*bone*. She wondered what kind of animal bones they were and who would use such a thing as wind chimes.

She pulled against the restraints. The door was so close. She imagined tipping over the chair, breaking the wooden frame, and slipping free, running out the door into the woods, back to her mother. Back to safety.

Wood boards creaked. A tall, lumbering shape appeared in the doorframe. Gemma screamed at the sight of it. A man, but deformed, one half of his torso and face swollen to the point of bursting. The size of the swollen half put the man off-balance, and he leaned to that side. It was as if another person lived inside him and was trying to get out. The thing considered her with the one eye it had on the normal side of its face.

"Get away!"

The thing seemed genuinely hurt by her words.

More footfalls sounded as a second figure entered the room.

"Now, that's no way to talk to your Uncle Cade, child."

An old woman stepped past the deformed Cade. She looked about seventy-years-old, possibly older. Barefoot and dressed in a faded yellow sun dress. Grey-white hair down to her waist. Skin almost the same complexion but wrinkled like old calico. She stood before the girl and smiled, revealing only a few tartar-flecked teeth.

"You got your momma's spirit, no doubt." She motioned to the monstrous man. "Cade, you come in here and take a load off."

He hobbled to the nearest chair, the floorboards crying out beneath his misshapen steps. He dropped into the chair while keeping his one good eye on Gemma. The woman put an arthritic hand on his bulging shoulder.

"You be wondering where you are? Who we are?"

Gemma swallowed and glanced at the door, thinking about what other terrors might appear there. Her heart pounded in her ears.

"There ain't nowhere for you to go out there, girl. Besides, you're perfectly safe here."

The rope cut into Gemma's wrists. "You kidnapped me."

"Kidnapped? No, sweet thing, I brought you home. Where you belong. Where you and your momma belong."

The girl struggled to calm her racing heart and mind. Who were these people?

"Please, you have to let me go."

The woman picked up one of the chairs, placed it in front of her, and sat. Gemma smelled the dirt on her captor. It was caked under her fingernails, trapped in every crevice of her knuckles.

"Come on, child. You're home now. There ain't no need to fear your old grandma."

"What?"

The woman smiled with satisfaction, creases emerging around her yellowing eyes. "I can't believe my baby girl, Selena, has a girl of her

169

own—and a pretty one, too." She turned to Cade. "You can see the family resemblance, too?"

Gemma wanted to scream at the thought, to vomit, to run away. She pulled on the ropes. "You have to let me go!"

The slap came without warning, her grandmother's bony hand like steel. Tears welled up in the girl's eyes, but fury filled her grandma's.

"You don't ever talk to me that way, girl! You're more like your momma all right—a disobedient little wench! You don't make demands of me in my own house, do you hear?"

She tasted blood as the old woman's gaze continued to burn, along with her vile words.

"You're lucky I don't just gut you like a fish. But that wouldn't bring my Selena back to me. So, I'll just have to promise to keep you whole … " She lifted Gemma's chin with a crooked finger. " … if you promise to show me and the rest of your kin some respect. You understand?"

The girl nodded. The old woman's fierce scowl softened.

"Good. Good. We're gonna get along just fine." She toyed with Gemma's hair and wiped the tears from her cheeks. "Now, tell me, what name did your momma give you?"

"G-Gemma … "

"Hmm. Gemma. A pretty name for a pretty girl." She pointed a finger at herself. "My name is Davina, but you can call me Grandma, or Mother." She turned to the behemoth. "That there is your Uncle Cade. He's your momma's brother. Your momma's got a sister, too—Asha. She's only a few years older than you. Right now, she's out fetching some water. She'll be back home in time."

Davina moved back to the table. "Their daddy's sleeping right now, but maybe, if he's up to it, he'll come out and get a good look at you." She smiled again and clapped her hands together in excitement. "Oh, it's just like a regular old family reunion, isn't it, Cade?"

A string of drool slipped from Cade's lips to the floor. Gemma wanted to turn away or close her eyes to his grotesque nature, but she was too scared to do anything. As she looked at him, she could tell he felt as trapped as her.

"It'll be wonderful to have us all back together," Davina said. "We've all missed Selena so much."

"Who's Selena?"

"Your momma, of course."

"Her name is Stephanie."

The very mention of the name sent Davina's face into a grimace, as if the utterance was an affront to her every breath.

"Well, that ain't her name, not the one I gave her!"

Gemma feared another slap as Davina stormed back toward her.

"Selena might have thought she'd have a life on her own, but her true life is here with us, serving the Black Lord!"

She struggled to understand, to not panic, and start screaming for help. Davina and Cade were mad, backward strangers who must have kidnapped her for ransom. They couldn't have been related to her mother. As she thought about it, she realised she'd only ever met anyone from her father's side of the family. Her mother never mentioned who raised her or where she came from. Almost as if it was forbidden.

The memory of the dogs came rushing back, the horrific dead dogs that brought her to this place. They'd been in her dreams, in her mother's. Could these people be responsible for all that? Could they be telling the truth with their talk of black lords? She looked at the old woman and the twisted Cade and wondered: *Is my mother a monster?*

Davina smiled with glee, and Gemma feared her grandmother knew what she was thinking.

"It's funny, I can usually see inside my kin's heads, but not you, girl." She *tsked*. "Must be that muck-blood in your veins from your daddy." She frowned. "Oh, I'm sorry about him, child. He seemed like a brave man, but my dogs had to do what they had to do."

Gemma's stomach roiled. "They … they killed him?"

"They're such good boys."

At a whistle from Davina's cracked lips, the hounds skittered into the cabin. The mere sight of them sent a shiver through Gemma. The creatures sensed it, immediately racing to sniff her all over. She winced at the view of their insides, their stink threatening to make her sick.

"Oh, they got your scent now, girl. They know you're a part of the family."

Gemma started to sob, helplessness setting in. She wanted her father, but he was dead, and her mother was nowhere to be seen. If this Selena was her mother, why would she ever come back to be with this horrible family? But Gemma didn't want to be there either, and she certainly didn't want to die so she had to try and find a way to reason with them.

"What do you want from me?" she said.

Davina interlaced her fingers. "It took me a long time to track your momma down. She didn't make it easy. She had some good protection on her, but what she didn't consider was the power of blood. Our family blood. You see, while Selena's amulet kept herself from view, once she became pregnant with you, *you* became visible to me." The old woman smoothed down Gemma's hair. "You're our blood. It took a while, but we reached out to you, and your blood shone so brightly, girl."

Her gentle touch became a vice-like grip, almost twisting a clump of hair from Gemma's scalp. The girl shrieked in pain as Davina pulled her head back. Gemma could see the hate in her eyes and smell her fetid breath.

"And we're gonna use your blood again to woo Selena back here. It might just be a few drops at first, but if your momma don't come running home, we might just shed it all until she does. The Black Lord expects us to keep up our end of the bargain, and it's been far too many years. Selena's his prize you see, so she'd better come home. Not just for her sake but for yours too."

She laughed then, a wet cackle bubbling up from deep within her foul heart.

"Welcome to the family, girl."

173

5

The cabin of the truck still carried the scent of Luke's cologne, and it tore Selena up inside. She sat in the driver's seat and barely knew Azamir sat next to her. There were so many thoughts racing through her head that she didn't have the luxury to grieve. She stared at the keys in her hand, at the fish shaped Gone Fishin' keychain she'd bought Luke several years ago. It was meaningless now.

"What are you going to do?" Azamir said.

She turned to study his face. Now, in a better light, he looked about twenty-years old, fresh-faced apart from the thick, black stubble on his chin, no doubt his spider bristles showing through. His eyes were a deep brown. He was the textbook "dark and mysterious" type. If only people knew the truth.

"I really don't know. One part of me thinks I should just drive away and keep driving."

"You could do that," her familiar said, offering a smile, "but I know you're not going to."

"Oh, you do, do you?"

"I've known you for many years, since you were a little girl. A determined little girl who stood up to her mother."

Selena looked through the windshield to the mound of dirt where Luke now rested. "That was a long time ago. I know before I said I wanted to kill my mother, but maybe that was all bravado. I don't want to. I never wanted to be part of their world. I was just born into it. That's why I ran away. Started a family of my own."

Azamir held her hand. "Your mother took all that from you, but you don't need to go back down that path if you don't want—"

She wiped away tears. "But haven't I done that already by summoning you? Doesn't that show intent?"

He smiled. "You summoned a friend, that's all."

"You say I don't have to go back to the darkness, but I don't have a choice. *She* made the choice for me."

They stared at the burial mound for a moment until Azamir said: "I remember a little girl who didn't want to hurt anyone. Isn't that the real reason you ran away?"

She put the keys in the ignition and started the truck, giving the accelerator a hard rev. "Pretty sure I buried that little girl about an hour ago." She put the truck into drive. "The only little girl I care about now is Gemma, and she's out there somewhere in the hands of that bitch."

"So, that's it, then?"

"Yeah, that's it."

He sniffed and sat straighter in his seat. "Okay. You know that I'll help you get Gemma back."

"Thank you."

"I just want to say, for what it's worth, I'm sorry the little girl I know and loved had to die."

Selena accelerated onto the dirt track, away from the burial mound, pondering the journey ahead.

"Me, too, Az. Me, too."

The remnants of the storm lay scattered along the skyline as they drove into the city limits. The city had been Selena's home ever since she fled her family. It had been a place of innovation and hope, but now she feared it would soon fall into the same darkness that had once ruled her life.

Azamir wound down his window and put his head outside like a dog. He was her pet, after all. The sight made her smile for the first time in a while, but it would probably be her last because of what she was about to do to get her daughter back. She steered the truck away from the main highway into the city, heading instead for the suburbs.

"I need to go home, to prepare."

Her familiar brought his head back inside. "You don't think your mother will follow you there?"

She shook her head. "I figured it out on the drive. My mother couldn't find me for all these years because of the amulet, right? So, she must have used blood magic, must have divined for family blood. It would have taken a while, but she obviously found Gemma when she came of age."

He rubbed his bristled chin. "So, what's the plan, then? Are we going to hide out in your house? Fortify it?"

"No, not the house—me."

"You?"

"It's been a very long time since I've practiced, and I need to get back in the game. Body, mind, and soul."

He frowned. "But once you start that process, won't you attract her attention?"

"Maybe that's what I want."

"Can I give you some advice?"

"Isn't that why I brought you with me?"

Azamir smirked. "If I were you, I wouldn't go home. You need a neutral space. You see, once I had this rival who tried to take over my domain. Every night he'd sneak into my cave because he knew I was out hunting. But I knew he would try that so while he was out searching for me in my cave, I dug a tunnel into his." His smiled widened, almost in pride. "It took me several nights but, ultimately, I created a trap web right under his own house."

Selena chuckled. "Where he least expected it."

"Exactly. By the time he figured it out, it was too late. So, you sense there might be a coven in the city, right? That's where you should start building our web."

She raised an eyebrow. "Our?"

"You want my help, don't you?"

She thought about Azamir's plan. Holing up in a hotel or even an abandoned warehouse in the city would help her find the source of any covens. A pang of guilt burned in her chest at the thought of returning home, the loss of her husband still raw. No, home wasn't an option. She needed to push aside the pain and concentrate on getting stronger. Getting even.

"Okay, we'll go with your plan, Az. Thank you."

"You're welcome."

"But I need you to do a few things for me while I find us a place to hide out."

"Like what?"

"I need you to find me some clothes and put out some threads on where to find this coven."

The city streets were not unlike the threads of a spider's web, Azamir realised.

Did that mean the people walking and driving on them were his prey?

After agreeing to go back to the city, Selena had dropped him on a corner of one of the main streets and ordered him to start the search for any sign of the coven.

Immediately, he'd noticed people gawking at him. People in suits drinking their lattes, engaging in gossip. How human existence had come to this he didn't know, but it made them more susceptible to temptation or finding themselves lost, or worse.

He licked his lips. It had been some time since he'd last fed, especially on a human. No, Selena—his master—had given him a task to complete. To find the darkness amongst the mundane places of the city. The perfect job for a creature such as him. Smiling to himself, he lifted the collar of his coat then crossed the street in the direction of a local bar. He stopped when a thought occurred to him: A bar was too obvious. Witch-folk, as he knew them, were all about sacrilege. Their goal was to defame.

Azamir scanned the street, letting the steady throng of people pass by. If he were a witch or warlock—not just a simple backwoods practitioner—

where would he call home? He thought back to all the times he'd been summoned by acolytes and apostles of the dark. Once, he'd been conjured into a basement, another time, a library. Those fools had been amateurs—and tasted as such—but he was looking for people who knew how to blend in with the ordinary.

He walked down the block to an intersection. He ignored the peddlers and the food truck purveyors, focusing on the bank on the other side of the crossing. The aura around the building on the corner was unmistakable. What a perfect place to entice and corrupt. Humans and their money. He walked across and stepped through the door of the New Alliance Trust Bank.

The inside was all marble floors and timber furnishings. For all intents and purposes, a place to exchange currency. But given the scent stinging his nose, Azamir knew that money wasn't the only collateral here. He studied the customers lined up to request a transaction. All appeared normal, even the bank tellers. The ones he sought were in the back, lurking. But how to get behind the counter?

"Can I help you, sir?"

Azamir turned to the man beside him. Dressed in a heavy jacket, ball cap, and sporting a pistol on his hip, staring at him strangely. Azamir realised he probably looked suspicious. He looked the guard up and down.

"Are you a security guard?"

The man slowly placed his right hand on the gun holster. "Can I help you?"

"Why are you answering a question with a question?"

This took the guard by surprise. "Sir, if you don't have any business here at the bank, I'm going to have to ask you to leave."

"Oh, but I do have some business here at this … uh, bank."

The guard squinted. "So, you have an appointment?"

He smirked and leaned in closer, spooking the guard who was about to pull his gun.

"I'm seeking a transaction of … let's say … a secretive nature. An exchange of non-corporeal currency. If you know what I mean." He winked in the hope that the guard would know what he meant.

"What?" the guard's face contorted in confusion.

Had he made a mistake? It had been many years since he'd taken human form. Perhaps he'd used the wrong words? Had he been wrong about the bank being a nexus? He had to get out of the bank before the guard shot him, forcing him to change back into his natural state and kill everyone inside.

'Harold, I believe I can help this gentleman."

The woman in the black pants suit seemed to appear beside them. She smiled at Azamir, and then to the guard.

"You go back to your post, now, Harold," she said.

The guard shuffled away, puzzled by the entire situation. Azamir observed the woman. Up close, she exuded power. Flawless skin and shining hair. He thought she was also perfectly proportioned for a woman of her age—at least on the surface. Those kinds of curves weren't acquired by natural means. She offered him her hand.

"Helene Kolbe. I'm the manager here. You're in need of some special services?"

He shook her hand, and he knew she could tell what he was. "What kind of services do you provide?"

"All kinds. Is there something in particular you require—or that your master requires?"

The familiar savoured the feel of the bristles on his chin. "You have a vault, yes?"

"Of course. Do you—or your master—need to make a deposit? Or a withdrawal?"

Azamir got a good whiff of the woman's power. "Can I make an appointment?"

6

Selena booked a room in the Plaza Hotel in the heart of the city and instructed Azamir to meet her there. Because of their *familiarity*, they shared a kind of telepathic bond and could sense each other's inner voice. The distance was limited—they had to be in the same place, or at the very least, the same town.

She waited for him to return, occupying her thoughts with views of the city. From the twelfth floor, she could see everything—except what she was looking for. Amongst the crisscross network of skyscrapers and asphalt streets, the coven hid in the dark places.

The coven, or covens, in the city were offshoots of her mother's temple in the woods. Disciples she'd sent out decades earlier to spread her dark word by whatever means necessary. Selena wondered how many innocent people they'd corrupted in the city, how many places of authority they'd infiltrated. The thought sickened her.

The guilt returned in a wave. Her thoughts were hypocritical. How could she pass judgement now when she ignored the darkness for so long? While she played happy family, evil spread its tendrils. No, she wasn't just protecting herself, she was protecting Luke and Gemma.

But what of them now?

Moving away from the window to the bar fridge, she retrieved a small bottle of scotch and can of cola, mixed it hurriedly into a glass and swallowed it down. She savoured the burn in her throat. The battle of wills with her moral centre was becoming tiresome. She just wanted feel numb. The freshly made bed was so enticing. If only she could slide between the soft sheets and lapse into a deep sleep.

Visions of Gemma intervened. Her little girl in the grip of terror. The sun was setting, and soon, her only child would be amid literal darkness. Selena could picture her daughter crying, recoiling from the old crone's wicked sneer. The ache of helplessness pulled at her gut, and she screamed and hurled the glass into the wall, sending shards into the rug and splashes of scotch over the curtains.

There was a knock at the door. Selena froze. No doubt someone heard her cry out, heard the shattering glass. A muted voice travelled in from the other side of the door.

"It's Azamir."

Through the peephole she saw the demon in the hall, holding what looked like a suit bag. She let him in but couldn't look him in the eye.

"Everything okay?"

Selena went back to the window, chewing her nails.

"You took your time."

Azamir tossed the suit bag onto the bed. "Well, I had to find you some clothes." He sniffed the air. "What happened in here?"

She collected the shards. "I dropped a glass. It's nothing." She scooped the pieces into the wastebasket.

Her friend saw the trails of scotch on the wall. "Right. Well, it wasn't easy, but I found a nexus site."

"You did? Where?"

He put his hands on his hips, seemingly proud of his achievement. "The bank on 48th Street—National Alliance something or other. There's definitely some dark energy there. Pretty sure the manager's a witch."

"That makes sense. A bank is discreet, secure, but also vital to people."

"I'm surprised you never picked up on it before."

She sat on the edge of the bed, thoughts and plans racing through her mind. "We did all our banking online and not with that bank."

"Online?"

"The internet. On a computer. Like a web that goes around the world."

"Oh, very cool. Well, I got you an appointment. Tonight."

"You did what?"

He slipped off his coat and undid the top button of his shirt. "An appointment with the manager. I told her you wanted to make a deposit." Again, he was proud of himself.

"Az, I never told you to do that! I just wanted you to find the place."

He held out his hands to placate her. "Hey, they were getting suspicious, so I had to do something. You wanted to go there, right? To confront them? Besides, I'll be there to back you—"

Selena stood and ran a hand through her hair. "I can't believe you did that!"

"Why?"

"Because I'm not ready!"

He recoiled at her tone. "You told me about how you held those dogs back with a water charm. You're ready—"

"Those were dogs! Not a coven with God knows how many defences! Jesus!"

She paced the room, Azamir watching.

"Look, I'm sorry, okay? We'll get you ready. There's still time."

"You'll get me ready? You've been a big help so far."

He sighed. "I know you're scared—"

She whirled on him. "I'm not scared!"

"Okay, okay. We'll figure it out. *You'll* figure it out."

Selena smoothed her hair, dried her sweaty palms on her jeans, and took a deep breath. She pointed at the clothing bag.

"What's that?"

"Oh. Well, you gave me your credit card to by you some clothes." He leaned down to unzip the suit bag and pulled out a grey blouse and matching pants. "What do you think?"

She scoffed and crossed her arms. "You're kidding, right?"

"Why? What's wrong with it?"

"I'm not wearing that. I'll look like an accountant or something." She gestured at him. "We'll look like twins, for god's sake!"

Azamir held up both items. "At least you'll look the part."

She noticed another garment underneath when Azamir picked up the outfit. "And what's that?"

He lifted a waist-length black leather jacket, zips and buckles worked into the sleeves.

"Oh, you like this?" he asked.

"Yeah, I like that."

✦

Selena was lost in the bathroom mirror. She'd showered and slipped on a towel, let the steam coalesce around her and, somehow, been captivated by her reflection.

There was only one way she was going to take on her mother and her minions. She was going to have to lose herself, entirely.

She wiped away the condensation. Her face appeared distorted, misshapen. Ugly. It was just for a moment, but she thought she looked like her mother.

Water dripped from the faucet, a deafening toll inside her skull. *Drip, drip, drip.* The sound made her want to scream, to smash the mirror into a million pieces. She imagined picking up one of the shards and driving it into her throat.

Do it.

The voice ran through her, a shuddering cry from the other side of the glass. Selena felt it more than heard it.

Her mother's voice.

Mirrors were powerful conduits between the real world and the spiritual. Doorways from one soul to another. From mother to daughter.

Selena ...

The old crone's voice swirled in the shadows of the reflection. Like it was coming from deep within the crevices of the earth.

Selena ...

Echoes in the room, echoes in her mind.

"Get out of my head," she muttered.

Through the steam and mist on the glass, she saw her mother, all unkempt hair and sallow skin. Crooked teeth gleaming.

Are you going to come back home, girl?

Swallowing hard, she gripped the edge of the sink. "What have you done with Gemma?"

In the murk of the mirror, Davina cackled. *Done to Gemma? Me? Nothing. I've done nothing to my granddaughter.*

"She's not yours."

Oh, but she is.

"You need to let her go."

If you come home.

Selena grimaced and tasted blood. "No."

Then, the girl stays. Her for you.

"No."

Don't you talk to me that way.

The mirror cracked beneath the fury of Davina's voice. A piece of glass fell into the basin. Selena caught her horrified reflection there.

You insolent little cur! You think you can still talk to me like that? You were always the same disobedient whelp! I wanted to beat that out of you, but your father didn't want you harmed, couldn't have you harmed! But that was then ...

The shard called to Selena.

Now, I have Gemma. So, maybe I don't need you. Maybe I'll teach Gemma in the ways of shadows and souls, hmm? What do you think about that?

Her hands trembled.

"Don't you fucking touch her!"

She's mine now!

The force of Davina's power wavered through the reflection.

You think yer just gonna come back here and take her home? She cackled again, and more pieces of glass slid into the drain. *You don't have it in you! You never did! Because you're weak! Why your father thinks you are good enough for the Black Lord escapes me. You're worthless! Unfit! You should just kill yourself and leave Gemma to me!*

Selena clutched the largest shard, tears distorting her vision. She wanted to drop it, but her hand wasn't hers to control. She had to do something to stop herself.

Do it! Davina's voice boomed.

She raised the shard, her terrified gaze following it up and up.

You think you're a witch?

The urge was so strong, the pressure pushing the razor edge into her palm, stinging, bleeding.

You're just the Devil's whore!

The cold fragment pricked the skin of Selena's throat. Outside, she knew Azamir was completely oblivious to what unfolded in the bathroom. How her master was about to end her own life.

"Az ... " she whispered.

Blood trickled down her neck.

Do it! Davina shrieked.

Azamir was right outside.

Do it!

If she could just call to him.

"Az ... Azamir?"

The bathroom door crashed inward, and Azamir barged in. He wrestled with his master to wrench the glass from her hand. They fell to the tiles, him on top of her, crying out for her to release her grip. Davina cackled, the sound threatening to drive her to madness, to suicide. If she could just let go, it would all go away. If she would just let go.

Let go!

Her familiar's voice broke through. "Let go! Master, let go!"

The room fell silent. Davina's voice was gone, leaving only a shattered mirror and Azamir holding her in his arms. He tossed the shard away and pulled her close.

"What were you going to do?"

She looked up him with baleful eyes. "It was her. The bitch was trying to kill me."

Clambering to her feet, she stared at the blood on her palm and realised how close she'd come to death. She caught her reflection in the faceted glass one last time and turned to her familiar. It was time.

"Blood for blood."

7

After nightfall, they surrounded themselves with candles and a protective circle.

Selena sat inside the circle while her familiar, being a demon, sat outside it. She contemplated the tasks ahead, watching the flickering flames intently, forcing down the after-effects of the attack she'd survived mere hours earlier.

"What's our next move?" Azamir asked.

From where the pair sat near the end of the two double beds, they had a view of the city lights. The majestic skyline did little to push down the uncertainty she felt. The candlelight was all she found strength in. The flames and her friend's counsel.

"If I'm going to beat her, I need to think like her," she told him.

"Right, and what does that mean, exactly?"

She gazed into the flame. "My mother has been the one to make the first move every time. First, she took Gemma, then she tried to kill me. She's baiting me, calling me out."

"Of course she is. She knows the extent of her power, but do you know yours?"

Selena licked her lips and tasted salty sweat. "She doesn't know that we've located one of her covens though. So, we should just stick with the plan of hitting it. Hard."

Azamir snapped his fingers. "Exactly."

His human mannerisms constantly astounded her. He had hundreds of years of experience after all. She turned to him. "But we can't just go in without some big guns."

He looked around the room. "We don't have any guns."

"It's a figure of speech, Az."

"Oh, right."

She stood and paced the perimeter of the circle. "So, I need to strengthen my armour, my resolve."

"And how would we do that?"

She sat back down and observed the flames. The light and heat accumulating around them. "Fire," she said finally.

"What?"

"I remembered how to harness water, right? What if I can learn how to harness fire—specifically hellfire?"

Azamir looked from Selena to the candles and back again. "That's not hellfire. That's regular fire."

"I know that. I don't want just regular fire. I need hellfire. That's what you're going to help me get."

She watched the recognition play across his features. He may have been a demonic spider-man, but he wasn't stupid. She knew he understood what she was asking, where she was going with her plan.

"You want to go to Hell ... and steal hellfire?"

"Not exactly."

A wave of excitement built, and she paced the circle again. "What if we opened a door to Hell?"

The candles sat at specific points along the arc of the protective circle, shimmering above the rug.

"Stealing hellfire isn't like lighting a candle, Master. It's extremely dangerous."

"You think I don't know that? It's exactly the reason why I need it."

Her familiar was the one pacing now. "You're just going to open a portal to Hell here, in this hotel room?"

"Well, I can't very well do it out in the hall!"

He held out his hands for her to take. "Master, you don't have to put yourself in danger like this. Let me do it. I could go down grab some hellfire and come back."

"You know it doesn't work like that." She let go of his hands. "The one who wishes to wield the power must be the one to claim it. Like I said, I am not technically going to go to Hell to get it. I'll still be rooted here on Earth."

Azamir swallowed. "It could kill you."

"My mother just tried to kill me! I know the risk, but if I'm going to have any chance of standing up to her, I need to do this!"

"Okay, okay. I don't doubt you can do it, I just worry that you might go too far and not come back."

Selena's eyes narrowed. "I understand, Az, but if this is going to work, I need you to do exactly what I say—without question. Do you understand?"

Azamir resembled a wounded dog. "Yes, Master. What would you have me do?"

"I need a grimoire of sigils."

"Sigils?"

"Witches marks. Icons of power and protection."

"So, the grimoire will help you open the portal to Hell?"

"No, the grimoire contains the sigils. My mother may have treated me like shit, but she shared a lot of knowledge with me and my siblings. I remember her telling us about grimoires. The one about sigils is one that stuck in my memory."

"What will the sigils do?"

"They'll stop me from getting pulled into Hell when I open the portal."

He raised an eyebrow. "Well, we'll definitely need those, then."

She slapped his shoulders. "Yes, and you're going to tattoo them on my skin."

They waited until after dark to start the first ritual.

Azamir acquired more candles and filled almost every available space in the room. He drew the curtains and gathered water in an ice bucket, an apple from the mini fridge, and a steak knife from the drawer.

Selena didn't have the time or the luxury to prepare the ritual in the traditional manner. She had to make do with what was available. He handed her the items as she stood in the circle, his expression forlorn.

"Is that everything?" he said.

She considered the items, running her thumb along the edge of the knife. "They're fine."

"You're ready?"

"Yes, but let's go over it one more time."

He checked the curtains were completely drawn. "You're going to steal the *Notas Diaboli—The Marks of the Devil*—from Harvard's collection by opening a portal to there. This, in turn, will be good practice for the second portal to Hell. But before you do that, we have to read the grimoire, find the right sigils in it, and then I'll tattoo them onto your skin using this tattoo gun and ink." He held up the gun and ink for emphasis. "Once you have the tattoos, you'll have enough protection to extract the hellfire and, in theory, be strong enough to defend yourself against anything the coven throws at you when you meet them in"—He glanced at the alarm clock on the bedside table which read 7:07PM—"a little under two hours."

The bucket of water was placed between her feet. "You forgot the inherent risk of touching the grimoire."

"Oh, how could I forget that? I can't physically touch the book with my bare hands because it's bound with the skin of a demon. *You* could touch it, but you need to stay inside the circle, and the grimoire can't go in the circle because of the whole demon-skin thing."

She pointed to the metal tongs on the bed. "Which is what they're for."

"Got it." Azamir gave a thumbs up.

Selena took off her new jacket and tossed it out of the circle. Beads of sweat were already forming on her bare shoulders, but she was ready.

"Okay, Az, here we go."

She held the knife in one hand while her other hand was palm open.

"I seek the doors obscured, passages unseen," she said. "*Obscurata fores peto, meatus invisibilis.*"

She squeezed the blade with her free hand until it pierced the skin. Drops of blood splashed into the bucket of water.

"This blood is the key. My offering to the keepers of paths not taken.

Hic sanguis clavis est. Munera mea custodientibus semitas non sublates."

The air quivered before her, a smudge on the fabric of space. She held the apple up to it.

"This comes from the earth. Let it be the point to open one door to another. *Hoc provenit a terra. Esto punctum ostium alteri aperire."*

The smudge sharpened and cracked to become a fissure of light, a split that swelled. Azamir smiled and fidgeted with excitement.

"Show me the way!" Selena cried. *"Ostende mihi viam!"*

Reality ripped apart. A void hovered outside the edge of the protective circle, almost to the ceiling. Selena squinted, trying to peer through to the other side. During the ritual, she'd visualized the place in Harvard where the *Notas Diaboli* grimoire was secreted.

"Do you see it?" her friend asked.

On the other side of the void was a darkened room. Shelves of ancient books lined the walls behind locked doors, but one sat separate in a large glass case atop a small brass lectern.

"Yes!"

"Great, now grab it!"

Selena frowned. "It's in a case."

"Break it, then."

"The place is probably alarmed!"

"No one is going to know it was you. Just slip your hand through, break the glass, and take it!"

She took the knife in her hand and plunged it through the void. There was a rush of air, from cold to warm. With all her strength, she stabbed at the glass, shattering it. To her surprise, no alarm sounded.

"Take it now!" Azamir said.

Holding the tongs, Selena bent through the gap and grabbed the grimoire. The book was larger and heavier than she thought, and she found it difficult to get a grip on it. Around her, the edges of the magical doorway shifted.

"Jesus, it's gonna slam shut." Azamir pulled off his coat and bunched it up in his hands and held it close. "I don't know why we didn't think of this before. Toss it to me and get back in here!"

Noise like crackling electricity rang in her ears. Squeezing the tongs tight, she wrenched the book from its resting place and flicked it through the opening, where Azamir was waiting to catch it, his hands protected by his coat. Selena landed on her ass in the centre of the protective circle. The void slammed shut with the sound of crackling thunder.

"God damn, I hope no one next door heard that," Azamir said.

Selena smiled excitedly at him cradling the grimoire in his coat.

"That was close!"

The *Notas Diaboli* was centuries old. Hewn from the flesh of a demon—a Duke of Hell—it contained a record of every witches' mark ever found during the burning times. Meant to be a simple catalogue of information, it became a grimoire in 1887 when occultists unlocked the curse by foolishly deciding to handwrite a facsimile of it. Now, Selena hoped to use the curse to her advantage.

The flesh jacket was faded, rough and flecked with tears and scars. Like it had been slowly rotting for centuries but without emitting any putrescence. Selena knelt inside the circle to get a closer look at it.

"I learned about this book from my mother. She'd even considered stealing it herself when I was younger, but it was moved around so much she could never narrow down its location."

"You beat her to it," Azamir said.

"Yeah. Okay, it's time to open it up."

The tongs in Azamir's hand quivered above the book. Selena saw the trepidation in his eyes.

"It'll be fine, Az. We're just taking a peek."

He nodded and gripped the edge of the front cover with the tongs. The book opened with a low creaking sound, flesh rubbing on flesh, ancient papyrus shifting for the first time in probably decades. The opening pages fell with a whisper.

"Oh, I think the pages are flesh, too," he said.

"Okay, turn to some of the witches' marks."

He carefully turned past the title page until he reached a spread of icons and shapes splashed across the surface.

"Is it written in blood?" Selena said.

"Looks like it."

She pointed at one of the marks—a large circular, split with a brush stroke on the diagonal. The stroke ended with an upward hook.

"It says: *scutum*," Azamir said.

"*Shield,*" Selena explained before pointing at another mark that looked like a triangle of intersecting spheres.

Craning his neck, he read the scrawl beneath the mark. "Um, it says: *tertius oculus.*"

Selena grinned wildly. "*Third eye!* Oh, this is perfect!"

He shared a smile of his own. "You still know your Latin after all these years?"

"The way my mother literally beat it into me, how could I forget?" She handed him her cell phone. "Now, take photos of everything in the book. Then, you're going to start tattooing them onto me. We have to get that hellfire."

Her familiar's gaze widened. "Are you absolutely sure about this?"

"Definitely. I'm gonna burn my bitch of a mother into the ground."

8

Every jab of the needle was a knife to Selena's soul. Her skin a canvas for dark forces.

She'd instructed Azamir to start with a protective sigil so she could take down her circle. Tattooing it into her hand outside the circle enabled her familiar to do the inking without any risk of harm. Once that sigil was complete, she erased the circle and moved to a chair near the window. She slipped off her tank top so he could start a large summoning sigil on her back, which would allow her to more easily open portals. The needle burned with each piercing of her skin. These were no normal tattoos, after all.

Azamir worked mostly in silence, only occasionally asking if she was okay. Of course, her every response was a lie. Every step of her plan to get Gemma back was an ordeal, but she had to be strong. She had to become powerful by letting herself go.

The tattoo gun droned on, pricking her back over and over. Selena stared at the one on the palm of her left hand. A straight line with a loop at one end. A sigil to protect. On the top of her hand Azamir had tattooed a V-shaped sigil which allowed her to touch the grimoire. She flicked through its pages while her familiar worked.

Will it work when I face the coven?

She glanced at the clock: 8:10PM. Less than an hour before she put the sigils to the test. Would two sigils be enough to protect her when she opened the portal? Her heart raced, panic rising to the surface. Azamir shifted the tattoo gun, and the needle bounced off her spine.

"Jesus! Fuck!"

"Sorry! Sorry!"

Selena turned away from him. "What the hell are you doing?"

"I'm sorry. I'm doing the best I can."

"Well, if you fuck it up, it's both our asses!"

Azamir turned off the gun and put it on the bedside table. "Maybe we should take a break?"

She stood, her body rigid with pain and frustration. "We don't have enough time. We have to meet these coven assholes in like forty minutes. I need that hellfire!"

He put his head in his hands. "I can't keep doing this," he muttered.

"You have to! You vowed that you would help me."

Her familiar's form abruptly swelled and morphed, transforming from man to demon spider in mere seconds. The gargantuan arachnid took up the entire bed and released a long, loud hiss—a hiss of rage. She heard his arachnidian words in her mind. Their connection was stronger than ever.

"*I don't want to be party to your destruction.*"

Selena eased back. "Okay, Az, just calm down."

The spider stomped its many legs on the bedspread. "*I've gone along with your plan long enough, Master. Your anger with your mother could jeopardize everything. Your daughter's soul—and your own!*"

"So, you would just have me give up, Az?"

He moved from side to side, chittering in contemplation. "*No, but ... perhaps a pact could be made?*"

"You're joking, right?"

"*What if you went back to your mother? Not in surrender or compliance, but from a strategic standpoint. Remember what I told you about my enemy? You could get close to your mother—and Gemma. Keep her safe and get stronger over time. Launch an attack on your mother from within?*"

She scoffed. "I can't believe you're going over this again. She's already tried to kill me. If I turn up at her front door, she'll likely kill me outright or torture me and make Gemma her new acolyte. I am sure as hell not gonna let that happen to her!"

Azamir backed his enormous frame up against the bedhead, drawing his legs as if in some sort of defence.

"*What if ... you contacted the Black Lord ... asked him for aid?*"

The witch swallowed down a tremor of fear. "No, no. Jesus, Az, he's the whole reason I ran away in the first place!"

"*I know but—*"

"But nothing! I'm not going to beg that son of a bitch for help. Not in a million fucking years!"

The spider-demon drew down, twisting and contorting back to its human avatar. There was more fear and sincerity in just his two eyes.

"Okay, Master. I apologize."

She sat and stared out the window again. Far below, humanity moved on, oblivious to the dark forces in their very midst. Cars and buses of people who didn't even believe witches were real. People, ordinary people, couldn't sense the occult unless they sought it out, and few rarely did. They couldn't even sense what was going on in this hotel room.

"She killed my husband, Az. She took my Gemma. Tried to make me kill myself. So, I'm going to start taking her world from her."

He kept his head down. "Yes, Master."

"Now, I don't want to hear about this anymore. Help me finish the sigil, then help me finish my mother."

Once Azamir finished tattooing the summoning sigil on her back, she instructed him to drive her to the city and park outside the National Alliance Trust Bank. She could see the soft formaldehyde-coloured lighting coming from inside and wondered what sort of coven waited within its walls. Schemers, no doubt. Which meant she had to be prepared for anything. Azamir turned to her after several moments of silence.

"Are we just scoping the place out, for now?" He checked his watch. "There's about fifteen minutes before our meet-up, and you don't have your hellfire—"

"No need to worry about that, Az. I know what I'm doing." She could tell he was confused.

"Are you altering the plan, Master?"

"No, I still plan on meeting them at 9 PM, and I still plan on getting my hellfire."

Azamir's mouth widened when he understood. "Oh, you're not going to open the portal inside the bank, are you?"

Selena held up her left hand to display the protective sigil. "When I walk in there, I'm literally going to have the upper hand."

Azamir blinked. "Wow. That's insane … but also kind of smart. But you'll protect me, too, right?"

"Just stay close."

✪

Helene Kolbe sat in her office, flanked by two bodyguards. She watched the CCTV images of the man and woman approaching the bank's front doors.

She had no idea who the woman was, but Helene remembered her companion from their previous meeting. Helene wondered if the man was her bodyguard. Or perhaps a partner in crime? She glanced at her own guards, a pair of tall, muscled bouncer-types.

"Let them in and take them down to the vaults. That way, if anything happens, we can clean up the blood."

The bank manager stood to smooth her suit jacket. She faced the wall behind her desk and traced a sigil in the air with a finely manicured finger. The wall faded away like it was never there at all, revealing a descending staircase. Her heels clacked on each step, echoing inside the secret space.

After-hours visitors were not uncommon in Helene's bank. Criminals often did their business at night. Spellcasters occasionally came to conduct business. Helene wasn't certain this particular customer was a practitioner, but she sensed something different about her. If the young woman was only just new to the shadow game, perhaps she could take advantage of that?

She reached the bottom of the stairs and entered a large vault room. Large green floor and wall tiles accentuated a floor-to-ceiling twenty-four-bolt Diebold vault door. To the right of the door's centre were two linked boxes for combination mechanisms, and to the left, a four-movement time lock. A standard vault door, fashioned in the early 1900s, but the *other* vault behind it was far more secure and protected items far more valuable than money or gold.

Another metal door on the wall to Helene's right unlocked with a clank of metal, and her guards entered with her guests. The young woman wore a black leather jacket and denim jeans, her sable hair pulled tight into a ponytail. She didn't look like a witch. Her familiar wore the same full-length black trench-coat and black suit he'd had on when she'd first encountered him. He was better dressed than her own guards and more handsome.

Helene gave her guards a glance, indicating for one of them to come and stand beside her and the other to stay flanking the new guests. In truth, it was more of a mental command than a glance. She offered the young woman and her companion a welcoming smile.

"Welcome to the New Alliance Trust. My name is Helene Kolbe. I'm the manager here."

The young woman stepped forward and offered her right hand. "Stephanie. Stephanie Markson. And this is my business partner, Alex."

She took Stephanie's hand and immediately sensed a surge of energy. "Nice to meet you, Ms. Markson. I already met your partner this afternoon. So, what can I help you with this evening?"

The woman tried to study Stephanie's face in the low light. There was clearly something about the young woman's eyes, as if she'd seen them before. The impression the young witch gave was off-putting.

Stephanie looked to the vault. "Well, I've heard great things about your bank and its reputation as a safe place to deposit certain rare items."

Helene gestured to the gleaming vault door. "Indeed. As you can see, we're quite secure. You have something to deposit?"

She saw Stephanie's eyes narrow. "I do." She turned to her companion, who carefully produced a large book from inside a satchel he'd been holding. He passed it to Stephanie. "This grimoire recently came into my possession," she said. "I want to keep it somewhere safe."

"The *Notas Diabolis*? That is indeed rare." She reached for it but Stephanie kept it close. Helene smiled and stepped to the vault door. She waved her hand, and the door washed away like mercury. Beneath was the true vault, rusted red and etched with all manner of runes and sigils. "This is one of the most secure vaults in the country. Of course, it has the price to match. Are you a member of any recognized coven, Ms. Markson?"

"I used to be."

"Really? Which one? Perhaps I know it?"

A wry smirk crossed Stephanie's face—one of impudence.

"Perhaps you've visited it yourself, Ms. Kolbe?" Stephanie said. "A little cabin in the woods. Petunias on the front porch?"

Helene waved her hand again and the shadow vault dissipated back to its modern façade. Who was this girl? She turned smiling, trying to feign ignorance, but the girl's prying stare hinted at a secretive nature. Very few knew about the cabin—the one true church of the Black Lord.

"Hmm, I can't say that I have heard of that one. In the woods here, you say?"

"No, not here, the next state over. West Virginia."

Helene folded her hands behind her back, issued a silent signal to the guard behind her. "Oh, a lovely part of the country. Sadly, it's been many a year since I've been down that way. Far too busy running this establishment, you see." She stepped closer and glimpsed some hesitation in Stephanie's gaze. "Tell me, Ms. Markson, have you ever considered selling your grimoire? I know of someone who be most interested in acquiring it."

Stephanie smiled, and Helene recognized the smirk. It reminded her of someone whose smile often set her blood running cold.

"Would that be Davina Kolbe?" Stephanie said. "Your sister?"

Helene chuckled, the realisation finally coming to the fore. "Selena? I haven't seen you since you were a little girl. If this was meant to be some sort of cosy family reunion, I'm afraid you've come to the wrong place."

She snapped her fingers, and the room plunged into darkness.

9

They came at Selena from the dark. The vault room was a shadow world, and she quickly realised Helene had conjured it into reality. Or perhaps it had never been a vault room in the first place? Wherever it had gone, there was little time to ponder it as bestial growls converged around her.

"Azamir?" her familiar didn't answer. Another voice did.

"You thought you could just waltz in here and attack me?"

The growls swarmed from left to right and back again. The bank manager's guards were more than hired muscle. Helene's voice wavered in and outside Selena's skull, taunting and playing with her psyche. This witch was no novice.

"My incubi are going to tear you apart … unless you hand over that book and reveal who you are!"

The book. She had no sense of the room, or up, or down. The darkness pervaded everything. The only feeling she had was that of her own flesh, and that the book was no longer in her arms. She must have dropped it. The sigils on her palm and back. She had to act.

"Take her!" Helene ordered.

A long-fingered, clawed hand reached out from the gloom to clasp her wrist. Scalding hot, like a vice of molten steel. She cried out in agony and tried to pry herself free of the incubi's grip, only for the second demon to grab her other hand. The dark dispersed, and she found herself suspended in the air, the two ashen skin incubi, holding her aloft. They were lesser demons but still more than capable of rending her limb from limb. She looked anywhere but their scarlet maws only to discover the floor beneath squirmed with thousands of maggots.

Helene emerged from the edges of the shadows. Her business suit replaced by a tattered gown of ebony lace and silk. Her true face was gaunt and pale, cheekbones pushing against the skin. Grey hair draped over her shoulders, eyes holding all the colour and power, the irises gleaming like burning coals. She took Selena by the throat with a withered hand.

"In here, you're mine," Helene said. She noticed her niece was no longer in possession of the grimoire. "Where's the book? If you're hiding it I'll let my boys here have their way with you. Would you like that?" The incubi's chests heaved at the prospect, only for their master to quieten them with a raised finger. "So, last chance. Tell me what you've done with the book or you'll be defiled in every way imaginable."

Selena frantically scanned the floor for the grimoire. "I don't have it."

"Now, we both know that's not true." Helene glanced at her demons. "Boys."

The incubi twisted Selena's arms, and she screamed. The bones of her forearms creaked with the strain. She couldn't worry about the grimoire. She had to fight back by any means necessary.

"My boys won't be bothered if you're in pieces—they'll still fuck you if you're a bloody heap on the ground."

She spit in Helene's face, only for the witch to slide out a forked tongue to taste it. "So defiant. Maybe I'll have a taste of what's left when they're done with you."

Selena turned her left hand out to show the witch her tattoo. "Got to hell, you fucking bitch! *Defendere!*"

A blinding light erupted from her palm, so bright the shadows in the room shrieked in tune with her captors. The illumination was brief but long enough to temporarily blind all in the space except, of course, the light-bearer. The demons recoiled, releasing their hold on her. She dropped to the crawling floor. Helene staggered about, desperate to see anything but the burning white light in her eyes.

"Kill her!" she said. "Kill her!"

Hunched down, Selena focused on the sigil still pricking under the skin of her back. She concentrated on its shape: the sideways oval with a circle inside, like two sides of a wound, showing the path from one side to another. The summoning sigil. Once it formed in her mind she spoke:

"Porta ad inferos!"

A searing pain shot along Selena's back, sending her body in a wide-open arc. Her cry split the space above, the very skin of reality. Through the gaping laceration she beheld the fires of Abaddon. Ragged cliffs and stones all ablaze, reaching to a sulphurous sky. Blood rained down onto silhouettes of naked souls writhing and exclaiming in a river of offal and bone.

"What do you think you are you doing, you stupid girl?"

Selena had one hope. She pushed Helene back and thrust her hand into the portal. Searing heat crawled along her right hand and arm. Stifling a scream was pointless. Nothing could hold back the pain she felt. She opened her eyes and watched the flame licking and circling her hand. The hellfire was hers. Beyond the inferno, through the portal, a clutch of demons perched on a cliff realised what she was stealing and took flight in her direction. Selena had to close the portal fast.

Helene's vile hands cloyed at Selena's hair and pulled her head back, exposing her throat to a razor-sharp athame. She pulled her blazing hand back through the portal, which closed, and then slapped her hand into Helene's face. She unleashed its power with a single word:

"Immolare!"

The room erupted into a single sphere of destruction. Scarlet and gold incandescence swelled to consume the two incubuses. Selena dropped and covered her face yet still felt compelled to watch the creatures burn. She prayed Azamir was nowhere near the flames. Embers fell and sailed, catching on Helene's frock. She could do nothing to stop the fire's progress as it blackened cloth and flesh. The witch's screams were even greater than the violent rush of the firestorm.

The hellfire burned out as quickly as it was ignited. Nothing remained but a vault room full of ash.

Selena picked herself up and assessed the damage she'd inflicted. Where once shadows had made the room temporarily black, the fire had scorched it permanently. Against one wall stood the charcoaled corpses of the incubi, mouths agape in sheer terror and suffering. Yet, there was no third corpse. Had Helene escaped? Even if she had survived, the burns would leave her wishing she hadn't.

The moment Selena realised she was safe and alive, her arms seemed to wake up to the burns they'd suffered. She peeled back the scorched jacket sleeve and gasped at the injury, her arm red raw and bearing the marks of one who'd wielded unearthly flame. The sight made her want to retch, so she quickly covered it. She'd need a healing spell to recover and a way to safely use the hellfire again without losing her arm in the process. Then, a new fear pushed the pain aside.

"Oh, God—Azamir!?"

She trudged through the carpet of ash, scanning it for any sign of her friend.

"Azamir!"

Something stirred in one corner of the room. On instinct, Selena raised her left hand, activating the defensive sigil. The protective light revealed Azamir in his miniature spider form, so small and fragile but alive. He emerged from a darkened corner, his many legs wrapped tight around the grimoire.

Smiling, Selena scooped him and the book up into her arms. "Oh, Az, I thought I killed you!"

He thrust one of his legs at her. "You almost did!"

"How did you manage to hide the book?"

"I went small as soon as she cut the lights."

She smiled and shook her head at him. "Of course you did."

The spider scuttled up her arm. "Master, what was all this for? It didn't seem to go to plan."

Selena wiped soot from her face and stared at the seared vault doors. "No, not exactly, but I knew there would be a coven here. I'll admit I never expected my aunt to be running it, but I wanted to see what I might be up against. To see if they knew about me."

She ran her hand over the doors and a scarlet shimmer ran across its surface, a sign that something was hidden beneath. Energy shivered against her fingertips.

"Maybe this wasn't a complete failure, though."

Azamir perched on her shoulder. "Why do you say that?"

The shimmer spread across the space, peeling back like oil on water to reveal the true entrance. Selena realised the spell Helene had used to lock the door was anchored in blood magic. It could be opened by the Kolbe family's dark DNA.

The doors opened onto a large space, stacked high with shelves of ancient tomes, priceless paintings, amulets, and other cursed trinkets collected over many centuries. The combined power in the vault washed over Selena in a blazing wave.

"Master, this is incredible! With the fire and everything in this room you could destroy your mother. You could rule the coven!"

Selena swallowed hard. The prospect of being in control of everything was a significant temptation.

"No ... " she said after a moment. "I don't want all of this. I don't want to be corrupted ... like my mother. I only want to save Gemma."

Azamir turned his eyes to her. "But you could do it all, Master. Save Gemma. End your mother for good."

"But how much would I lose?" she asked him, and her familiar fell silent.

On one of the shelves, she saw an athame. Obsidian glass with a silver handle. Cautiously, she reached out to take it. The blade gleamed in her palm.

"That's all you're taking?" Azamir asked.

The dim wail of emergency sirens rolled in from outside and Selena secreted the blade into her coat pocket. With a wave of her hand, she closed the vault—and all its temptations—possibly forever.

"Come on, we need to get out of here."

The sound of sirens from approaching fire engines echoed through the streets as Selena and Azamir fled the scene in her pickup.

Her body ached with pain and exhilaration, adrenaline and the remnants of dark magic coursing through her veins. She sat in the passenger seat while Azamir drove, going back over the events—the power she'd gained and unleashed. There was no going back now.

She'd dealt the coven a significant blow, one that would ripple all the way back to her mother in the cabin in those horrible woods.

Oh, God I was so stupid for going to that coven! What will it mean for Gemma? Will Davina kill her in retaliation?

A pair of fire trucks hurtled past them, their lights painting Selena's face and burned hand an even brighter red. She looked at her hands, one emblazoned with a sign of power, the other wearing all the hallmark signs of having used an even greater force. Azamir's voice broke through the noise of the emergency vehicles.

"Are you feeling all right?"

"I don't know."

He kept his eyes on the road. "Your hand ... does it hurt?"

His very mention of her hand brought the pain rushing back, the sensation like the skin was still burning with hellfire. The forbidden fire was seared into her soul.

"Just keep driving ... " she said, "we have to get back to the hotel."

"Master, what you did ... it was incredible. You incinerated them. And now you have access to that vault."

Selena relived it in her mind, plucking the fire from Hell, the contorted souls, the demons locking their gazes onto her. They saw her. They knew who she was. They'd tell their Black Lord—Belphragon. She put her head out the window, trying to let the rush of air calm the fear in her heart.

"Az, stop. Just keep driving ... please."

She saw Azamir glance at her right hand. "Fuck, the power of that flame. I just can't believe you got it. What did it feel like?"

Selena recalled raising her hand to Helene's face, the feeling of the fire erupting from her fingertips. The fire trucks were long gone, but she could still hear the sirens. What would the firefighters say when they saw what she'd done?

What would her mother think?

What of Belphragon?

"Stop ... " she muttered.

Azamir frowned. "What did you say?"

The skin of her right hand screamed. She saw the veins beneath the surface had changed shape, twisted into arcane symbols.

She'd become the right hand of Hell.

"Stop the car."

"What? You want to stop?"

"Stop! I'm gonna be sick."

"Oh, shit!"

Azamir slammed on the brakes and brought the truck to a shuddering halt. Selena opened the door and dropped to the sidewalk. She retched like she was trying to force the unholy power out of her body, but it was trapped in her now, in her very soul. In that moment, helpless and afraid for her daughter, she imagined her mother had won.

Selena was a little girl back in those horrible woods all over again.

10
1995

Young Selena's bedroom was thick with shadows. Spent candles lay in pools in the corners, trapping the carcasses of insects like amber. Cold air leaked in through the gaps in the floor and walls, urging her to pull the blankets tighter around herself. The bucket beside her bed was rank with the evening's waste. She so desperately wanted to be rid of it, but that would mean venturing through the house where, no doubt, her mother waited.

The sound of birdsong drew the girl to the window, where soft morning light was waking the world. There was so much beauty outside, yet so much ugliness within the four walls of the place she was meant to feel at home. The cabin was hell on earth to Selena, a temple to horrors from which there seemed no escape.

She pulled back the covers and moved to the edge of the bed. The wooden floor was freezing, and she only thin socks riddled with holes to keep it at bay. They had nothing but the shirts on their backs for they gave everything to the Black Lord—Belphragon.

His name made her shiver. She'd glimpsed him once during a worship ritual. His tall, skeletal silhouette backlit by a wall of flame. The demon had called her by name, and she'd screamed, a mistake she'd later paid for. Selena rubbed the scars on the backs of her legs, the slaps of her mother's whip still stinging in her memory.

Selena despised them all: her father, her siblings, Belphragon. Most of all, she hated her mother. *One of these days, I'll kill her,* she thought. She imagined standing over her mother's corpse, peering down with satisfaction. Heart pounding, Selena pictured stabbing Davina over and over with a black athame, tearing open the old woman's abdomen, pulling out her entrails and raising them to her lips.

She swallowed such feelings down, forced the thoughts away. Her emotions had taken on a will of their own ever since that worship ritual, when the Black Lord had raised his barbed finger her way. Davina had seen it as a blessing that Selena had been chosen by Belphragon for a *special task*.

In the days following, Davina had doted on the girl. Even her father, usually indifferent, had expressed interest in his eldest daughter. Selena dreaded to think what was intended for her future.

It was yet another reason to escape. Selena pushed those thoughts down, too, lest the Black Lord was listening. The door handle creaked, and the girl gasped.

"Why is this door locked, child?"

Her mother's voice was harsher than the air in the room. Selena quickly padded to the door and unlocked it. Davina's lined face, dismayed, yet curious, appeared in the gap.

"Let me in girl," she said.

Selena pulled open the door and withdrew, letting her mother scan the interior.

"You didn't answer me. Why is this door locked?"

"A-Asha's been coming into my room at night … into my bed. I needed to sleep."

Davina grabbed her wrist and squeezed until she cried out in pain. Her rancid breath fell on her ear.

"You don't ever lock this door again, do you hear?" There was malice in Davina's yellowing eyes.

Selena nodded, mute with fear. Davina released her daughter's hand and collected the bucket from under her bed. The liquid sloshed around inside.

"This will make a fine offering to the Black Lord," she said. "He will welcome it, knowing that it comes from his chosen. Praise Him."

Davina glanced the girl's way, and Selena, now afraid not to speak, said, "Praise Him."

Her mother smiled her almost toothless smile. "Good girl. Now, you dress for the cold. You and your sister will do some chores before we perform a ritual. You understand?"

"Yes, Momma."

She watched her mother leave before dressing in silence. Tears streamed down her cheeks, but she stifled any sort of exclamation. She dared not make her sadness known, not to her family, nor the Black Lord.

As her mother always said, *"Tears are a sign of a weak soul, and weak souls are worthless."*

Selena, her sister, Asha, and brother, Cade, ventured into the woods to collect water and berries and to check on the rabbit traps before breakfast. To any outsiders, these would have looked like normal, everyday tasks for a family living at one with nature, but everything Selena's family did was in service to the Black Lord.

Their every word, every thought was meant to serve him. Selena walked through the woods with her siblings in silence, picking the berries and placing them into a wicker basket she carried. Despite her dark thoughts, she couldn't help but admire the shards of morning shining between the trees or the scent of pine in the air. Asha, however, was less interested in their surroundings and came to Selena's side and dropped some berries into the basket and a whisper in her ear.

"Is it true, sister?" Asha said, her pale blue eyes widening with curiosity. "Is what true?"

She leaned in closer. "That you're going to be given to the Black Lord?"

Selena glanced at her brother, busy checking for rabbits in a trap, to make sure he wasn't in earshot. "What do you mean?"

"Well, I heard father tell mother that you've been chosen, that you're going to become the Black Lord's servant."

"Whore more like," their brother Cade volunteered as he lifted a rabbit from its cage. The animal writhed in his hands until he snapped its neck with a violent twist.

Selena grimaced at Cade's act and his words. "You're wrong," she told him.

He fastened the rabbit's legs with some twine and slung it over his shoulder. "You're kidding yourself if you think you know what *servant* means, Selena."

Asha whispered again. "I heard mother say that your blood has come. What does that mean?"

Selena cringed, almost dropping the basket. "Asha!"

"It means Selena's going to be the Black Lord's sex slave," Cade told his younger sister.

Asha frowned. "Sex?"

Their brother strode past them, a vile grin on his handsome face. "You know the sounds you hear at night coming from mother and father's room?"

"Stop it, Cade!" Selena warned. "You don't know anything."

He laughed and walked in the direction of the cabin. "I obviously know a lot more than you."

Cade's mockery followed Selena all the way back to the cabin. Was what her brother said true, or was he just tormenting her like he always did? The worship of the Black Lord had intensified over the past few weeks; animal sacrifices, storm-calling, even summoning of spirits, but were her parents truly planning on letting Belphragon take their eldest daughter as his own?

When they arrived back home, their father was waiting. He stood at the foot of the stairs, his gaze locked on his children. Lars was old, but strong, his bald pate only emphasizing his imposing stature. Strangely, he was dressed in his ceremonial tunic and clutched his ceremonial machete. His expression was one of impatience, which to Selena and her siblings was a terrifying notion. Where their mother was cold, Lars was calculating.

"Put the water and food inside and then come to the gathering tree," he told them.

The gathering tree was an old, sprawling oak behind the cabin, near the entrance to the woods. None knew exactly how old the tree was, but mother often spoke of how she believed its seed had been planted by their forbearers. Its branches were grey and cracked, the leaves never green. The tree appeared dead, but something very elemental kept it alive.

Selena had once climbed it and swung from it on a rope tire, but now, being much older, she understood just how frightening the tree was. When she found her father standing beneath it, that fear was amplified a hundred-fold. Mother stood by his side, ever-present and always willing.

"Come and sit," Lars said.

Asha sat close to her sister, while Cade sat cross-legged on his own, eagerly awaiting his father's next command.

"Our worship ... " Lars began, "our reverence ... has left much to be desired."

He struck the machete into a wooden stump and let it rest there. Selena was well aware of her father's passion for worship, his devotion, but she'd never seen him so ... detached. Sweat already stained his tunic.

"You children, I fear, are starting to lose faith."

Cade stood, appalled. "No, father, we share your devotion. We swear!"

Lars placated him. "I blame myself. Perhaps I haven't instructed you enough. The Black Lord knows your mother and I have tried, but I feel like I have failed all of you."

Now, Asha rose to object. "No, father, please. You are the most devoted of teachers. A true servant of the Black Lord—and a wonderful father."

Their mother stood in the shade of the tree, ever so calm. Like she was waiting for something to happen.

"There is a way to remedy my mistakes," their father said, "to beg his forgiveness." He reached down and pull the machete from the stump. "At the very least, to prove that I am indeed truly devoted."

Asha and Cade shared worried looks, but Selena kept her eyes locked on Davina. The old crone stepped forward and embraced her husband and kissed him. It was the first time Selena had ever seen them express their love in such a gentle way. Then, Lars handed Davina the blade and knelt before her by the stump.

"Father, no!" Cade was in a panic, but he dared not move. He knew a ritual was taking place.

Asha sobbed, but Selena was frozen as her father placed his arm on top of the stump.

"You're going to have to help your mother more with the chores," Lars said. "See that you do."

Davina raised the machete over her head. Asha and Cade's gasping breaths filled the air.

"Praise Him," Davina said.

Lars closed his eyes. "Praise Him."

Then, the blade came down.

11
2024

Detective Corrinne Walsh stepped under the crime scene tape into the National Alliance Trust Bank and immediately tasted ash in the back of her throat.

The entire interior of the bank was tainted with the acrid smell of smoke, and likely would be for many months to come, but it compared little to the underlying stench of death. The fire department had long gone after extinguishing the fire in the vault room, but what remained, only the police would be able to determine.

Fire was usually the arson squad's area of jurisdiction but not when the fire left behind human corpses. The incident at the bank looked like homicide. As she made her way through, Walsh passed a pair of crime scene officers scraping soot off a wall and stepped around water dripping from the ceiling. She ventured down an internal staircase to the vault room, the level of scorching increasing by degrees as she descended, darker and darker, the walls becoming almost black with each step.

The smell intensified along with the blackness, a thick, sickly sweet tang of burned flesh and fat that overpowered all others. It made her eyes water. She cleared her throat and popped a fresh mint, hoping to taste anything other than the remnants of the dead. It helped somewhat, but nothing prepared her for the sight of the vault room.

The space was wall-to-ceiling black. Water dripped and pooled on every surface. Some of the tiles had cracked and fallen in the intense heat, the pieces floating in the puddles. The concentration of forensic techs was greatest here, men and women dressed in bright white protective jumpsuits, desperately collecting any fragments they could. Fire was the bane of their existence because it was all-consuming, destroying evidence with every lick of flame. Even the human body.

One of the officers was crouched in a corner, the word CORONER in large black lettering across the back of his jumpsuit. This was the person Walsh needed to see to make sense of things. She stepped toward him, carefully placing her feet where there was little to no debris. When she was just a few feet from him, she beheld the bodies he examined.

The pair of corpses almost blended in with the wall. Caught in a violent rigor, their hands twisted up close to their bodies, the skin black on the surface, yet cracked and split, revealing blood-red viscera beneath. Their faces were more skeletal, the thin layers of flesh peeled back by the heat around their mouths in a rictus grin. The blackened sockets gazed widely at nothing. Walsh sucked her mint and turned away from the sight, internally filing it in the part of her mind she planned to purge later.

"Hey, Jonesy, what you got for me?" she asked the man at her feet.

The coroner jumped, startled. "Jesus, Walsh! You scared the crap outta me!"

Walsh chuckled. "*I* scared *you*. But these guys don't?" She gestured to the charred bodies.

He pulled down his mask to reveal a bearded smile. "Sorry, was just deep in thought."

"I can see that. So, any of those thoughts about what the hell happened in here?"

Jones stood and took in the room. "Well, that's the thing. We haven't exactly worked out how the fire started yet."

"Really?"

"No, and we can't even pinpoint where it started."

The detective studied the corners of the room and craned her neck to take in the ceiling. The scorch marks seemed to be all the same level of intensity, a uniform level of burning that touched every inch of the space.

"Any indication of an accelerant or explosive residue?"

"Not upon first glance, but we'll have to put some samples through the spectrometer for a closer look."

Walsh popped another mint and nodded at the bodies. "What about them?"

"Well, they're male, but the fire burned away their clothing, and there's no trace of anything that could identify them, like IDs or wallets. The fire must have been extremely hot. We'll just have to get them to the morgue and take X-rays of their teeth and hope they pop up in any dental records."

She slipped her hands into her coat. "Hmm, you're not giving me much to go on here, Jonesy."

"Hey, I'm not a miracle worker. All I can do is open 'em up and see what's what."

Her eyes focused on the bodies' skeletal hands. "Could they have started the fire?"

"Possibly. But this fire … I dunno. Like I said, there's no sign of any accelerant, but the sheer intensity of it … how it burned everything."

Walsh headed back to the stairs. "Well, it can't have just started by itself."

"No, it can't." He pulled his mask back on. "Hey, it's good to see you back."

"Yeah, me, too."

"How's the shoulder?"

"Not too bad. Thanks, Jonesy. Now you get to the bottom of this, you hear? And let me know when you're about to do the autopsy. I want to sit in on it."

"Will do, sicko."

She smiled. "You know it. I live for this shit."

Walsh went back upstairs and made a beeline for the security room. Inside, two officers combed through CCTV footage on a laptop. As she entered the room, a twinge of pain ran through her shoulder, the gunshot wound making itself known. She braced herself against the doorframe, embarrassed when she noticed the pair observing her distress.

"You okay, Detective?" the one with the laptop—Ramirez—asked.

"I'm fine," she replied, shrugging it off and moving to his side. "What have you got for me?"

Ramirez made himself comfortable in the chair and turned his laptop so she could see it. The vision on the screen was distorted, a mishmash of grainy pixels and bars of digital noise.

"Not a hell of a lot, I'm afraid. The fire set off the overhead sprinklers in here and, in turn, the electrics, which affected the hard drives where the footage is stored."

"They didn't have it backed up to the cloud?"

"We're looking into that."

Walsh tsked. She couldn't believe her luck on the first day back on the job. "So, there's nothing?"

"I didn't say that. There's some footage I was able to extract, but it's only a few minutes before we think the fire started based on when the alarm was tripped. Here, take a look."

The blue-grey vision on the screen showed five people standing in the vault room. Three men and two women. The faces weren't close enough for distinct facial features, but Walsh could tell there was tension between the parties.

"Do we know who any of them are?"

He pointed to the woman in the pantsuit. "We think this is the bank manager, a Ms. Helene Kolbe. No idea about the others. We'll have to take the footage back to the lab and run it through facial recognition."

"And this bank manager's nowhere to be seen?"

"Correct."

Her eyes narrowed on the people in the footage. The other woman had her back to the camera and was only partially in profile.

"Can you play it for me?"

The vision began and showed the two women talking. The supposed bank manager was very animated, her hands moving about in an odd sweeping motion.

"What's with all the gesticulating?" Walsh asked.

Then, the screen went black. The detective looked at Ramirez.

"That's just before the fire we think," he said.

Walsh frowned. "It's almost as if the CCTV was switched off."

"Or the power was lost when the fire started? We'll know more when we examine the footage more closely."

She patted him on the back. "Thanks, Ramirez. Let me know if you find anything."

Corrinne sat in her car outside the bank, virtually immobilized by the pain in her shoulder. From the rearview mirror a woman whose life had been irrevocably altered by two bullets looked back at her. Someone who'd aged ten years in just six months. She massaged her shoulder, trying to ease out the tightness in the skin. The rough edges of the scar tissue came through her blouse, making the memory of what created it even keener. Almost as if the slug remained inside her, embedded in the meat and bone.

The memory played out in her subconscious, her weapon raised on the killer, his pointing back with equal tenacity. The muzzle flashes turning everything black. The coppery taste of blood mingled with the smell of gun smoke, like wet sawdust. Then, the pain, in varying degrees ever since. She'd taken down a killer but almost lost her life in the process. He was gone, but he'd left an indelible mark on her—body and soul.

Walsh opened the glove compartment and retrieved a bottle of Vicodin and dry swallowed two pills. She took deep breaths, praying the pain— and the visions—would subside. Making the pain go away would get him out of her head, at least for a while.

She thought of the victims, splayed out in pools of blood, put on display by a madman. They'd endured so much more pain than her, but at least it came to an end. The killer, too. That's what hurt her the most, that he'd died when she'd lived, and that she never got to find out why he butchered them at all.

Her cell rang and cut short her melancholy. The screen showed it was her lieutenant—Brady. She put it on speaker and concentrated on not letting her pain and fear overwhelm her.

"What you got for me, Walsh?" Brady's gruff tones echoed inside the car.

"Two bodies, male and what looks like a transaction gone wrong— maybe."

"What, a robbery?"

Walsh rubbed her shoulder. Thankfully, the pills had started to numb the wound.

"Hard to tell. The manager's missing so it could be a hostage situation or just a straight-up killing. There're two potential suspects—a man and a woman we've got on some dodgy CCTV footage."

She heard Brady slurp his coffee. "So, what's your next move?"

"There're some cameras on the street outside the bank. We're gonna scan those for the suspects. Maybe we'll get a hit on their faces or a vehicle. I'll put out a BOLO for them and the manager."

"Sounds like a plan." He paused, and Walsh braced herself for his next question. "How are you doing … with the pain and it being your first day—"

"I'm fine, Lieutenant. This case is a good distraction."

"Good. Good."

"Is that all, sir?"

Rustling papers sounded through the speakers. "Uh, almost. OPR came back to me on your shooting. They deemed it a clean shoot. You're likely going to be put forward for a commendation."

A montage of violence surfaced behind Walsh's eyes: bloody viscera, the empty stares of beautiful eyes, and a vile, shit-eating sneer in the dark. It reached its crescendo with the booming sound of two guns being fired.

"Walsh?" Brady's voice pulled her back to reality. "Did you hear what I said? Balkovich isn't killing anymore because of you."

"Don't say his name." Walsh didn't even realise she was crying.

"Sorry."

She glanced at her reflection. "Yeah."

"You can take comfort in the fact he can't hurt anyone anymore. That you brought him to an end."

"Lieutenant?"

"Yeah?"

"Why do you think he did it?"

"Because he was a fucking psycho, that's why."

She wiped away the tears. "You never wondered if there was more to it than that?"

Brady sighed. "No, and I don't think you need to either. You took him out and that's it."

Walsh started the car. "Thanks. Listen, I gotta go."

"Okay. You sure you're all right?"

"I'm fine."

12

Davina hobbled down the stairs to the cabin's basement. Each step was a knife in her legs, so she whispered an incantation, and the pain abated—at least for a while. Age had made her body weary, the *struggle* getting harder and harder with each passing year.

Her time—and her family's time—was running out.

Despite her frailty, she was still strong in mind and spirit, empowered by her devotion to the Black Lord. Yet, Belphragon was becoming impatient. He'd called in his debt, and it would have to be paid in full, one way or another. She reached the bottom of the stairs and waved her hand. Dozens of candles erupted into life. The light revealed an earthen floor and a shrine against one wall—a crudely carved wooden statue of a horned demon—the Black Lord himself. Beneath it, a large, dull, circular silver platter and a long, black athame of obsidian glass.

In one dank corner something stirred, a rustling or dragging through the dirt toward her. Then, a voice.

"Davina, is that you?"

The severed head of her husband, Lars, crept out of the shadows, the tendons and veins of his neck reaching out like legs, scraping and pulling him closer.

"Yes. I've come to talk," she said, moving to the shrine.

Lars crawled to her and wrapped a spindly vessel around her ankle. "It's been too long ... " His voice, once smooth and commanding, was as dry as the dirt he slept in.

"I have the girl, Lars," Davina told him.

"Selena? She's come home?"

"No, her child, Gemma."

Lars slipped between her feet. "I have a grandchild? I must see her."

Davina kicked Lars' head back, and her husband hissed in pain. "We need to talk about what we're gonna do, Lars! Selena still defies me after all this time. Even her gifts linger, along with her hatred of me."

Lars slid back to her. "Of *us*. She hates all of us, for lying to her."

"She knew what her purpose was!"

"She knew she was a servant, not that she was intended to be the Black Lord's bride."

Belphragon's statue seemed to mock Davina. The candlelight dimmed as if in response to the old crone's continued failures.

"Selena was always a selfish girl, even before the Black Lord singled her out. She's not made the same sacrifices as you, or me, or Cade."

Lars reached her leg and wrapped his viscera around it again. "Our sacrifices were not in vain. They were to appease the Black Lord. Offerings of devotion—"

"They were just to buy us time! And look what we have to show for it!"

She picked him up off the floor and held him to face her. His eyes had turned milky white after so many years in the dark. Skin so pallid. Yet, his caress was still so gentle.

"You've given so much, Lars," she said. "I don't know how much more we can give."

"If we don't fulfil the Black Lord's pact, he'll take everything."

"We need to force Selena to come home. Or bring her home ourselves."

Lars smiled toothlessly. "Perhaps we could offer this Gemma to the Black Lord instead?"

Davina grinned back. "The threat alone could be just what we need to get Selena back."

Lars coiled his tendrils through Davina's hair, pulling her closer. "You always were the wisest of us," he said.

They kissed, the pact they made to each other and the darkness unwavering, even in the face of disfigurement and damnation.

A spark of light fractured the gloom of the basement, and Davina and Lars turned to it, startled. The light took on form—the shape of something human. Lars slid back to the dirt and, in a panic, retreated for the nearest shadow. Davina stood her ground, prepared for anything. A body fell from the light at her feet—a woman, clad in scorched black clothes, still smouldering. A gasp issued from its lips:

"Sister ... "

Davina recognized the woman despite her extensive burns. "Helene!"

She turned her younger sister over. Half of Helene's body was burned, reddened flesh weeping and bleeding. She reached up with a blackened hand.

"Help ... me ... "

"Who did this to you?"

Helene coughed, her scalded throat barely managing the sound. "S-Selena ... and her familiar ... "

Davina cradled Helene, gently picking away threads of singed hair from her sister's raw face. "Selena?"

Helene tried to shake her head. "She ... said her name ... was ... Stephanie ... but I knew that ... was a lie ... "

Lars scurried out from his hiding place. "Are you sure it was Selena? What did she look like?" he asked.

"The same dark hair ... piercing ... eyes ... "

Davina probed her memory for the name Gemma had said. "So, she did hide her name from us?"

Her sister nodded and gasped, desperate for any lasting breaths.

"Selena!" Davina faced her husband's head. "Our long-lost daughter!"

Helene clutched at Davina's dress. "She ... she brought forth ... hellfire."

Lars recoiled. "What?"

The old woman shook her sister. "Hellfire?"

"It ... almost ... killed me."

Lars' veins cloyed at Davina's skirt. "She hasn't forgotten the ways at

220

all! If she's strong enough to summon hellfire—"

Davina's leathery face twisted into a scowl. "It looks like taking her child might have rekindled Selena's dark gift." She pulled Helene closer. "Did you see any sigils upon her, sister? Do you know if she had a book?"

Helene was slumped in her sister's arms, dead. The burns had claimed her. Davina sighed and bent to kiss her forehead.

"Belphragon tolle hanc animam in explexum tuum."

Belphragon, take this soul into your embrace.

Lars placed a tendril on Helene. *"Laudate Eum."*

Praise Him.

Davina laid Helene softly onto the earth, then stood, her hands squeezed tight into fists.

"What are we to do, my wife?" Lars asked.

"If the bitch wants a fight, then let's give her one."

The woman, Asha, looked so much like her mother, Gemma thought that they could have passed for twins if it weren't for her pale countenance.

Gemma pulled gently on her restraints as Asha spoon-fed her hot broth. The girl stared into Asha's eyes, careful to remain compliant and unsuspicious. If she was to escape, she had to play the perfect hostage. These people—her apparent relatives—were unstable, and there was no telling what they would do to her if she wasn't a "good girl." Abruptly, Asha put the spoon down.

"Stop looking at me," she said.

Gemma averted her gaze. "Sorry."

"I know what you're doing." Asha placed the bowl down and folded her hands in her lap.

"What am I doing?"

"You need to stop thinking about it."

"About what?"

"Escaping."

She tried to relax, but Asha's eyes seemingly searched Gemma's mind. Davina had displayed a similar ability earlier. Was it a part of their magic?

"I'm not trying to escape—"

"Good. Because if you try, my mother will kill you. Do you understand?"

Asha took the bowl to the sink. Behind her, the two undead hounds lay on the floor, keeping guard. Every time Gemma looked at them, she wanted to be sick, the very sight of them repulsive. She turned to the front door, preferring the world outside.

"You're doing it again," Asha said.

"I'm not … Just leave me alone."

Asha chuckled and came back to sit before the girl. "You're just like her."

"Who?"

"Selena. You're defiant like she was. Righteous."

"So, what if I am?"

Asha smiled, revealing yellowed teeth. "It's not going to help you."

"I really don't care what you think, so you might as well just stop talking."

Her aunt grabbed her by the hair and yanked. "You little slut. You think you're so much better than us? You think your mommy's gonna save you? She's not. She's going to die, and then we'll do whatever we like with you. Maybe we'll make you our slave, or maybe we'll just serve your insides up to the Black Lord. How would you like that, hmm?"

Gemma laughed but, on the inside, she feared her aunt's every word. Yet, she had to hold onto the defiance. "Who sounds like their mother now?"

Her words must have stung because her aunt slapped her in retaliation. "That's enough!"

Asha stood and retreated as the old crone entered the room. Cade was in tow, dragging his misshapen form across the floorboards. When Gemma looked at Davina's face she saw unbridled rage.

222

"You'll not lay a hand on the girl again, Asha, you hear?" Davina turned her hand, and Asha clutched at her belly, falling to the ground in pain. Her screams quieted the birds. Moments later, Davina released her daughter from the grip of agony, but it left her dazed and panting. Then, the crone's gaze turned Gemma's way. "Yer momma's putting up a fight, it seems."

The girl perked up, straightening in her chair. Davina came to stand before her.

"She burned my sister to death, murdered two of her incubuses, set a whole building on fire."

Gemma was emboldened, imagining her mother setting fire to her enemies. All to save her daughter. Defiance and self-righteousness manifesting as power.

"Yer momma might think that she's gonna win this war—"

"She will!"

"She's already lost, girlie." Davina bent and licked her cracked lips. "The moment she used her dark gift she gave up her soul."

Gemma's heart pounded. "What?"

"Selena's damned herself. She used hellfire for you, girlie. Went to Hell itself to steal it, and do you know what that means? The Black Lord knows what she did, and he'll be coming for her."

"No!"

Davina smoothed Gemma's hair with a gnarled hand. "But don't you worry, child. I'm gonna send her big brother Cade to bring her home, where the Black Lord will be waitin'."

"No, please!"

Cade loomed, his body suddenly swelling, expanding in height and girth. More monstrous. Davina's cackle soared along with him.

"We'll all be one big happy family real soon!"

13

Selena stared at her hand, red with fierce burns of hellfire. Yet, there was still no pain. She was numb to it, accepting of the fact it meant she was now gaining more power.

She sat on the floor in the hotel bathroom, drying off from the shower, indifferent to the chill of the water beading on her skin. All she could think about was the fire in the bank, the ochre and crimson flames consuming everything in almost an instant.

Her wedding band was stark against the rawness of the burns, and beneath the burned flesh, the sigils of power, etched there by the forces of Hell. Dozens and dozens of marks, brands left by the fire. Constant reminders of what she'd unleashed. Of what Hell had granted her.

The limb erupted into flame as if in response to her thoughts. At first, she flinched in panic, scrambled to her feet. The flames licked along her slender fingers, and she watched them dance, the fear slowly becoming fascination. There was no pain from the hellfire, as if the initial burning had left her immune. Slowly, she closed her hand into a fist, and the flames were extinguished.

It was hers to control, by will alone. A wry smile passed her lips. Davina had never dreamed of wielding such a force. But Selena knew the extent of her mother's powers. The hag could still call upon formidable forces of darkness. Even the Black Lord himself. No doubt she would do just that if threatened. Which begged the question: Would the hellfire be enough to destroy her? To get Gemma back?

She traced the sigils on her left palm with a finger, turned to the mirror so she could see the one on her back. She needed more. More protection, more strength. More will.

Her eyes caught the glint of the light on the pieces of shattered mirror from when her mother tried to break through her defences. She picked up one of the large shards and ran her thumb along its edge. A thin line of blood followed. For the first time in a long time, her mother's lessons came flooding back, the old woman's words escaping her own lips:

"Devotionis significat sacrificium."
Devotion means sacrifice.

Selena locked the door. She couldn't have Azamir coming in. Not this time. No matter what. She let the towel drop to the floor and took in her naked flesh. Milky white, stretch marks along her belly from when she carried Gemma. She considered those marks alongside the sigils and burns. She'd bore marks for her daughter before, and she'd do it again.

The broken glass kissed her breast. Selena let the blood flow, calling on all the powers of Hell as she did. She'd show her mother the true meaning of devotion. She'd sacrifice everything, just like Davina did all those years ago.

1996

The snows came early that year, along with a deep, dark cold their hearth could barely keep at bay.

Selena and her siblings had been at their mother's mercy. Days of chores and foraging, followed by nights of foul benediction. Davina wailed all hours, stalking the house unclothed and offering blood, spit, and excreta to the Black Lord. She and the others had no choice but to make offerings of their own and, on one freezing fall evening, their mother's demands reached the darkest depths.

Davina gathered her children before the hearth, tossing bone and blood into the cauldron, the aromas pungent against the earthy scents of sweat and fear. Selena tried to mask her terror and thoughts of leaving it all behind, but there was no escaping the sacrifices that needed to be made in his name.

She looked to her brother Cade, who buckled under the weight of the cabin's shadows, but this only served to draw his mother's ire. The old crone grabbed him by the hair and dragged him toward the hearth.

"Do you know how much your father has given? Do you?"

Davina held Cade's face near the fire, close enough for the heat to sear his cheek. His screams echoed throughout the cabin, yet still their mother's voice rose above.

"What are you going to sacrifice, boy? What pound of flesh will you give to him?"

She brandished a small thin-bladed knife and pressed it to Cade's throat. Selena yelled at her mother to stop while Asha sobbed in a darkened corner.

"P'raps it's time for you to prove your devotion, boy?" She pried him away from the hearth, left him wincing on the floor. "Prove your worth!" She tossed the knife, let it clatter on the floor next to her son. Cade immediately grabbed it and stood to face her.

"What, are you going to kill me, boy?"

"I fucking hate you, you fucking bitch."

Cade lunged at his mother, but she side-stepped him and took hold of his wrist, twisting it with a sickening *snap* of bone. Her dark gift—her devotion—had kept her strong. She brought Cade to his knees and pulled him to the cauldron, its contents steaming and overflowing onto the floor.

"You hate me, yes, but do you love him? Do you have the strength to love him?"

Selena rose and moved toward them in a bid to stop the madness. "Mother, please stop! He didn't mean it!"

"You'll stay there if you know what's good for you, girl!"

Davina bent Cade's right arm behind his back with one hand and reached for the ladle with the other. "You need to be cleansed boy. You and yer sisters. You all need to drink his elixir!"

She raised the ladle to Cade's lips, pouring the boiling liquid down his throat. The boy writhed, gagging and spluttering against it, but the essence was already inside him, changing him. Cade released a harrowing moan and collapsed, his body contorted in horrible pain.

Before Selena's eyes, her brother's limbs swelled, the muscles ballooning, veins bulging as if they would burst. Even his face, once handsome, was left a bulbous mask of agony. He reached for his sister with a gargantuan hand.

226

"Help ... meee ... "

His eyes were the only thing in his body left unchanged.

"Seleeennaaaa!"

She ran for the door, out into the wretched cold, Davina's high-pitched laughter at her back. The snow rose almost ankle deep, but she didn't care. She couldn't save Cade, or Asha, or even her father. Only herself.

Tree branches, dusted with snow, lashed her arms, sprayed her face, and turned her nightgown damp. Her panicked breaths bloomed in the air, but she couldn't stop, wouldn't stop, not even as her mother's voice resounded even closer.

"You get back here, girl!"

The very sound of the witch-mother's voice urged Selena on. She'd never run so fast in her life. The tree branches became gnarled hands, grabbing at her hair, her clothes. She slapped them aside and kept running until she came to a clearing, a snow-covered swath of land that spread out toward the mountains. Cragged black shadows against a violet sky, scattered with stars.

It was in the centre of this field that Selena beheld a small, illuminated dome—a tent. She ran to it as if it were a beacon that would set her free. It didn't seem real until she touched it.

"Hello? Please, help me!"

Two silhouettes moved within the tent, one of which quickly unzipped the opening. A man and a woman peered out, confused and terrified.

"Oh, my God, it's a girl!" the woman said.

Selena was so grateful to see the woman, to see her concern.

The man, large and bearded, stepped out and took Selena's hands.

"Jesus, she's freezing. Casey, grab a blanket." He looked into Selena's eyes. "Are you all right?"

Oh, Selena was so grateful to see anyone other than her family.

"Please ... " she said. "My mother, she—"

"Your mother?" the woman named Casey said. "Is something wrong with your mother?"

A voice came from above them.

"Pay no heed to the girl."

Selena screamed, as did the woman named Casey, at the sight of Davina hovering twenty feet above the tent. The moon painted her naked form but couldn't penetrate the dark malevolence in her eyes.

"Yer trespassing here on this land," she told the strangers. "You've committed a grave sin in the eyes of the Black Lord."

Selena gasped as her brother, gigantic and filled with rage, charged at the people who would have set her free.

"And for that ... " Davina said, "you will be punished."

The strangers' hands were bound with barbed wire and their clothes torn away, but Davina didn't cover their mouths because Selena knew she wanted to hear them scream.

Cade, his body and mind reduced to monstrous instinct, had beaten the man into submission, and the woman had complied out of sheer terror. At his mother's instruction, Cade had dragged the captives back to the cabin, down to the decrepit basement. Selena had little choice but to follow.

The man pleaded for Davina to let them go, but they'd been damned the moment they'd camped on their land, the moment they'd touched Selena's hands. Davina led Selena down. Asha, too. They would be witness to the offering for it would also serve as a warning to the family that there would be no escape.

Not ever.

Cade placed the man and woman before the altar and its demonic statue of their Lord. He shuffled to his place at the foot of the stairs, a sentry guarding a holy place. Davina pushed Selena into the dirt.

"This is yer doing, girl. You brought these two into our home. Don't you forget."

The bearded man looked up at the old woman, blood pooling in his left eye. "Please ... we're sorry ... just let us go ... "

The matriarch backhanded him across the jaw, and he spat blood. "You shut yer mouth. This is a sacred place!"

"Please ... don't hurt us!" the woman begged.

Davina moved like a striking snake to grab the athame from the altar, slicing it across the woman's cheek in one fluid movement. Her shriek of pain roiled inside the basement.

"You do not speak, whore!"

The man tried to stand, to attack Davina, but again, she was too fast with the blade. In one swift swipe of her arm, she opened his throat, the torrent of blood turning the floor to mud. The woman's screams were relentless howls of grief and horror. Selena tried to cover her ears, but the sound shook her very bones. She wanted the noise to stop, for everything to stop.

"Kill her, then, girl, and it will!"

Selena opened her eyes. There stood Davina, offering the blade.

"Kill the whore!"

The woman's cries rose higher and higher, hysterical, feverish. There was a moment where her eyes met Selena's and, in that moment, they begged Selena to fulfil her mother's command.

Selena turned to the old witch. "No."

Davina sneered, her disappointment becoming anger, then rage. She moved to the woman and plunged the knife into her right eye. She dropped dead, her blood joining her lover's. The old crone retrieved the silver platter and collected some of their blood onto it, letting the liquid drip from the tip of the athame to pool.

"*Hunc sanguinem domion offerimus nigro,*" Davina intoned.

Asha stepped forward. "We offer this blood to the Black Lord."

The statue moved, turning its head toward the sacrificed couple. Davina presented it with the platter.

"*Hoc donum accipere.*"

"Accept this gift," Asha whispered.

The pooled blood shrunk, consumed by an invisible tongue.

"Defendat nos!"

Asha raised her hands in reverence. "Protect us!"

"Defendat nos!"

"Protect us!"

"Laudate Eum!"

"Praise Him!"

All Selena could offer were tears, tears for the souls she'd damned for all eternity, and when the statue turned to look her way, the girl knew he would gladly accept her tears, too.

14
2024

The heady scent of formaldehyde followed Walsh like a ghost all the way down to the morgue. It had been many months since she'd had a reason to visit its sanitized and polished halls, but the strangeness of her first case since she came back called to her. Through the viewing windows of the main doors, she saw the coroner, Jones, preparing his tray of dissecting tools.

When he noticed her, he invited her in with a gloved hand. The chemical fragrances were even stronger when she stepped inside, but it did little to mask the aromas emanating from the pair of corpses laid out on the slab. The two male bank victims, charred almost beyond recognition.

"Good morning, Detective. Nice of you to join us," Jones said.

Walsh sniffed. "Yeah, I really wouldn't dream of being anywhere else."

Smirking, Jones gripped a scalpel. "You ready for me to proceed?"

"Knock yourself out."

The coroner started the Y-incision on the first body, the blackened torso skin splitting to reveal pinkish meat beneath. Walsh chose to examine the gleaming steel cabinets and the evidence jars within instead.

"No one available to assist you today, Jonesy?"

"Hannah's off sick so it's just me but, thankfully, there wasn't an influx of new bodies overnight, which is a first."

"That *is* a first."

Jones peeled back the flesh to expose the rib cage. He retrieved the bone shears and snipped the bones down each side, the harsh clicks of the shears ringing in Walsh's ears.

"Hmm, as expected, the lungs show signs of smoke inhalation."

"So, they were alive during the fire? No explosion killed them?"

He leaned closer to peer into the chest cavity. "I see some external damage to the bodies but not enough to prove fatal on its own. I'll crack open the skull. It should show evidence of extreme heat."

Walsh tried to think about something else as he worked, slicing through the scalp and peeling the face down to expose the skull. The violent whir of the bone saw set the detective's teeth on edge and sent a twinge through her shoulder wound.

"I heard you were cleared in the shooting?" Jones said, not taking his eyes off his grisly task.

"Uh, yeah."

"Must be a relief."

"Yeah, it is."

He carefully removed the brain from its resting place. "You don't really sound relieved."

"Well, I guess I never wanted to be put in that position in the first place."

"Understandable, but you were just doing your job." He turned the brain over in his hands.

"Is that all I was doing?"

He glanced up at her. "I meant no offence, and by no means was I trying to trivialize what happened."

"I-I know. I just wished it didn't turn out the way it did."

"I'm sure those poor girls wished things had turned out differently for them, too. What you did was give them justice. Closure."

She ran a hand through her sandy hair. "Look, I appreciate what you're trying to do, but can we just get back to the matter at hand? Do you have a cause of death or not?"

He placed the brain on a scale and took down a measurement. "Okay. Well, I'd say they both succumbed to the smoke before the fire did the rest."

"So, we can rule out an explosion?"

"Well, like I said at the scene, forensics are scanning for trace evidence, chemicals, and the like—"

The dissected corpse sat upright, its heart and lungs spilling out onto the floor. Before Jones or Walsh could react, the body reached for the coroner and clamped its jaws around his throat.

"Jesus Christ!" Walsh fumbled for her weapon, overwhelmed by the sight of a dead man—eviscerated—attacking her friend.

Jones' eyes were wide with terror as the corpse dragged him to the floor and feasted on his neck. Walsh pulled out her pistol with shaking hands, her mind racing in confusion, fear, and the memories of six months past. She aimed the gun at the hollow skull of the corpse as it leaned over Jones, who's lights were going out.

She squeezed the trigger, emptying the magazine into the thing eating her colleague. Each slug entered its back, nine bloodless holes. At first, Walsh didn't think the thing even registered the shots until it turned away from Jones to fix its blank gaze on her.

Its eyes locked onto her soul, a lifeless stare of recognition, not unlike the eyes of the man she'd shot dead six months ago. The very concept distracted Walsh just long enough for the thing to stand, push her down, and flee the mortuary room.

A dead man walking.

The last thing Walsh glimpsed before the darkness of unconsciousness claimed her was Jones struggling for his final breath through the hole in his neck, his voice stolen by a torrent of blood.

✶

When she came to on the floor of the morgue, Walsh discovered two paramedics leaning over her. She took a deep breath, that became a scream. Flashes of the creature tearing Jones apart brought it all back—the panic, the disbelief, the terror. It wasn't until she saw the familiar face of Lieutenant Brady that she felt safe.

"Walsh, it's me! It's me!"

She sat up and reached for him, the confusion in his lined face matching her own.

"Jones!" she said. "Jones … he—"

"I know … I know. What the hell happened, Walsh?"

The creature rose in her memory, turning to face her, flesh dangling from its lips.

"I-I don't know how to explain it! Oh, God!"

Brady gestured to the paramedics. "Guys, can we get a bit of space here?"

They backed away. Behind them, scores of detectives and uniformed officers milled about in equal disbelief. They were all looking to Walsh to make some sense of the chaotic scene. Brady rubbed his moustache, his look of concern almost the same as the one he'd displayed to her when she'd shot the killer, Balkovich.

"Oh, God, Lieu … It just doesn't make any sense."

He helped her from the floor to a chair. From that vantage point, she could see forensics as they took samples from Jones' corpse.

"Try and explain it to me," Brady said.

She wiped away tears. "I-I came down to observe … Jones … doing the autopsies on the bodies from the fire … "

Brady nodded, listening intently so she continued.

" … he … he'd just finished opening up the first one when it … it … "

"What?"

"It … The man mustn't have been really dead. I-I don't know … he just sat up ... and attacked him. Jesus, Lieu, it killed him!"

Brady licked his lips and watched the officers carefully place his coroner in a body bag. "Do you know how fucking crazy that sounds, Walsh?"

Walsh noticed something shift in Brady's gaze, changing from confusion to disappointment.

"Lieu ... I swear to you I'm not making this up."

He frowned, his disappointment on the cusp of anger. "I should never have signed you off to return to work."

"What?"

"Where's the burned body?"

"The body? What?"

"The man who attacked Jones, where did he go?"

Walsh's heart sank, and her fear turned a cold knot in her gut. "I told you ... he must have still been alive ... and the autopsy must have ... brought him back ... "

Brady pinched the bridge of his nose. "Stop ... "

She looked to the other dissection table. "There were two of them ... oh, God. Where's the other body?"

"It's in the morgue. We'll have to get someone else in to do that autopsy."

"No, no. You can't ... Lieu ... you need get rid of it. Incinerate it!"

"It's evidence, Walsh, for Christ's sake."

"You don't believe me?"

"That's enough Walsh." Brady stood and scratched his thinning hair before turning to the group. "Get out!"

The people in the room froze.

"Everyone, get out, now!" Brady said again.

Walsh sat shaking as the room emptied of people. She caught their wayward glances, felt their judgement. The last people to leave were the forensics techs, their white coveralls flecked with Jones' blood. Brady paced, the ramifications going far beyond the death of one of his staff. Then, he stepped before her.

"You must know how this looks?"

"Sir ... I'm telling the truth—"

"How can someone, who you witnessed have their brain removed, magically came back to life and kill Jones? How am I supposed to believe that?"

Walsh moved to stand, to reason with him. "Sir—"

"Sit down!"

She fell into the chair. Her heart pounded in her ears while the smell of Jones' blood coagulating on the floor permeated everything.

"Sir ... please ... I swear that's what happened. What reason would I possibly have to lie?"

Brady snapped, thrusting his finger in her face. "Maybe because you're a detective with PTSD from a previous officer-involved shooting? Because you came back to the field too goddamned early, and you've fucking snapped?"

He might as well have slapped her. She fell cold in the chair. Her story was insane, but it had happened right before her eyes. She wiped tears on the back of her sleeve and took a long, slow breath.

"Are you going to suspend me, then, sir?"

"I don't know what the hell I'm going to do with you, Walsh." He leaned on a nearby table and stared at the pool of blood. "All I know is that I have to call Jones' wife."

"What are you going to tell her?"

He turned. "I honestly don't know."

"What about the missing body ... and the other one? What are you going to do about the other one?"

Brady shook his head. "Fuck me. First, a bank fire with no discernible cause and two bodies, and now my coroner is dead."

"Again sir ... am I suspended?"

"You fired your weapon. And Jones is dead."

"I told you why I fired my weapon."

"Because a zombie killed him."

Fresh tears flowed, but Walsh wasn't going to let her resolve fade entirely, not when she was being questioned.

"I know what I saw," she said.

"You know what you *think* you saw."

A moment passed, a silence that only emphasised the tragedy unfolding in the room. Tragedy and distrust. Walsh found the courage to break through it.

"Sir, suspend me if you feel you must. I'll go peacefully. But all this started at that bank with the fire. The bank manager's still missing. The suspects are still at large. There are still questions that need answering, and maybe, just maybe, if we find those answers, it will help prove what went on here."

Brady put his hands on his hips. "You honestly expect me to let you stay on the case after this?"

Walsh unclipped her badge from her belt and presented it to him. "We can work it together, or you can do it alone. It's your choice. But I stand by what I said. You know that wound in Jones' throat wasn't caused by a bullet from my gun. I don't understand what killed him, but I think whatever weird shit happened at that bank will explain it. That woman who fled the bank can answer everything."

15

Walsh and Brady stared at the bank of television screens in the security room, mesmerized by the grainy footage glowing against the dark. Brady wanted proof of Walsh's claims, and the only place she could think to start was the precinct's security cameras.

Cameras were located in strategic locations throughout the building: hallways, bullpens, and some office spaces, but other areas were off-limits, like the morgue. While the cameras couldn't see inside the morgue, they were angled toward the entrance and external hallway. Therefore, Walsh surmised, the person—or thing—that killed Coroner Jones should appear in the footage escaping the scene.

Should.

The detective's heart pounded as her eyes tried to make sense of what was displayed on the screens. The tape displayed the time—4:58:12 PM and a view of the morgue door, which was wide open. At 4:58:22 PM the screen showed Walsh entering from the adjacent hallway.

"When I went in, Jones already had the bodies on the slab," she told Brady, not taking her eyes off the screens.

"That's what you said."

They watched the time counter click over from 4:59 to 5:03.

"You say Jones had started the autopsy by this time?" Brady asked. "What were you doing?"

"Observing. Talking to Jones."

"About what?"

"His findings."

At 5:08 PM, a series of flashes erupted from inside the morgue.

"Those are your gunshots, correct?"

Walsh swallowed. "Yes."

Brady covered his mouth with a hand and stepped closer to the nearest screen. When the counter reached 5:10:23 PM, a shape appeared in the doorway, a shifting blur of red and black, a streak of movement resembling human form.

"Pause it," Brady said.

She turned to him after pausing. "There. Do you see it?"

"I don't know what I see, Walsh."

She closed her eyes for a moment, recalling in her mind what the footage wasn't showing. The undead man tearing at her friend's throat.

"Press play." He leaned in so close his eyes reflected the screen.

Walsh clicked the button on the remote, the footage shifting forward frame by frame. The figure in the morgue doorway transformed with each passing second, the blackened shape becoming a shadow, then a wisp of smoke, and then nothing. Like it was never there at all.

"Jesus Christ," Brady rubbed his eyes.

She paused the tape at 5:11:02 PM. "I know what you're thinking?"

"Oh, you do?"

"You're thinking there's something wrong with the tape. That it's corrupted somehow. That you'll have to get forensics to run a fine-toothed comb over it. I'll save you some time now and admit that, yes, I fired my gun and that ... " She pointed at the wisp of smoke on the screen. " ... is the thing I fired at."

Her boss' face shifted from confusion to frustration, his brow a twist of furrows. "This is fucking insane."

"Yeah, it is."

"I mean, how am I supposed to understand this, let alone explain it to the top brass? That a fucking corpse killed my coroner, and then just up and vanished?"

Her eyebrows raised. "So, you believe me?"

"I don't know what to believe. But something's definitely off with this case."

"Not just this case, Lieu."

"What do you mean?"

"Seeing this ... whatever this is ... makes me wonder about Balkovich."

"Balkovich? What does he have to do with this?"

"His killings. The ritualistic nature of them. His ... his evil."

"Walsh. The guy was a fucking nutcase. A psychopath. Nothing more. Just another serial killer."

She shook her head, her gaze wandering back to the wisp in the footage. "That's what I kept telling myself, too—until tonight. This ... this isn't psychos or thrill-killers. This is some sort of strange ritual, just like Balkovich. What happened with him and what happened here tonight is real fucking evil, and I don't know how we can keep denying it exists."

It had been more than thirty minutes since Selena went into the bathroom. Her silence troubled Azamir greatly. The last time she'd locked herself away her mother had tried to kill her, but now the silence left him even more concerned.

The little girl he knew was no more. Davina had seen to that. He understood what taking the dark path did to a person, to their soul, but he hated what it was doing to Selena. Of course, they'd been apart for many years, but he always sensed that she was safe. Living the life she wanted. The knowledge of it gave him comfort.

He knew it was strange for a demon to have such thoughts and cares, and he guessed Selena had changed him, too. Regardless, he had a responsibility to fight for her. Including this very moment. He knocked gently on the bathroom door.

"Selena, it's me. Is everything okay in there?"

Azamir listened intently and stared at the door. After the last time he'd burst in, he'd made some slight repairs with some duct tape, but if he had to go in again, it wouldn't take much to force.

"Selena?"

The lack of response was like a physical rift. He knew she was keeping her emotions close to her chest, keeping them secret.

"Why won't you talk to me anymore?"

He heard something clatter and immediately remembered the broken mirror. He knocked again.

"Hey, can I come in?"

The silence was like a knife.

"Selena ... Mistress ... please, just let me help you."

The door opened, and Selena emerged fully clothed in a tank top and jeans, the heavy coat completing the ensemble. Azamir noticed her hair was still damp, her face flushed and slick with sweat.

"Is everything all right?" he asked as she brushed past him.

She gathered the grimoire and the newly acquired athame. She wondered whether they would be enough. Should she have armed herself with more weapons from the vault? "It's time to go," she said. "Get your things."

"Where are we going?"

"Wherever I tell you to go."

His mistress' tone had changed, become cold.

"Selena, what's wrong?"

"What's wrong is that you keep asking me questions."

"I'm only worried about you—"

Azamir flinched when she slammed the grimoire down on the table. The room trembled.

"Well, don't be. I don't need you to worry about me. I just need you to do what you're told."

The demon blinked, astounded by Selena's fury. She stood there, rigid, her jaw tight, fists clenched. A trickle of blood ran down her wrist and dripped onto the rug.

"Selena, you're bleeding!"

The blood trailed down her hand, fascinating her. Azamir noticed her tank top was also stained with bloody splotches.

"Why are you bleeding?"

She took a step back when he approached. "It's none of your concern."

"None of my concern?"

"We have to go. I have to get Gemma back."

"Selena ... "

"I can't just sit here. I have to find her!"

He reached out to her. "Mistress ... what have you done?"

"Stop ... "

"You're bleeding. Let me help you."

"Stop it!"

Her voice knocked Azamir off his feet. He fell to the bed, startled. Even her words carried significant power. He climbed off the bed and stood before her.

"The sigils ... what did you do?"

"What I have to ... to save Gemma!"

Azamir felt his human form ache with guilt, hot tears on his cheeks.

"At great cost to yourself."

"That doesn't matter anymore. All that matters is Gemma."

"Oh … Mistress … no."

Selena pulled back her left coat sleeve. Blood-smeared sigils, large and small covered her forearm. She opened her coat and lifted her top, revealing more finely carved symbols on her abdomen.

"No … "

She hid the mutilations away. "Isn't this what it's going to take to get my daughter back?"

He covered his face, but her defiled flesh was etched into his mind. "You don't see what you're doing."

"I know exactly what I'm doing, and I need you to just accept it."

"Can't you see that you're doing exactly what Davina would do?"

"Yes! I need to think like her, be like her."

He dropped back onto the bed, defeated. "So, you've forgotten that it was only hours ago that you told me how much you doubted yourself? That you didn't believe you could stoop so low?"

"So low? I've risen above that. I realised what I needed to do, and I did it."

"You've sacrificed who you are, Selena. Sure, you might get Gemma back, but she's not going to recognize you anymore."

He saw something slip in the witch's gaze, frustration becoming spite. By the time he realised the impact of his own words, the hellfire was already behind her eyes. The same fire exploded from her right hand, sending him crashing into the wall. He lay there gasping, smoke curling around his face. Wincing, he watched his mistress walk to the door. Her final words to him hurt the most.

"I don't need you anymore. I set you free."

When Davina looked at her granddaughter, she saw only bait, a sacrifice waiting to be made. The matriarch watched the girl quiver in her chair, on the verge of tears, her soul starving for a release that would never come.

Unless Selena came back home.

She approached Gemma with a small bowl of oatmeal but, immediately, the girl recoiled.

"I'm not hungry," she said, turning her gaze from the offering.

"Oh, I know what yer hungry for … Just not nourishment."

Gemma chose to stare at the floor, but this wilful arrogance only spurred the old woman on. "You think giving me the silent treatment is gonna save you?" She grabbed the girl's chin and pulled her gaze back. "What if I just cut yer tongue out, hmm? Maybe that would get you to open that pretty little mouth of yers."

"Do what you want. I don't care anymore."

"Yer tears say otherwise." she took one of Gemma's tears with her thumb, watched it run, and then licked it. "Tastes like fear."

The girl's eyes were pitiful. "What made you like this?"

The old woman sneered. "My devotion to the Black Lord. He made me who I am."

"So, what, you just decided one day to be evil? To be a Devil worshipper?"

"We've worshipped for generations. My momma passed it down to me, and her momma passed it down to her."

"But what for? What's the point?"

The girl wasn't ignorant, just defiant. "There are forces you don't understand, child—"

"All I understand is that you torture people. That you kidnap kids and turn them into monsters."

"Because the Black Lord wills it."

A smile crossed the girl's face along with a shake of the head and, for the first time, Davina thought she glimpsed Selena in that smirk.

"Does he? Or do you just do it 'cause you like it, 'cause you're actually the one who's the monster?"

"Maybe I am, and maybe I need to remind yer mother of that."

She turned away and raised a pointed finger at the air. Slowly, she drew a circle, the very space cracking apart, bleeding. With a sweep of her flabby arm, Davina opened a wound in the world. Through it was an alleyway in the city her daughter and granddaughter called home.

Back in the cabin, heavy footfalls announced Cade's arrival, his bloated frame ready to step through the entrance his mother had created. She stood on tiptoes to kiss his maligned forehead.

"Now, you be a good boy for yer momma and go collect yer sister."

Cade raised a swollen foot over the edge of the portal, stepping from the cabin to the dirty backstreet on the other side. The scent of asphalt and the distant blaring of car horns oozed through the gateway. Davina looked back to Gemma and knew the girl wished she could break free of the bonds, leap through the portal, and warn her mother. But it was too late for all that. Davina took Cade's hand before he stepped through.

"You seek her out, and you bring her home, you hear? Whatever it takes. Don't let no one get in yer way."

"Please, don't hurt my mother," Gemma said.

Davina savoured her fresh tears and offered her a mocking grin. "Only if the Black Lord wills it."

Then, Cade stepped over the threshold, and the laceration between one nightmare and the next was sealed—possibly forever.

16

Selena sensed a shift in reality, a shuddering wave passing from one plane to another. Something was coming.

She stopped in the hallway outside her hotel room and listened intently to the hum of the earth. In truth, it was more of a feeling than a sound, her heightened gifts turning her body into a tuning fork to elemental forces.

Something had opened a door and walked into the city from elsewhere. Was this the moment? Was her mother finally coming to confront her? No, she'd never be the one to take that first step, to leave the veritable safety of her den.

Shaking off the trepidation, Selena walked to the elevator and pressed the down button. Thoughts and scenarios raced through her head. She pushed those aside and reached out with her mind to try and ascertain the approaching threat. Yet, a force cloaked its identity from her. All she could sense was the sound of footsteps, the unyielding procession of an unstoppable thing. She knew that sound.

The elevator pinged open, and she stepped inside, pressed the button for the lobby. She hesitated. Should she instead go back to the hotel room where it was safe? No, she had to go. Besides, Azamir would be there, licking his wounds, and she had no time for that. Every second Selena wasted was another round of torment for Gemma. It was time to take a stand.

The elevator doors opened to a lobby littered with late night guests checking in and staff taking bags. She hoped to slink out the front doors unseen, unheard, but she caught the eye of the concierge, who immediately ventured out from behind reception in her direction. A thin, weaselly little man.

"Madam, a word please … " he said.

Selena tried to slide past, but the concierge had done this dance before.

"I need to get past."

"Madam, I'm sorry, but we've received some complaints of noise coming from your room."

Shit, I knew I should have made the room barrier stronger!

"Yeah, yeah, I'll keep it down," she told him.

"There have been reports of things being broken. Is everything all right?"

She sensed a rumbling beneath her feet, a dragging *THUMP-THUM-THUMP*. The concierge seemed not to be aware of it.

"Madam?"

She glanced over his shoulder to the front doors. Through the revolving glass doors, she saw passing cars and people. All seemingly normal, nothing untoward. When Selena tried to move past the concierge again, he persisted.

"If damage has been done to the room, you may be charged for repairs or replacement—"

Memories of the ritual circle, broken mirror, and Hell itself appearing inside the room came to Selena's mind.

"Look, just add it to the bill. I need to be somewhere."

THUMP-THUMP-THUMP-THUMP.

There was a screech of tires, followed by screams of terror. Selena and the concierge turned to the doors. Outside, people ran in a panic, falling over themselves to get away from something.

"What's going on out there?" The concierge nodded at the two security guards, who moved to investigate.

THUMP-THUMP-THUMP-THUMP.

Selena grabbed the concierge's arm. "You have to get everyone out of here!"

He frowned, his expression wavering among annoyance, confusion, and fear. "What?"

On the other side of the doors, the streetlights revealed the shadow of a gigantic, lumbering shape heading for the hotel. The guards were paralyzed by the misshapen form, its drooping mounds of naked flesh, and drooling cavernous mouth.

"Cade," Selena whispered.

A moment later, the revolving doors exploded inward, glass fragments becoming bullets, striking the security guards and sending them flying across the foyer. Selena's brother burst inside, breaking the doorway apart like it was made of matchsticks. Screams erupted from the guests and the concierge, who ran for cover. Selena, though, stood her ground, even though the sight of Cade mortified her.

He was more monstrous than the last time she'd seen him, obviously fuelled by their mother's malevolent influence. His great feet squashed the injured guards, the snapping of their bones competing with the screams of the fearful. She locked eyes with him and thought of the runes on her skin, willing them to ignite.

Cade, somehow attuned to her intentions, gripped one of the nearby four-seater lounges and hurled it into Selena, sending her crashing hard to the floor. The witch slid along the tiles into a wall, the wind knocked out of her. Through the blur of pain and threatening unconsciousness, she failed to see Cade charging in her direction until the last minute.

She raised an arm in self-defence, but Cade was fast despite his size. He took hold of her arm and lifted her into the air as if she were a rag doll. When he tightened his grip, only pain—not spells—could pass Selena's lips.

Her brother wrapped his other bulging hand around his sister's throat, the fingers slick with vile perspiration. Cade pulled her close, forcing her to look into his eyes—the only part of him still human. She gasped for breath, searching for any semblance of humanity he might have left.

"C-Cade ... please ... "

Blood-tainted spittle slipped from his lips along with a moan, a plea of his own.

"Please ... " Selena said. "She's ... controlling ... you."

Black stars burned inside Selena's skull. She couldn't pass out now or she'd be done for. She'd never see Gemma again.

An enormous force slammed into them, and for a moment, Selena felt nothing but the air around her. All she knew in those few seconds was that Cade no longer had hold of her. Then, she hit the floor. She rolled, toppling at speed until a column stopped her momentum. Something inside her broke, possibly a rib, and the pain wrenched her back to the now. Her eyes focused on the sight before her—Cade pinned down by a colossal ebony spider. Azamir.

Her familiar looked her way with solemn eyes, his voice in her head. *"Run, Mistress! Run!"*

Selena scrambled to her knees, ready to go to Azamir's aid, but his voice—his exclamation—pushed her back.

"No, Mistress! Leave now!"

Cade released a bellow of his own then unleashed a fist into Azamir's abdomen. The familiar cried out in pain, which instantly diminished any Selena felt. She raised a hand, ready to incinerate Cade to protect her guardian, but they were too entangled in violence. She couldn't hurt Cade without hurting Azamir, too.

The familiar fought back, striking Cade hard across the face with one leg, then biting him with his great pincers. The pair rolled about, crashing into the reception desk, then scaling the wall, up and onto the chandelier, only for their weight to bring it crashing down with a thundering boom of glass and steel.

Selena felt helpless as the equally matched beasts snarled and hissed, slathered in each other's blood. One determined to kill, the other born to protect.

Her brother ripped off one of Azamir's legs, and the familiar in turn, bit off one of Cade's arms. Rage or survival drove them on, Selena's familiar pushing her brother into a wall, wrapping his pincers around Cade's chest, but the deformed giant seemed to swell in retaliation, matching Azamir's size, punching back, tearing, howling, relentless.

Cade was going to kill her friend, and she cried out in fear. "Azamir!"

The great arachnid fell onto his back. Cade leapt for him, but Azamir was ready. Thick web erupted from his spinnerets, catching Cade midair. With his remaining legs, Azamir spun the freakish behemoth, coiling him tight. Selena smiled. Cade dropped to the floor, struggling to move, and Selena knew this was her chance to bring the battle—and her brother—to an end. She rushed in, hand raised.

The giant howled, the ferocity of his scream shaking the very foundations of the lobby. The overhead fire sprinklers burst, showering everything. Again, Cade grew, larger than the great spider, so large the webbing tore. Cade reached for Selena with gargantuan fists, and Azamir stepped between them, pushing his mistress out of harm's way.

Cade's fist struck Azamir's head, and the arachnid fell, motionless. The giant, his body pulsating with anger, came for his sister once more, and seeing her friend lying on the floor, Selena considered for a moment letting him claim her.

Until she heard Azamir's voice one final time. "I'm ... sorry ... Mistress ... but you must ... run ... "

Selena's shriek of grief was a wall of sound and light, an explosion that blasted Cade out of the lobby, through the shattered doors, and across the street into darkness. The force of her cry took almost every ounce of her strength, but not as much as the sight of her familiar's body, broken and lost forever.

With tears streaming down her face, she honoured his final wish—his last hope—and ran.

Detective Walsh thought a bomb had been responsible for the devastation inside the Plaza Hotel, until the concierge started talking about a giant spider.

The man's statement would have been absurd—should have been—if it weren't for the thing she saw killing her coroner mere hours before. Walsh was quickly realizing that her worldview was coming apart, that darkness and evil were making themselves known.

Trails of bitter smoke coiled in the air over the remains of the hotel foyer. The scene reminded her of the inexplicable bank fire, another incident that involved the mysterious woman. It couldn't be a simple coincidence.

She stepped over a fallen piece of concrete pillar and headed toward the body in the centre of the chaos. Her lieutenant stood over the corpse, the same look of consternation on his face. His gaze moved from the body to the shattered surroundings and back again.

"What the hell happened here?" he said.

Walsh crouched to get a closer look at the dead man. His face was a pulpy mess, one arm torn from its socket, and chest crushed. The man had clearly suffered before he died.

"Looks like he took a hell of a beating," she said.

"Like he's been run over by a tank."

"Or attacked by a giant spider."

Brady turned to her. "What?"

"The concierge. He said a gigantic spider and a goliath got into a fight in the hotel." She gestured at the carnage. "Caused all this."

The lieutenant looked to the street and saw a gaunt looking man in a waistcoat talking to a uniformed officer.

"Is he high?"

Walsh opened the dead man's coat. "I don't know, Lieu. Other witnesses said the same thing."

"Mass hallucination, then."

"Hah, maybe."

"What the fuck is going on in this city?"

She gasped at the sight of something long, black, and spiked protruding from the corpse's left torso.

"Maybe I'm hallucinating, too."

Brady knelt beside her, only to recoil from the sight. "What in Christ's name is that?"

Walsh stood, eager herself to move away, yet her eyes were transfixed. "I think ... it's a spider leg."

"You're shitting me."

A crumbling of concrete dust underfoot startled the pair as a uniformed officer ran to their side.

"Detective. Lieutenant. We're getting reports of another incident happening about two blocks from here."

Brady ran a hand over his balding pate. "Jesus, what now?"

The officer blinked in disbelief. "Reports of a giant man chasing a woman along 54th and 6th. They said the woman was throwing flame from her hands."

17

The streets were a lurid blur as Selena ran, streaks of red and yellow, a cavalcade of faces and vehicles. The witch's frantic breaths soared above the bystanders' cries of confusion and the blare of car horns. She side-stepped taxi cabs, careful not to slip on the rain-soaked asphalt. She couldn't fall now, not with a demon on her tail.

She glanced over her shoulder as she bolted to the other side of the street. Behind her, about fifty feet away, the gargantuan Cade followed. The screams of the public followed him like his entourage. He was getting closer, so much closer that fear was taking root in her mind.

Fear roiled in her gut, made it hard to think how to escape. Amidst her terror was grief at the loss of her Azamir. Guilt that she'd rejected him only for him to make the ultimate sacrifice. Selena shook the thoughts from her head and the rain from her hair and pushed on, legs aching, lungs burning, desperate to flee.

The shriek of twisting metal stopped her cold, and she whirled about to witness Cade pushing aside a car like it was a sheet of drywall. In a panic, she raised her arm and ignited the runes with a curse.

"Incindere!"

A sphere of flame burst from her palm and struck her brother in the chest, hurtling him back into the same car. His heavy frame crushed the hood as if he was a human wrecking ball. She didn't stop to admire her work, running hard down the street because she knew Cade would get back up. He'd chase her to the ends of the earth.

Selena pushed between a man and a woman filming the madness on their phones. She had to find safety, a place of sanctuary where she could breathe and think of her next move. Another car horn blared to her right, the sound deafening. She ran through an intersection and gasped at the sight of a church on the corner—a stone cathedral with a tall spire piercing the swirling grey sky. If she could make it to the church, she could hide. Find a way to defend herself.

Avoiding another procession of traffic, she made for the gates of St. Stephen's Cathedral. At the top of the stone staircase, a sliver of candlelight beamed out from the gap between the tall double doors.

She slapped her burning hands against them, cried out for someone to let her in. To her relief, they parted, and a beleaguered priest looked out at her from the other side. Selena charged in and closed the doors behind her before he could utter any objection.

"Are you all right?" the priest said, looking her up and down. "Do you need help?"

She flicked back her wet hair. "Something ... *someone's* following me."

The priest raised a bushy grey eyebrow. "Do you need me to call the police?" He looked to the church doors, a whirlwind of emergency sirens echoing through them from outside.

"No! No cops!" Selena said, pacing the aisle.

"I'm sorry, but are you okay? You look terrified. I might be able to help if you just tell me what's going on?"

She gripped the priest's arm, saw the gentleness behind his eyes. "You have to get out of here. You and anyone else who might be in the church. Right now!"

The clergyman trembled beneath her hand. "What? Why?"

"I don't have time to explain! You just have to leave now!"

His gaze dropped to her forearm, to the rune scorch marks. "Oh, dear Lord. What happened to your arm?"

She pulled him closer, so close she could smell the fear in his sweat. Within herself, her frustration rose, and a heat emanated from her eyes— the hellfire. The priest suddenly looked mortified.

"Get. Out," Selena growled.

The priest made for the front doors, but a great pounding from the other side halted him. He faced Selena, seeking instruction, understanding.

"Better not go that way, Father," she told him.

The doors pounded again. The priest howled in fright, running past Selena, up the aisle, his legs belying his age. Once she was certain he was gone, she faced the doors, which shuddered a third time. She pulled off her coat, swallowed her fear, and focused on the runes. If Cade wanted a fight, she was going give it to him. She wasn't going to die here.

The doors crashed open, and Cade burst inside with a guttural roar. Wind and rain came along with him, the droplets adding a further chill to Selena's skin. He charged at her so fast she had no time to react. He thrust out his arms, sending her soaring through the air and coming down to land hard on the rows of pews, toppling half of them like dominoes.

Pain seared Selena's ribs and back, and she lay on the marble floor panting in agony—but not for long. The thudding of Cade's deformed footsteps jerked her back to awareness, and she scrambled to her knees, just in time to see her monstrous brother launch into a second charge.

The pews flew apart like leaves as the beast-man ran through them. The staccato *boom-boom-boom* of their impact thunderous inside the cathedral. Selena put her weight on one knee and aimed her hands at Cade's vile face. She never saw the pew clutched in his right hand until it was too late.

"Incindere!"

Cade swung the pew like a baseball bat, the sparks of Selena's spell casting the end of it ablaze. The flaming weapon struck the floor in front of her with a burning *whoosh* of heat. The witch was lifted off the ground again, back through the air until she crash-landed before the altar.

Blood pooled in her mouth. Her skull pounded with the threat of swirling unconsciousness. She was faltering, her body nothing more than flesh regardless of all the power she wielded. Gritting her teeth, Selena lifted herself onto all fours and turned her gaze to the behemoth that was her brother.

The creature stood amongst the fallen and splintered pews, waiting, taunting. Even as a twisted thing, Cade's intelligence remained. Perhaps? Her brother raised the flaming pew ready to strike, only for Selena to exchange spells for reason.

"Cade, stop!" she said.

Her brother lowered the pew and cocked his hideous head to one side.

"Remember what I said. Mother is using you like she always has!" Selena said.

He let the pew rest on the floor, the tongues of fire spreading to some

252

of the other surrounding seats. Selena feared it wouldn't be long before the entire church went up in flames.

"Look at yourself!" she pleaded. "Look at what she's done to you!"

Cade glanced down at his hands, one so swollen it was fit to burst, the other an arthritic assemblage of talons. She wondered if there was indeed recognition behind his eyes. Did she have any hope of getting through to him?

"Brother, please. I can help you. I can help return you to the way you were, if you can help me save Gemma from our mother."

The monster groaned, let his massive arms fall by his side. Then, he spoke through foamy lips.

"Do you think your brother is the one in control?"

Davina.

Their mother spoke through Cade, the beast-man's dislocated jaw flopping and jutting about with each word.

"Cade is doing my bidding, girl. A will servant to his mother and the Black Lord."

Selena spat blood on the floor. "You've cursed him."

Cade laughed, wet and deep, his entire body shaking. "I've helped him reach his full potential. He is glorious."

Hot tears burned on Selena's face. "Cade, if you're in there," she said, "I just want you to know it's not your fault and that ... I'm sorry."

Thunder rolled in from outside, along with the ring of emergency sirens. Selena had to act now.

"And, Mother ... "

Cade cocked his head again as Selena raised both hands to the church ceiling.

" ... know that I'm going to end you. *Turrim flammae!*"

A column of fire exploded from the floor beneath Cade's feet. The flame burst with ferocious light, curling around and through him, soaring up to the cathedral's arched ceiling. The beast-man screamed, but Selena heard her mother's wails as well, and she took some pleasure in that.

The tower of destruction slammed into the roof, shattering stone and timber, the fragments raining down to crush Cade to death. Sadness filled Selena's heart, but only for a moment as the power she'd exuded broke the cathedral apart and fire and ash and smoke came once more, threatening to send her into Hell's maw, too.

※

Walsh pulled her car up to St. Stephen's Cathedral just as the ceiling collapsed beneath a shimmering bolt of flame.

The detective leapt from the car without a second thought and ran in the direction of the carnage. Disbelief and fear clashed inside her mind as she pushed her way through the terrified crowd. What she craved through all of this—the bank, the coroner's death—was understanding. She was prepared to jeopardize her own safety to get it.

Smoke and embers billowed out from the church. A group of onlookers stood in awe, succumbing to the spectacle. Walsh ran past them, ignoring their cries and the danger within. She unholstered her pistol with one hand and covered her mouth from the smoke with the other, before stepping into what might as well have been Hell.

Much of the church ceiling and roof lay in a gigantic pile of rubble. Fires burned in almost every corner, creeping up the columns and transforming the pews to charcoal. Enormous cracks pervaded the marble floor, and stained-glass windows were shattered. It was like an act of God—or the Devil.

The sound of someone coughing drew Walsh's gaze—and her weapon. Through the murky curtain of smoke, a shape pulled itself out from under a fallen piece of timber. Walsh raised her Glock.

"Police! Don't move!"

The figure raised its hands. Walsh could make out the long dark hair and a tattered waist-length coat. Even in the low light, the detective recognised the woman as the one from the bank. Before she could utter another warning, the woman faltered on her feet and collapsed, seemingly unconscious.

Walsh couldn't believe her luck.

When Selena came to moments later, still inside the smoky ruins of the church, she realised she couldn't move her hands. She rolled onto her side, only to discover a woman pointing a gun at her head. Selena tried to push aside the mental fog, but the battle had left her weakened. There was no getting to Gemma—not now.

"You were at the bank," the woman said.

Selena groaned, the cold steel of handcuffs stinging the brands on her arms. "What?"

"You destroyed the bank, set it on fire."

"I did ... what I had to."

"Including destroying this church?"

"You're ... a cop."

"Detective Walsh. I've been looking for you."

Selena needed to get to Gemma. She squeezed her right hand, desperate for some spark of power, but there was nothing.

"Please ... you have to let me ... go. They're going ... to kill her."

"Who? Who's going to get killed?"

"My daughter ... please!"

The woman reached down and hauled Selena to her feet. The threat of unconsciousness swirled inside Selena's skull. There was no way she had the strength to make another run for it.

"Well, you can tell me all about it down at the station where you're no longer a danger to anyone."

"You need ... to listen to me. It doesn't matter where you take me because ... the danger is still coming."

18

The basement of Gemma's grandmother's house was pungent with the scent of old death, and the girl was terrified they were going to bury her beneath it.

In a new fit of rage Davina had ordered Asha to untie Gemma from the chair and drag her down the steps. She was becoming increasingly unhinged with each defeat. Gemma's mother—Selena—seemed unstoppable. Which begged the question in Gemma's mind: Why wasn't she here now, saving her only child?

The earthen floor of the basement was cold between Gemma's toes, the very air dry and dank with dark promise. She stood in its centre, shivering as Davina paced, running her gnarled fingers through her colourless hair. In one corner, Gemma noticed a bronze statue glinting in the sconce-light—something demonic. Did they really worship the Devil?

To her left, Asha fidgeted and stifled a sob. She didn't know exactly what had occurred to upset Davina so. All she knew was the monster Cade hadn't returned from his mission.

"That bitch!" Davina said before slapping a hand against the stone wall. "That fucking bitch!"

Asha bit her fingernails. "W-what happened, Momma?"

Davina moved along the wall, whispering to herself, "There has to be another way ... show me O' Lord ... show yer faithful servant ... grant unto me yer wisdom so that I may destroy your enemies."

Gemma watched silently, petrified by the tension in the room. The statue's eyes appeared to follow her. Asha stepped closer to her mother.

"Momma, did something happen to Cade?"

The old crone ignored Asha, instead dropping to her knees in the dirt before the shrine.

"Great beast! I implore you to come to our aid! Give us wisdom and strength! Do not forsake us in this time of woe!"

Davina's anxiety was infectious, turning Asha's fidgeting into uncontrollable trembling. "M-Momma, please ... "

She whirled on Asha, closing the gap between them with supernatural speed.

"Yer brother failed me! He's dead! Selena killed him!" She wrapped those arthritic fingers around Asha's neck. "Is that what you wanted to hear?" When Asha's eyes flooded with tears, Davina shoved her to the ground. "You stop yer whining, or I may just send you to do my bidding next."

The old woman turned her jaundiced eyes to Gemma, and the girl backed away, dreading the thought of those same twisted fingers around her own throat.

"I fear there's no other choice," Davina said. "We are forsaken. Lost."

The icy stone wall pricked at Gemma's back, along with a cloying stench of emptiness.

"There's only one thing left to do." The old woman's hand reached closer. "A sacrifice will have to be made. Consequences be damned."

Gemma saw the sheen of sweat on Davina's palm. "No ... " the girl said.

"No!"

Davina spun about, her ruminations cut short by a guttural male voice. There was a scraping sound, low to the ground. The noise came from another corner, darker and filthier. Shapes, like twigs or roots, but coloured the shade of blood, slipping from the shadows. Twisting and pulling into the ground. Gemma shrieked as the same shadows parted, revealing human flesh—a decomposing, disembodied head, severed, yet impossibly alive. She locked eyes with it as it crawled her way.

"If we kill the girl, we've lost," it said, as it crept toward Davina.

"We've already lost, Lars!" the old crone replied.

Gemma squeezed her eyes shut and reopened them only to find the nightmare was still very real.

"The girl is our only bargaining chip," Lars wheezed. "Kill her, and Selena's rage will engulf us all."

Davina sat in the dirt and let the undead head approach. It wrapped its veins around her wrist.

"I don't know what to do, husband," Davina said, her voice shaking for the first time.

"You should have come to me," Lars told her.

"I know." Davina cradled him. "I thought the Black Lord would guide me, but I fear he ain't listening."

A rotted vein caressed Davina's wrinkled cheek, and bile rose in Gemma's gullet.

"The Lord will listen to me," Lars continued. "If the Lord wants to invoke his pact, then he'll have to hear me."

"What should we do?"

Gemma gasped when Lars' bleached eyes shifted her way.

"If the Lord wants a bride, I say we give him one. We know the police have Selena, so we'll send the dogs to finish her."

The girl's heart quickened when Davina and Asha's eyes bored into her, too. "W-what?" she said.

Lars slinked out of Davina's embrace and scuttled to Gemma, the veins and tendons eagerly inching a path to her through the muck. His deathly blue lips smiled in anticipation.

"If we can't give the Black Lord Selena, we'll give him her daughter."

Asha crawled closer. "A trade?"

Davina smiled too. "Blood for blood."

Lars' wet tendrils slipped around Gemma's ankle, and she screamed. Behind the malevolent trio, a crack opened in the wall, flooding the room with the glow of a landscape of vicious flame and the howls of eternal suffering.

And Gemma realised they were going to drag her to Hell.

When Detective Walsh studied the woman through the two-way glass she felt an undeniable sense of dread.

The way she sat shackled to the table in the interrogation room, fidgeting and anxious, emphasised her physical appearance; the dark circles under her eyes, the bloody burn marks on her arm. She'd clearly put herself through hell, but to what end? Walsh, for the first time in her ten-year career, was afraid to find out.

She pulled out her notebook. Her suspect had only provided a first name—Stephanie. Walsh had read the woman her rights at the church but, so far, she hadn't asked for an attorney. There was no doubt, however, that her suspect wanted to be somewhere else.

Walsh was going to use that fact to her advantage. When she put her notebook back in her coat pocket and turned back to the two-way glass, she found Stephanie making direct eye-contact from the other side—bearing the wild-eyed stare of someone terrified.

"What the hell is your deal, lady?" Walsh whispered.

The door to the viewing room opened, and Lieutenant Brady stepped inside.

"So, this is your girl, huh?" Brady said.

"Uh, yeah. Gave a first name of Stephanie but no surname. No I.D. We're running her mugshot and prints right now."

Brady approached the glass. "So, you think this one set the fire at the bank and murdered those guys at the hotel?"

"Don't forget the explosion at St. Stephen's."

Brady turned. "We mustn't forget that. Apart from the pancaked corpse, no one else was hurt, but I'm told the cathedral is toast."

"Damn. I guess we'll add arson to the list of charges."

"What's your strategy here, Walsh? You've told me she seems on edge. How are you going to get her to confess?"

She sighed. "I don't really have anything specific. I mean, look at her. She looks ... well, desperate. The marks on her arms, do they look self-inflicted to you? And what the hell are they anyway?"

The lieutenant shook his head. "She looks like a whacko to me. Maybe we should get her a psych-eval?"

Walsh came to Brady's side. "Oh, no. I don't think she's crazy. Frustrated. Scared even. She said something about someone wanting to kill her daughter."

"She could be lying."

"Could be."

Brady huffed. "Well, it's your job to find out. So, get to it."

Walsh nodded and left the room, exiting one door and opening another that led to her suspect. Selena locked eyes with Walsh again when she stepped inside. The detective sat opposite and opened the file they'd accumulated on Selena: arson reports, surveillance footage. Walsh spread the documents out and began her questions, deliberately choosing not to look the woman in the eye—yet.

"Would you like a water? Coffee?"

"I need to get out of here."

Walsh reached over and pressed a button on the wall-mounted recording device. "This is Detective Corrinne Walsh, badge number 7621. The date is May 12th, and the time is 10:12PM." Walsh looked up at Stephanie. "Can you please state your full name for the record?"

The woman put her head in her hands and sighed. "I don't have time for this ... please ... "

"And I don't have time for your bullshit. Name."

"Selena Kolbe."

Walsh frowned. "You told me your name was Stephanie?"

"It's Selena, okay? Selena."

"Why would you give me a false name?"

"Selena is my real name. I changed my name to Stephanie all right? Look, I need to get out of here."

Walsh glanced at the file. "Well without I.D., Miss Kolbe, you're going to have to stay here until I verify who you are. But before that I'd like to remind you of your rights. Should you wish to have legal representation present—"

She shifted in the chair, the handcuff chains rattling on the table. "I waive my rights. I just want you to hurry up and get this over with."

The detective raised an eyebrow. "So, you *do* have somewhere else to be."

Selena leaned back. "This is all just a waste of time, mine and yours."

Walsh waved a hand over the contents of the file. "This says otherwise. I mean, what's this all about?"

"I told you, I'm looking for my daughter."

"You said someone was trying to kill her? Is that why you were at the bank? Were you paying a ransom for your daughter?"

"No. For Christ's sake you need to let me go!"

She gestured at Selena's arm. "Did you do that to yourself?"

Selena pulled the sleeve of her jacket down.

"Are they brand marks?" Walsh continued. "What do they mean? Why would you do that to yourself? Is this what you meant when you told me at the church that you did what you had to do?"

Her suspect sniffled and picked at her fingernails, but Walsh carried on.

"What I don't see amongst all this is the why. Why you did all of it. That's the part that doesn't make sense."

Selena sighed once more. "It's beyond you."

"What does that mean exactly?"

"If you think you're going to wear me down with these inane questions, then you can save your breath."

Walsh grabbed two photos from the file—one from the bank vault surveillance footage and the other from the hotel incident. "The guy who was with you in the bank? This is him here in the hotel, too, right? Deceased." She glimpsed a shift in Selena's demeanour, an expression of deep pain. "Who was he to you? A brother? A partner? A lover?"

"Shut up."

Walsh retrieved a third photo—a closeup of Selena's companion's body. A gloved hand holding up a long black shape protruding from the victim's torso.

"Here's a pretty inane question for you, Miss Kolbe: What the fuck is this thing coming out of your buddy's rib cage? Because, to me, it looks like a spider's leg. But that's not possible, right?"

Selena slammed her hands on the table, startling the detective. "Listen to me!" she said. "You have to let me out of here!"

"That's not going to happen, lady."

"No, please listen! You think you want the answers, but you don't! Believe me! You need to let me go so I can find my daughter or they'll come for me.

"Who's coming for you?"

Unless you let me go, there'll be more horrors—and you don't want that!"

"All I want is the truth! Tell me who they are, and we can help you."

"You can't help me, and the truth you want? It's all bullshit. All this law and order and rules you believe in? It means nothing. All there is now is chaos."

Walsh watched a tear roll down her suspect's cheek. "If they've taken your daughter then you definitely need police help. Let me help you. What have you got to lose?

Selena wiped her face with the back of her hand. "If you don't let me go, I'll lose her, I'll lose everything."

There was a tap on the glass, and Walsh turned quickly for the door, collecting the file. "I'll be right back."

Brady met Walsh in the hall, much to the detective's frustration.

"Lieu, I'm in the middle of getting her to open up," she said.

"She's just feeding you a bunch of hokum. 'All there is now is chaos?' What the hell is she even on about? I told you, she's crazy."

Walsh led him farther away from the interrogation room. "She truly believes what she's saying. And there's the stuff about her daughter. What if this is all connected to a kidnapping?"

"What if she's making it all up because she's crazy, Walsh?"

"Lieutenant, you can't label suspects like that. It's not the seventies anymore. And what about what happened to Jones? Or the fucking spider in the hotel? Or have you forgotten about that?"

"No, I haven't forgotten about that. I just feel we'd be wise to get a psychiatrist down here. I say we charge this Selena woman with arson and put her in lock-up until—"

A scream shattered Brady's and Walsh's concentration, and the pair immediately turned and ran for the squad room, guns drawn.

"What the hell was that?" Brady said.

There were more screams, the sound of glass breaking, and the growls of something unnatural. Walsh and Brady continued down the hall carefully, only to come to an abrupt stop when they saw an officer wielding a shotgun run across their path about twenty feet in front of them.

Brady turned to Walsh. "Was that Sergeant Marshall? Did he have a shotgun?"

"I don't know, Lieu."

Gunfire boomed, the sound of a 12-gauge.

"Jesus Christ! What is going on?"

Multiple screams rang out, followed by another volley of gunfire, but beneath it all, the call of some beast barking.

"Has one of the tracker dogs gone wild? Gotten out?" Walsh asked.

"I'm going out there," Brady said. "You get your suspect secured in interrogation and don't come out until I give you the okay, got it?"

Walsh gripped his arm. "Lieu, are you sure you don't need back up?"

Brady didn't answer, he simply ran off in the direction of the chaos.

Chaos, Walsh thought. Isn't that what Selena had warned her about?

She turned and ran back to the interrogation room because she knew only Selena would be able to make sense of the madness her boss was running into.

19

Trails of blood led Brady to six dead officers lying in the middle of the squad room floor.

Brady knew them all and not just by name. The pang of sadness and guilt he felt was only eclipsed by the horror of seeing his colleagues—and friends—torn apart. Some he could only identify by their badges, their faces mauled or even torn off.

Sparks flew from one of the overhead lights shattered by shotgun blast. The other lights that worked flickered on and off, casting the entire bullpen in a staccato sheen. Brady's eyes found it hard to adjust in the low light. It was hard to see anything other than the spatters and streaks of blood that covered almost every surface. What on earth could have been responsible for such carnage?

He walked slowly around one of the bodies and picked up the phone receiver on a desk to call downstairs. To his dismay, the line was engaged.

"Where the hell is everyone?" he whispered.

A long snarl answered him, and he whirled about in the direction of the hallway that led to the restrooms. The lights continued to flicker on and off, illuminating a silhouette one second and darkening it the next. Brady squinted at the low, squat form as it padded out into the squad room. It announced itself with another long, low growl.

"It's a fucking dog," Brady breathed.

The light washed over the rottweiler, revealing its eroded maw, protruding ribcage, and two iridescent red eyes. The thing shouldn't have been alive, but there it was, walking toward him.

"What the fuck are you?" Brady said and aimed his pistol at the creature.

The canine ceased its procession, and Brady almost believed it was sizing him up. With only ten feet between them, he was able to get an even better look at it. The dog definitely shouldn't have been alive. The thing breathed despite its lack of lungs, and even with burning coals for eyes, it could still see its prey. Brady could also see the blood on the thing's putrescent muzzle—the blood of his fellow officers. He aimed his Glock at the dog's head.

"I don't know what you are, but I'm going to end you for killing my friends."

The undead mongrel growled in defiance. Brady replied by squeezing off two shots. The sound echoed inside the lifeless space as the rounds sent the dog flying and tumbling along the floor, leaving behind a streak of brackish blood. The creature didn't even cry out in pain.

"Now, fucking stay dead, you piece of—"

Brady heard the rhythmic scrape of claws on the linoleum and released a gasp of disbelief as the same dog trotted back up the hall. He was about to fire again when more growls approached on both sides. Two more decomposing mutts.

"What the hell?"

The hounds circled him, calculating, their heads low and vacant eyes filled by some unearthly light. Brady's heart pounded in his ears, fear taking hold. The Glock was slippery in his hands, yet it was his eyes he felt had betrayed him. He couldn't comprehend what he was seeing. Three dead dogs animated by some ungodly power.

One of the dogs jumped on a desk and, on instinct, Brady turned and fired. His shot simply passed through a hole in the dog's cavernous abdomen, finding purchase in the wall behind it. None of the impossible animals even flinched. He swore the creatures shared a look of understanding— that it was time to attack.

"I'm not going to go out like this, not without a fight," he told them.

All Brady could think about was that Walsh had been right all along. There were dark forces behind everything that had happened: the bank, the death of his coroner, the hotel. And it all centred around this Selena. But were these undead dogs her doing or someone else's?

He had to give Walsh time to find out. With his free hand, he slowly reached for his cell and typed a text to his detective.

DOGS HAVE ME CORNERED. GET 2 SAFETY.

The nearest dog dropped from the desk and padded purposely in his direction, the other two joining it on either side as if they were flanking him. Brady remembered a dog from myth, Cerberus—the three-headed dog that guarded the gates of Hell.

Smiling, he pointed his gun at the snarling one in the middle and squeezed the trigger.

When Walsh heard Brady's agonized screams, she ran for the door to go to his aid, but her suspect's words stopped her cold.

"You'll die if you go out there," Selena said.

Walsh considered the hollow almost nonchalant way Selena told her. Brady's screams echoed from the hallway, and she reached for the door handle.

"I have to help him," she replied.

"If you open that door, you're dead."

She turned to Selena. "Is that a threat?"

"There's nothing you can do for your friend. I told you this would happen if you didn't let me go."

The detective trained her gun on Selena when she could no longer hear Brady's cries. "You're doing this, aren't you? Somehow."

"No."

"Don't fucking lie to me! You're responsible for all of this!" Selena shook her head, and all Walsh wanted to do was pull the trigger, and she would have if the fierce growling and scratching from the other side of the door didn't rip the thought away. "What the fuck is that? What's out there!?"

Selena intertwined her fingers on the table. "My mother sent them."

"Your … your mother?"

"They're the family pets, only they're long dead."

Walsh kept the pistol aimed on her. It was the only way she could still feel in control of the situation. "I don't understand … "

"I told you it was beyond you, didn't I?"

"Tell me what's going on for Christ's sake!"

"She's a witch."

"Who?"

"My mother. She's a witch. She raised me and my brother and sister to be witches, too. All in the service of a demon from Hell."

The image of the monster tearing open and gorging on her coroner's bloody throat stabbed at Walsh's mind. She let her gun arm fall.

"They're ... real, then?" she said.

"Very real."

The growls intensified, along with the fierce scratching. Walsh pointed her gun back at the door.

"And out there, those things, they're real, too?"

"Yes, and unless you uncuff me, they're going to get in here and kill us."

The cop pushed strands of hair from her sweaty brow. "But ... you ... you said you're a witch. How do I know the things out there don't really belong to you? That they're not really here to help you escape?"

"Because those things out there kidnapped my daughter and killed my husband. My mother sent them to bring me home or to kill me. Either way, that's not happening because I'm going to destroy them first."

Walsh sniggered. "This ... this is all so fucking insane." Selena nodded, but Walsh continued. "Yet, somehow, it all makes sense."

"What do you mean?"

Low snarls rolled in under the door and desperate sniffing for the scent of fresh kills. Walsh didn't even feel the smile creep across her face.

"Hours ago, a dead man—one of the burn victims from the bank— came alive and killed our coroner. Right in front of me. Then, the same body just up and ran out the door." Walsh saw a wave of recognition in Selena's eyes. "Before, I couldn't explain any of it, but now I can. It makes sense because of you."

The creatures slammed into the door, startling them both.

"Let me out of these cuffs!" Selena said.

"You killed those people in the bank with some sort of spell, didn't you?"

"Jesus Christ. There's no time for this. Uncuff me."

267

Growls and scratches filled the room, the door rattling on its hinges.

"You killed those people for your daughter?"

"Yes! Now, for God's sake, set me free!"

Walsh pointed the gun at Selena again. "My friend and my boss are dead because of you."

Panic reigned on Selena's features, and for some reason she couldn't understand, this made Walsh happy.

"Look, I'm sorry. I'm sorry about your friends. I didn't plan for any of this to happen. I was happily living my life until my bitch of a mother found me and took my little girl. I got dragged back into a world I never wanted any part of in the first place."

The door cracked under the force of the hounds' desperation. Through the splintered opening, Walsh glimpsed their vile yellow fangs and burning eyes.

"You may have had your hand forced, Selena, but you have to take responsibility for what you've done, for the lives you've taken!"

The witch's eyes narrowed. "Release me, and I will."

The door split, teeth biting down on the edge of the crack, tearing to find a way inside. To kill. Walsh fished the handcuff key from her pocket and tossed it onto the table. Selena pressed it into the lock when the door suddenly exploded inward. Walsh sucked in a deep breath and opened fire as the three dogs bolted inside the room. The bullets splattered their flesh, knocking them onto the floor, but they recovered in seconds.

"What the fuck?" Walsh said.

"Get behind me!"

Walsh scurried into a corner, unloading her gun until the magazine was spent. Out of the corner of her eye, she saw Selena raise her scorched arm, the marks on the skin glowing with impossible light. The dogs launched themselves at her.

"Shut your eyes!" Selena said.

Walsh squeezed them closed.

"*Incindere!*"

Light and heat assaulted Walsh's eyelids, her entire body, as if she'd stepped into a car in the middle of summer. Curiosity—and fear—forced her to open her eyes and see the unthinkable. Sparks caught on the dogs' fur, becoming waves of concussive flame. The force pushed Walsh back into the wall, almost knocking the wind out of her. The stink of burning fur assaulted her nostrils, but still, she couldn't look away from the spectacle. The creatures howled as they combusted, trapped in the throes of a blistering rigor. The fireball seemed to lift the beasts off the floor, the heat contorting their meagre frames to the point of breaking. Their howls rose higher and higher in time with the rush of flame, writhing and splitting until they were nothing more than smoke and ash. When the spell was done, only falling embers remained.

Walsh looked up at Selena. "You ... you obliterated them."

"You're welcome."

Selena helped the detective to her feet.

"How ... how did you do that?" Walsh said, breathless.

"Does it matter?"

Walsh holstered her weapon. "I ... don't know." She watched the embers fade. "You were right. This is beyond me, but, at the same time, you've opened my eyes."

Selena raised an eyebrow. "And saved your life."

"Huh, yeah."

"So, you'll let me go." It wasn't a question.

"What?"

"I have to go. They've got my daughter."

The detective stared at the ash on the floor, then the marks on Selena's arm. Yet, it was the sheer determination in the woman's eyes that Walsh truly understood.

"One more thing before you go?"

Selena swallowed. "What's that?"

"These demons ... they can possess people, right?"

"Sometimes. Why?"

Corrinne Walsh sat on the edge of the scarred table. "Some time ago, I pursued a killer. He butchered several women, and the circumstances were … strange, not unlike everything that happened over the past few days. So, I'd like to know, how likely is it that this killer was one of these demons?"

Selena smiled. "After everything that's happened, after what you just saw, does that question really need answering?"

Walsh pinched the bridge of her nose. "I … I don't know what I just saw. I mean, what the hell just happened? Zombie dogs … corpses coming back to life … you casting a goddamned fireball. Is that what I saw? I don't know what I saw … "

Selena reached for Walsh. "Don't do that to yourself?"

"Don't do what? Go crazy? My boss just died. Countless officers. How do I explain what happened without sounding like a lunatic?"

Selena stepped to her, and Walsh noticed a shift in her gaze, a ferocity. "Then leave it unexplained. Say it was me and that I escaped."

Walsh raised an eyebrow. "Seriously?"

"This all started with me. Let it end with me."

"Just let you go?"

Selena nodded slowly. "You can say I struck you."

"Right."

She stepped closer. "But don't ever come after me—or I'll do to you what I did to those dogs. Understand?"

Walsh smiled nervously. "Got it."

The witch returned the smile, the tension fading. "That's what you tell them—that I threatened you. It'll sound better that way."

The detective chuckled. "Thanks for fake threatening me. Well, I guess you'd better high tail it outta here."

Walsh watched as Selena waved her scarred hand, opened a fissure in the air, and stepped through. It closed with a wisp of black smoke. Walsh smiled anew.

"Yeah, give 'em hell."

20

Hell is memory.

Selena's portal opened into the cabin, but not in the now. It appeared newer, the air thick with remnants of trauma yet occupied only by figments of the souls that had once occupied it. She felt its cold caress as she stepped through, like she'd fallen into an ancient, bottomless pit. Her assumption that her mother had interfered with the transference became truth when the old crone's voice filled her head.

"You think you can just waltz in and take her back?"

Selena turned, frantic to get her bearings and find the source of her mother's voice. She stood in the kitchen, the light trapped between afternoon and dusk. The hearth was unlit, and motes of dust floated about, unable to escape from the den of inequity that was once her family home.

"You've always been selfish," Davina said from the black depths of the hearth.

Selena stared into the dark void where fire should have been. She raised her right hand, eager to fight the old crone with flame of her own.

"*Incindere!*"

Nothing happened. Selena stared at her hand, the runes simply scars with no semblance of life. Davina's cackle rose out of the hearth.

"Stupid girl! Yer stolen power has no effect in here."

Selena spread her fingers, mentally demanding a spark, anything.

"Yer in my world now, girlie, or have you forgotten that?"

The young witch's hand, the arm she'd disfigured, was dead weight. "No. This can't be happening."

Two arms, pale and flecked with countless liver spots, emerged from within the darkness of the hearth, then a face like grey leather, strands of white hair framing jaundiced eyes. It was a face Selena hadn't seen in twenty years.

"Oh, but it is." Davina stood upright, breasts swaying beneath her decrepit gown as if she'd not changed in all her years. Selena's heart thrummed in her throat so hard she could barely speak, but speak she did.

"No … "

Davina stepped closer. "I hold all the strings here, Selena."

She flicked a bony finger, and Selena's hands and arms went rigid by her side. Reduced to a statue, with Davina her sculptor. Her mother came face-to-face, leering, smiling around rotted teeth.

"You were doing so well," she looked her daughter up and down. "Being smart by staying away. Hiding. But then all this power you've stolen went to yer head." She poked Selena in the chest.

Selena gritted her teeth. "I didn't steal … anything."

Her mother scoffed. "Oh, so you just went into Hell and asked them to give you some flame, and they just gave it to you? You really think that's how it works?" She put her head back and laughed, wet and long. "Yer even more stupid that I thought."

Davina walked around her cackling, her body odour making Selena want to retch.

"Yer Gemma will be better off without you."

Selena squeezed her hands into fists, trembling. She called upon the forces within herself to act, but she was numb. Davina was in almost total control of her body. All Selena could manage was her voice.

"If you don't let my daughter go, I'll kill you."

Again, another cackle. "She's not yer daughter anymore, Selena. You see, once I've gotten rid of you, I'm going to raise her as my own."

"NO."

The old crone whispered in Selena's ear, her breath fetid and cloying. "And when she's ready, when she's flowered, I'm going to give her to the Black Lord."

"NO. NO."

Her mother almost danced a happy jig around the room. "Oh, yes! And you, my girl, won't be able to do anything about it because you'll be damned to the lake of fire you stole from! For all eternity!" She shifted across to Selena in an instant. "Because that's what you deserve for being the conniving, disobedient little cur you've always been! Oh, and I'm going to take so much pleasure in watching you burn!"

There was so much hatred in Davina's gaze, a wanton lust for revenge. Had there ever been any love in those eyes, Selena wondered. She tried to recall any moment from her childhood where her mother showed care or compassion for anyone other than the Black Lord. There was only ever blood and pain because Hell was a memory.

The phrase sang in Selena's head—and gave her an idea.

"Can I … can I speak?" Davina's eyebrows lifted as if she was about scold her again, but Selena persisted. "Can I speak freely … Mother?"

The salutation startled the old woman and, for a moment, Selena thought she softened. "What are you—?"

"I'll do it," Selena interjected.

"Do … what?"

"I'll give myself to him."

Davina took a step back. "What?"

"If you promise not to hurt Gemma, I'll stay and fulfil the pact." Selena watched the cogs turn inside her mother's head, hopeful.

"Do you think I'm stupid, girl? You'll say anything to get free."

"No, Mother. Listen, I know I ran away. I know I didn't obey you, but I swear I've come back because I realise I should never have left. Look at everything that's happened. It's obvious you're the only one who can keep me and Gemma safe."

Selena's tears flowed, and Davina reached up to take one drop on her thumb and taste it. The old woman savoured the flavour.

"So, you came back here thinking we'd take you back with open arms, is that it?"

"I came back because I was scared. Scared of everything that's happened because … because of my foolishness. I lost Gemma and Luke … and Azamir and Cade because of it, and I'm scared I'll never be able to repair the damage I've caused."

Davina stared at the hearth. "Yes. You are scared. A scared little traitor.

273

To me, to yer family, to yerself, but most of all, to the Black Lord."

Sobbing, her body still frozen Selena shuddered with sadness. "I'm sorry, Mother. I was just … afraid."

"Scared and weak is what you were."

"Yes, and I'm sorry."

The old woman sighed. "I thought I'd raised you better. All of you."

Selena sniffled. "We were just … just scared to fail you."

Davina turned to her. "Fear was the only thing you kids would heed." She tapped her chest. "But I knew in here that the fear would make you strong, prepare you for what was to come—your servitude to him."

The young witch bowed her head "I'm sorry I failed you. That we failed each other."

Her mother grimaced. "Each other? Yer the one who shamed me! Made me look like a fool when you ran away!"

"I only did what you taught me!"

The matriarch stomped her bare feet on the floorboards. "You never listened to a word I said, none of you! Yer father left everything to me. Left me to … "

Selena raised her head slowly. "I remember what it was like for you, mother. Trying to fulfil all those roles—of mother, wife, and servant. It must have been so hard for you. So frightening."

Davina sat in a chair by the hearth and stared at the dirty floor. "I-I did the best I could," she said.

Selena felt a twitch in her right arm. "But you were afraid it wasn't enough, weren't you, Mother? You were afraid that the Black Lord wouldn't think it was enough."

There were tears in Davina's eyes. "Yes … "

Her hold was slipping, Selena sensed it in her fingertips. "I was afraid, too, mother. Don't you remember?"

The old woman nodded. "I-I had to pass it on … "

"I know you did." Selena clenched and unclenched her fingers. "But you have to know what it did to me."

Her mother looked at her with tearful eyes. "I had to. I had to do it because the Black Lord is the only one who matters."

Now, Selena thought. Now was the time to act. She could finally move. She lifted her freed arm and placed it on Davina's shoulder.

"I know, Mother. I know he's the only one you truly love. But I'm sorry ... because Gemma is the only one who matters to me."

The hand on Davina's shoulder belonged to the young woman who ran away.

This didn't make sense to the hag. She believed she was the one in control, not the one who abandoned her family on purpose.

"How did you do that?" Davina asked, noticing how much fire there was behind the young Selena's eyes.

"You let your guard down, Mother."

Davina rubbed at the hairs on her chin. "Hmm, I guess I must have. I did teach you well."

"Actually, you taught me nothing. I did all of this myself. I did it because you gave me no other choice."

Something shifted in the hearth beside Davina, a soft orange glow between the sleeping coals.

"I made the choices for you, all through your life," Davina said. "I thought you knew that."

"Those weren't choices, Mother, they were rules we had to follow. Or else."

The hearth came back to life, but who was breathing fire into it, Davina wondered.

"Or else we all would have felt his wrath," the old woman said. "I had to follow rules, too, you know."

The girl squeezed her shoulder. "Don't you want to know why I ran away?"

"I don't care."

"I think you do, Mother."

Embers grew and became sparks, promising a release of rage.

"Go on, then, tell me."

"I ran way, not because of the pact you made, but because there was no love in this house. No love in anyone's hearts, and that's all I ever wanted."

A tongue of fire slinked out from between two coals. "We had the love of the Black Lord … " The girl withdrew her hand, attracting Davina's gaze. "What are you doing?"

"Did you ever love me, Mother?"

After a moment, she said, "I gave you a purpose. I fed you. I clothed you. I put a roof over yer head. I gave you knowledge."

"Yes, you did all those things, but did you do them out of love … for me?"

Davina stared at the embers, dancing against the dark. "I'm not going to say sorry if that's what yer after … but I'll give you something else."

Davina closed her eyes and cast a shadow across the room. Cast it long and cold toward her daughter.

"Can you feel my love of darkness, child?" Davina said.

Davina's shadow hand slipped around Selena's throat.

Her daughter sucked in a panicked breath as her mind's eye was plunged into the murk. Davina was playing one last trick, one final desperate attempt to survive.

Selena whirled around in the nothingness. The dark night of Davina's soul had no doors. Yet there was an echo, the old crone's cackle of deceit. The abyss morphed to liquid, the inky quagmire closing in and rising up Selena's legs and waist until it became hard to breathe. Hard to move.

"S-stop it … mother," Selena said, her voice soundless in the gloom.

The pool kept rising, touching her chin.

"Give up, girl," Davina said. "Take the Black Lord. Take him into you."

The ebony pool lapped at Selena's lips, begging to seep inside.

"Drink him, girl! Drink!"

Selena dove down into the black, the pressure squeezing against her from all sides. The Black Lord's blood looking for any way in. But Selena would never let it in. She'd never drink like her mother did.

So, she summoned the spark and drove the darkness away.

Davina's shadow was thrown out of Selena's mind back to the cabin and the blazing fireplace. Slick with sweat from the attack, the crone gasped when the young Selena stood between her and the hearth. The girl's rage had gone, her expression one of acceptance.

"You tried to convert me mother, but all I'm after is understanding. To understand why you would bring me into a world only to torment and damn me?"

The old woman turned her yellowed eyes to the girl. "Because it's what my faith, our faith, demanded of me."

Selena smiled gently. "And now you know why I ran away."

The hearth erupted with a sphere of fire. Davina glanced down and saw the runes on the girl's arms shimmering with fierce light. For the first time, she felt proud of her daughter. Her child placed a hand on her face.

"Now you know that everything I've done, and everything that I'm going to do, is because I love my daughter, Gemma. Goodbye, Mother."

The wave of heat exploded from the hearth and enveloped Davina like a small sun. Swarmed with flames, the old woman left the chair and fled, leaving molten footprints on the floor. As she ran, the sparks and embers caught on the curtains and the dinner table, coiling upward to the rafters, sending the Kolbe family cabin to Hell where it belonged.

Davina never once cried out in pain, and Selena didn't shed anymore tears as she let it all burn.

21

Flame, embers, and screams assaulted Gemma as she was dragged into Hell.

It was the Hell she'd always imagined in her deepest nightmares, the

Hell she'd read about in school. The one her parents never talked about was real.

Gemma stood paralyzed with her captors, Asha and the hideous Lars, on a cliff face that overlooked the infernal landscape. The scarlet horizon blazed on forever, raging with a relentless immolation. Rivulets of sweat ran down the girl's face and back, soaking into her clothes.

Beneath the burning sky was a vast sea of churning, boiling blood. Within its waves, millions of damned souls thrashed and shrieked, drowning endlessly, choking on their sins, scalded by all their wrongdoings.

She couldn't look away from the ghastly spectacle, could barely breathe or speak. The horror of the unfolding reality was too much for her heart and head, so much that she feared the sights would drive her mad. Would she be cast into the fire? Was that Lars' plan, to just throw his granddaughter into the lake? Would the scorching heat melt the flesh from her bones? Would they just leave her here to burn over and over, forever and ever? Would her mother be able to find her?

"Mom?" Gemma didn't even realise she'd spoken until Asha answered with a laugh.

"I remember the first time I saw Hell," she said. "Mother brought me here after I forgot an important step in one of our rituals. She brought me to this very spot, the Valley of Regret, but after five minutes of being here I learned very quickly not to make the same mistake again."

The girl's tears mingled with her sweat. She tried to swallow the fear, and the resultant inhalation of heat singed her throat. Asha leaned in, smiling.

"You want to know a little secret about Hell?"

Gemma wanted so much to blink away the vista before her, to block out the vision of the ever-shifting lake of fire.

"It's all in your head." Asha giggled.

Lars scampered up onto a rock. "That's enough, Asha. We cannot stay here. The Black Lord is expecting us."

Lars skittered down a narrow path between two, high, craggy cliffs.

Glistening red creatures, bone-thin and adorned with tattered, fleshy wings, peered down on them. Even at a distance, Gemma could see their tooth-filled maws dripping with hunger and hear their long talons scraping the desert sands. She was too terrified to move, but Asha gripped her arm and pulled her forward.

"Come now or I'll let those things have their way with you."

The girl had no choice but to comply. There were no veiled threats in the heart of Hell. So, she let her aunt lead her, trying so hard not to shed a tear, let alone scream. Gemma never wanted her mother more than this moment. If she could take back every dishonourable thought, every childish argument, just to have her back, she would.

The path opened onto a large circular piece of shadowed ground, surrounded by a series of caverns, hungry black mouths that oozed ash and brimstone. Gemma covered her nose, the stench almost buckling her at the knees. Again, her aunt laughed mockingly.

"You never really get used to the smell."

Lars appeared at Gemma's feet, and the girl almost cried out; she dared not bring any attention to herself.

"Silence," he said. "The Lord approaches."

The hills swarmed with more of the haggard, gargoyle-like figures Gemma glimpsed on the cliffs. Hundreds of demons, their crimson hides scarred with old and fresh wounds, cavorting and squealing like beasts contemplating slaughter. The girl watched their frenzied ruckus, their pulling and clawing at each other like some macabre ecstasy. She wanted to look away, but there was nowhere to turn, nowhere to run.

Then, the screams became a song, a depraved symphony of soaring, croaking ululations. Gemma covered her ears, but the sound ran through her bones and, despite her promise not to, she screamed—and the concert stopped. When she finally found the courage to look up at the cliffs, every monstrous eye was upon her. Ravenous and waiting.

Asha whispered in her ear, "I think they like you."

"Quiet!" Lars ordered, swiping at Asha's shin with an appendage.

A figure emerged slowly, regally, from one of the caverns. Gemma's gaze was fixed upon it. Bone thin and at least eight or nine feet tall. The thing had no flesh on its frame, but its skin remained affixed, drooping like robes from its limbs and back, or a grotesque cloak, fit for a king of Hell. Two enormous horns grew out of its eye sockets and curled back over its head, contorted into the form of a crown. It walked slowly toward them, the flayed flesh robes dragging bloodily through the dirt.

"The Black Lord," Lars breathed. "Belphragon."

Gemma was fused to the spot, too terrified to move as Asha, Lars, and all the gathered hordes of Hell bowed in Belphragon's presence. The demon king shuffled ever closer, its horned eyes locked on her. Gemma saw even more of its features; it had no mouth, it was simply a skinned corpse, still bleeding and reaching for her. She instinctively retreated.

"Don't move!" Lars said, keeping his head low.

The tips of Belphragon's fingers pointed at Gemma, the Black Lord's blackened nails dripping blood.

"No! Stay back!"

The demon king snarled from deep within.

"Do not speak." Asha seethed and, for the first time, her own fear shone through.

She took another step back as Belphragon stretched out his spindly arm.

"Get away from me!"

Belphragon's muffled roar surged through the horde, and they all dropped to their bellies. The Black Lord stamped his feet and lashed out to grab Gemma's arm and hoist her. Her scream echoed almost as high as those of the damned.

She writhed and kicked, but Belphragon's might held her fast. Forced to stare at him, she observed every scar and blood vessel in his face, every gouge in his ocular horns. Even without a mouth, she still feared he would devour her. The demon smelled of offal and malice, and she would have retched if not for his grip around her throat.

Astonishingly, her insectoid uncle came to her aid, bowing at the Black Lord's feet. Belphragon let the girl fall to the dirt and turned his eyeless head in his servant's direction. Gemma sucked in hot air while they began their bargain.

"My Lord, if I may ... " Lars said as Belphragon circled the party. "I realise this soul, this girl, is not the one that was agreed upon."

Belphragon paced behind Asha, and she clutched her arms tight around herself; Gemma, now able to breathe, could virtually taste her aunt's fear. It was as strong as her own. Lars moved about on his morbid digits, always keeping his eyeline low.

"Yet, this girl, I can confirm, is of our blood," he continued.

The demon king turned its attention back to Gemma.

"She is, in fact, the daughter of the one who was meant to be your betrothed."

Gemma gasped. "What?"

The hellion stepped toward Gemma once more.

"Selena, I regret, has betrayed us ... betrayed you, my Lord. She has forsaken our coven, killed many of our kin, including my son." A tear ran down Lars' disembodied face.

The Black Lord craned its head to consider Gemma, the viscera and tendons in its flesh slipping and sliding in the congealed blood.

"To that end, my Lord, Selena is no longer our offering."

Gemma scrambled to her knees. She was prepared to run—she didn't know where she would go, but she was not going to stay here.

"Instead, we offer you Selena's child. Her *only* child. The maiden, Gemma."

The girl gaped at Lars. "No ... No!"

Her uncle crept forward and pressed his lips to Belphragon's cloven feet. "She is yours, my Lord."

"NO!"

She stood to run, but Asha had been lurking behind her. Before Gemma could react, Asha punched her in the jaw, knocking her back into the dirt.

Black stars exploded behind Gemma's eyes, but her aunt's jibe still broke through the haze.

"You're not going anywhere, you little bitch."

Belphragon peered down on his new prize, yet the deal was not yet done. Again, Lars grovelled in the dirt.

"I ... *We* have laboured ... toiled and worshipped you for generations. We've given our blood, sweat, and tears to your cause."

The Black Lord grunted with impatience, choosing to ignore Lars and instead admire the semi-conscious girl at his feet. Still, Lars continued.

"Respectfully, my Lord, we ask that you grant us our rewards, the ones you promised us when our pact was made."

The demon king turned his horned gaze to Lars.

"We want what's coming to us," Asha interjected, and the creature whirled back to face her, his featureless visage somehow expressing displeasure. She stepped back, bowing low.

"Forgive my daughter's impertinence, my Lord," Lars said. "It has been a very trying time for the family."

The lord of Hell considered the three of them in silence. Gemma, who eased out of unconsciousness, clutching her head. She sobbed when she realised she hadn't just been having a terrible nightmare.

"Please ... " she said. "Please, let me go."

"Shut up!" Asha replied.

Belphragon's growl silenced them both. He reached out his hand to Gemma, only to then turn it in Lars' direction.

"Oh, thank you, my Lord," Lars whispered.

An invisible force took control of him, and he wheezed in ecstasy, or pain, Gemma couldn't tell which. His head arched back as the appendages— the florid veins and tendons he'd used as legs for so long—grew before Gemma's eyes. More blood vessels sprouted, then the feathery trails of nerve endings. Organs bloomed within them, the sight eventually forcing the girl to look away. Yet, there was no escaping the sound of growing bone and creeping flesh or Lars' cries of delight as he finally returned to the man he'd once been.

When Gemma turned her eyes back, she found her uncle standing, naked before his master, the first words passing from his reborn lips:

"Praise Him," he said, weeping new tears.

Asha bowed along with her father. "Praise Him," she said.

And the hordes of Hell joined in their chorus.

"PRAISE HIM!"

22

The portal opened onto Ossuria—the Hill of Bones, a towering mountain of carcasses that touched the boiling clouds in Hell's caustic sky.

The bones belong to Hell's most demented sinners, people who'd committed the vilest of acts. Every shred of their flesh had been torn off piece by piece, leaving nothing but a skeleton to be tossed onto the great ash heap. Billions, trillions of bones stacked high for all to see.

Selena observed it from the shadows, carefully secreting herself in a narrow gorge, the high walls blocking out the blood-red glare of the atmosphere and, thankfully, some of its blistering heat.

She had always been prepared for this moment, the inevitability that she would have to step into Hell, but still she was afraid. Afraid for her daughter. She looked at the Hill of Bones and prayed that Gemma's body wouldn't end up a part of it—or her own. The only way to survive this voyage, Selena knew, was to plan. She couldn't simply walk out with Gemma safely tucked under her wing. There was survival, and there was survival in Hell.

You could lose yourself in Hell, in part, or the whole. It could rend your flesh but leave your soul, or it could harvest your mind and send you back a gibbering fool. It was all a matter of degree.

Selena wiped tears from her eyes and chided herself. Tears wouldn't help Gemma. There was no time for fear, not in this place. Fear was a stronger scent than even burning flesh in Hell, and unless she got her fear under control, the demonic denizens of Abaddon would be able to smell her on the wind.

So, she needed to come up with a plan.

No doubt her father was going to present Gemma to Belphragon. To Lars, completing the bargain was paramount to his family's survival. Would the Black Lord accept such an exchange? Selena didn't know. Despite her many years of service, she'd never met the demon king face-to-face. Only her parents had. This made the entire situation unpredictable.

Selena smiled. No, she didn't know the Black Lord's inclinations, but then he didn't know hers either. She could use that to her advantage, couldn't she?

First, she had to find Gemma and the remaining members of her wicked family. Finding one soul in the nine circles of Hell with its billions was almost impossible.

Almost.

Selena raised her inscribed arm and scanned the runes carved into the flesh. She literally had the language of Hell at her fingertips. She just needed the right piece of script, the one that would give her the map of all of Pandemonium.

"*Ostende mihi viam,*" she said.

Show me the path.

The runes flared with light, only to quickly fade. Nothing. *The wrong turn of phrase perhaps.*

A crescendo of distant screams were carried on the wind, and Selena jerked in shock. Fear. *Remember, they can smell it.* She took a breath of rancid air, then another, focusing on staying calm, staying focused.

"You've come this far. Don't fold now," she whispered.

She turned her arm in a bid to find the right rune. All she wanted to know was how to get around Hell.

"Why is this so difficult?"

Hell.

"That's it," she said.

Emblazoned on her arm was the language of Hell, which meant there had to be a word for it—a name. There were many names for Hell: Abaddon, Gehenna, Hades, Pandemonium. But what was the symbol for it? She turned her arm over and whispered the names she knew.

"Gehenna."

Nothing.

"Abaddon."

Nothing.

"Hades."

"Tartarus."

"Sheol."

The runes were silent. Selena scratched at them in frustration, drawing blood and fresh tears.

"How could I have been so stupid to come here?" she said, on the verge of sobbing. "I'm so sorry, Gemma."

The tears came, along with the fear. Screams echoed from all around, a wavering sea of pain and torment, seemingly close and miles away at the same time. Selena wanted to give in, walk to the nearest cliff and fall into a pit and accept that she'd failed. She couldn't save Gemma, not ever.

She scrambled to her feet. No, that's the fear talking. Don't listen to it. You're in control. You have the power of Hell in the palm of your hand. Use it.

She closed her eyes and pictured the runes in her head, flicking through each one, looking for the icon for Hell.

"Hell is memory," she said.

Thoughts of her mother came, of how she'd tormented her with visions of her ugly childhood. She opened her eyes and glanced around the vista of damnation, at the souls in the throes of everlasting punishment. Forced to relive their past sins over and over, to remember what they did, who they'd wronged. Again, and again and again. The worst punishment you could ever imagine.

"Hell is memory … "

Selena gazed at the top of her forearm and whispered a new incantation, the word she knew described Hell more than any other.

"Memoria."

Her skin thrummed, and a rune, in the shape of a diamond, looped through with a circle, gleamed with light and blood. Selena winced in pain as the symbol activated like the tolling of a great bell. The pulse spread outward, across all of Pandemonium like the first rumble of an approaching storm.

To her horror, the screams of the damned fell silent.

"Oh, shit."

Every soul, every demon would have heard the true name of Hell being called.

They would know exactly where to find her.

Lars saw Belphragon turn his crowned head to the east, toward the Hill of Bones, seconds before he felt the tremor in his feet.

"Someone has called Hell by its true name," Lars muttered.

"Selena?" Asha asked.

Lars kept his head low. "Possibly."

"No. That means that mother is—"

"Hush. What's done is done. We can't dwell on it now."

The Black Lord brought his attentions back to Lars, looking to him for an explanation. Lars averted his eyes from his master's stare. The patriarch instead looked to his granddaughter. The timid girl scanned the horizon, overwhelmed by so much fear that Lars could taste it in the back of his parched throat. The last thing she needed was to feel any semblance of hope that her mother would be coming to save her.

"Asha," he said. "Go to the Hill. Find your sister and kill her."

"No!" Gemma made to run, but Lars grabbed her and pulled her close.

"Your mother is cunning, but she won't do anything rash once she sees we have you."

Lars watched Asha run into the distance, slowly becoming a plume of dust on a blood-red wasteland.

Belphragon came forward, and the head of the Kolbe clan felt the demon king burrowing into his mind. Failure was not an option. The Black Lord lifted his hand to the cliffs, to the gathered hordes, and all burst into a frenzy, running down the rockface in the direction of the Hill in a thunderous pounding of hooves.

The great demon lord was not going to leave anything to chance—and definitely not to a Kolbe.

The demon throng was a swarm of black on the incarnadine sky, and Selena knew they were coming for her.

She crouched low behind a pile of rocks and scanned the horizon. Demons in their hundreds, like black flies, approached on high. She could run and hide, but there was no doubt they would eventually track her down. She glanced at her arm, pondered if its power would be enough to keep them at bay when they attacked.

Then, she glimpsed another shape much closer, walking across the abandoned plain—a solitary figure, not lost but resolute. Even at such a distance, Selena knew the figure's face, its gait. When she blinked, it was gone, leaving only a puff of ebony smoke in its wake.

Selena turned when a voice sounded at her back.

"Hello, sister."

Asha sneered at her older sister, her tattered gown flicking in the scorching winds. She looked like Davina, only much younger and bone thin. Selena tensed, readying herself for the attack to come.

"You're looking well," Selena jibed.

Her sister laughed. "The mutilated arm suits you. I didn't realise you were into self-cutting."

"Are we really going to do the witty banter thing?"

Asha craned her neck to look over Selena's shoulder. "I'm just buying time until the horde gets here. It's going to be so much fun watching them tear you limb from limb."

"Maybe. Maybe they'll go for you, too?"

"You're forgetting that you're the only one not under the Black Lord's protection."

Selena smirked and wiped her sweaty brow on the back of her hand. "The only one the Black Lord protects is himself."

"Not from where I'm standing."

The howls of the demon flight reached them like a shrieking hurricane of hunger. Selena knew she only had moments before they reached her.

"If you're so sure he's protecting the coven, Asha, then why didn't he stop me from killing Davina?"

Asha's sneer became a hateful scowl. She stepped closer to her sister. "So, it's true, then. You killed her?"

Selena held up her right arm. "With this. She was powerless in the end. Weak." She saw Asha's lips quiver with rage. "She was weak … just like you."

Asha clenched her hand into a fist. "Oh, you think I'm weak?"

"I did what you always dreamed of doing but couldn't. I killed our mother."

Asha lowered her head, her eyes cold and dark despite the fury of the hellscape. She was malice personified, and Selena admitted to being intimidated, that mocking her might not have been the wisest choice.

"Then, sister," Asha said, "let's see who is truly the better, shall we?"

The younger Kolbe sister's eyes glowed red, and Selena felt her innards twist and turn, a pain that buckled her at the knees. Her guts screamed as if they'd become snakes, coiling and biting at her insides. Selena tasted blood and spat a clutch of straight pins into the dirt. She vomited more and more of them, the thin pieces of steel shining red in the spreading pool of filth. She struggled for breath as the pins kept coming. Asha cast a shadow

288

over her.

"You look good on your knees, sister. Maybe I won't kill you, after all. It might be more fun getting you to kneel before our father and the Black Lord instead."

All Selena could feel was the pins in her gullet, and all she could see was the torrent of blood but, in her mind, she remembered there was only one form of magic Asha had ever been adept at—curse magic.

Selena swallowed the pins down and reached out with her burned hand to grip Asha's ankle. She looked up at her sister with a bloody red smile on her face.

"You forgot the one thing about curse magic, Asha … "

Asha tried to pull her leg free of Selena's hand as the runes illuminated.

" … it only works if the victim believes it's real."

The pins vanished, so, too, the pool of blood, but before Asha could utter another word, Selena said one of her own, igniting her hand. Hellfire spiralled up Asha's shin, quickly catching on her gown, the conflagration racing higher and higher until she was a living column of heat and light. The young witch's cries joined those of the approaching horde. Selena released her grip, and Asha ran in a meaningless attempt to escape until, finally, she dropped to the ground, dead.

Still, Selena didn't have time to admire Asha's smouldering corpse. Screeches to her left and right drew her gaze. The winged hellions fluttered to land on the craggy cliffs one after another, carefully sizing up their intended prey. Their glistening, scarlet bodies heaved with anticipation and raspy, hot breaths. They considered Selena through glowing eyes, like they were seeing a long-awaited meal for the first time.

The witch raised her hellfire arm at them. "Try it, and you die," she told them, only to have one of them reply with a hoarse laugh.

"We are born of flame, witch," it said.

"It can't hurt us!" said another.

The first demon flapped its wings impatiently. "You stole hellfire. It does not belong to you!"

The second one pointed at her. "We will take it back!"

Selena aimed her arm at the demon. *"Incindere!"*

The hellfire enveloped the creature. It arched back its head, releasing a long guttural sigh, the flames easily being absorbed into its skin. Selena gasped.

"Oh, that was really stupid, Selena."

The first demon took to the air toward her. "Take back the flame!"

Other members of the swarm followed, dozens of them leaping from their perches. Heart pounding, she turned and ran but several were on her in seconds. She toppled to the ground and rolled onto her back to kick at the attackers. The demons pulled at her pants, slashed her coat, and almost lifted her into the air. When one of them yanked her by the hair, she screamed, and it leaned in to hiss in her ear.

"Give it baaaack!"

Demonic claws scraped her skin, and she writhed and pulled against them, but there were too many. She was soon pinned down and forced to watch as the leader straddled her. It smiled with a mouthful of needlepoint teeth.

"Foul witch stole the flame! Return it or die!"

The horde joined in, chanting, "DIE! DIE! DIE!" pulling at Selena's tattered clothes. The witch tried to think through the pain and terror, to mentally summon any of the runes to activate, but her arm may as well have been made of lead. The hellions' talons picked into the skin of her arm, pinching it, hungry to get it off.

"Give it!" the leader said.

Selena let her arm fall slack. She stared at the fiery sky, ready to take her punishment.

"You can have it," she said, "if you let me live."

The demons looked at each other in silent contemplation until one of them spoke, a forked tongue slipping between its cracked lips.

"Master wants her dead!"

"No!" the leader protested. "The Kolbe man wants her dead, Master said to stop her."

Selena trembled beneath them as they bickered. All she wanted was a chance to escape. One more chance to save her daughter.

"Kill? Or stop?" another demon said.

"Is stop killing?"

"She stole the flame. Did the master want it back?"

Selena grimaced and held her arm out to them, and they screeched in startlement.

"Do what your master says. Take it."

The leader grabbed Selena's wrist and put it to his mouth. "The witch stole the flame! We must take it back!"

Pointed fangs pierced her skin just above the elbow, and she screamed. Warm rivulets of blood ran down her arm and spattered her face. She heard the *crunch* of bone, felt the pull of ligaments and the tearing of meat—until the darkness claimed her.

The same agony brought Selena back to consciousness but on the verge of death.

She sat bolt upright, the pain searing though her body hotter than the surrounding inferno. The demons, though, were gone, leaving her to die. Eventually, once she could control her breathing, she found the courage to look down at her arm.

It was a raw stump, the flesh shredded and chewed to the bone. Blood oozed steadily from the wound, soaking into her clothes and caking the dirt to mud. She opened her mouth to scream again, but nothing came. The shock left her mute. The demons had taken back what belonged to Hell, and she was now without a weapon.

Selena rocked back and forth in time with the throb from her phantom limb. She didn't know what to do or how to think. Her body demanded to just give in to the suffering and die.

Gemma needs me, she thought.

Gemma.

The witch looked to the horizon. The horde was far in the distance, returning to their master. Her daughter was there waiting, hoping. This was Selena's last chance.

She turned and leaned on her only arm, the simple movement sending a fresh jolt through her entire body. Taking in a deep breath, then another, she pulled in her knees. After several more breaths, she stood, staggering under the weight of pain-induced vertigo.

"I'm coming, Gemma," she muttered.

Through the misery, Selena tried to recall the incantation for getting from one place to another quickly, the same spell Asha had used to surprise her mere minutes before. It was called *shifting* and was one of the first spells Davina had ever taught them, but now, the magic escaped her.

"I'm ... coming."

Squeezing her eyes closed to block out the pain, she remembered. It wasn't about visualizing where you were going but rather the why. You also had to know and see where you were going. She staggered in the dirt, a precipice a few feet in front of her.

"Gemma ... " she said.

Her daughter was the why. Why she'd endured so much, and why she'd willingly endure much more yet.

"Gemma ... "

Selena reached out to the horizon. "Gemma ... "

She shifted, the landscape a sudden blur of red as if an invisible hand had picked her up and moved her. The witch came down hard in the dirt, the force leaving her groaning and shuddering. Black fog filled her senses, but she got up to discover she had, in fact, relocated from the cliff to the wide open plain. In essence, she was halfway there.

Biting back a new wave of agony, Selena turned her wavering vision—and her heart—in the direction of what she wanted most in the world. She closed her eyes and tried to shift again.

"Gemma ... " she said. "I'm coming."

23

The hordes gathered in the wild plain and made a throne out of their bodies for the Black Lord to sit upon.

From his perch, Belphragon studied the girl, Gemma, covetous, yet cautious. There was something about the child that captivated him beyond the flesh, something prophetic. He turned his attention to the Kolbe patriarch, the one who'd brought her to him.

Their association had been long, his devotion unwavering—until now. With a taloned hand, Belphragon called the one named Lars forward, and the mortal quickly scurried to kneel before him. The demon king delved into the Kolbe servant's mind, filling it with questions, mainly why the girl's mother had defied his father ... and the Black Lord himself. Lars grovelled in the dirt.

"The naivety of youth, my Lord. My daughter was always defiant," Lars replied, his face down.

The monarch of Hell probed further, deeper, and Lars cringed.

"Yes, perhaps it would have been wiser to punish her sooner, my Lord. Yet, we always believed she understood the consequences of her defiance."

Belphragon snarled, and Lars bowed his head lower still.

"A sacrifice? Well, yes, my Lord, we could have considered Selena as a blood offering, but we felt she was best placed as your bride ... "

The demon bent down, his great head so close to Lars Kolbe's that the man shook with doubt and fear. The servant's chin dug into the dirt.

"The girl ... Gemma ... is a simple exchange, my Lord. Blood ... for blood. She is a suitable offering, I assure you."

Gemma's keening distracted the Black Lord. The girl's suffering should have aroused him. Instead, it was aggravating. The horde of demons echoed her pleas for release, mocking sobs that became hysterical laughter. The demon king roared, the skin where his mouth should have been stretching almost to the tearing point. He stood and thrashed the demons that were his throne with his bare hands, killing them instantly. The other demons recoiled and fell silent, daring not to move.

Lars Kolbe lay prostrate in the dust as Belphragon charged toward his granddaughter, eager to inflict the same rage upon her. Her terror was pathetic, and he considered destroying her then and there. Yet, at the same time, he knew nothing would come of it.

He felt duped, a fool in his own kingdom. Angered further, he wrapped his long-fingered hand around the girl's throat and spoke into her tiny mind. The girl's eyes widened at his power, and it took her a moment to reply.

"I-I don't know where my mom is."

He pushed again, her eyes rolling back in her skull.

"I ... swear ... I don't know."

Belphragon dropped Gemma, frustrated by her truth. She was not worthy to be his bride, not even for sport. Until, there, wallowing in the dirt, she challenged him.

"I-I don't know where she is. I don't know why she's left me here. I don't even know who she really is. All I know is that she's lied to me my whole life." She wiped away tears. "She's a monster ... just like you."

Again, the girl's truth was undeniable. He let her speak.

"I'm not going to be your bride, so you might as well kill me."

He reached out to her. He would snuff her out, he would snuff her and her grandfather out, and then tear the earth apart just to find the one named Selena.

Screeches of alarm from the horde put a hold on the demon king's wrath. He whirled about to find a woman, torn and bloody, staggering toward them. The one he'd been waiting for. Selena.

The girl at his feet rejoiced.

"Mom?"

✹

Gemma's mother resembled a walking corpse. Ragged and broken, shuffling in the dirt, Selena Kolbe was unrecognizable. It wasn't until she spoke that Gemma was certain her mother had finally come.

"My Lord … " Selena said. "I beseech thee … "

The witch's appearance became more evident as she approached, and Gemma cried out when she saw her mother was missing her right arm. Gemma wanted to run to Selena and hold her, but all she could do was look on in horror.

With each painful step, Selena spilled blood, and the scorched soil soaked it up like so much water. The sight of her agonized Gemma; her mother had endured Hell to rescue her. She thought about all the horrible things she'd said about her to Belphragon, that her mother had abandoned her. She wanted to tell her mother then and there that she was sorry she ever doubted she would come. Guilt and fear kept her silent.

"I beseech thee … " Selena said again, her voice cracking.

The Black Lord somehow stood taller, and Gemma thought he would destroy Selena in an instant but, strangely, she realised the demon king was curious. Her grandfather shifted onto his knees, his hateful gaze now on the witch who'd forever defied him.

"You infernal wench," he said.

Belphragon barked, raising a hand in threat at Lars. The man quickly buried his face in the soil. Gemma watched her mother do the same, falling to her knees, a shattered woman.

"My Lord … " She held out her arms in surrender, splashes of blood dripping from her right arm. Bleeding for her cause. "I come to you … not as a mother … "

Gemma wanted so much for her mother to look at her, but she saw every ounce of Selena's strength was reserved for the creature before them.

" … but as your servant. One who has failed you."

Lars cried out from the ground, "She admits it, my Lord. Selena has wilfully disobeyed you, as she has done our family."

The Black Lord stamped his feet, sending up a spray of ancient dust and ash. Lars kept his head down but raised his hands in placation.

"This woman is unfit to be your servant," he muttered. "She belongs with the damned in the lake."

Belphragon addressed Selena, and Gemma felt his voice burn within her, too.

"*Witch.*"

Gemma saw Selena lower herself to the ground. She didn't know what her mother was doing. Was she truly surrendering?

Belphragon's voice pushed all her thoughts aside.

"*You have committed sacrilege, witch,*" the demon said. "*Why should I not let my hordes rend you down to your bones?*"

Selena kissed the dirt. "My Lord, you have every right to punish me for my insubordination but, my Lord, please do not punish Gemma."

Gemma shivered at the mention of her name, yet still, her mother would not even offer her daughter a single glance.

"Mom?" she whispered desperately.

Belphragon's horns turned to Gemma, and she went rigid, trapped in mind and body by the demon's will, only permitted to watch and listen.

"*The child has been brought to me in your stead. Blood for blood.*"

Gemma saw Selena look up.

"And in doing so, my father has not fulfilled the terms of the covenant he made with you," Selena stated.

"What?" Lars interjected.

The Black Lord seethed, clenching a hand and releasing a pulse of energy that opened a crack in the ground. Lava oozed out from beneath the surface and crept snake-like to form a circle around them all. No one was going to escape the hearing—or his wrath.

"*I demanded a soul. A vessel to host my spawn on Earth,*" Belphragon said.

Lars lifted his gaze. "And I have brought you one, my Lord. The girl is sufficient."

Selena, determined, rose to her knees, grimacing in pain. "My father made a pact with you all those years ago, my Lord. By bringing my daughter here, he has broken that pact."

Lars stood. "You filthy wretch." He ran at Selena, knocking her down.

Gemma screamed as the madman slipped his sweaty palms around her mother's neck.

"You defiant whore," Lars said. "After all we have done for you. You've ruined everything."

Gemma tried desperately to move, her eyes shifting from the struggle before her to the demon lord. Why was he refusing to intervene? Lars squeezed tighter and tighter as Selena gasped for air. The girl's heart pounded in her ears, the threat of losing Selena becoming too much to bear. A coil of heat welled up inside her, a power lying dormant within that arose through her voice.

"MOM."

The fury of Gemma's cry thrust Lars off her mother, sending him sliding through the dirt to collide with a rocky outcrop. Gemma's surge of strength built up again. Before she could understand how, she had broken free of Belphragon's hold and was running to take Selena into her arms.

"Mom!"

Selena was limp in Gemma's embrace, a doll smelling of blood and sweat.

"G-Gemma?" her mother said.

The Black Lord howled, and Hell shook, the very ground beneath the women shuddering. Belphragon dragged his claws and split open the earth. More lava spewed out, spreading fast toward them.

"ENOUGH."

Lars came to, shaking off the impact to rush at Gemma and Selena a second time. "You have no say here."

"NEITHER DO YOU."

Belphragon's power gripped Lars in the air. He was a puppet on invisible strings. With a curl of his fingers, the demon king undid Lars Kolbe's resurrection, the man's skin desiccating and shrinking over his bones until it tore like paper. Shredded strips of flesh fell to hiss in the flowing lava.

The patriarch screamed as he fell apart, his body twisting and tearing. Blood poured from ruptured veins, spilling to the soil. Pieces of him crumbled into a pile of ragged, ichor-slick viscera. Gemma closed her eyes to it and pulled her mother close when the Black Lord swung the same destructive hand their way.

"Honor ... the pact ... my Lord," Selena said.

"Mom?"

Belphragon halted, listening.

"You ... can have me," the witch continued.

"Mom, no!"

Selena slipped free of Gemma to kneel before Hell's regent. "I'll be your bride ... if you let my daughter live."

Gemma's sight blurred with tears. "Oh, my God. Mom, please don't do this."

Her mother locked eyes with Belphragon. "Let Gemma live and send me back to be your emissary on Earth. Your conduit."

The demon lord lowered his gaze, and Gemma imagined him doing to them what he'd done to her grandfather. Selena spoke one last time.

"Honor the pact ... and I'm yours."

Belphragon waved his hand, and a black cloud swarmed in around them, a swelling miasma that swallowed all light, sense, and thought, and Gemma asked herself: *Is this death?*

24

The black cloud parted to reveal they'd travelled to the place where Luke had died.

Selena looked down to see her right arm had been restored, her wounds healed by the power of Hell. She watched the mist curling off the tops of the trees into the sky above and stood steadfast with Gemma at her side. The smell of pine filled the air and light rain fell on her new bare skin, but she felt no goodness in it. They'd escaped Hell itself, yet Selena didn't feel free because this beautiful place would always be one of mourning.

She looked at the patch of earth where she'd laid Luke down. He was there waiting for her, she thought, but there were still so many things to do. Finally, Gemma broke the silence.

"Mom, what happened?"

"A new pact."

"What … what does that mean?"

"That we're alive."

Gemma shivered beside her, and Selena realised her daughter couldn't comprehend the future that lay ahead for them.

"I can't believe what you did just to save me," she said.

Selena faced Gemma as a gust of wind tousled their hair. "I didn't save you, Gemma." She watched the girl's eyes widen.

"What?"

"You have to save yourself."

Gemma pushed a wet strand of hair from her face. "I-I don't understand."

"No, you don't. Not yet." She took Gemma's hands in hers. "But I'm going to teach you. I'm going to make sure you're a survivor."

Gemma pushed Selena's hands away and hugged herself. The girl looked so thin, Selena thought.

"But I thought all of the bad things were behind us now. That we're free."

Her mother smiled and turned back to Luke's grave. "I thought I'd left it all behind, too, Gemma. But then it all came rushing back. I should have known that you can never escape your past. Family is forever."

She felt the girl's hand on her shoulder. "Mom, you won. We're safe now. Why can't you see that?"

Selena rested her hand on Gemma's cheek. The girl's eyes gleamed with brightness—and innocence, still.

"Gemma, listen to me. I— *We* have a new responsibility now. A promise we have to keep, and I'll need you to help me fulfil it. You already have the power in you. Even the Black Lord knows it."

Her daughter withdrew as she struggled against the realization. "What if I don't want to?"

Selena crouched next to the grave. "You're still not really hearing me. Even after everything that's happened. Everything I had to do. You still don't want to hear me."

Gemma crossed her arms. "Mom, please, just stop it. I just want to go home. Can't we just go home and … live?"

Selena stood and took Gemma by the shoulders and shook her. "You've got to be stronger than this, Gemma! You can't be weak!" She saw the girl's features soften with fear, her inquisitive eyes scanning her own.

"You sound like her," Gemma said. "Like Davina."

Selena let her go and studied the trees again. She could sense their collective heartbeat, feel the roots burrowing into the earth. The soul of the world was a cold, dark place.

"I guess I do sound like her," she said. "That's what mothers do to their daughters—give them their voice. Pass on their words, good or bad, to the next daughter, and the next." She looked up at Gemma. "You need to hear those words, Gemma, the words I have to tell you. Okay? Even if they come from a place of darkness. Do you understand?"

Gemma closed her eyes, and tears fell. Selena caught one and pressed it to the girl's lips.

"I will save you, Gemma, with my words. Words are everything. They have so much power. We have to give those words, and more, to ourselves—and to him. There's no way we can avoid it."

Selena took the girl's hand and led her to Luke's grave. She interlocked her fingers with Gemma's and held them over the patch of wet earth.

"I love you, Gemma. That will never change."

Their hands hovered over the grave.

"Do you know what true love really is?"

Gemma shook her head and shivered against the cold.

Selena squeezed the girl's hand. "It's just one word."

A red pearlescent flame flared around their hands.

"Sacrifice."

Gemma gasped in surprise, but her mother wept because she'd lied to the girl—the first of many lies that were to come. To Selena, true love was more akin to fate. The fate of a mother willing to lose everything in order for her daughter to survive. A cycle of fate.

The flame dripped onto the grave, and the body within stirred with life. Selena whispered in her daughter's ear:

"Family is forever."

Publication History

"The Bedlam Stones," *This Sublime Darkness and Other Dark Stories*, Things in the Well Publishing, October 2019.

"The Book of Last Words," *This Sublime Darkness and Other Dark Stories*, Things in the Well Publishing, October 2019.

"The Darkness at the End of the Tunnel," *Specul8: Central Queensland Journal of Speculative Fiction*, Issue 4, July 2017.

"Daughters of the Veil," *The End of Halloween*, September 2016.

"The Droste Effect," *This Sublime Darkness and Other Dark Stories*, Things in the Well Publishing, October 2019.

"Dura Mater," *Nightmare Fuel Magazine*, April 29, 2023.

"Hell-O-Ween," *Australian Reader Halloween Special*, October 2009.

"Light House, Dark House," *Lighthouses*, Black Beacon Books, September 2015.

"This Sublime Darkness," *This Sublime Darkness and Other Dark Stories*, Things in the Well Publishing, October 2019.

"The Yellow House," *Under Twin Suns: Alternate Histories of the Yellow Sign*, Hippocampus Press, July 2021.

About the Author and Artist

GREG CHAPMAN is a horror author, editor and artist based in Brisbane, Australia.

Greg's fiction and art has received wide acclaim from readers and critics of the horror genre since his first publication in 2011.

In 2024, his collection *Midnight Masquerade*, published by IFWG Publishing International, won an Australasian Shadows Award and he is also a Bram Stoker Award finalist, with his debut novel *Hollow House*, making the shortlist in 2016.

His most recent short story collection, *Black Days and Bloody Nights* is also a finalist in this year's Australasian Shadows Awards. He's currently co-editing the Halloween anthology *Samhain Screams*, due for release by Black Beacon Books in October.

His artistic endeavours include designing book covers and creating illustrations for various publishers and authors in Australia, the United

About the Author and Artist

States, and the United Kingdom. He was recently named as a finalist in the Best Artist category of the British Fantasy Awards. The first graphic novel he illustrated, *Witch Hunts: A Graphic History of the Burning Times*, written by Rocky Wood and Lisa Morton and published by McFarland and Company, won the Superior Achievement in a Graphic Novel category at the Bram Stoker Awards in 2013.

Greg was also the President of the Australasian Horror Writers Association from 2017-2020.

www.ingramcontent.com/pod-product-compliance
Lightning Source LLC
Chambersburg PA
CBHW030246030726
47493CB00023B/611